Delicious Torment
(A Miranda's Rights Mystery)
Book II

Linsey Lanier

Edited by

Donna Rich

Editing for You

Second Look Proofreading

Gilly Wright
www.gillywright.com

ISBN: 1941191134
ISBN-13: 978-1-941191-13-2

DELICIOUS TORMENT

The second book in the emotional story of a stubborn loner looking for her stolen daughter.

What happens when your old flame turns out to be a killer?

At a ritzy steeplechase Miranda Steele discovers the body of a beautiful young horse breeder, her face brutally crushed by the hooves of her favorite stallion. Torn between leaving town to search for her daughter and continuing to work for her sexy, ace investigator boss, Miranda doesn't want to get involved. But when the dead woman's sister begs her to take the case, Miranda can't ignore her powerful need to set things right.

Even more puzzling, Parker is strangely aloof about the case, not at all like himself. As she looks into the incident against his wishes, Miranda begins to realize that her boss has a past he doesn't want her to unearth.

For more information visit www.LinseyLanier.com

CHAPTER ONE

"Did you see that move?" Miranda Steele gritted her teeth as she watched a masculine hand slide up a shapely thigh under a calico sundress a few tables away.

"Unfortunately, yes." Parker pretended to study his Dom Pérignon. "Were you able to capture it?"

"Every disgusting slither." She grinned with satisfaction, adjusted the broad brim of her flouncy silk hat, and murmured under her breath. "Thanks to this fancy equipment, courtesy of the Parker Agency."

Tucked under the crown of her hat was a state-of-the-art mini camcorder, so light she barely felt it. The camcorder was surreptitiously attached to a viewer hidden in her sunglasses. A very cool surveillance toy.

It gave Miranda a thrill to be sitting here with her sexy boss, ace investigator Wade Parker, CEO of the ultra-successful Parker Agency, at the ritzy Northwinds Steeplechase outside of Atlanta, acting as if they were just having drinks at an outdoor pavilion. With its linen-covered tables, its view of the rolling green fields, the Vivaldi wafting from concealed speakers, no one would imagine they were really gathering evidence on a couple of brazen cheaters.

"Have one." Parker nudged a china saucer of appetizers toward her. Peppers laced with chipotle and wrapped in jalapeno bacon.

"Don't mind if I do." She picked one up by its miniature skewer and popped it in her mouth. It burned, but nothing she couldn't handle. "Bland," she shrugged.

Parker chuckled. Ever since she'd challenged him to a pepper-eating contest at a local restaurant, he'd been testing her endurance. "I'm pleased at how quickly you've picked up the feel of the equipment." He sat back and sipped from his glass, peering at the lovebirds across the way. "Excellent work, so far." His low Southern murmur was as smooth as Jim Beam and juleps.

Involuntarily, the corner of Miranda's lip turned up. "Thanks."

She'd never had a real career before, and she liked detective work. She was glad Parker had asked her to work this case, even though it was partly an excuse to be with her.

"What's the first rule of covert surveillance?" he said so softly, she barely heard him.

That was a quick one-eighty. "Don't get made," she whispered. "So?"

"So why are you so tense?"

"I'm not tense," she hissed through her teeth.

"My mistake," he said dryly and set down his glass.

Watching the bubbles rise in the amber liquid, she exhaled and rotated her shoulders, even picked up her drink and took a sip. Maybe she was too tense. She really wanted to nail this guy.

"That's better," Parker smiled. Then he nodded casually to an acquaintance passing by their table.

Easy for him to say. Ease and charm came naturally to the cagey investigator. Especially earlier this morning, when they'd had to make polite conversation with the women of his social circle while they'd trailed their frisky targets all over the steeplechase grounds. Women who thought Miranda's presence here with Parker proved she belonged to the species *goldus diggerous*. But at least she hadn't gotten as many cold stares as she once had from the horsey set.

Could be the front-page news coverage of the murder case she'd just solved, where she'd saved a young girl's life. A battle with a monster that left her cold and numb—and with twenty-five stitches across her chest.

A half-groan, half-giggle came from the woman in the calico sundress. The man just about drooled over himself as he draped an arm across the back of her chair.

"Smile for the birdie." Miranda narrowed her eyes at the frisky subjects. These two belonged to the "horsing around" set.

The man was Anthony Lloyd Witherspoon. Young, clean-cut, dressed in an expensive beige suit. An upwardly mobile banker type from CK&G. The woman, tanned and carefree, with long, dark blond hair, was Farrah Simmons, a local well-to-do with connections to the steeplechase. Her stylish hat, like Miranda's, was in deference to the Ladies' Hat Contest, something of a ritual at equine events, Parker had explained.

Miranda caught the insignia on the woman's tote bag. "Canterbury Stables is Simmons's horse farm, right?" She remembered that from the file.

Parker nodded imperceptibly. "She's part owner with her family."

Miranda angled her head. "Got the bag. Nice extra bit of identifying evidence."

"Outstanding."

Witherspoon reached up casually to caress Simmons's neck. The woman turned to him with an I'm-all-yours smile and gave him a full-lipped kiss with a bit of tongue. Would have been a charming scene—if Witherspoon weren't married to somebody else.

Miranda growled under her breath. "That's right, buddy. Go for it. I've got you covered."

"Down, tigress." Parker's low laugh caressed her ear. "You're enjoying this, aren't you?"

She caught herself before she could smile, shrugged instead. "You know I don't like cheaters." Especially after trailing the bastard on her last case who'd been sleeping around on a friend. As well as beating her.

"And you know I don't either. But are you sure you can focus? Perhaps this exercise is a bit much after—"

"I can focus just fine." She fidgeted with her paper napkin and shot her boss a wary look. Why did Wade Russell Parker the Third have to be so darn sexy?

Those sharp, Magnum-gray eyes that could both warm you with passion, then freeze with disapproval. The salt-and-pepper sprinkled through his dark hair that he wore just over his ears. His finely tailored, dark blue suit. That distinguished, middle-aged face. That irresistible magnetism. No wonder he could turn the head of every available woman in Atlanta—a fact she had witnessed more than a few times. Since the death of his wife three years ago, Parker had been the most eligible bachelor in town.

He leaned in a little closer, those steamy gray eyes of his brimming with testosterone-fired attraction. "Are you *sure* you're alright?" He let a finger trail down her arm.

Miranda swallowed as goosebumps bombarded her flesh. She cleared her throat. They'd talked about this. After her recent ordeal, she couldn't take much more than a casual friendship, even if they had gone through that ordeal together. Even if they had slept together just a few weeks ago.

"Yes. I'm just peachy." She shifted away and concentrated on her targets. "This outing *is* business, isn't it?"

He sat back again, his gaze still piercing. "Absolutely. Why would it be anything else?"

Liar.

Yesterday afternoon, when he'd plopped the file on her desk and asked if she wanted to work this weekend, she knew he had something up his sleeve. This assignment didn't call for the chief investigator and president of the Parker Agency and his best trainee.

This morning, when he'd picked her up in his midnight blue Lamborghini, held the door for her, told her the form-fitting red-and-white sundress he'd given her to wear as a "disguise" looked stunning with her dark hair, she knew this excursion had all the trappings of a date. Parker was making an excuse to be with her, trying to keep her from moping around her apartment alone this weekend.

While the camera caught Pretty Boy and Simmons gaping at each other again, he leaned in and exhaled against her ear. "You're doing an excellent job."

She shifted in her chair, ignoring the chill bumps skittering down her back at the warmth of his breath. "Thanks, but you already said that."

"Did I?"

In a deft move, he slipped an arm along the back of her chair, with a lot more charm and subtlety than Witherspoon. "You've come a long way since you started at the Agency, Miranda."

Too soon, Parker. "Really?" she asked, finding her voice had gone hoarse.

"Yes, you have."

"Thanks," she said. Again. And reached for her glass. She put it down again.

She couldn't get down another swallow of wine. Her throat was too tight. Their bland conversation was too heavy with the subtext of things neither of them wanted to talk about. The horrendous fight they'd had three weeks ago. The day she'd stormed out of his office, never intending to come back. The day he'd saved her life.

How long would she stay in Atlanta and keep working for the Parker Agency? The jury was still out on that one.

Parker inhaled patiently and leaned back to study the woman beside him. He removed his arm from the back of her chair, but it took all his restraint to keep from taking her in his arms and kissing the daylights out of her right then and there. After mourning Sylvia's death for three years, he had finally fallen in love.

But it was too soon. He was too aware of her pain. Of those dark, tempestuous feelings that simmered just below her surface. Those emotions had given them a decidedly rocky start. He had to give her space and time to settle in again. Work was what she needed now. Nothing hazardous, of course. Not yet. Just a small case or two. Something to rebuild her spirit.

He longed to see that spirit back in full bloom. She had tremendous strengths. A keen eye. A sharp mind. The persistence of a bulldog. And she had a few weaknesses. Those, he would handle. Once he finished training her, she would be one of the finest investigators the Parker Agency had ever had.

Not in all his years as an investigator had he ever met anyone quite like Miranda Steele.

She was a kindred spirit. A defender of the defenseless, driven by his own fervent passion to protect the helpless and avenge the innocent. No one had ever touched him so deeply. Or exasperated him so thoroughly.

Stubbornly, Miranda beat back the lusty emotions her boss had aroused. This wasn't a date, no matter how much Parker wanted it to be. She was on assignment. And Witherspoon and Simmons were rubbing noses like Eskimos. She tilted her head and once more allowed the mini cam to "capture the memory."

Then she scowled. Would this evidence be enough? "These shots aren't like catching them together in the sack," she complained. "Do you think they'll be enough for Witherspoon's wife to take him to the cleaners?" Poor woman.

Parker waited a beat, sipped his drink. "What makes you think our client is female?"

She blinked at him. Huh? "Does Witherspoon swing both ways or something?"

Almost imperceptibly, Parker shook his head. "Objectivity, Miranda. *Mr.* Simmons is our client. It's Farrah Simmons who's the primary cheat. Witherspoon is single."

What? "That wasn't in the file. I'd have seen it."

"Yes, you would have. I left it out."

Her mouth fell open. She glared at Parker. "You what?"

"I wanted to see if you'd ask. You didn't. You assumed." He gestured toward the targets.

Miranda snapped her head back in place and thought of the pages in the file. There had been several references to "the client," with no name specified.

"The client" thought Witherspoon had been seeing Simmons for about a month. "The client" thought they had been sweethearts in college. "The client" reported that Simmons was an old flame. Miranda had assumed "the client" was Witherspoon's wife.

She exhaled an exasperated huff. "You trying to show me up, Parker?"

"Not at all." He chuckled, those sexy laugh lines forming at the corners of his eyes.

She shifted in her seat, grinding her teeth. "Oh? So what's with the double-cross?"

"It wasn't a double-cross. It was a test."

She arched a brow. "A test?"

"A lesson in objectivity. Without objectivity, you risk going off on tangents. You waste valuable time." He reached over and patted her hand. "Don't take it to heart. Everyone brings their own biases to a case. Every investigator has to learn his or hers."

"Ever the teacher, aren't you?" She pulled her hand away and ran her fingers over the condensation on her almost untouched champagne. "I'm not biased."

"Not even a little bit after all you've been through?" There was tenderness in his voice. He knew her too well.

She'd been through a lot, but that didn't make her unfair. "Mighty thoughtful of you to point that out."

Parker frowned, annoyed she wasn't getting the point. "Miranda. You're tough, sharp, and you have an uncanny instinct for cutting through bullshit and getting to the gritty truth underneath. But…sometimes you jump to conclusions too quickly. You need some objectivity. Objectivity can protect you. Objectivity can—"

"Don't tell me. Save my life?"

"Yes."

He'd said similar words to her before. She sat back and blew out a breath, wanting to lambaste the sneaky PI. "So is this case for real? Or is it just an excuse for a date?"

His eyes flashed with insult. "Of course, it's real. James Simmons paid the Agency a large sum to verify his suspicions about his wife." The furrows in his brow deepened. "I wouldn't bring you out here on a ruse. Or for a 'date,' as you put it."

"Hah," she snorted. "Tell that to someone who was born yesterday." She wished she could get up and walk away, but her unbiased professionalism kept her butt in her seat.

His jaw tightened. "Your reaction merely underscores my point."

"Oh, it does, does it?"

"You need more objectivity. This isn't personal, Miranda."

"Isn't it?" she said a little too loudly. Then she sucked in her breath when she saw Witherspoon glance their way. "Uh oh."

"Don't look surprised."

"I know that," she hissed. She looked away. "Did he see us?"

Before Parker could answer, Simmons rose, gave Witherspoon an affectionate tweak on the nose and strolled away.

"Where's she going?"

"Not sure."

With a long-legged, decisive gait, Simmons strode past the tables, heading toward the far end of the track near the barns.

"Checking on her family's horses before the race?" Miranda hoped.

"Probably."

She glanced back at the table. Witherspoon got to his feet, tossed some bills on the table and started off in the opposite direction. Crap. "Are they on to us?"

"I don't know, but we can't lose them." Parker rose. "You follow Simmons. I'll stay on Witherspoon. If I don't call you, we'll meet back at our seats near the finish line in one hour. Just before the races begin."

"I'm on it." Miranda rose and nonchalantly fell in behind Simmons, keeping a reasonable distance between them.

She felt awful. If she screwed up this assignment just because she'd let Parker get to her, she'd never forgive herself. She had to concentrate. Throwing off the bad feeling, she focused on the thrill coursing through her veins.

Now there was a real chase.

CHAPTER TWO

Miranda followed the quick-paced Simmons across the uneven ground, cursing the high heels she'd worn. And the gall of Parker for pulling that little "test" on her. And for denying he had ulterior motives for bringing her here.

Okay. So she'd jumped to conclusions about Witherspoon. Detective work brought out the hunter in her. But she wasn't biased. She knew women could be as nasty as men. Hadn't she gotten into as many fights with one sex as the other, during her barhopping days?

If Simmons suspected she was being followed, she didn't show it. She strode past the press tents, waved casually to a group of friends relaxing in lounge chairs, wended her way around bales of hay that marked the paths to the paddock. She marched past fences where jockeys and trainers were warming up their horses, finally taking a turn toward the large barn that boarded the steeplechase contestants.

Miranda was right behind her, still fuming. Objectivity. She had objectivity.

Open-minded. That's what she was. Okay, she was working for Simmons's husband, not Witherspoon's wife. Simmons's husband was the one who'd hired the Parker Agency. But what if he wasn't a very good husband? A neglectful man could give a wife a wandering eye. What if he was like the abusive jerk Miranda had been married to?

Simmons was nearing the barn now. It was a long, brown wooden structure with open stalls, so the horses could poke their heads out and get plenty of air. Not fancy at all, which surprised her. At its near end sat a boarded-up structure, like a lean-to, with a dark opening for a door. Must be where they kept supplies.

Miranda's heart sank. Simmons would probably just give her prize steed a pat on the nose and head for the stands, making this excursion nothing more than a good walk. All they'd have was the footage of the monkey business at the pavilion. They'd have to put in more hours to catch Simmons and Witherspoon in the sack together.

And then something strange happened. As she reached the building, Simmons ducked into the lean-to.

If Miranda had blinked, she would have missed it. But she didn't blink. She headed for the enclosure. As she reached it, a low, sensual moan greeted her ears.

Already? That was fast. Someone must have arranged to meet Simmons in there. Her heartbeat picking up, she strolled casually past the door, then stopped and pressed herself against the side of the lean-to. Holding her breath, cautiously she peeked through the opening.

Next to some riding gear, Simmons had some guy pressed up against the wall. It wasn't Witherspoon. This one had dark hair and was shorter. Another old flame from college? He had Simmons's skirt hiked up to her waist, and his hands were all over her ass. Simmons was unbuckling his belt.

Two lovers? One cheater cheating on another cheater? Simmons's husband must have never heard of Viagra.

Making sure she wasn't seen, Miranda reached up to turn on the high-powered directional microphone hidden in the ribbons of her hat.

Lover-Number-Two's pants slipped down around his ankles as Simmons straddled him. *And they're off.*

They both groaned and pawed each other. One thigh rubbed against another. *And it's Lover-Number-Two on the outside.* Breathing heavily, Simmons attacked with her tongue. *The filly takes the lead.* They kept at it. Miranda tilted her head, suppressing a giddy thrill as she captured a good half-minute of nice, x-rated footage. They both were moaning, on the point of orgasm. *Heading for the home stretch…they cross the finish line.*

There you have it, ladies and gentlemen of the jury. Didn't have to be Witherspoon. Cheating was cheating. Miranda hoped Farrah Simmons had a good lawyer.

Pleased with herself, she straightened and leaned against the wall a moment to catch her breath. How's that for objectivity, Parker? No matter how she felt about the people involved in a case, she did her job.

She was just about to head for the track when she heard the sound of a horse.

Not the normal neighs and snorts you hear around a steeplechase, but a fierce, frenzied whinny. A wild screech pierced the air. Then sharp banging, like a round of gunshots. She felt the vibrations through the wall behind her. Along with the sensation of icy fingers snaking down her nerves.

Something was wrong. Bad wrong.

A man shouted. People began to dash toward a stall down the way, yelling like the barn was on fire.

She turned and watched a heavyset man rush to the angry horse. "Whoa, Calypso. What's wrong, boy?"

Another man reached up and grabbed at the animal's rope, but it pulled out of his hands. "What's the matter with him?"

"He's going berserk."

Miranda caught a glimpse of a horse's head bobbing up and down in the stall. Then he reared into the air, as if he'd suddenly gone mad. As if the enclosure was suddenly too small for him and he was frantic to get out.

The heavyset man reached for the beast's halter, but couldn't catch hold of it. "I don't know what's wrong," he shouted to the other man. "I left for only a minute to get a bottle of water. He's never acted this way before."

The horse came down on his front legs. He ducked his head, and the sharp bang, bang of his back hooves hitting the stall shattered the air once more. There was another sound, too, like a dull thud.

A crowd started to gather.

"What's going on?"

"What's wrong with that animal?" a woman shouted.

Another man dared to step close enough to take a look at the enclosure. As soon as he did, his hands shot in the air. "There's someone in there! Get that horse out."

"Unhook the latches."

There wasn't much of a barrier for the door. A movie-theater-like rope and a piece of canvas stretched over the opening.

Someone got it open, and the chestnut bounded out, snorting furiously, his beautiful coat shimmering with sweat in the sunlight. He bucked and kicked his long, graceful legs in the air, as though hornets were attacking him.

The sight was as dazzling as it was bizarre.

Three strong men seized the animal's halter. Another peered into the stall "It's Ms. Langford," he shouted. "My God, what was she doing in there?"

Shrieks came from the curious onlookers.

Panic pumping through her veins, Miranda raced for the stall, pushing her way through the swarm of people. When she got to the barn, she peered through the mesh wire that fenced in the upper part of the enclosure.

The sight took her breath.

Freshly torn and splintered by Calypso's hooves, loose boards hung from the back wall. The wood was punctuated by gaping holes. And there in the hay, beside the wall, lay the body of a woman.

Miranda glared at the gawking crowd. "Isn't anybody going to do anything?"

Too stunned to speak, the onlookers blinked at her.

CPR. Her training took over and she marched into the stall, went straight to the body. But as she leaned down, she saw the blueness of the woman's skin. A finger against her throat told Miranda she was dead.

Good Lord.

She'd seen dead bodies before. Too many, recently. The bodies of children. But that didn't stop her gut from wrenching hard enough to give her a jolt of pain, her mind from reeling fast enough to make her wobble. She struggled to get hold of herself, forced herself to breathe, as she took in the scene.

A girlish, blue-flowered sundress was wrapped around the dead woman. White gloves covered both hands. Delicate, short curls, as red-gold as Calypso's coat, lay tangled and matted in the hay.

Mid-thirties maybe? Hard to tell from the face. The fragile cheekbones that must have been beautiful a few minutes ago were now broken and bruised in a lacerated mass of bleeding flesh.

Her eyes were open. Sea green. Cat-like. Mangled from the injury, they seemed to gaze in two directions at once.

A smashed straw hat lay upside-down next to her hand as if she'd just taken it off. Except that it, too, had been crushed by the animal's hooves. There was something under it. A piece of paper?

Miranda felt dizzy. The stall suddenly seemed cramped and close. A strong scent of booze came from the body, but there was also a mix of animal odor, the smell of death, and…a man's cologne?

"Desirée," a voice murmured behind her.

Miranda spun around and saw a man standing behind her in the hay.

Tall and rather thin, he was dressed in jeans, a tangerine suit coat and teal-and-green tie. The festive colors seemed garishly out of place at this scene, like a dish of rainbow sherbet in a morgue. But the tie was askew, his coat a bit rumpled, almost like he'd slept in it.

His streaky, bleached-blond, shoulder-length hair was thick and wild, and there was stubble under his lip. Tears stained his cheeks. His eyes blazed with shock and grief.

He reached out for the woman as he stepped forward. "Desirée darling, what have you done?"

Instinct took over and Miranda got to her feet. "Don't come any nearer, sir."

Rainbow Sherbet focused on Miranda with a glazed look, as though he hadn't seen her until now. "I have to talk to her. I have to tell her something."

Too late for that. The poor guy was in shock. She took a step, stubbornly blocking him.

His face grimaced in anguish. "Let me pass. I have to talk to her. I have to tell her I love her." He lunged forward, his long-fingered hands awkwardly trying to push Miranda aside.

"No, you don't, buddy." She grabbed his arm, quickly twisted it behind his back in a classic move she learned long ago in one of her martial arts courses. She'd never dreamed she'd have to use it in a situation like this.

"Let me go." He struggled, pulling against her. "Don't you understand? That's my wife lying there."

Miranda softened her grip, her heart going out to the dude. She couldn't let him go, even though she knew he hadn't meant to attack her. He was out of his mind with grief. "I'm sorry, mister. But I can't let you touch anything. You'll contaminate the evidence."

His glazed eyes flashed with terror. "Evidence?"

"Yes, evidence." It might have been a bizarre accident, but sooner or later, the police would be here to investigate.

"Mr. Usher," a voice barked from outside. "What the hell are you doing in there?" A large man in a beige uniform ducked under the rope someone had put back up to keep out the crowd and took Rainbow Sherbet by the arm.

Thank God. "Are you with Security?" Miranda asked. "We have to secure this stall."

The man ignored her comment and reached for her arm. "You, too, lady."

What the— "Hey, watch it, buster. I'm with the Parker Agency."

"I have orders to clear the area." Without even acknowledging her claim, the big man pushed her and Rainbow Sherbet toward the narrow opening.

Outside, a small troop of uniformed guards was holding back the throng of onlookers.

"What's going on in there?" a voice demanded. "What happened to that woman?"

"Everyone stay back," the big man boomed. "The police will be here shortly to investigate."

"Investigate," Miranda said. "That's what I was doing." Or starting to.

As if he had wax in his ears, the guard shoved both her and the man out the door and into the crowd. Still in her grasp, Rainbow Sherbet twisted away and headed toward the far end of the stables.

"Hey," she cried. "Shouldn't someone be questioning that guy?" But he'd already disappeared into the sea of people.

Fitfully, Miranda scanned the scene as she reached under her hat and turned off the camcorder she'd just realized had been running the whole time.

Calypso and the men who'd tried to control him were gone. The mass around the barns had swelled with trainers, jockeys, vendors from nearby booths. There were spectators in suits, in bright dresses and the omnipresent hats. A host of hungry reporters from the press tent were there, too, itching for a story. Was the whole world here?

The teeming throng pushed her farther away from the stable, but Miranda had to get back in there. She was struggling to reach one of the guards, when the crowd parted like the Red Sea.

In the middle of the opening, Parker appeared.

Alongside him strode Lieutenant Erskine, Chief Detective of the Atlanta PD, and behind him several other police officers who must have been locals. It didn't take long for Parker to spot her. They had a sort of telepathy in stressful situations. He shot her a warning look that told her to stay put and out of trouble.

What the hell? Now she was pissed. *What's wrong, Parker? Am I not 'objective' enough to help out?* Again, she started to muscle her way back to the stall until she felt a tug on her arm and spun around with a gasp.

Sea green, cat-like eyes. Short, reddish-blonde curls. Girlish, blue-flowered sundress. White gloves. Straw hat. The same woman she'd just seen lying dead in the stall? She inhaled, her throat constricting.

"They say that's my sister in there." The words came out in a hoarse Southern accent.

Sister? Miranda focused on the woman. Her eyes were red and filled with tears. The lines around them told her she was probably in her early forties. Older than the woman lying in the hay back in the stall. She wore a dazed look. Shock.

The woman pressed a trembling hand against her chest. Even in her panic, she had the air of a Southern aristocrat. "I'm Delta Langford. Desirée's sister."

That explained it. "You...you look a lot alike."

She gestured awkwardly toward her too-sugary garment. "Desirée and I always dress alike for the Steeplechase. It's our...tradition." She gazed about with a wild stare, then fixed on Miranda. "Is it true? Was it *Desirée* in the stall?"

Slowly Miranda nodded. "Desirée Langford. That's the name I heard."

"What...what happened?"

Miranda didn't think she should be the one to give her the details. "There was an accident."

"Someone said she was trampled by one of our horses."

"I'm not sure." Miranda didn't really know who the crazed horse belonged to.

The woman shivered. "Is she...is she...really *dead*?"

Miranda gritted her teeth, hating to be the one to deliver the news. But she couldn't lie about that. "Yes, ma'am," she said softly.

With a shriek, Delta Langford put a lacey handkerchief to her mouth and closed her eyes. "Oh, dear God. Dear God!"

Gently Miranda reached for her arm. "I'm so sorry for your loss, Ms. Langford." She wished she could say something more comforting. She wasn't usually so touchy-feely with strangers, especially upper-crust strangers, but her heart went out to the poor, bereft woman.

Suddenly Delta Langford glanced around with her catlike eyes, as if she didn't want to be overheard. She grasped Miranda's arm and nudged her to the side of the barn, giving them some privacy from the grumbling crowd. "You're Miranda Steele, aren't you?"

"Yeah," Miranda answered cautiously.

"I recognized you from your picture in the paper."

She winced. Her first case at the Agency had made her semi-famous in Atlanta. She liked it better when nobody knew who she was.

"You work for the Parker Agency, don't you?"

She nodded.

Delta Langford leaned toward her. "Ms. Steele, I need your help."

"My help?" Involuntarily, Miranda backed away.

Nervously, Delta Langford glanced over her shoulder. She was looking more unstable by the minute. "I don't know what just happened to my sister, but I know *he* had something to do with it."

"He?"

"Ferraro Usher."

Miranda frowned.

Delta Langford sobbed into her handkerchief and gestured toward the barn. "I saw you coming out of barn with him just now."

Rainbow Sherbet. The dude with the colorful clothes and wild hair that she'd just had in an armlock. The security guard had called him Usher. Delta Langford must have been in the crowd, watching the commotion. "That's right, Ms. Langford. He said Desirée was his wife."

"*Ex*-wife." Her catlike eyes grew dark, she began to wring the lace hanky in her hands and mutter, half to herself. "The way that man carries on, you'd believe he really loved Desirée. But he'd just as soon destroy her. I know he had something to do with this." She wept again.

Miranda's investigator's ears perked up. The woman thought it was *murder*?

She recalled Usher's bewildered expression in the stall. He'd wanted to tell Desirée he loved her. Guess he still carried a torch for her. Sad. "He seemed pretty upset." As much as Delta was, though they both appeared a little strange to Miranda, even under the dismal circumstances.

"That man is often upset. He's a temperamental artist, as if that's an excuse," Delta Langford sneered bitterly. "Desirée's life was always in an uproar when she was married to him."

"I'm so sorry." Miranda glanced back at the barn. Police stood barring the entrance, refusing to answer the questions the desperate onlookers and reporters were shouting at them.

The woman in the stall had been kicked in the head by a horse. How could the guy dressed like a dessert parfait have caused that? "It looked like a freak accident to me."

"This was no accident," Delta insisted, darkly. "Ever since that man came into Desirée's life, he's caused her nothing but pain. It was because of him she drank too much. He got her into using drugs. Oh, my poor, poor Desirée."

"Whoa. This was way too much information. "Why are you telling me this?"

"Because you understand, Ms. Steele."

"Me?"

"That story in the newspaper. I read about your courage. Your own ex-husband. How did you face him? What nerve that took."

Miranda rubbed her arms. Yeah, she'd faced her ex, that vicious, abusive jackass. She wanted to tell Ms. Langford it was nothing, but that was far from the truth.

She'd had nightmares about it. The knife blade flashing through the air. The pain of its slash across her skin. The taste of her own blood. She had a new memory to replace the day he'd put her daughter up for adoption and tossed Miranda out in the snow. Parker was pushing her to go into therapy, but she didn't need a shrink. She knew where Leon Groth really was. Lying in a hospital room on life support, waiting to die.

"Look, lady—"

"Ms. Steele, I want you on this case." She said it more like a command than a request.

What case? Miranda shook her head. "I appreciate the compliment, but I don't take work for the Agency."

"You're turning me down?"

Miranda wasn't convinced it was murder. Besides, she couldn't take on a case by herself. She'd gotten in enough hot water for going out on her own the last time. "If you want the Agency's help, you need to contact Wade Parker," she told the distraught woman as gently as she could.

"I can't do that."

"Why not?"

A funny look came over her face as she uttered an odd half-laugh. "Wade Parker's a man. He wouldn't understand. Not the way you do."

That was different. Most people would jump at the chance to have Atlanta's top detective on their case. Most women would jump through a hoop of fire to be in the same room with Parker.

"Please, Ms. Steele." The woman's green catlike eyes pleaded with her, pulled on her heartstrings.

"Uh." Miranda shifted her weight and glanced toward the stall where Parker had disappeared. Snooping around a little was one thing, taking on a client was a different matter. She wasn't a full-fledged investigator yet. She couldn't speak for the Agency. Parker would have her head.

Once more, Delta Langford reached for her arm. "Ms. Steele, I need you to bring Desirée's killer to justice."

Justice. The word evoked powerful urges. The same impulses she'd felt on her last case. The need to act. To do something. To set things straight. What if Delta Langford was right? What if Ferraro Usher had killed her sister? If it were true, Miranda would love to be the one to put him away.

She looked back at the stall, considering the idea. At that moment Parker stepped out of the opening. His gaze went straight to her. He gestured for her to join him.

Saved by the boss. She turned to the woman. "Sorry, Ms. Langford. I gotta go." She hurried away as fast as she could.

"Ms. Steele," Miranda heard her cry out. "Is there a way to get in touch with you?"

"You can contact me at the Agency," she called back over her shoulder. Then she was out of earshot.

Whew, that was close. But deep down, Miranda hoped Delta Langford would phone her.

CHAPTER THREE

Desirée Langford's bizarre death turned what should have been a festive afternoon into something eerier than a scene from a Greek tragedy.

When the Northwinds Steeplechase officials announced the afternoon races were canceled, shock and anger rumbled through the throng on the field like an impending earthquake. Several of the stunned spectators shouted blind accusations, blaming anybody they could think of for the terrible mishap. The trainers, the coordinating committee, the security staff. It got so tense, Miranda was glad there was an army of security guards and cops around.

The only folks who weren't upset were the reporters. They had a nice, juicy story for the evening news. *Wealthy Heiress Killed in Bizarre Horse Accident.*

But was it really an accident?

Miranda leaned back against the plush leather passenger seat of Parker's Lamborghini, glad to finally be heading home. Parker had been pleased with the evidence she'd gathered for the Simmons case, especially when she'd told him about Lover-Number-Two, but he hadn't mentioned anything about what was now the main event—the body in the stall.

As they sped past rolling green fields, Miranda stared out the window thinking of Delta Langford. "Did you and Erskine have a nice reunion in the barn?" she said finally. Parker's relationship with the police Lieutenant could be strained at times.

Parker shot her a wary look. "After Witherspoon left the grounds, I was heading toward the barns to find you when the Lieutenant spotted me and told me what happened. I offered to help."

Uh huh. "Why didn't you want me in the stall?"

He sighed, his gaze steady on the Interstate traffic, which was lighter than usual. "I thought it was too soon for you. It was an ugly sight, to put it mildly."

Dang straight, it was. "So you think I'm too much of a wuss to handle it?"

Parker stiffened. "'Wuss' is the last word I'd use to describe you, Miranda."

"If it had been anyone else from the Agency," she said, letting her annoyance show, "even another trainee, you'd be glad to get them involved. You'd say it was good experience."

Parker tightened his grip on the steering wheel. Miranda Steele was the most defiantly stubborn woman he had ever met. "We've already been over this, Miranda. I don't want you near any violent cases until some time has passed."

With a grunt, she glared out the window. Parker could be so darn irritating when he was trying to protect her. But he didn't know she'd paid her respects in the stall before he got there. If she kept it that way, maybe this could turn into a case, after all. He wouldn't keep her off it if Delta Langford called the Agency and asked for her specifically, would he?

She cleared her throat and forced a calm tone into her voice. "So you and Erskine examined the scene. What do you think happened?"

He gave her a suspicious glance as he slowed to let a pickup truck pass him. "At first sight, it appeared to be an accident. The deceased had been kicked by her horse. Then we noticed the body smelled strongly of alcohol."

She remembered that. A couple in a Fiat convertible passed them. Parker didn't change his speed. The Lamborghini could make mincemeat out of that Fiat. He was stretching out their time together. Two could play that game. She'd make him talk.

"Alcohol?" she asked innocently.

"Ms. Langford has a history of alcohol and substance abuse. The swelling around her eyes and the color of her skin indicated recent drug use. The coroner will be able to determine more details. But right now, Lieutenant Erskine believes cause of death is suicide."

Really. Miranda sipped at the soda Parker had bought her before they left. "Not an accident, then."

"No."

"Are you still involved in the investigation?"

"No. Erskine merely wanted temporary backup due to the crowd. He's been asked to work with the local police."

She took in what he'd just told her. After several minutes, they neared the city and the scenery grew dense with subdivisions, office buildings and strip malls.

Delta Langford insisted Usher had influenced her sister to use drugs. Had they made her want to kill herself? "Erskine thinks it was a suicide just because Langford was a user?"

Parker shook his head. "There was a note."

The corner of white she'd seen in the hay. She'd thought it looked like a piece of paper. "Under her hat."

The centrifugal force tugged at her stomach as he cruised along the interstate's off-ramp. Glass structures towered over the trees. He glanced at her with that piercing look of his. "How did you know that?"

She shrugged. "I have my ways." His own line didn't sound so smooth coming from her lips. "What did the note say?"

He shot her another suspicious glance. "It appeared to be handwritten by Desirée. It implied she was tired of living. She wanted to die beside her beloved horses."

She wrinkled her nose. "That's weird."

"Not so strange. Though horses and steeplechase racing were her passion, Desirée Langford was given to depression."

"Her passion?"

"Her family owns Aquitaine Farms. She was one of the top thoroughbred breeders in the country." He changed lanes as they merged onto Peachtree Road and headed toward her apartment building. "Her loss is a blow to the racing community."

"Even more strange to do it today," she murmured.

Traffic grew heavy. Parker slowed. "She may have wanted to make a statement. The woman was moody. She had a bizarre personal life. She was known for her peculiarities."

"Such as?"

"Wild parties, experimenting with drugs, and a bad temper."

Just like Delta told her. "How do you know so much about her personal life?"

He gave her a sidelong glance. "I've known the Langfords since boyhood."

Okay. She'd wondered if Delta Langford was in Parker's social circle. So why was she so hesitant to talk to him about her suspicions? Miranda decided not to pursue that line of questioning. "According to Erskine, then, it wasn't the kick from the horse that killed Desirée, it was the drugs she'd taken."

"That's what he suspects. The coroner's exam will confirm it. Or not."

Miranda shook her head. "The woman shoots up, guzzles down some booze, writes a suicide note, then goes out to her favorite horse's stall and waits for him to kick her in the head to finish the job? On the day of the Steeplechase?" Didn't seem right, even if she were depressed.

She watched Parker staring at the car in front of him. He didn't buy it either. "According to the trainer, Calypso is a spirited animal. But something provoked him."

"What?"

"Anything could set off a nervous horse. The unfamiliar surroundings, the crowd, a child. The kicks might have been pure coincidence."

"Why did she stand behind the horse? Wouldn't she know better?"

"Good question. But if the drugs were hallucinogenic, as Erskine suspects, she might not have even realized where she was."

"Too buzzed to duck when a hoof was heading for your face." If she were lucky, too numb to feel the hit.

"They'll know more when they do the autopsy." He came to a stop at a light, turned and gazed at her keenly with those sexy, steel-gray eyes of his. "You didn't answer my question."

She titled her head. "What question?"

His eyes narrowed. "How did you see the suicide note?"

She shifted in her seat.

"Miranda?"

Man, he was pushy. "What was I supposed to do, Parker? Right after I got those shots of Simmons and Lover-Number-Two, the commotion started in the barn. It was only natural to go and have a look-see. When I saw the body, I thought I could revive her. But when I ducked into the stall, I saw she was dead. That's when I noticed a piece of paper sticking out from under the hat."

Parker inhaled as he gazed at the obstinate woman in his passenger seat. It was just like her to step right into the thick of trouble. If he didn't love her so much…he wasn't sure what he'd do with her.

Her red-and-white surveillance hat lay in her lap. Her dark curls had come down and fallen around her shoulders the way he liked. As always, her deep blue eyes with their sharp, black lashes spoke volumes to him. She was still fragile after her ordeal a few weeks ago, though she wouldn't admit it.

Today's incident was a tragedy. He had wanted to protect her from it, shield her from any more pain than she'd already suffered, but her independent spirit made that difficult. Yet, her stubborn tenacity was one of the traits he admired most about her. One of the traits that made him care so deeply for her. One of the traits they shared.

He studied her quietly. "What else did you see?"

Miranda pursed her lips. Parker's look went straight through her. He could get anything out of her with that look. But there wasn't much to tell. "I saw the body," she murmured. "Like you said. It wasn't pretty."

"Anything else?"

A honk came from behind them. Miranda pointed up. "The light's green."

He stiffened. "I see that." He moved through the intersection. "Go on."

She raised her hands innocently. "A weird-looking dude. Desirée's ex-husband."

He nodded. "Ferraro Usher. He's an upcoming artist. What was he doing in the stall?"

"Same thing I was. Looking at the body."

Parker drove in silence until the Colonial Towers building rose before them. He turned into the parking lot. "How did Usher seem?"

Seem? How could she explain that dazed glare in the strange man's eyes? "Confused. Shocked. The security guard pushed us out before we could get acquainted. You know Usher, too?"

"Slightly. I've been to a few of his shows downtown." Frowning, he pulled into a space and stopped the car. "How did you know his name?"

Good grief, he was persistent. She ran a finger along the edge of the window. Might as well fess up. He'd find out sooner or later. "Delta Langford told me."

His brow rose. "The deceased's sister?"

"Yeah. She recognized me from the newspaper and approached me. In her opinion, what happened to Desirée wasn't an accident. She thinks Usher did it."

He leaned forward with interest. "Oh? And why does Delta suspect him?"

Miranda stared down at her hat. Good thing she'd stopped the tape after she got kicked out of the stall. Wait a minute. Why had she been holding back? If she told Parker the details, he'd want to take the case.

She turned to him, excitedly. "Delta said her sister was unhappy with Usher. It sounded like they had a pretty rocky relationship. According to Delta, it was because of Usher that Desirée drank and took drugs." She played with the hat in her lap a moment, watched Parker's face grow thoughtful from the corner of her eye. "She, uh, asked me to take the case."

He inhaled with surprise. "What did you tell her?"

Miranda chewed on her lip in irritated frustration. It wasn't such a crazy idea. "I told her to contact the Agency."

He nodded curtly. "I'm proud of you."

"Thanks." She shot him a half-sneering smile, sat back, stared out at the lawn. A thin man strutted by with a white poodle on a leash. Must be one of her neighbors. She waited a beat. "I think it's worth looking into," she said tightly.

His face grew grim as he turned off the ignition. "We can't."

"Why not?"

"Simple. She hasn't hired us."

"She sort of hired me," she countered. Sure, it was a stretch. There was no money and no contract. Not even a verbal agreement. But Miranda wasn't the type to be bound by details. "What if I paid Mr. Ferraro Usher a little visit? You know, on my own. Just to feel him out, and—"

"Unless Delta Langford comes to the office and signs the requisite paperwork, there is no case." Parker's deep Southern voice was firm as Gibraltar.

Folding her arms in disgust, Miranda watched the eager poodle pull her neighbor by the leash to a side road that ran behind the building, nose to the ground. Yeah, always something holding you back. "Why not?" she said through gritted teeth.

His broad shoulders stiffened. "Investigating on your own wouldn't do any good. Without a client, nothing you discovered would be admissible in court. You know that."

She narrowed her eyes, suspicious. "It's more than that."

He sighed. "Delta and Desirée's father is Eli Langford. He's one of the city's top real estate developers."

She thought back to a night when Parker had taken her to dinner. From a view overlooking the city, he had pointed out his father's many projects. Wade Parker, junior was a local real estate mogul. "Eli Langford is your dad's rival?"

He nodded. "My father's chief competitor. Though we've known each other all our lives, our families have never been close."

Miranda knew Parker's gift for understatement. "Not close" probably meant a long-standing feud between the wealthy families. But even that wouldn't keep the Wade Parker she knew from investigating a murder like this one. "There's more to it, isn't there?"

She watched his jaw twitch uncomfortably. A rare occurrence for Parker. "Let's just say Delta Langford and I have an unpleasant history."

An unexpected rush of jealousy shot through her. Parker was a heartbreaker, after all. So that was why the woman didn't want to ask Parker to take the case. But she still wanted Miranda. The jealousy turned to a flush of pride.

"We'll have to let the police handle this one," Parker said sternly. "Besides, it's too soon for you."

"What do you mean, too soon?"

"You know very well what I mean."

Her ordeal with her ex.

Now he was being overprotective. That was for her to decide. Hadn't Parker admitted that she'd solved a high-profile murder? Hadn't he offered her a promotion under his supervision? She stared out the window. The thin man and his dog were two small specks under the far trees. She'd better go before she slapped her sexy boss. But she didn't move.

Her gaze wandered to the tall red brick building that had been her home for a little over two months now. If you didn't count the time Parker made her so mad, she'd moved out and been on her way to another state. She'd been lucky to get her apartment back.

She turned to him and caught his gaze drinking her in. His mind had moved on to those other things that occupy a man like Parker. Bedroom thoughts. "Have you made an appointment with a therapist, yet?" he asked tenderly.

Wrong guess. She bristled, then was touched by the concern in his eyes. She shook her head. "Uh-uh."

Parker sat back, his face thoughtful. He was in no hurry to leave. He drummed his fingers on the wheel. "As I've suggested before, it might help get you through this time, if you saw someone."

She'd been to shrinks before. They'd helped at first. Now she thought most of them were full of crap. She smirked. "Might help if I didn't keep running into dead bodies."

Leaning toward her, he took her chin in his hand, his eyes filled with concern. "I'm sorry you had to go through that today."

His tenderness shot straight through her. She didn't try to escape from his hold. His look made her think of a night not too long ago when, right on the white-columned entrance to her building, he had accosted her with a round of sensuous kisses. And caresses in places that made her mouth water.

"I'll be okay."

He reached for her hand. She let him cradle it gently. "As your employer, I'm concerned with your health."

Sure. All business. He'd tried that ploy before. "I'm fine. I just need to get over this cold numbness." Except for the mixed irritation and attraction she felt toward Parker, and the sudden interest in this case, she'd waded through the past two weeks, as if her heart was packed in cotton.

"Is that still lingering?" Parker asked.

She nodded. Her fight to the death with her ex, Leon Groth, had left her anesthetized. A shrink who'd seen her in the hospital had said that was normal, but she couldn't shake the mood. "I just wish I could feel something."

He leaned closer, the warmth of his tender smile giving her a glow she couldn't deny. "What does this make you feel?"

Her breath caught as his lips captured hers. His touch was gentle, as though he were afraid of bruising her.

She didn't feel so fragile. Hungrily, she kissed him back. As if on autopilot, her hands reached up and dug into his hair. Oh, that hair of his. She'd missed the feel of it. Thick, clean, without a speck of styling gel. The style of Parker's hair was inherent, natural. The style of his kisses was a kind of refined wildness.

She moaned as his mouth moved over hers, arched her back as his hand skillfully slipped to her breast while his tongue played over her lips and sent tingling sensations through her whole body.

He had a point. She could still feel passion.

It was their first kiss since her trauma. Two weeks ago, just after she'd been released from the hospital, she'd sat in a bistro with him, intending only to discuss the possibility of going back to work for him. But they'd ended up playing footsie under the table. She'd pulled back, gotten hold of herself. Her old demons were too much for her to handle at the moment.

She'd thought he'd understood. They'd agreed to dinner together once a week. But that soon turned into twice a week. And then there was the Steeplechase today, which he pretended to be just business. No wonder they called him the Silver Fox.

His warm breath fanned her cheek. His pressure increased, then lightened again, as if he were suddenly deciding even this was too much for her.

He pulled away, not wanting to push too hard, she guessed. He let his gaze wander out the window. "You know, I've never seen your apartment."

She must have misread him. He wasn't backing down, just warming her up slowly for the kill. She wasn't ready for that.

She laughed, attempted to straighten her hair. "I wouldn't want to shame you, Parker. My digs are so much fancier than yours."

"You haven't been to my penthouse, either." His tone was suggestive.

"You know what I mean."

His look grew warm, edged on searing. "I do. I remember it well."

It was his father's mansion where they had slept together. Where she'd first known what sex could be like with a man like Parker. It seemed like ages ago. But she still felt the sting of the bitter fight they'd had there where she'd told him it could never work between them. She had no intention of going back to that house.

She cleared her throat, picked up the hat that had slid down onto the floorboard. "Okay if I keep this over the weekend?"

"Of course."

She reached for the door handle.

His fingers traced her hand again. His eyes ran over her figure, her face. "How would you like to meet my father?" he said at last.

His father? She grinned. "The infamous Wade Russell Parker, junior?"

"Yes. I'm going to visit him in the nursing home tomorrow afternoon. Come with me."

Another excuse to be together. She ought to say no. "Nursing home?" She raised a brow. Parker had told her his father had checked himself into a place like that with a heart condition several weeks ago.

"It'll only be a short visit. We can have an early dinner afterward."

She couldn't let him go on concocting ways to see her. "A nursing home sounds too much like a hospital. You know how crazy I am about those places." She'd just spent almost a week in one.

He gave her a penetrating look. "You don't have to go if you're uncomfortable."

She was about to say she'd take a rain check. Then she gazed into those Magnum-gray eyes. Cool and hot at the same time. Not many women could say no to Parker. She could, but she didn't want to hurt his feelings.

"Sure," she shrugged. "It'll make up for not letting you *see* my place."

He chuckled. "I'll pick you up tomorrow at two."

She nodded. "It'll be interesting to meet the great and powerful real estate mogul who sired you."

With Parker's laughter in her ears, she opened the car door and got out while the getting was good.

Parker watched her lithe figure and shapely legs under the swirling skirt all the way to her doorstep. His heart swelled with desire, tenderness, and sheer love for the stubborn, feisty woman.

He reached for the ignition. Only a matter of time, he reminded himself. Only a matter of time.

CHAPTER FOUR

Those steamy, sultry kisses of Parker's still burning on her lips, Miranda stepped off the elevator and hurried to her tiny apartment. Struggling to force the man's charms from her mind, she changed out of her sundress and into a comfortable pair of jeans and a T-shirt. Then she got herself a beer from the fridge and settled down before the laptop she kept on a card table that took up about a third of her living room.

The laptop was new. She'd bought it with the bonus Parker had given her for solving the Taggart case. It had all the latest bells and whistles and was a lot faster than her old piece of junk. Right now, she was glad of that—she needed the upgrade to run the special software.

Carefully, she peeled off the Velcro rim of her flouncy steeplechase hat, pulled out the wireless receiver and hooked it up to a USB port. She fired up the special software and after a few mouse clicks, the day's activities began to replay before her eyes.

Simmons and Lover-Number-One sucking face and sipping drinks under the colorful umbrellas. Simmons marching toward the stables. Simmons going to town with Lover-Number-Two. She fast-forwarded through the images.

Hold it. There.

Desirée Langford's body in the hay.

Miranda had gotten a good shot of her with the hat camera. That poor, bloody, disfigured face. Once more, her stomach clenched at the gory tissue. An ugly sight, as Parker had said. The camera moved to the crushed straw hat with the corner of the suicide note peeping out from under it. Strange place to put a note like that, she thought.

Usher's voice scratched through her speakers. "Desirée..." She paused the film as his features came into view. Tall. Wild hair. Rumpled tangerine suit coat and teal-colored tie. Slowly she went through the film frame by frame, studying the man.

Thin, expressive brows. Large, round eyes, the color of seaweed, stunned with shock and horror. They were bloodshot. Pupils dilated. From coke?

Weed? Or just pure grief? He sniffed and wiped at his nose. He kept opening and closing his other hand in an agitated way. Not just grief.

What else did that look of his mean? Bewilderment from the loss, of course. And probably drugs. But even in his dumbfounded stupor, he seemed to know something. Something more than met the eye.

A small scar, about a half-inch long, ran along his right cheek. Interesting. He didn't seem to be the fighter type. He seemed the arrogant, pampered type. The type who liked attention and was used to getting what he wanted. And if a woman didn't give it to him?

Miranda knew what a cruel man could do to your psyche. Had Usher driven Desirée Langford to suicide? Or had he killed her more...directly? She felt a chill go through her.

Objectivity.

She was reading too much into this.

She sat back and blew out a breath. All she had was speculation and too many unanswered questions. It didn't look like she'd be getting any more information. Not with Parker's "unpleasant history" with Delta Langford, whatever that meant.

Feeling spent, she reached for the mouse and shut down the program. Maybe Parker was right. It was too soon to get involved in something like this.

She got up, grabbed her beer and strolled into the small bedroom. She stared down at the plain rented furniture. Unopened boxes sat on the floor. She hadn't completely unpacked since she'd come back to the place. Indecision had made her unable to put everything away. If she wasn't going to stick around, what was the point?

She put the beer on the dresser and bent down to open one of the boxes. Her breath hitched at the sight of gift-wrapped packages that greeted her like old friends. Pink, blue, yellow paper. Ribbons that had yellowed and flattened over the years.

Gifts for Amy. The baby Leon had taken from her thirteen years ago, just after she was born. Her only child.

She knew what was in the boxes. A teething ring and a pink seahorse for the bath, when Amy was one and two. A stuffed monkey for when she was four. A baby doll for when she was five. A Barbie for when she was ten.

Over the years, Miranda had lovingly picked out each treasure, wrapped it, stuffed it into cardboard boxes with the others, dragging them around as she moved from place to place, from one construction job to another. One day, she told herself, she'd be able to give them to her daughter in person.

A month and a half ago, she'd thought that day had come. She thought she'd find her daughter in Atlanta. She'd thought she'd come closer than she ever had. But it had turned out to be a lie. Now finding Amy seemed more impossible than ever. A hopeless dream.

She wiped her eyes. Long ago, after Leon had thrown her out and she was in the sanitarium, a shrink told her she was having an identity crisis. Back then, she'd decided to remake herself.

And she had. She'd studied martial arts, kept herself fit, taken construction jobs so she could stay strong and pick up tips on how to fight from her coworkers at the local bars after work. No man would ever hurt her again. She was strong inside and out.

Strong enough, she'd been able to face Leon.

Back then, she'd also promised herself she'd find Amy, but it was better that she hadn't. Leon wanted both of them dead. At the thought, that cold numbness stole over her.

Maybe she was having another identity crisis. She put the packages back and closed the box.

Maybe it was time to settle down and do something with her life. She'd taken the job at the Parker Agency to find her daughter, but it had turned into more than that. Parker had put out some feelers, but he'd come up with zip. Maybe…it was time to give up the search for Amy.

She blinked, tears stinging her eyes. She brushed at her nose. Crap. She hated crying, even when she was alone.

She got up, took a swig of beer. So should she settle down or take off again? She'd never been indecisive about moving before. It was Parker's influence. Why couldn't she walk away from that man?

He'd saved her life. Given her an interesting job. Loaned her some money she hadn't finished paying back. The least she could do was put in a few more months in PI training. Yeah, she owed him that much.

She rubbed her eyes, too tired to think about it. She needed a nap. Feeling more listless than ever, she shoved the boxes into the corner and lay down on the bed.

Maybe one day, she'd have the strength to get rid of them.

CHAPTER FIVE

Miranda had never liked hospitals. A nursing home, its institutional second cousin, wasn't the coziest place to spend a Sunday afternoon.

So how had she ever let Parker talk her into visiting his father here? she wondered as she followed him down a long corridor to a door labeled "Wade Parker, junior."

He opened it for her, and she stepped inside, expecting to find a sickly old man, laid up in bed.

Instead, she did a double take.

Gold-framed paintings hung against walls paneled in dark mahogany. Black leather chairs sat in a tasteful arrangement, a Persian rug on the linoleum floor. The four-poster bed was covered with a chinchilla quilt. Baroque music came from overhead somewhere. The smell of expensive cologne masked any hospital odor. The masculine decor was more like a rich man's library than the room of an invalid on his deathbed.

At the far end of the room, a wheelchair faced curtained floor-to-ceiling windows that opened to a small veranda. The head of its occupant peeked over the back.

"Father?" Parker murmured.

Slowly the wheelchair turned. Miranda resisted the urge to whistle. The man in the chair had a head of thick, pure white hair, impeccably styled, a matching mustache, crystal blue eyes. Dressed in a fine gray suit, a deep red Ascot at his throat, he was almost as good-looking as his son.

He steepled his hands and raised a carefully groomed brow that was the same pure white as the hair on his head. "Have you finally come to pay your respects to your ailing father?" His Southern accent, deeper than Parker's, oozed old world charm.

Irritation flushed over Parker's face. He glanced around the room. "Not too ailing to completely redecorate. Does the staff allow patients to alter their room this way?"

Parker's father gave a confident smirk. "Money always coaxes administrators to bend the rules, son." He waved a hand in the air as though dismissing the topic. "That's not the reason I asked you here." He caught sight of Miranda and charm spread across his face. "And who is your lovely companion?" Before Parker could answer, he raised his hand again. "Wait. I know." He pressed his palm to his heart. "Can this be the daring young woman who recently saved my son's life?"

Miranda shifted her weight. It was bad enough to be recognized from her picture in the paper. Lord only knew what Parker had told his father about her.

She stepped forward, extended a hand. "Glad to meet you, sir."

The elderly gentleman grasped her hand with both of his. "Ms. Steele, isn't it? Miranda Steele?"

She nodded.

"How can I ever repay you?"

Man, he was laying it on thick. She pulled her hand away and shrugged. "Your son and I are even. He saved my life, too."

He shook his head. "That's his job. He's always saving people's lives. It's rare when someone has to save his."

"It's my job, too." Sort of.

He nodded. "That's right. You're his employee. The Parker Agency is fortunate to have someone of your talent and spunk," he eyed her up and down, "and good looks."

The night they spent in his father's bedroom, Parker had told her what a notorious ladies' man his father was. The old gentleman's flirting was kind of charming. "Thanks, Mr. Parker," she said, trying to brush him off gently, "but I'm just a regular gal."

He studied her. "You must be special, or my son wouldn't be with you today. Would you, Russell?"

"Russell?" Miranda couldn't hold back a smile. Parker didn't mention his dad called him by his middle name.

Parker shot her a scowl and evaded the question. "You'll find Ms. Steele can be very stubborn when you try to change her mind about anything, Father."

Miranda grunted. "Me stubborn? You ought to take a look in the mirror."

Mr. Parker chuckled. "I see what you mean, Russell. You both share that characteristic."

Parker strolled to the small stainless-steel refrigerator in the corner and began inspecting its contents. "How could I be anything else, with you as my father?"

Might have known it would be a family trait.

"A good point. Oh, do help yourself, son. I'm well stocked, as always."

Loaded with champagne and caviar, Miranda guessed.

Parker went through a couple of shelves. "Perrier Jouet. Champagne truffles. Exotic cheeses. Pastries. This doesn't seem to be the diet of a heart patient."

Mr. Parker laughed. "My son, the perpetual investigator."

Miranda eyed the two men before her. She could sense the quiet tension beneath the male banter. Parker had told her once that his father had disinherited him when he became a cop. That had been a long time ago, but evidently there was still fallout. How else would two closely-related, bullheaded ladies' men get along with each other?

Mr. Parker smiled infectiously. "You're right, Russell. My genes were generous to you." He turned to her and spoke in a near whisper. "Don't be too stubborn, Miranda. If you are, life can dole out some bitter lessons to set you straight."

Sounded like he regretted the rifts between himself and his son. "I'll try to remember that," Miranda said.

Mr. Parker cleared his throat and moved his wheelchair to the middle of the room. "And speaking of being stubborn, that brings me to the reason you're here today."

Parker closed the refrigerator door. "I'm here simply to visit my ailing father, though he doesn't seem to be ailing after all."

"Nonsense. I asked you here to discuss the house."

Parker moved to the window and stared out of it. "I told you before, father. I don't want the house."

What house?

"You must take it. My accountant advises me that if I gift the house to you, the tax benefits will be enormous."

"I'm sorry, Father. I can't do that."

"You're screwing up my financials, Russell."

"Is that the only reason, Father? I would think you could make much more selling the house than you would gain on taxes."

"What house?" Miranda asked, though she thought she already knew.

Parker was silent. She watched his jaw tighten.

"The Parker estate in Mockingbird Hills, of course," his father answered since he refused to. "Our family home."

Oh, that house. The place where they'd made love. The place Parker had asked her to move into with him.

Parker exhaled in frustration. "I can't take the house, Father. I have my reasons."

Mr. Parker grunted. "It's been in our family for generations, son. It's a historical landmark."

"Then donate it to the historical society."

He tapped the wheelchair arm with his fist. "How can you be so crass? How could you ask me to give away our family home?"

Miranda looked down at her shoes, stinging with guilt. Was she the reason Parker didn't want the mansion?

Parked sighed, annoyance in his breath. "You seem well enough, Father. Why don't you keep the house? What are you doing in this nursing home, anyway?"

As if on cue, the door opened, and a nurse entered the room with a tray filled with little plastic cups. "Meestre P," she chided in a thick accent. "You didn't tell me you were having visitors."

The elderly gentleman's face brightened. "I wanted to surprise you, my dear."

My dear? Miranda and Parker stared at the woman open-mouthed.

Though she might be pushing fifty, the lady looked more like a movie star than a nurse. Her bright blue scrubs hugged her figure, the low-cut top revealing a tan, ample bosom, in a Sophia Loren sort of way. Her dark hair fell in luxurious strands around her shoulders.

She moved seductively to a coffee table and bent to set down the tray. "It's time for your afternoon pill, Meestre P."

She pronounced the initial like 'pay.' Hmm. What was that accent? Eastern European, maybe?

Parker's father wrinkled his face. "Oh, but Tatty, you know how I hate swallowing those nasty things."

She clucked her tongue at him. "Now, now, Meestre P. How will you ever get better if you don't take your medicine?" Her tone was motherly, half-teasing.

Miranda raised an eyebrow and looked at Parker. He gave her the same look. Their thoughts mirrored each other.

Parker's father turned his wheelchair and gleefully raised an arm. "Russell, Ms. Steele, this is Tatiana, my nurse. She's from Ukraine."

That explained the accent.

The woman smiled and nodded as she dutifully poured a glass of water from a pitcher and handed her charge one of the small cups.

Parker's father gave her a loving look. "Must I?"

She returned his gaze. "We don't want our blood pressure to go up again, do we, Meestre P?"

He gave her a wink, then downed the pills, wincing at the taste of them. And the water. He was used to stronger drink, no doubt, judging from the stash in the fridge. "She takes excellent care of me."

He wrapped an arm around the nurse's waist before she could get away. She seemed both embarrassed and enchanted by the gesture.

Parker's father turned to her and spoke in unintelligible words Miranda could only guess were the nurse's native tongue.

The nurse scowled at him, her laughter music as she shook her head. "You speak my language so badly, Meestre P. Your accent is poor, and you just called me a swine."

"Forgive me, my darling. My tongue fumbles. It was meant for other things." He grabbed her hand, opened it and gave her palm a full-mouthed kiss.

Tatiana sucked in her breath as her eyes widened with shock. "I must go. I have other patients to attend." With that, she wrested herself from the gentleman's grip, nodded to the company, picked up her tray and left the room.

"She leaves such a glow," Parker's father murmured after the door shut.

Mr. P, Miranda thought—a cute nickname for him.

"Is that why you checked yourself into this place, Father?" Parker demanded. "To chase skirts?"

Mr. P scowled. "How vulgar, Russell. It was the only way I could have the time to win Tatiana over. My feelings for her run deep."

"Indeed?"

"I mean it this time. Very well, yes, I did come here just to seduce her at first, but it backfired. I fell in love. Tatty and I have a bond like I've never felt with a woman since your mother."

Parker stared at him, unable to reply.

"We're getting married."

He was even less able to speak after that announcement. Miranda felt for him.

"That's why you have to take the house, Russell. I can't live there anymore. It wouldn't be fair to Tatiana. Too many memories for me. You can understand that, can't you?" He eyed Miranda.

She felt as though he could see straight through her.

Parker turned away. Biting back his anger, he clasped his hands behind his back and stared blankly at one of the paintings.

This visit had certainly turned out well, hadn't it? He had wanted to bring Miranda here to give her what sense of family he could. Instead, it had turned into a...surprise wedding announcement?

And an argument over a piece of real estate that did nothing but dredge up bad memories. Not the least of which was the day Miranda had walked out on him.

Other disturbing visions ran through his mind, as well.

He saw the mansion in Mockingbird Hills, with its spacious rooms, its halls, its grandeur, and its very walls seemed to echo with long-ago quarrels with his father. The squabbles after Parker's mother died when he was sixteen. The bitter wrangling during his senior year in high school, when he began to date Laura Turner, a young woman his father said was beneath him.

Laura. His first love. His first case.

She'd been taken from him too soon. Before they'd had even a chance to begin a life together. They'd been dating only about six months, when one dreadful night just before his high school graduation, she went missing. Her body was found a week later. She'd been brutally raped and murdered. In a blind reaction, Parker had joined the police force, making his father livid. His only son was to follow in his footsteps and take over his business, not become a lowly beat cop.

Parker could still hear their bitter shouts, their brutal exchange in the library. He could still see himself racing up the grand staircase to his room, packing a bag, storming out the front door, never to return.

His father never had understood that Parker had to join the police to find Laura's killer. That he blamed himself for what had happened that night. That beside himself, there was only one other person he could blame.

Delta Langford.

He ran a hand through his hair, forced himself back to the irritating present. *Getting married?* To an immigrant nurse? Of course, he had nothing against the woman, but when had Wade Parker, junior changed his mind about the requisite social status of a wife?

Forcing composure into his tone, he turned back around. "That's precisely why I don't want the house, Father. There are too many memories for me, as well."

The older man held his gaze a long moment. Parker thought he saw remorse in his eyes. He, too, remembered the arguments. "That was a long time ago, Russell."

He shook his head. "I'm sorry."

Miranda watched the somber lines in Parker's face and felt his pain streak through her own heart. She didn't know what caused that pain, but she knew it was deep. Parker had secrets. Things in his past he'd only hinted to her. The night they'd spent in that house, when young neighborhood girls were being murdered, couldn't help how he felt about the place. Not to mention their awful breakup in the elegant kitchen. There was more to it than that, she sensed. But still, he couldn't be serious about getting rid of his family home.

She decided to shake him out of his sour mood and forced a laugh. "Hey, maybe I should take the house."

She meant it as a joke to cut the tension in the room, but Mr. P blinked at her as though she'd just invented electricity. "Where are you living now?" he asked.

She frowned. "Colonial Towers."

He grimaced. "That slum?"

"Hey, it's not that bad. Okay, it's pretty small, but it's home sweet home." For the time being.

"Russell, why are you letting her live in Colonial Towers?"

Parker scowled. "Father—"

Mr. P waved a hand in his direction. "Never mind. What are you paying?"

"Excuse me?"

"Don't be shy. I'm a real estate professional."

"Private, not shy." But he could probably guess. She told him.

He rubbed his chin thoughtfully. "A fair price. I'll sell you my house for the same monthly payment."

Miranda snorted. "What?"

"I deal honestly."

A ten-bedroom mansion in one of the best neighborhoods in Buckhead for the same as her studio apartment? Had that frisky nurse given her patient too much medication? Then Miranda saw the gleam in the wily wheeler-dealer's eye. Ah, that was it. Mr. P had picked up on her off-hand remark and decided to run with it.

Make Parker take the house by pretending to sell it to her for cheap. Pretty cagey.

Okay. She'd play along. She grinned at him. "Sounds like a plan."

"This is ridiculous, Father," Parker grumbled.

Working like a charm already. She held back a smile, as she put her hands on her hips. "What's so ridiculous about it?"

Parker fixed her with a glare that went right through her. "Are you sure you want to tie yourself down like that, Miranda?"

She pursed her lips, feeling the barb. He knew she hated the thought of putting down permanent roots. But what did it matter? The deal was just a ruse.

She glanced over at Mr. P and saw another twinkle in his eye as he watched the sparks between them.

She turned to face him. "So what kind of deal do you have in mind, Mr. P?"

His white teeth sparkled with delight. "The typical deal. We'd have to arrange financing, allow you to have the customary inspections done, have the papers drawn up."

Papers? Miranda gulped. She glanced over at Parker. His expression hadn't changed. This wasn't real, she told herself, but better make it look good.

"I was thinking of a lease-to-own agreement." She'd had one of those for a house outside Cincinnati years ago when she'd toyed with the idea of settling down there. For about eight weeks.

Slowly Mr. P nodded. "Sounds good. Rent for six months before deciding to buy?"

"With an option for an extension."

"Of course."

Parker wouldn't buy that she intended to stick around for six months. "And one week's notice if I decide I don't want to buy," she added.

Mr. P's cagey smile gleamed brighter. "Agreed. What a shrewd negotiator your associate is, Russell. Ms. Steele, have you ever considered a career in real estate?"

"Not for me, but thanks. Is it a deal?"

He stretched out his hand. "Absolutely. I'll have my lawyers draw up the papers."

Papers. There was that word again, sending an icy tingle down her spine. Relax, she told herself. The way Parker was fuming under the collar already, it wouldn't take long for him to tell Mr. P to call off this phony deal. There would be no papers.

She took Mr. P's hand, and they shook.

Parker stood watching them, hidden fury painting his handsome face. Miranda had never seen him so unsettled. "This is a terrible idea, Father," he said darkly. "Miranda can't live in the Parker mansion."

"Why not?"

He bristled. "For reasons I don't care to go into with you."

Miranda knew the reasons. He meant she couldn't live there alone. Without him. He was protecting her from the trauma she'd gone through when she'd stayed at the place. Another incentive for not letting her go through with the purchase. Icing on the cake.

"It's okay, Parker," she told him flatly. "I'm a big girl. I can handle it."

Parker ground his teeth and studied his father and the woman he loved—despite how much she continued to exasperate him. She needed to heal. To stay away from triggers like his family estate. After what happened when she was there, the place would only make her relive her past. He couldn't allow her to live in that house, to stay there alone.

He was about to tell his father he'd reconsider taking the place, when he saw them exchange glances and his powers of observation finally kicked in.

Of course. This was a ruse. A ploy to get him to take the house. His heart suddenly warmed. Miranda Steele might not admit it, but she cared enough about him to strike a deal she didn't really want with his father, so he wouldn't lose his inheritance. Or at least, pretend to strike a deal.

She wouldn't go through with it. He knew the part of her that wanted to be strong, independent, free of others. But he also knew the part she denied and hid. The part that was tender and vulnerable and needed other people. The part of her that longed for roots and more permanent ties.

She'd been alone and adrift for over a decade. She needed stability. She'd just given him the opportunity he'd been looking for. Two could play this game. He'd call her bluff.

He folded his arms and struggled to hide a smile. "I warn you, Father, if you persist in this venture, I'll have to see my lawyer."

His father waved a hand and chuckled with glee. "Ms. Steele, I'll have *my* lawyers contact you in a few days."

Miranda glanced over at Parker again. Rock of Gibraltar. He hadn't budged. What the heck? "Sure. Whatever you say, Mr. P."

"It's a new day, Russell. We're both turning over a new leaf in our *affaires de coeur*. It's time for some changes."

With a victorious tilt of her chin, Miranda turned to Parker. Then she caught the self-satisfied look in his eye. Huh? Had he guessed what she and Mr. P were up to? He was an ace investigator, after all, well schooled in reading body language.

Nah. He'd give in sooner or later. It might take a little time, but he'd never let her go through with signing any papers.

She hoped. And yet, from the sneaky look on his face, the Silver Fox might have a plan of his own up that debonair sleeve of his.

CHAPTER SIX

As private investigators' offices go, the Parker Agency was an anomaly. Nothing like the one-room holes-in-the-wall in old detective movies on *The Late Show*. No, Parker's company took up several floors in the Imperial Building in downtown Buckhead, and included a large gym for the employees, training rooms, upscale executive offices, and a massive, mazelike cube bank.

If that wasn't enough to say "rich and successful," the whole place was done in a classy blue-and-silver décor, complete with Art Nouveau paintings and potted plants.

For IITs, Investigators In Training, mornings at the Agency were filled with calisthenics, martial arts, and lectures on topics like collecting evidence, report writing, and criminal law, while the afternoons brought background checks and routine insurance work at their desks.

It was the cushiest job Miranda had ever had. But by Wednesday morning after the steeplechase, as she got a cup of coffee, turned on her computer, and scanned her emails before class, she wondered why she was still hanging on here.

Maybe it was time for another road crew job. Maybe in Missouri.

Absently, she touched the spot on her chest where Leon, her psycho ex-husband had cut her. She'd had another bad dream last night. Running down a dark hall, gasping for breath, desperate to escape the grimy, greedy hands that clawed at her.

She'd woken up in a cold sweat.

She put down her coffee cup and stared at her computer screen, willing the dark memory away. But her mind only replaced it with the image of Desirée Langford lying dead in her horse's stall. Had Desirée been attacked like that? Had *she* been killed by a crazy ex-husband? The thought made Miranda feel a strange kind of bond with the dead woman.

She drummed her fingers on the desk, scanning the outline for today's lecture Detective Judd had emailed. *Interrogation Methods*. Sounded interesting. Something she'd had experience with, though mostly on the receiving end.

She was halfway through the twelve-week training course required for IITs. Finishing it would mean having to make a real commitment to the job, to the Agency, to Parker. She'd never intended to stay on that long.

But now she was about to become a homeowner, thanks to the conniving Mr. P. Nah, Parker wouldn't let her buy his family home right out from under him. He just didn't want to admit she had the upper hand. He was probably working out the details with his father right now.

Then she thought of that look in Parker's eye. His little "test" about objectivity. That steamy kiss in his car after the steeplechase. He could be just as cagey as his father. Was the sneaky investigator up to something? The day she walked out on him, out of that gorgeous mansion of his, he'd said he was in love with her. And her feelings for him were…too confusing to think about.

All right, she might be insatiably attracted to Parker on a physical level. And maybe more than that. He'd been good to her, treated her better than any man ever had. But a relationship could never work between them. She'd made that clear. She had too many issues. They had too many differences. Why didn't Parker see that?

The man was too stubborn for his own good. If he had any tricks up his sleeve about this house business…well, maybe she'd have to get serious about turning in her resignation.

"Time for class." Curt Holloway's lanky form appeared over her cube wall.

"Ready, Steele?" As always, Dave Becker was at his side.

Her two best buddies at the Agency, the pair had befriended Miranda on her first day and she'd been secretly grateful to them ever since.

Per the company rules, they were both clad in suits and ties. Of course, Miranda was in a suit, too. A black, form-fitting number with a slit so high up the skirt, it would make Gen, Administrative Head of the IITs and Parker's only daughter, send out a fuming email reminder about the dress code, when she got a load of it. Gen and Miranda weren't exactly best buds.

"Interrogation Methods." Holloway bounced up and down on his toes with excitement. Tall and thin, with a habitually suspicious air, Holloway was a former Marine from Texas.

His cohort rolled his eyes. "I know all about that after my last job." Becker's accent was nasally Brooklyn.

A short, nervous little guy with a large nose, big expressive eyes, and thick dark brows, he reminded Miranda of a cross between Groucho Marx and Joe Pesci. He'd worked in Collections before coming to the Agency.

"This is different." Holloway bent his knees to give Becker an elbow in the ribs. "This is interrogating *criminals*. I'm going to get an A on this assignment."

Becker gave his buddy a punch on the arm. "You won't score higher than me."

"Oh yeah?" Miranda closed her email, grabbed her notebook, got to her feet, and sashayed past the pair. "We'll see who gets the highest score."

"Are you telling me you went straight to your desk this morning?"

"Sure. Like I do every morning."

Miranda leaned in toward her suspect. Becker squirmed.

After a long, boring lecture, Detective Judd, the large-bodied senior staff member with a head of thick, wavy gray hair, had announced to the class that the cucumber sandwich he'd brought for lunch had been stolen. He suspected one of the IITs. Their assignment was to find the culprit.

After grilling all her classmates, she now had her buddy Becker in a chair at the front of the class and was proceeding to skewer him. "No stopping at the water cooler?"

"Nope."

"No ducking into the break room for coffee?"

His lips twitched. "I wasn't in the mood today."

Dang if he wasn't tougher than she'd thought. She was sure of her facts. She even had an eyewitness.

She turned her back to him and strolled toward the whiteboard. "So how come Smith over there saw you with your head in the refrigerator?" She peered hard at him over her shoulder.

His big dark eyes bugged out, but he didn't answer. He rubbed his palms over his thighs. She was making him even more nervous than usual and felt a stab of guilt. Judd had warned about giving in to feelings like that.

She took a deep breath, put her hands behind her back, and paced back toward him. "Did you forget to bring your own lunch?"

His thick black brows shot up. He ran a finger under his collar. No answer.

She stopped pacing right beside his chair and got in his face. "Were you...*hungry?*"

"Not a bit." He grinned awkwardly, gnawing on his lower lip.

She had him. With a frown, she pointed at his mouth. "So what's that piece of green stuck between your teeth?"

"Huh?" Right on cue, Becker's stomach growled, loud enough for everyone to hear. The class broke out in giggles.

Becker threw up his hands, as if he were being arrested. "Okay, okay. I took Detective Judd's lunch out of the fridge and ate it. I was going to pay him back."

Miranda let out a breath, glad this assignment was over. The faces of her classmates were a mix of admiration and jealousy. Especially Smith, who'd never liked her.

From the corner, Detective Judd nodded, looking smugly pleased. "Excellent work, Steele. You get an A."

"You really got me good, Steele," Becker moaned on the way back to their cubes.

"What do you mean? You did a great job playing the thief."

"I should have held out longer, but I just couldn't." Becker was so easily intimidated, she'd thought she could get him to confess to the O. J. Simpson case, but he'd held his own, even though all the evidence pointed to him.

She gave him a nudge. "C'mon, you put up a heck of a fight, Becker."

He shook his head.

"You wouldn't have confessed if your stomach hadn't growled."

Becker's cheeks turned a shade of red that clashed with the décor. "Or gotten cucumber stuck in my teeth." He scraped at his incisor with a fingernail.

"I can't believe you actually ate that sandwich," Holloway said as they rounded the corner where a tall potted palm stood. "Yuck."

"Detective Judd told me I had to, or it wouldn't be realistic. If only I'd checked in the mirror."

"Don't be so hard on yourself, buddy." Holloway shrugged a shoulder toward Miranda. "Can't forget she's a pro."

Somehow her colleagues had gotten the impression she had years of PI experience. She'd never corrected it. After cracking the Taggart case, she had a feeling they wouldn't believe her, anyway. When she'd returned to work less than a week after her knife fight with Leon, she'd gotten a standing ovation from her class, which was humbling and embarrassing at the same time.

"Oh, I don't mean it that way, Steele," Becker said in his nasal accent. "I'm glad to know the pro in the class."

"Likewise," Holloway chimed in.

She came to a halt at her cube and glanced inside. The red light was blinking on her phone. A message from Parker? Her heart skipped a beat. No doubt he'd come to his senses and was ready to tell her the deal for the mansion was off. She knew he'd cave.

Holloway leaned over and peeked at her phone with a bet-that's-from-the-boss look. Becker and Holloway worshipped the ground Parker walked on.

Jeez. She grinned at her buddies awkwardly. "Guess the boys at Quantico need some advice."

Holloway's cheeks colored, but Becker's chin dropped. "Quantico?"

She rolled her eyes and gave him a punch. "Stop with the sucking up, you two. You're making me nauseous."

With a cough, Holloway looked down at his shoes. Becker studied the floor.

Crap. Now she'd hurt their feelings. She had no tact at all. "You did fine in class, Becker," she insisted. "You had me doubting the evidence for a while."

He looked up again, his eyes hopeful. "Did I? Really?"

"Sure. Judd wouldn't have picked you to play the bad guy if he thought you'd cave easily."

"Yeah, you got a point." He nodded about five times.

Both he and Holloway wanted to do well at the Agency. She couldn't help it if this detective stuff came easy to her. Maybe always feeling like she was on the other side of the law gave her an inside perspective.

"You two want to grab some lunch?" Holloway asked.

Becker's face grew pensive. "Nah." There was a faraway look in his moody brown eyes. "I've got a peanut butter sandwich at my desk. I'll just eat that. Talk to you guys later. Thanks for making me feel better, Steele." He stuffed his hands in his pockets and ambled away to his own cube.

She stared after him. That was weird. Becker loved going out to eat in the Buckhead restaurants. "I wasn't trying to show him up, Holloway."

"It's not that."

"What is it then?" she asked.

Holloway looked around in that suspicious way of his. "He'd kill me if I told you."

Miranda shrugged, turned toward her cube. "Suit yourself." She didn't want to pry.

Holloway touched her arm. "You know those skip-tracing exercises we did in class a few weeks ago?"

She thought back. "Yeah." When they'd first got computers.

"Remember he tried to find a girl he dated in high school?"

She nodded. "Uh huh."

"Well, ever since then, Becker's been kind of hung up on the idea."

She folded her arms. "What idea?"

"The idea of finding his old girlfriend. He spends a lot of time searching on the computer for that girl. He makes calls back home asking about her. He even spent money on one of those 'Find Your Classmates' ad."

"Good grief. Most of those sites are bogus. The Agency's databases are a lot better than those online ads."

"That's what I tell him, but he won't listen. He keeps saying she was the love of his life. He's really carrying a torch for her."

"Old flame, huh?"

"Yeah, he's got it bad. I told him he should bury those old memories. But he says he can't. You know how it is."

Not really. Miranda's "old flame" had tried to kill her.

"Wish there was some way to take his mind off the past."

Take your mind off the past. That would be a good trick.

"Hey, you don't know anybody we can set him up with, do you?"

"Huh?" Holloway was definitely barking up the wrong tree if he wanted help with that. She made it a point not to get emotionally involved with anyone. She didn't have girlfriends. "Sorry," she said flatly. "I'm not the social type."

"Sure. Just thought I'd ask." He looked down at his feet, scuffed at the carpet with the toe of his long shoe. "So, you want to try the new Italian deli down the street?"

She was about to say yes, when she remembered the message on her phone. "Uh, I think I'm going to be busy for a little while, Holloway. You go ahead. If that place is good, I'll go next week."

He looked almost as let down as Becker. "Okay, but I think you're missing a great chicken parm sandwich." Guilt stung her as Holloway shrugged and moved down the hall.

She just wasn't good with people. Not when it came to being friends. Shaking it off, she settled into her chair, tapped her fingers on the desk beside her phone. Parker would want to have a talk with her. He'd probably take her to lunch and gently, in that suave way of his, explain why he couldn't let her take the house.

She'd have to let him go on and be sure to act disappointed. But not too much. She didn't want him to change his mind.

With an eager grin, she picked up the receiver and pushed the button. The recorded voice gave her a jolt.

"Ms. Steele, I hope you've reconsidered taking my case." The familiar Southern drawl had the same mix of sadness and demand Miranda had heard this past weekend.

Delta Langford.

Miranda's heartbeat picked up. "My poor sister's body is barely cold and already Usher is contesting her Will because she didn't leave him anything. All he cared about was her money. That must be the reason he killed her. He was such a brute. If only you could have seen how cruel he was to her. How miserable he made her. Ms. Steele, you're the only one who understands. You have to help me."

The voice paused for a long moment, as if Delta were deciding her next move. "I need to talk to you in person. Come to the funeral this afternoon. It will be at Saint Simon's. Please." The message ended with a beep.

Miranda stared down at the phone and shivered. Usher was cruel. He made Desirée miserable. She knew how that felt. Images of that weird, bleached-blond dude in the tangerine coat brutalizing Desirée Langford shot through her mind. If he had killed her...

Funeral. Quickly, Miranda reached for her keyboard and brought up the *Atlanta Journal-Constitution* on her computer. Sure enough, there was a story about Desirée Langford's service this afternoon. It was at one o'clock. She clicked the link for a map to Saint Simon's. She'd have just enough time to grab a bite and get over there.

"Steele."

Miranda almost took a sky dive through the ceiling. She spun around.

Gen.

Parker's daughter was head over the IITs and she'd hated Miranda from the day she started at the Agency. She especially despised Miranda's relationship with her father, though she'd softened a bit after Miranda had saved his life.

But from the flash of her dark eyes and the tinge of her complexion that made her short blond hair look even blonder, Miranda had a feeling that was wearing off.

She decided to act formally. She sat up straight. "Yes, Ms. Parker?"

Gen's eyes narrowed. "Someone wants to see you."

Now? She glanced at the clock on her computer. "Can it wait? I've got to meet someone for lunch."

"No, it can't," Gen snapped, irritated at not being immediately obeyed. "You'll just have to cancel. Or be late."

"Okay. Guess they can wait for me." Gritting her teeth, she got up and followed Gen down the long hall.

They wended their way around a corner and down another hall, until they reached a huge meeting room. Miranda stared at the closed paneled doors. She'd heard this was where the board met, but she'd never been in here.

With the expression of a drill sergeant with indigestion, Gen reached for the handle and gestured her inside.

Gingerly Miranda stepped through the entrance and noticed several suited men milling around near the credenza at the end of a long meeting table. Were they who she thought they were? She swallowed, suddenly feeling like she was breathing through cotton. Goosebumps sprang up along her arms. Her nails dug into her palms.

Then she recognized the white-haired gentleman standing in the middle of the suits, this time sans wheelchair.

With a huge smile, he stepped toward her, arms outstretched. "Ah, Ms. Steele. How good to see you." Purring with Southern charm, he clasped both her hands, which were still clenched.

"Hi, Mr. P." Her voice cracked.

He was perfectly dressed in a sharp-looking, light colored business suit, and looked as fit as a twenty-year-old. Guess he had a fast recovery, now that he had his—uh, affairs settled.

"Are you ready for your closing?" he crooned.

She opened her mouth, but no sound came out. "Closing?" she managed to gasp, finally.

Mr. P smiled smoothly. "Why yes, Ms. Steele. My staff has everything prepared." He gestured gallantly toward the suits.

"They do?" Parker wasn't calling off the deal?

"Yes, of course," he chuckled. "Are you ready to sign the papers?"

"*Papers?*" As in legally binding documents? What happened to their secret conspiracy? Icy fingers dancing down her spine, she leaned toward Mr. P and whispered. "Where's Parker?"

He waved a hand. "Oh, just over there."

She glanced up as one of the lawyers stepped aside and saw Parker in the corner leaning against the credenza, his arms crossed over his sexy broad chest, a sly look of satisfaction on his handsome face.

She narrowed her eyes at him. That scoundrel. Had he seen through her charade about buying the house? He must have. He was calling her bluff. No wonder he looked so smug.

And Mr. P was letting him? No. She got it now. Mr. P was calling Parker's bluff right back. And she was stuck in the middle of a family feud. A battle of the wills between two powerful men, both used to getting their way. What had she been thinking? Good thing she'd asked for a six-month rental agreement. She refused to be tied down. Or let Wade Parker the Younger win this one.

With a careless shrug toward her boss, she turned to his father. "Okay, Mr. P. Let's get on with it. Where are the papers?"

Mr. P grinned with delight. "Eager, are we?" He snapped his fingers. "Sullivan?"

As she sat down, the lawyers gathered around the table like hawks. The one named Sullivan slid a thick contract in front of her. Swallowing, she opened it and squinted at the tiny print.

She drew in a tense breath. This wasn't real, she told herself. Picking up the pen one of the suits had set before her, she waggled it in Parker's direction.

Without budging from the corner, he watched her steadily with those deep gray eyes, eyes the color of the barrel of a Magnum, as if daring her to go through with it.

Hah. She turned back to Sullivan. "Where do I sign?"

"Several places, actually." His voice was dull and lawyer-like. He pointed to the first line.

In a minute, she'd break out in a sweat. Miranda exhaled and met her boss's steady-as-Gibraltar gaze. "You sure you want me to do this, Parker?"

From across the room, he shot her a cavalier, iceberg-like smile. "It's entirely up to you, Miranda. I don't tell my employees how to spend their money."

She smiled back at him through gritted teeth. What a stubborn mule he was. Was he really going to make her go through with this? So what if she signed papers? It was only a six-month rental agreement. Okay. If that was what it took to make Parker come to his senses, she'd do it. She'd play hardball with him.

She eyed Sullivan. "Where's my escape clause?"

He looked bewildered. "Escape clause?"

Mr. P chuckled. "Ms. Steele is very shrewd, Sullivan." He turned a page and tapped a paragraph with his finger. "Right here. You may void the contract at any time during the first six months with one week's notice."

She read it over again carefully. "No strings attached?" It didn't look like it.

"None whatsoever."

She looked up at Parker. No reaction. Crap.

With a grunt, she picked up the contract and began wading through the mumbo jumbo. It wasn't like it was the first time she'd seen a legal document. She'd carefully read every rental contract she'd ever signed, which were quite a few, making sure no shifty landlord was taking advantage of her and that she wouldn't be overcharged.

She noted several passages written in Mr. P's favor. He was no fool. But nothing she couldn't live with. Everything looked pretty kosher. There was even something about Mr. P supplying a part-time staff. Guess he thought the house was too big for her and he wanted to keep it in good shape. Fine. Whatever.

She set down the papers, picked up the pen and tapped it on the polished tabletop. "You really don't mind?" This time she played the Southern belle and batted her eyes at Parker.

It was so out of character for her, he had to fight back a grin, but he gestured gallantly. "Be my guest."

Angry shivers ran down her arms, down her back, up again. She'd get Parker for this. Hadn't he heard payback's a bitch?

Okay, no more stalling. She took a deep breath and turned to Sullivan. "Where do you want my John Hancock?"

As the lawyer pointed and turned, pointed and turned, pointed and turned, she scribbled down her name, initials, current address, whatever he asked for.

Just before she thought she was going to get writer's cramp, he reached the last page. They were done. Sullivan gathered up the papers as one of the other suits handed her a set of keys.

With a grunt, she shoved them into her pocket. *Take that, Parker,* she thought, glaring at him. *Be as smug as you like. Once what I just did sinks in, you'll be begging me to give back your house.*

And she bet it wouldn't take six months.

As the lawyers packed up and drifted out of the room, Miranda glanced at her watch. She had about twenty minutes to get to Saint Simon's. Wait—wouldn't Parker and his dad be going, too? Not good.

She eyed Parker's father. "Terrible news about Desirée Langford, isn't it, Mr. P?"

He shook his head, his expression growing serious. "Dreadful. In business, Eli Langford is my worst enemy, but I certainly feel for his loss."

She nodded toward Parker and tried to sound casual. "That's right. Your son mentioned that you and Langford are rivals."

He scoffed, straightening his jacket. "That's putting it mildly. We bid against each other on properties, and it can get mighty ugly at times, but that's the least of it. The truth is, I can't stand the man."

"Really?"

Mr. P shuddered, as if thoroughly repulsed. "Not an ounce of finesse. Has all the civility of a German U-boat. And the way he's raised his daughters." He shook his head.

Now he'd piqued her curiosity. "What do you mean?"

Mr. P rubbed his white mustache with his manicured fingers a moment, shot his son a wary glance, as if weighing how much he should say. "The girls' mother died when they were in their teens. Eli immediately took up with another woman he'd been seeing on the side for years. After that, he paid little attention to his daughters. While they were growing up, he ignored his girls, let them run wild in their teens. When they inevitably got into trouble, his method of discipline was to belittle them in front of his friends. I've seen him bring both of them to tears in public more than once."

Miranda felt her skin prickle. "Good grief. He sounds like an ogre."

Mr. P's crystal blue eyes turned dark, as all the charm drained from his face, replaced by anger and insult. "Eli Langford is a brute of a man. It's no surprise what happened to Desirée."

Miranda cast a glance at Parker. A story like that ought to bring out the rescuer in him, but today his face was a rock.

She turned back to Mr. P. "I read in the paper the funeral's this afternoon. Guess you and Parker will be going."

His thick white brows knitted together as he pulled at his lapels again. "Uh, no. Eli and I can't be in the same room together without arguing. Unlike him, the Parker family has some sensibilities. It would be cruel to make an appearance at the service. We have sent flowers and our condolences, though."

Emerging from the corner, Parker finally broke his silence. "As the Agency has," he added. "Unfortunately, given the tension between us, it would be ungracious for anyone in our family to attend. And for anyone in this office." He eyed her carefully.

She met his gaze. Did he sense she had plans? Didn't matter. He wouldn't be there and what Parker didn't know wouldn't hurt him.

But she moved her head up and down, like a good little employee. "Sure, I understand. I guess the police concluded their investigation." They wouldn't have released the body otherwise.

Parker nodded sternly. "They determined it was suicide. They found high levels of PCP in her bloodstream."

"Angel dust? So she took an overdose."

"Yes, tragically."

Or she was given one. Miranda bit her lip and looked down on the carpeted floor, taking in his words. Did Parker really buy that? Why wasn't he getting involved?

"Well, I'd better get back to work." She picked up her copy of the contract and held out a hand to Mr. P.

He shook it heartily. "A pleasure doing business with you, Ms. Steele." His voice was warm again. Genuine, and as musically Southern as his son's.

Miranda gave him a wink. "Likewise."

She shot a fake grin at Parker. "See ya later, boss." Then she turned and headed back to her cube.

After waiting a few minutes, she looked around and found the coast clear, then quietly pulled her purse out of the drawer. There were no classes this afternoon. She could finish the skip tracing she had to do later.

After running her fingers through her thick hair and straightening her clothes, she slipped out of the back without anyone seeing her. She wouldn't be gone long. Not more than a couple hours. Parker would never be the wiser.

Good thing she was already wearing black.

CHAPTER SEVEN

The high gothic columns of Saint Simon Episcopal echoed with the strains of somber organ music that was punctuated, after a pause, by the hollow coughs and stifled sobs of the crowd seated down below. In dark clothing, too warm for this time of year, a subsection of Atlanta's wealthy grieved the loss of one of their own.

One so young, so vibrant, with so much success and promise, that this age-old ritual only served to underscore what these mourners had in common with the rest of humanity.

Death.

The Grim Reaper knew no difference between the affluent and the needy. Between the glamorous and the plain. Between the pampered and the poor. On his playing field, everyone was equal.

Everyone was a loser.

At the end of a long aisle, a robed priest stood behind a gilded altar, surrounded by pale statuary that stretched to the ceiling. Before the altar, a small forest of sympathy lilies, remembrance wreaths, and floral arrangements sat on flimsy stands. In front of the foliage the closed silver casket sat, covered with a huge spray of what must have been a hundred red roses. Along with the other flowers, they perfumed the air.

Lovely. Silent. Alone.

The music ended and the minister moved to an ornate podium. He began to speak, attempting to soothe the grieving listeners with images of the hereafter.

Miranda scanned the crowd. Delta Langford was in the front row, a dark, wide-brimmed hat, thick with black netting covering her face. She lifted a black lace handkerchief to her lips to smother her sobs. Beside her, a large man with dark gray hair put an arm of comfort around her. Eli Langford, Miranda surmised.

She thought of what Mr. P had said about the man. He didn't seem like the brute who had humiliated his daughters in public when they were teens. Had

44

they mended their fences over the years? Or was it this tragedy that had forced Eli to show some affection? In any case, the scene only made Miranda feel even more sympathy for Delta.

Across the aisle, down a few rows, Miranda recognized Ferraro Usher, Desirée's ex. He sat stiffly, his long blond hair combed and pulled back in a band, his clothes dark and muted, like everyone else's, instead of the colorful garb he'd worn at the steeplechase. His eyes bore straight ahead, as if he were in a trance.

The minister finished. The organ crescendoed. Pallbearers appeared to bear the casket away. The assembly rose, formed into rows and followed it down the aisle.

Outside, Miranda lagged behind the processional, wondering whether to follow it into the cemetery. She hadn't learned much yet, so she decided she might as well.

The ceremony at the gravesite was just as bleak. She stood off to the side and watched the family, now seated under a blue canopy erected by the funeral home.

The crying was louder out here. Delta's. Eli Langford's. Usher's. Especially Usher's. When the priest sprinkled the coffin with a handful of dirt and bade the victim farewell, Usher broke down in bitter sobs.

The awful sounds made Miranda think of her mother's death over a decade ago. She had been just twenty, married to Leon a little over three years. She hadn't spoken to her mother in months. A stern, detached woman, she rarely communicated with anyone her own age, let alone the daughter she had nothing in common with. A co-worker had found the body and called the police.

Miranda had been numb. It was the first death she'd experienced in her family. She didn't count her father's abandoning her when she was little. Her father was still alive, for all she knew. At the time, she'd felt bewildered, lost. She'd reached out to Leon, but there was no comfort there. He didn't talk to her either. Didn't hold her. Later that night, she remembered him yelling at her again for something she'd forgotten to do.

Suddenly, her mind snapped to three weeks ago and she was back in that wine cellar with him. The gleam of his knife slashing at her. The smell of old wine. The terror crushing her chest. The pain shooting through her back as she fell to the hard, stone floor.

With a jolt, she came back to the present. The priest was announcing that there was food for everyone in the Fellowship Hall.

She glanced around, self-conscious. Maybe Parker was right. Maybe she did need a shrink.

She peeked at her watch. Food, huh? She hadn't had lunch, and she hadn't made much headway so far. Might as well check it out.

She turned to follow the others and felt someone come up beside her. "Oh, Ms. Steele. You're here. You got my message. Thank you for coming."

It was Delta Langford.

Miranda nodded silently. *Wouldn't have missed it for the world* didn't seem appropriate.

"Does this mean you'll take my sister's case?" she asked, a pitiful quiver in her voice.

Guilt pricking her conscience, Miranda thought about what Parker had said earlier. "The police think it was suicide."

Delta stopped walking and blinked at her. Then her catlike gaze bore into Miranda with the intensity of a stalking leopard. "It wasn't suicide," she hissed through gritted teeth. "I know Usher did it. My poor sister. What he put her through. And now she's gone." She gasped a sob into her black lace handkerchief. "He has to pay, Ms. Steele. Someone has to make him pay for what he did to her. Only another woman could understand. You know what we go through at the hands of men who say they love us."

The woman sure knew how to push her buttons. But she'd better come clean. "Look, Ms. Langford, I have to be honest with you. I'm not authorized to take cases for the Agency. I have to go through Parker."

Her eyes took on an even wilder look. Almost like panic. "Isn't there some way around that? You're an excellent investigator. You just solved a high-profile murder."

The woman knew how to play the ego card, too. Miranda blew out a frustrated breath. "Why don't you come into the office tomorrow and talk to Parker about it?"

Delta took a step backward, hugging herself tightly. "I couldn't do that."

"Why not?"

She looked away. Then began to talk quickly. "I don't want my father to know. I've had two failed marriages, Ms. Steele. The last one nearly ruined me financially. To protect me, my father keeps an eye on my bank account. He'd know if I wrote a check to the Parker Agency. An investigation would be too much for him right now."

Miranda felt her stomach twist. Delta Langford was living with her father? And he handled her finances for her? This family was bizarre. But she knew the real reason the woman didn't want to go to Parker was that "unpleasant history" he'd mentioned.

"You could talk to one of the other detectives," she suggested gently. Senior investigators could take on cases. Maybe Judd.

Delta's eyes grew watery. "I want *you*, Ms. Steele. You're the only one who truly understands." She lifted the lacey black kerchief in her hand as if speaking to it. "My life has been so difficult over the past few years. Now my dear sister is gone. Murdered. And I'm the only one who knows it." She pressed the hanky against her face and began to sob again.

Miranda shifted her weight, her heart breaking for the poor women. Well, she'd come here to snoop around, hadn't she?

"Look, Ms. Langford, while I'm here, I'll do a little preliminary investigating."

Delta raised her head, hope spreading over her face. "Will you?"

She'd try. "I can't promise you anything, but I'll see what I can find out."

"Oh, thank you, Ms. Steele." She reached out a gloved hand and squeezed her arm in that crushing, emotional grip.

"Don't thank me yet. In the meantime, while I'm here, pretend you don't know me."

"I beg your pardon?"

Miranda lowered her voice. "If a certain somebody thinks we're pals or something, it won't be good."

She nodded. "Of course. I understand." She let go of Miranda's arm. "Thank you, again, Ms. Steele," she whispered, "Please let me know what you find out."

Miranda nodded, then watched Delta Langford turn and join the other mourners as they somberly moved into the Fellowship Hall.

CHAPTER EIGHT

The smell of garlic, basil, and baked bread made her mouth water as Miranda descended the stony steps into the cool of the hall. Two long tables stretched out on either side of the large, open room, both crowded with delicious-looking goodies. Already, people were busy serving themselves.

She hadn't eaten all day and since she had to blend in, she grabbed a plate and got in line.

She was digging into a pan full of cheesy lasagna covered with thick tomato sauce when she heard an accent just as thick and almost as Italian. New York Italian, that was.

"Well, if it isn't Ms. Congeniality herself."

Miranda looked across the table and met the murky stare of a woman about five-two, with short dark hair. She was dressed as a server in a black long-sleeved shirt with a black bow tie at the neck.

"Fanuzzi." Miranda hadn't seen her in ages. Well, at least a few weeks.

She folded her arms over her trim chest. "Guess after that splash about you in the papers, you don't have time for your old friends on the road crew."

Miranda winced. "Sorry. I kind of suck at relationships."

Her dark brows drew together. "I'll say."

Back in the day—before Miranda's job at the Parker Agency—Joan Fanuzzi had been the Dump Person on Miranda's paving crew, directing the hauling units around the job site, and Miranda had been a Lute Person. It was the best job she could get when she first came to town. Fanuzzi had always been nice to her, had acted like she wanted to be friends. Especially when she heard Miranda was working for Wade Parker.

Miranda had promised to keep in touch, but she hadn't.

She caught the cheese that was hanging from her plate, twirled it around her plastic fork, and scooped up some noodles with it. "Nice to see you." Quickly, she stuffed the forkful into her mouth so she wouldn't have to answer questions. It didn't work.

Fanuzzi narrowed her eyes at her. "What the hell are you doing at the Langford funeral, Murray?" She always called her Murray. It was a nickname the road crew had given her. "You trying to rub elbows with the local lords and ladies?"

Miranda glanced around, hoping no one had overheard the woman. She chewed the noodles, swallowed, and dodged. "I could ask you the same thing."

"Hey, I got business here. I'm the caterer."

Miranda looked over the tables again at the spread of food. There were a couple of younger helpers dressed in the same black shirt and tie Fanuzzi had on. "Caterer? What happened to the road crew? Did you lose your job?"

"Nah. But I got bills to pay. My ex can be slow with his child support. So I started this business on the side. I always wanted to cater fancy events."

"Really? I never pictured you as the domestic type."

"What are you talking about?" she said defensively. "My mother was from Tennessee. She taught me how to fry a chicken. But my specialty is lasagna. So?"

"So?"

"So what'd ya think?"

Guess she wasn't too mad for a compliment. "It's good. Delicious." Miranda eyed the table. "You got any hot sauce or anything?"

Fanuzzi scowled. "You gonna ruin my lasagna with hot sauce?"

"I like my food with a kick."

Now Fanuzzi looked wounded.

"Sorry. It's good. Really. Even without the kick." She put another bite in her mouth to prove it.

Fanuzzi put her tongue in her cheek and eyed her carefully. "You never answered my question."

"What question?" Miranda said, still chewing her last bite.

"What are you doing here at the Langford funeral?"

Miranda put down her fork, leaned over the table and whispered as quietly as she could. "I'm sort of working a case."

Fanuzzi blinked. "Really? Is Wade Parker here?"

"No."

She looked disappointed. Fanuzzi had gushed like a giddy teenager over the idea that Miranda was working for Parker.

Miranda wiped her mouth with a paper napkin and gazed over the crowd. Halfway across the room, huddled near a supporting column, Eli Langford was talking to a couple of men who looked like they might be business cohorts. Eli was large, heavyset, and dressed, as she would expect, in an expensive-looking solid black suit. He leaned on a cane for support and there were dark circles under his eyes. As he shook his head woefully, his jowls jiggled. He seemed to be in genuine pain.

Behind Langford, a door opened, and Usher strode into the room. He glanced about, but didn't speak to anyone. Finally, he sauntered toward the far corner and sank into a chair, stretching his long, lanky body as if every muscle ached with grief. Blankly, he stared out a window.

Miranda turned back to her former co-worker. She had to make sure she kept quiet. "Hey Fanuzzi, you want to help me out?"

Fanuzzi suddenly brightened. "Sure."

"I really need to mingle right now. But if anybody asks, pretend you don't know me."

Fanuzzi nodded, her dark eyes big. "Right. I get it. Never saw you before in my life."

Miranda smiled. She liked Fanuzzi. She caught on quick and seemed just as quick to forgive her shortcomings. "Thanks. Glad you understand. We'll keep in touch. I promise. Hey, maybe we can go out together this weekend."

Fanuzzi smirked. "Yeah, and maybe the Easter Bunny will bring me a basket of winning lottery tickets."

"Lighten up. I'll give you a call." Though she wondered herself whether she'd keep that promise.

"Sure."

Peering through the crowd toward the corner, she saw that Usher was still sitting there staring out the window. She tossed her paper plate in the trash, picked up a Styrofoam saucer of cake from the end of the table and headed for him.

Time to practice those interrogation techniques she'd learned about in class.

"My condolences," Miranda said when she reached Usher's chair.

The man didn't budge. As if he were deaf, he sat there, dark and brooding, his lower lip pouting, his eyes swollen. The sensitive, artistic type in mourning. Or giving a good imitation of it.

She cleared her throat. "Mr. Usher?"

He came out of his trance, turned his head. "Oh. Yes, thank you," he said with a dismissive, superior air. Then he squinted at her. "Do I know you?"

"I think we met once."

He peered at her more closely. The small scar along his right cheek moved as his jaw flexed. "Oh, yes. The arm wrestler at the Steeplechase." He didn't move to offer her his seat, unlike most men of the upper class. Miranda decided she'd rather stand. His eyes narrowed with suspicion. "Are you a friend of the Langfords?"

Miranda shifted her weight. "I know them distantly. I saw the notice in the paper and thought I'd stop by to offer my sympathy. It was tragic."

"Tragic," he repeated, looking straight ahead. He sniffed and swiped his nose. Then he began to mutter, as if talking to himself. "Tragic is an understatement. A beautiful vibrant life cut down in its prime. Desirée had so much to live for, so much to offer." His voice was soft, almost feminine on the surface, but it had a rough, edgy undertone. He rocked a little as he spoke, digging at his expensive pant legs with his long fingers, his arrogant air fusing with his agitated grief.

50

"But she didn't offer it to you?" Miranda asked quietly, allowing just enough sympathy to seep into her words.

He turned back, tried to focus on her. "What?"

"I heard you'd separated." She paused. "I'm sorry."

His shoulders slumped. "She left me. But I still loved her."

"She didn't feel the same?" She kept her tone soft.

Suddenly, he glared up at her. "I don't wish to discuss it with you—"

"Steele. Miranda Steele."

He pulled his long body up in his chair as if trying to get hold of himself. He gave her a condescending look. "Ms. Steele, I don't mean to be rude, but I'm beside myself today, as I'm sure you can understand."

Oh, no you don't. She wasn't going to let him weasel out of being questioned. He might seem genuine, but all that grief could be just crocodile tears. *Objectivity.* She could hear Parker's voice ring in her ears. "Maybe it would help to talk about it," she said as gently as she could. "What was your relationship with Desirée like?"

With a sigh, he stared out the window again. "We had no relationship. She divorced me. It was final three months ago."

"But you still saw her, didn't you?"

He didn't ask how she knew that. He simply shrugged again. "When I could. When she let me."

When you forced yourself on her, Miranda thought. Now things were starting to add up. Usher abused his wife, got her into using drugs, and when she tried to leave him and clean up her life, he stalked her, tried to get her to come back to him. When she refused, he decided no one else could have her either.

Would be an open and shut case if she had some proof. "Did you ask her to come back to you?" It was getting harder to sound soothing and sympathetic.

"A thousand times."

Just as she thought. "And when she refused, did it make you angry enough to kill her?"

Slowly Usher turned his head. His large, round, seaweed-color eyes blazed with indignation. "The police concluded my wife's death was a suicide."

"Right. From an overdose of PCP. Is that how you see it, since her life was so beautiful and vibrant? Do you think she'd do that to herself?" Her voice had lost its motherly quality.

He sucked in a short, outraged breath. "This is terribly rude of you, Ms. Steele. Are you investigating her death?"

She leaned over him. "Just curious about your opinion, Mr. Usher. Weren't you the one who introduced her to PCP?"

His mouth opened, his cheeks flamed with what looked like sheer dread. Guilty.

It took him a minute to recover. "I don't use illegal substances, Ms. Steele," he spat, straightening his coat. He rose and started to move into the crowd, his bloodshot eyes still shooting lasers at her. At his sides, he was still opening and closing his fists. Then he stopped and turned back. "If you think Desirée's death wasn't an accident, you should start with Dr. Kennicot."

"Who?"

"Dr. Gabriel Kennicot," he snarled. "Desirée's favorite horse vet. A man seventeen years her senior whom she worshipped since she was a teenager. Her 'old flame,' so to speak. He's the one she left me for. And he's the one with access to PCP."

She put a hand on her hip, resisting the urge to grab the haughty artist by the lapels and shake him. Instead, she stepped close to him and lowered her voice. "And what reason would Desirée Langford's veterinarian—slash, 'old flame'—have for killing her with PCP?"

A strange expression crossed Usher's face, the closest thing she'd seen on him to a smile. "An ancient reason, Ms. Steele," he whispered. "Jealousy. Desirée was about to leave him and come back to me."

The Georgia sun was settling in for the night, spewing a glorious spray of pastels across the sky above the silhouettes of buildings and treetops, when Miranda pulled into the Colonial Towers parking lot. With a tired huff, she got out of her car and made her way down the sidewalk.

Since the funeral that afternoon, she'd tried to work off the lingering frustration from her encounter with Ferraro Usher by running laps around the Parker Agency gym and doing skip traces at her desk, but the nagging questions had kept buzzing in her brain.

Desirée Langford left Usher for a veterinarian she'd been in love with since she was a teen? Surely Delta knew about this little love triangle. Why hadn't she mentioned it? Who was this veterinarian anyway? How did Usher know he had access to PCP? Miranda had done a little research before she left the office. Vets did use PCP, but it was rare, due to bad side effects.

Most importantly, was Desirée really going to leave the vet and go back to Usher? Or was that a figment of the artist's wild imagination? If Usher was telling the truth, then both men had a motive for killing her.

She needed to talk to that vet, but that would really be pushing it. She had to see Parker about taking this case. First thing in the morning, she decided.

She reached her apartment door, dug into her pocket for her keys and felt something funny. What was this? She pulled out the metal mass and stared at it.

Oh, yeah.

The keys to the Parker mansion.

She'd been so wrapped up in her investigation, she'd forgotten she was a homeowner now. Her shoulders slumped at the thought.

Shrugging off the urge to sulk, she opened her door and went inside. She tossed the keys on the counter, then looked around at her tiny living space. She put her hands on her hips, tapped her foot.

The Parker mansion had closets this size. Her whole apartment could fit inside its kitchen. It had several luxury showers she never had a chance to try.

She stared at the keys twinkling on the cheap laminate surface and remembered Parker's smug look when she signed the papers in the boardroom. Irritation bubbled inside her. If she didn't move in sooner or later, he'd know she was bluffing. She had to make the deal look good. And she sure couldn't keep up the rent on two places.

She strolled into her bedroom and studied the clothes and boxes in her closet. She had never kept too much stuff around. Made it easier to pick up and go whenever the urge struck her. Though she had more than usual now, after working at the Agency with its fancy dress code, it was still a manageable load.

Yep, if she was going to get Parker to take back his house, she had to make the threat of her living there real.

She reached under the bed for her duffle bag and began to pack. She'd call her landlord in the morning and cancel her lease.

CHAPTER NINE

It was past eleven when Miranda finally dragged the last of her bags up the grand staircase and into the master bedroom of the Parker mansion. She dropped the last duffle bag next to the boxes of Amy's gifts and sank down onto the luxurious mattress. Exhausted as she was, she flushed with the memory of its feel. This was where she and Parker had made love.

The room's blue-and-plum décor seemed more lavish than she remembered, the tall windows with their airy gauze curtains, more elegant. The naked Grecian statues, the cozy chair arrangement in the corner, the brass bamboo fountain gurgling in the other corner, all more sensual and seductive.

The mansion had a slew of bedrooms, all nicely made up and cleaned by the part time staff. Why had she chosen this room? She ran her hand over the silky, pure-white comforter beneath her and remembered the smell of Parker's skin, the texture of his hair as her fingers dug into his scalp, the wild thrusting of his body into hers, his gentler lovemaking later on that night.

Maybe this place was too much for her. But not in the way Parker had meant.

With a grunt, she forced herself up. Time for beddie-bye. Might as well try one of those fancy showers Parker's father had installed. She marched into the master bath.

Yep, just about the size of her apartment. The room was a maze of blue-and-gold ceramic and granite, accented with a forest of mirrors. The floor seemed to be heated and thick, pure white towels were piled everywhere.

She opened the shower door, and the sight took her breath away. More gleaming ceramic, with over a dozen shimmering showerheads. A control panel mounted on the wall. The area was large enough for a baseball team.

She peeled off her clothes, stepped inside and studied the touch screen. Body zones. Adjustable pressure and temperature. You needed a manual to turn it on. She pressed a button.

Hot water shot out of one of the showerheads, hit her on the side with full force. "Whoa," she giggled. "Too much." She tapped the button and it shut off. She tried a different one. Cold shot out from the other direction. "Wait a minute, brr." This was like wrestling an octopus. She turned it off, tried again. Something pulsed right between her legs. "Now you're getting fresh." She bet Mr. P had designed that feature himself.

She stopped the stream and glared at the controls. *Spa-luxury-routine*. That sounded good. Biting her lip, she touched it.

A nice, warm spray danced out from all directions with just the right pressure. She sighed. "That's more like it."

It self-adjusted, began working the muscles between her shoulders. Mmm, nice. After a few minutes, it adjusted again, began working down her back, her hips, her legs. Wow. She'd never felt anything so good. Well, not alone. Goldilocks should have had it so good.

She reached for the soap pump and a delicious odor of lilacs and mountain lilies filled the steamy air.

After about a half hour of ecstasy, the stream stopped. Relaxed and mellow, Miranda considered a second try, but she was already feeling like a prune. Better save some for the next time.

Thank you, Mr. P. Even if she weren't going to stay in the mansion forever, this was one shower experience she'd never forget.

She stepped out, dried off with a towel so thick it felt like a carpet, lifted a luxurious terrycloth robe off a hook and wrapped it around her. This was the life.

"Can't get used to it," she reminded herself as she padded into the huge bedroom and rummaged through one of her suitcases for a T-shirt and a pair of panties. Parker would come to his senses soon. He'd take back the house in less than a week, she bet.

And as soon as Parker moved in, she was moving out. She'd made it plain she wouldn't live with him. That could only lead to misery for both of them.

A large chandelier hung from the high bedroom ceiling, but Miranda opted for the muted light of the Tiffany lamp on the nightstand.

With a big yawn, she flopped onto the bed, sank her head into the thick satin-covered pillows. Hmm. Nice. "See, Parker? I'm just fine in this big, scary house." She pulled up the comforter and reached up to turn out the light. Wait. Maybe she'd leave it on for tonight.

She rolled over, closed her eyes, let her mind go blank.

The silent house seemed to groan.

Her eyes shot open. *Was that a creak? A footstep?* She sat up and listened hard. She could hear her heart beating. Her mind was playing tricks on her. After all, her last night here had been pretty horrific.

Stubbornly, she lay back down and closed her eyes. Morning came early. She let her mind drift to Usher's drawn, mournful face that afternoon. "Dr. Gabriel Kennicot's the one with access to PCP." Desirée's old flame, the vet. Had she been playing the artist and the vet against each other, the way Farrah Simmons played her lovers? Steeplechase images played in her head, began to blur. She drifted off.

What was that? She jolted up with a start. Was that...water running?

With a grunt, she shoved the blankets away, got up, and went to the bathroom. Had the fancy shower started a routine on its own? No, everything in here was still. Dry as a bone. Maybe it was time to see that shrink. Wait, she knew what it was.

That dang brass fountain.

She plodded back into the bedroom, crossed the floor, and fiddled with the contraption until she found a switch in the back. She turned it off. There.

A shiver went down her spine. She still heard running water.

Her heart pounding, she went for one of her boxes on the floor, opened it. Where was it? Not that box. She grabbed another and dug into it. There. Her fingers curled around hard wood and she drew out *Defender*. The thirty-four-inch Old Hickory solid maple baseball bat she used to sleep with when she lived in New York.

She turned toward the door and slapped it against her palm. She'd take care of that water bandit.

She stepped into the hall.

Soft nightlights glowed along the walls, but there was no sign of life. This couldn't be one of her nightmares. It was too real. The coolness of the hard wood under her bare feet was physical. And so was the persistent sound of that running water.

Gritting her teeth, she made her way down the hall. The sound of water grew louder.

Half way down the hall, she spotted light under one of the doors. She hesitated outside it, adjusted her grip on Defender, went through a few karate moves in her head. Swallowing her nerves, she reached for the handle and slowly opened the door.

Inside was another palatial, tile-lined bathroom. This one done in a sensual, oriental style with plum and lavender accents and shiny black trim. It was even bigger than the one with the octopus shower.

A huge sunken tub sat in the middle of the floor. It was filled with fragrant bubble bath, suds peaking high like the meringue on a lemon pie. Near the faucet sat a silver tray. On it was a crystal decanter with a champagne bottle, two tulip-shaped glasses, and a pile of strawberries.

Had Mr. P forgotten he'd sold the house?

Along one wall was an opening to another room. The sound of running water came from there. She stepped around the tiled partition and found an opaque glass door with Chinese markings on it, steam rising over its top.

Another shower. And someone was in it.

The dark figure maneuvered behind the panel, soaping itself. Too tall to be Mr. P, but the form looked awfully familiar. Miranda tightened her grip on Defender, slowly tiptoed toward the shower door. Her throat constricted as she reached for the handle. Do or die.

She threw it open. And gasped.

"Parker."

He turned, stood there gazing at her with the shower pounding down, hot steam rising from its spray, his grin as sly and smug as ever. "Good evening."

Her breath gone, she sputtered angry gibberish until finally coherent words shot out. "Parker, what in blue blazes are you doing here? You swore you wouldn't stay in this place."

She gaped at wet, salt-and-pepper hair, his firm muscles gleaming with beads of water, the dripping black hair matted on his chest. He had the strong, fit body of a martial artist, a fighter, a Southern gentleman. Fully-clad, he was a debonair man-about-town. Stark naked, he was…irresistible.

"I couldn't let you stay here alone tonight," he said with that coy, easy smile.

"I almost lambasted you."

Parker gazed at the irate vision before him. Her wild, tangled dark hair, her deep blue eyes flashing with fury. She was dressed temptingly in nothing but panties and a gray cotton T-shirt that caressed her breasts and revealed her delicious form. She'd thrown his timing off a bit, but otherwise, the plan of attack he'd hatched in his father's room at the nursing home was working beautifully.

He shook his head and chuckled. "I don't think so."

Miranda couldn't help glancing down. Clearly, she'd aroused him. She was about to say, "Guess you're glad to see me," when he reached out, grabbed her under her arms and lifted her off her feet.

Defender clattered to the floor. "What do you think you're doing?"

"I'd like a partner."

She spat water as he set her down in the tub and the spray hit her head, soaking every bit of her including her T-shirt and undies. "I've already had my bath. In the octopus shower."

"I have a fetish for clean women." He bent his head and captured her lips, the water peppering both their faces.

Fetish? Must be the same one she had. For a moment, she gave in to the delicious taste of his lips working over her mouth. That powerful physical attraction began to work its greedy fingers along the nerves of her solar plexus. But this wasn't the plan.

She broke free. "I really don't want another shower, Parker. Besides, I liked the one in the master bath better. The one with the multiple showerheads."

He laughed, drew her to him, pressed his lips against her cheek. "If you liked multiple showerheads, what's wrong with multiple showers? Or other things that come in multiples?"

"I really—I don't—"

He took her head in both hands, his gaze unyielding. "I think we've had enough conversation about it." Firmly he pressed his lips over hers, so she couldn't argue. His mouth was strong, demanding. She opened to it, surrendering to its powerful seduction. Part of her still fought him.

What was he doing in *her* house? He'd scared the daylights out of her. She should throw him out on his ear. Instead, she shivered with desire as exotic arousal pulsed through her. Dang, she had a weakness for him.

At last, he freed her lips and began working his way down her neck. His method of persuasion was working pretty well. She couldn't bring herself to protest. With a lusty groan, she rolled her head back, let the water wash over her neck while Parker's mouth attacked her shoulder and collarbone.

He lifted his head, his gaze lusty. His hands moved teasingly over her a moment, then reached for the edges of her wet shirt. Before she could protest, he'd pulled it up over her head. "You don't need this."

"What are you—?" She opened her mouth in shock, but he swallowed her reply with his own lusty, wordless one. Their lips still locked, he lifted her out of the shower, turned the water off with his foot and padded toward the bubble bath, their wet bodies dripped across the tiled floor to the sunken bath on the other side of the partition.

"What's this fancy tub around the corner for?" she murmured, half breathless. "You planning on entertaining somebody?"

"You threw off my timing, but yes." Kissing her again, he stepped into the water.

Hovering above the suds, Miranda wrenched her lips free again, tried to wriggle out of his grasp. "Now look here, Parker. This is fun and all, but I want to know what you're doing here—ahh."

She hit the water, and the warm liquid caressed her body, soothing as a mother's arms, smelling like wildflowers. He really knew how to get to her, didn't he?

He reached over her head for a strawberry, popped it into her open mouth. "Would you like a drink with that?"

"No, I don't want a drink," she grunted with her mouth full.

"Very well. Then we'll get right down to business." His hands disappeared under the water and the next moment her panties were gone. "You don't need these either." He tossed the wet fabric onto the floor.

"Now, look you. You can't break into my house and...oh."

He closed in beside her in the tub, went to work on her neck again, let his hands float to her breasts, giving her the welcome home he'd no doubt intended when he'd hatched this scheme.

She shouldn't do it, shouldn't let herself go, she told herself as she sank into the suds. But she let his skillful hands slide over her wet skin. He teased at her, stroked his fingers over her belly. This was a mistake. A very bad mistake. But as she ran her hands over the muscles of his arms, took in the clean scent of him, her heart clenched in her chest.

To heck with it. What choice did she have? She couldn't resist the intoxicating man with his intoxicating ways, his intoxicating smell, his intoxicating touch. He enthralled her, mesmerized her like no man ever had. She was helpless. Done for. Wondering if she could ever break free of his wizard's spell, she opened herself to him and his magic hands.

He slipped them around her, lifted her breast to his mouth, took it in. She went dizzy as delirious sensations danced through her whole body. Then she smiled to herself. He might be conquering her body, but she'd won the battle over the house.

Feeling victorious, she pressed her lips to him hard, turned him over with a splash.

"There's my tigress," he laughed.

"Feel my teeth." She bit him on the shoulder. Lightly, but hard enough to arouse him, as if he needed that.

"You devil, you." His eyes flashed and he spun her over, settled himself on top of her, the two of them splashing in the water like spawning salmon.

Her gaze met his and she was filled with desire so intense, she thought the tub might start boiling. "Don't make me wait."

"I don't intend to."

He entered her smoothly, like a bar of soap over wet skin. Then slowly moved inside her, deliciously. The sensation made her shiver and quiver and feel all too feminine.

Memories of the night they'd shared in this house bombarded her. Not the ugly ones, the beautiful ones. His gentle touch, his tender kisses that had grown strong and demanding with the need they both felt. Their bodies fusing, thrashing passionately on the silky sheets of his bed. She had felt so close to him that night. For a few hours, she had felt loved, protected. As if nothing bad could ever happen to her again. As if nothing evil existed.

But it had. Parker's lovemaking was only a temporary cure. Maybe knowing that was what made her unable to resist him.

His eyes were closed, his face was hard, full of unspeakable feeling as he came. She shuddered, joining him. They breathed in unison. She'd never known such intense pleasure as Parker gave her. He made her want more of him. Exactly what she shouldn't want.

He opened his eyes, watched her last waves of ecstasy, enjoying her pleasure. And the fact that he had been the author of it.

"Proud of yourself, aren't you?"

"Proud?"

"Don't men feel virile when they conquer a woman?"

"Conquering has nothing to do with it. When you let me make love to you, I feel very much alive."

"Because you've won."

"Because I'm close to you. It's more about bonding than bondage." His look grew intense. "But if you need further proof…" His lips fluttered down her neck again.

Keep your head clear. This could go on till dawn. She cleared her throat. "By the way, Parker, where are you spending the night?"

"Right here," he murmured, attacking her throat.

"So you're taking the house after all?"

"No."

Now he was pissing her off. She pulled away from his lips. "Then what are you doing here?"

One lip curled in a look that was definitely that of a conqueror. "Acting as your personal bodyguard."

"Bodyguard?" He was doing a lot more than guarding it.

"The Agency offers those services."

"I can't afford them. And I don't need to be protected."

"We could work out an arrangement." He was good with arrangements. "My payments would be reasonable." He went for her neck again.

She shifted away, fuming. "Speaking of the Agency, don't we have to be there in the morning?"

"You're right. I need to put you to bed." With that, he lifted her up and out of the tub, set her on her feet. Then he grabbed a thick towel and started to pat her dry.

"Hey, I'm not a child."

"Definitely not," he chuckled.

But his attention felt too good to stop. As he rubbed away, her mind drifted back to what she'd learned about Desirée Langford that afternoon. Now was a good time to bring it up. This was as vulnerable as Parker got. "You know, I've been thinking about the Langford case."

He stopped rubbing. "Case?"

Of course, he'd remind her that there was no case. Yet. "Her death," she corrected. "Maybe it wasn't Usher who wanted her dead. Maybe it was someone else."

"Oh?" His tone was flat. He began to dry her again.

"Desirée knew a lot of people in the horse industry. Anyone could have been jealous of her."

He put the towel around her butt and pulled it back and forth vigorously. "Do you have any ideas?"

She shrugged. "Could be anyone. Her vet, for example."

"Her vet." He continued to rub. "Is that what Usher told you when you talked to him at the funeral today?"

She grabbed the towel and yanked it out of his hands. "How did you—?"

He narrowed his eyes and gave her that piercing grin. "I recognized that look in your eye when I told you not to go. I knew you would, despite my order. So I followed you."

He took the towel again, reached for her. She jerked it out of his hands, tossed it on the floor. She was dry enough. "You *followed* me? I didn't see you at the funeral."

His expression smug and self-satisfied, he reached for another towel, began drying himself. "I stayed outside in the car. I saw you talking with Usher through the Fellowship Hall window."

She folded her arms under her naked breasts. "Oh, you did, did you? Well, I thought I did a pretty good job of questioning him."

He nodded. "From what I saw, you did an excellent job. But that's irrelevant. We don't have a case."

She gritted her teeth. "Seems like an ace detective could figure a way around that."

With a dark look, he wrapped the towel around his waist, reached for her and picked her up. At the moment, she almost wanted to pull a karate move on him and throw him to the ground.

"We'll discuss it in the morning," he said, heading for the door.

"What's wrong with now?"

"It's late." He carried her down the hall, past the paintings, the decorative wall sconces, the ornate doorways that led to a myriad of other rooms.

"Not too late for fooling around."

She felt his chest heave. "Miranda, I don't want to discuss it."

She wriggled in his arms, twisting to face him. "Why not? What's up with you and Delta Langford? What's this 'unpleasant history' between you?"

"Miranda, please."

"Tell me."

"There's nothing to tell." Those deep gray eyes looked weary as they trekked through the master bedroom door and into the soft lights.

Liar, she was about to say. But he'd stopped and was staring down at her boxes lined up along the foot of the bed.

"What's this?" he asked, suspicion in his tone.

"Nothing. I haven't finished unpacking." Now she was the one with something to hide. She wrestled herself out of his arms and grabbed the thick robe she'd left on the bed.

"I'll help you put these away." He reached for a box.

A streak of panic shot through her. "No. I'll take care of them." She seized the box he'd picked up. "Let go."

"Why?"

"Never mind." Maybe it was more embarrassment than panic, but she couldn't let him see these things. She gave the box a yank, but her move had too much force. The lid fell off and packages slid to the floor. "Crap," she muttered.

"Was it fragile?" He bent down and lifted one of the packages. It was wrapped in shiny red-and-blue paper, tied with a smashed silver bow. "What are these?"

Miranda sank down on her knees intending to stuff the packages back into the box. Instead, she buried her head in her hands. Might as well fess up. "They're gifts."

"For Amy." he said in a gentle whisper.

Slowly she nodded, gathering up the packages. "Birthdays, Christmases, Easters. I collected them over the years. I thought I might give them to her when I found her." She sniffed, rubbed her nose, but continued stuffing everything back in the box. "I don't think she'll need the rattle I got her when she was one, though. Maybe she'd still like the teddy bear I got her when she was five." Amy would be thirteen now. A young girl about to become a young woman.

"Oh, Miranda." Parker's arms went around her with such feeling and tenderness, she couldn't push them away. It was the first time in her life she had someone to share her pain with.

"Darling."

Her heart leapt at the word. No one had ever called her "darling." Not Leon. Not her mother. Maybe her father had a long time ago, but she couldn't remember it.

Parker held her close, kissed the coarseness of her thick, wild hair, touched the contour of her firm shoulder muscles, the softness of her skin betraying the softness inside. He loved that contrast. But his heart broke for her pain, the loss of her only daughter that had tormented her so long. He'd do anything in his power to take it away. But all he could do was distract her, as he was doing with this mansion. He'd live in this house with her, even with its sullied memories of his own past. They were nothing compared to hers.

He reached for her chin, turned her face toward him. "Won't you consider seeing a therapist? It might help."

Now she was the one who didn't want to talk about it. She shook her head. "They never help."

"You haven't found the right one."

Stubbornly, she rubbed her eyes. "Like you said, it's late. I'm tired."

He pressed his lips to her forehead. "Of course. We'll talk about it in the morning."

"Sure. Just like we'll discuss the Langford case." She got up and crossed to the bed.

He paused, studying her for a long moment. She could see the wheels turning in his head. "I'll...make a deal with you."

She turned to face him, folded her arms. "A deal?"

He nodded. "If you make an appointment with a therapist, I'll consider finding a way to take the Langford case."

She snorted. "*Consider finding a way?* That deal sounds a little lopsided to me."

His low sigh was more like a lion's growl, but he glanced down at the boxes and caved. "I'll start doing some preliminary research tomorrow."

Her heart did a little flip. "You mean it?"

"Absolutely."

Suspicious, she tilted her head at him. But it was the best chance she had. She'd take it. She reached out her hand. "Agreed."

He clasped her palm and pulled her onto the bed, making her laugh as he kissed her cheeks. This was going to be a long night.

What a way to seal a deal.

CHAPTER TEN

It's late.

The ice clinks and the whiskey shimmers in my glass as I drink it. The newsprint of the worn obituary stains my fingertips.

Why did she have to go? Why? She was so like me. We were soul mates. No, she wasn't like me at all. She was beautiful. Beloved. And now that beauty is gone from this world and all that remains are hearts broken from the loss. Such a tragedy. Such a waste.

But she had to go. Had to.

That beauty, that graceful loveliness, had to be destroyed. She caused too much suffering. Too much pain. *My* pain. She had to die. It was only right. She was too haughty, too self-serving, too arrogant for her own good.

Like that female detective. Prying, probing, snooping from the very first moment she was dead. Like her famous boss.

I hate them both so much. So much. As much as I hated her? Perhaps.

I take another mouthful of whiskey to steady my nerves. Yes, I do hate them as much. My hatred grows by the day. Soon it will be too much to bear.

I won't be able to contain it. I'll have to act.

I need a plan. Something no one will ever suspect. Something no one will see until it's too late. Something quick. Not painless, but quick. And decisive. And then the snooping detective and her egotistical boss will be…no more.

Just like Desirée.

CHAPTER ELEVEN

Sleeping with the boss on a weeknight sure made getting to work the next day hell.

Miranda wanted to throw the alarm clock against the wall when it went off the next morning. But when she lifted her head off the satin pillow and discovered the bed empty, instead she went downstairs and found her new bodyguard.

Parker was outside, sitting on a huge redwood deck built off the kitchen, that overlooked a magnificent backyard garden filled with lush green oaks and pines and a painter's palette of flowers.

He rose as she approached. Sweet as Southern molasses, with a dash of landed-gentry thrown in for good measure, he gestured to a tiled table under a vine-laced trellis, where coffee and croissants were waiting for her on fine bone china.

"Good morning," he smiled, pouring the rich hot liquid into a cup etched with a fancy gold pattern. He indicated one of the Adirondack chairs. "Join me?"

She pursed her lips, her mouth watering. "Are you still 'playing house,' Parker?"

Those Magnum-gray eyes locked with hers. "In a manner of speaking."

It was too tempting to resist. "Okay." Warily, she crossed to the table, sat down and let him kiss her on the cheek. Now that her head was clear, she wasn't about to fall for any more of his shenanigans.

"Have one." He set a delicate saucer before her with what looked like a melt-in-your-mouth croissant.

She took a bite, found it light, flaky, and filled with a soft, sweet cheese. So good, she felt herself slipping under his spell again. Recover. Now. She took a swallow of the rich coffee, cleared her throat. "Speaking of playing house, I guess now that you're here in your estate, I can move out."

She thought she heard his chest rumble, earthquake-like, but he merely sat back and sipped from his cup. "If you move out, Miranda, I'll move out. I think I made it very clear I don't want to live here."

"But you'll live here if I'm here."

"I'm only here for bodyguard duties."

The stubborn mule. "I didn't hire a bodyguard."

"The service comes with the house."

"Like the cleaning staff?" she smirked.

"Something like that. I'm sure my father would agree." His air was the one he used when questioning a suspect he had the goods on.

If she tried to explain this situation, Mr. P would probably laugh. So she'd have to put a good spin on it. "We'll see about that." She took another bite of the pastry, swigged down a final sip of coffee, stood. "Well, I've got to be off."

His dark brows drew together. "Breakfast too sweet for your taste? I apologize I don't have sliced jalapenos for the croissants."

She gritted her teeth in a forced grin. "The croissants are delicious. But there's no way you and I are going to the office together."

He stared off at the yard. "Ah, so you're afraid of gossip?"

"Dang straight." With Becker and Holloway taking the lead. She turned and scooted across the deck to the kitchen door.

"You needn't be concerned. I know how to be discreet."

She had to laugh. "Oh, yeah? And just what do you think Gen would have to say about us living here?"

The irritated befuddlement on his handsome face at the mention of his daughter, gave her a thin victory, but it lasted only a moment.

"By the way..."

She put her hand on the knob, sucked in a breath. "What?"

"Don't forget to make an appointment with a therapist this morning."

She turned back, resisting the urge to tap her foot on the cedar floor. "I haven't forgotten our deal. Don't you forget what you promised."

Parker kept his gaze on the garden as he fingered the coffee cup in his hand. "And if you want to be involved in the Langford investigation..."

Her heart clenched. "What?"

"Book more than one session with the doctor."

With the grunt of a charging rhinoceros, she spun on her heel, yanked the door open. As she stomped through it, Parker's confident chuckle rang in her ears.

On the drive to the office, Miranda had a good talk with herself. What was she getting into with Parker and this house business? Despite the fantastic sex, she was furious with him for showing up like he had last night. This was exactly the situation she'd told him she didn't want. She couldn't handle it. Why wouldn't he listen?

Maybe because of her mixed signals?

She'd let him pull every slick trick in the book on her last night. How did he get away with that? How did she let him push just the buttons that would make her succumb to him? She knew how. She cared about the man. Way too much. And he knew it. But that didn't change the fact that she sucked at relationships. That she couldn't believe love could last. Didn't Parker get that?

Oh, he got it all right. The sensual snoop knew exactly what he was doing. He wanted to live together to prove her wrong, and he was using the house to make it happen. That explained his smug, self-satisfied look at the nursing home when she made the deal with Mr. P.

She had a good mind to throw him out on his ear. She would have last night, but what's a girl to do when she finds a sexy, naked man in her shower? *What about the darn house?* It belonged to him. Surely Parker didn't have her owning the place in mind when he'd first asked her to move in with him. When was he going to break down and admit that?

She could wait him out, but as stubborn as the man was, that could take a long time. She could pack up and leave, but that would leave Desirée Langford's murder unsolved.

In her mind, she saw the troubling image of the young woman lying dead in Calypso's stall. That poor, disfigured face.

Who would do that to themselves? A woman like Desirée Langford wouldn't destroy her own face. Miranda didn't care what the police had concluded. That wasn't suicide. That wasn't self-destruction. It was hatred. A bubbling, raging jealousy. Like the jealousy she saw in Usher yesterday afternoon at the funeral. Or maybe like the jealousy of Dr. Kennicot the vet, as Usher claimed? If Desirée had two men fighting over her, either one of them could have killed her. Miranda was determined to find out which one it was.

She had to solve the case. It wouldn't be right to walk away now. But when she figured out who murdered Desirée Langford, she was moving out of that mansion for good. In the meantime, she'd have to think of something to keep the persistent, horny investigator-slash-bodyguard at bay.

She got to the Imperial Building early, before most of the other IITs, snuck in the back way, and even managed to make it to the coffee machine to guzzle down another cup of wake-up juice before anyone saw her.

She muttered to herself as she headed for her desk. "Okay, Mr. Smart-Ass-Ace-Investigator. You won this one, but you'd better do what you said."

As soon as she reached her cube, she yanked a phone book off the shelf and turned to the "Ps" in the yellow pages. There were a slew of names. Dr. Alton on East Paces Ferry. Dr. Alexander on Peachtree Dunwoody. Dr. Brown on Lenox Road.

She groaned. There were more shrinks in Atlanta than you could shake a neurosis at.

Closing her eyes, she plopped her finger on the page. Dr. Berkoff on Peachtree. Right down the street. Good enough. She dialed the number.

Earliest appointment was six weeks from now. Crap.

Try again. Dr. Campbell. Booked until August.

Okay, she'd go farther down the alphabet. Dr. Lindstrum. Twelve years clinical experience. Depression, Eating Disorders, Hypnosis. Whatever. She dialed again. This dude was booked until September. Anxiety must be on the rampage in Buckhead.

She tried the M's.

Six calls later, she'd reached the Z's and came up with zip. Every psychologist, psychiatrist, and counseling clinic was booked for at least a month. Was everyone in Atlanta phobic? The morning paper peeking out of her Inbox caught her eye. She grabbed it and started flipping. Bingo.

A big half-page ad in the Metro section. "Feeling stressed? Lonely? Depressed? We can help." Dr. Theodore Theophilus, Licensed Social Worker and Psychotherapist, was holding a group therapy session open to the public at one o'clock this afternoon. And best of all, it was free. She tapped in the number on her phone.

One spot left. She grabbed it.

Good enough. She sat back with a victorious grin. That ought to satisfy Parker, especially if Dr. T had regular sessions. When she got back from the shrink's, the Langford case was first on her to-do list.

CHAPTER TWELVE

Dr. Theodore Theophilus's rented space on the ground floor of a Piedmont Road office building was friendly in a medicinal, sterile sort of way. The large meeting room, with its linoleum floor, notices posted on the walls, and high, echoing ceiling, had the feel of a small gymnasium. Without the locker room smell, of course. That wouldn't do for Buckhead.

Instead, as Miranda walked through the doorway, she thought she caught a whiff of...sandalwood? The dude must be into aromatherapy.

The traffic had made her late and a circle of assorted victims, uh, patients, were already gathered around in a circle.

As she neared the group, she spotted a short, pudgy man in a sky-blue sweat suit with a bald spot on top of his head. The rest of his reddish hair stuck out in all directions, like he'd been playing with a light socket.

"Welcome." He waved to her, his bright blue eyes dancing with excitement. "Come join us. We're just about to start."

Two of the clients moved over and Miranda took a place in the circle.

"As I was explaining, we're about to have our 'Happy Time.'"

Happy Time? She looked around the group. It was made up mostly of women in their twenties and thirties, dressed in jeans and sweat clothes. They looked like an assortment of well-to-do Buckhead soccer moms with a lot to be happy about already. But anxiety disorder knew no monetary boundaries.

Still, Miranda felt a little out of place in her navy dress slacks and plain white blouse she'd bought to replace the one Leon had sliced up. Except for the skinny young-looking guy in a dress suit across the circle, who didn't look like he belonged here, either.

And who was that next to him? Miranda did a double take as she took in the young girl dressed in jeans and a plain green T-shirt. *Was that who she thought it was?*

Dr. Theophilus cleared his throat. "What is your 'Happy Time,' you must be wondering?" He chuckled, squeezed his hands together in a nervous gesture.

"Well, it's a time when you can return to a place in your childhood when life was joyous and carefree."

Sounded like what she'd heard called your 'Happy Place.' The phrase must be copyrighted.

An assortment of colored plastic balls of various sizes sat on the floor. Theophilus reached for a blue one that looked like a small Pilates ball and held it up. "So close your eyes, think of that time. And now, we're going to play catch, just like you did on the playground as a child."

Miranda's gaze wandered back to the young girl. *It couldn't be her, could it?*

Suddenly, the blue ball came sailing toward her head. Instinct taking over, her arm shot up, and she socked it hard with her fist.

"Hey." One of the patients ducked as the missile flew over her head and bounced against the wall with a smack. It ricocheted back and knocked the doctor right on his bald spot.

"Oh my," Theophilus squealed, rubbing his scalp, his free hand flapping as he chased after the ball. "We do have a lot of pent-up aggression, don't we?"

"Sorry," Miranda shrugged. "It was a reflex."

The young girl across the circle giggled.

Miranda recognized that sound. She stared at her again. It *was* her. Wendy Van Aarle. The girl whose life she'd saved. But with a very different look. No wonder she hadn't recognized her at first.

Gone was the Goth look with the dark makeup and clothes. Her hair was lighter, straighter, and cut in a grownup shoulder-length style. Her makeup had been applied with a light touch. Her complexion had color, instead of the wan shade she'd always had before. She looked like a new person. Miranda felt her heart melting.

Dr. Theophilus returned to the center of the circle with his ball. "Once again, I'm going to toss this to each of you." He turned slowly, addressing everyone, as if they really were kids on a playground. "Catch the ball and throw it back to me."

Guess she'd missed the instructions. The doctor tossed the ball to her. This time she caught it and tossed it back to him.

"That's right," he nodded and smiled, tossing the ball to the patient next to her. "Don't take it so seriously. This is 'Happy Time.' It's a game." He continued around the circle.

When she caught the ball, Wendy giggled again. One of the soccer moms joined her.

"That's right," Dr. Theophilus said. "Laugh. This game is supposed to make you loosen up, release your anxieties. Laughter cleanses the soul."

Cleanses the soul? Sorry, didn't bring my psychic soap, Miranda thought, catching the ball a second time as it went around again. If she'd wanted a workout, she could have done laps in Parker's gym. Well, you get what you pay for.

"Very good." Theophilus caught the ball and held it up. "This time, as I toss the ball to you, clap your hands. Remember, it's okay to laugh at yourself. C'mon, everyone. Clap."

The room began to fill with the sound of clapping hands and laughter. This was weird. Parker had better be working on the Langford case right now.

"Doctor," one of the soccer moms asked, "is this really going to cure my anxiety?"

He looked thoughtful. "It's a beginning, but if you really want to make progress, you can call my office and make an appointment. I have openings next week."

Miranda grinned. She'd just met her new therapist.

"Do you use behavioral therapy or a Freudian approach?"

"I just focus on getting you to your Happy Place."

The soccer mom beside Miranda frowned. "What about dealing with OCD? Working through childhood trauma?"

Theophilus shook his head. "All you need is to find your Happy Place. I'm writing a book about it. Tanya Terrance is interviewing me on the radio next week."

So that was his angle. Well, Dr. Phil had nothing to worry about.

As tempting as it was to fulfill Parker's bargain with this guy's openings, Miranda didn't think she could stomach weekly sessions with Mr. Happy Place.

Clapping and waiting for her next turn, she looked across the circle and caught Wendy's eye. The girl shot her a grin of recognition.

When Theophilus turned his back, Wendy grimaced at him. Miranda nodded and rolled her eyes.

She got an idea. As the ball came to her, she gave it another hard sock and sent it flying across the room.

"Oh, dear." Theophilus shoved his hands on his hips and shook his head. "We have to get rid of that aggression." Then he turned and trotted after the ball.

Miranda broke out of the circle and scooted over to Wendy. "What do you say we blow this pop stand? This is too freaky for me."

"Me, too," she nodded. "Good idea."

Before anyone noticed, they were out the door and onto the sidewalk outside. Miranda spotted an ice cream shop across the street. "Would you like a sundae? My treat."

Wendy lit up. "Sure."

Watching Wendy Van Aarle dig into a banana split in a rainbow-colored booth at Dilbert's Ice Cream Palace was anything but therapeutic, Miranda decided. The last time she'd seen the girl was when Leon slashed up her chest.

"So how are things with, uh, your family?" she asked cautiously.

"Better since we've been going to counseling." Wendy dragged her spoon neatly around the edge of the dish to capture the melted ice cream and syrup, then licked it with her tongue. "The doctor ordered us to spend more time together."

"So I heard." Parker had filled her in on the details after she got out of the hospital. "What were you doing at Dr. Theophilus's, uh," she circled the air with her finger, "'Happy Time' hour?"

Wendy smirked. "It was my mother's idea. She wanted to get her hair done and she needed a place to, like, park me." She rolled her eyes and took a bite of the strawberry ice cream. "That doctor was a total doofus."

"My thoughts exactly." Miranda felt a twist in her stomach. *Like, "park" her?* Was Iris Van Aarle neglecting her daughter again?

She watched Wendy make a dent in the scoop of chocolate. Her face was prettier without the heavy makeup she used to wear. Her highlighted hair fell just at her shoulders. Miranda imagined Iris giving her daughter a makeover, the two of them bonding together over lipsticks and eye shadows. "How are you and your mother getting along?"

Wendy scrunched her nose. "Well, it's summertime, so she's teaching me her cosmetics business. She calls it 'home schooling.'" Iris Van Aarle was owner and CEO of the fabulously successful company Iris Rose Cosmetics. Part of Miranda admired the woman. "I'm learning bookkeeping."

"Do you like that?"

Wendy lifted one shoulder. "It's okay. We might have to really home school in the fall, if I can't get into a regular school."

"That's too bad." It sucked that Wendy was being blacklisted because of what happened to her, but maybe staying out of school for a while was what she needed after what she'd been through. "And what about your dad?"

She scooped up some whipped cream and put it in her mouth. "He takes me to the golf course once or twice a week to practice my swing. It's pretty cool." Wendy's father was Shelby Van Aarle, the famous golf pro. It was an understatement to say Wendy's mom and dad had beaucoup bucks. But until recently, they had come up short when it came to things like support and affection and paying attention to their own daughter. Miranda still felt a lot of resentment about that.

"So you and your folks are getting on a lot better."

"Sure. We have dinner together at least three times a week."

"I see." Sounded real intimate.

Miranda studied Wendy's face. Was she really happier? Was she better off now that her parents were paying more attention to her? At least she was alive.

The thought almost brought tears to her eyes. Dang, she couldn't believe how much she cared about this kid. But then, it wasn't too long ago that she thought this girl was her own daughter.

"What about you? Do you have any friends your own age?"

Wendy licked at the spoon, studied it a moment. "They won't let me on a computer anymore. I never really had many friends. You know that."

"Yeah." It was something they had in common. They were a lot alike, both of them with a bitter-edged, jaded view of life. Miranda's had started to form when she was about Wendy's age, she guessed. When she'd realized how little her own mother cared about her. She'd never outgrown it. Life could be a real pile of crap sometimes.

"What are you doing these days?" Wendy asked. "Are you still working for Mr. Parker?"

"Yes, I am," Miranda said, surprised Wendy was interested. "I'm looking into the death at the Northwinds Steeplechase last weekend."

"I heard about that."

"Did you?"

She gave a short laugh. "My mother hid the paper when it happened. She thought I'd freak out if I saw it. But I snuck a peek. I heard her talking on the phone to Mrs. Taggart about it. She was real upset."

Miranda bet she was. Cloris Taggart was the Steeplechase coordinator and one of the women who had lost their own daughters last month. "It was terrible."

Wendy leaned across the table with almost a grin. "So what have you found out so far?"

Was she interested in the case? Miranda shrugged. "Not much."

"Didn't the police say it's a suicide? From a PCP overdose?"

Young people knew way too much these days. "Yeah, but we're not sure."

Wendy shrugged again, now acting as if it were the most boring topic in the world. Short attention span, Miranda guessed. Then the girl dipped up some of the soupy goo of the now half-melted sundae, and watched as it dripped off the spoon. "Don't you have to get drugs like that from like a criminal? Like maybe a gang person or something?"

She'd been concentrating more than Miranda had thought. "Maybe."

She licked the spoon. "So where did Ms. Langford get her drugs from?"

"Good question." The kid was sharp. She had a point. If Usher was into drugs, as Delta Langford said, no telling where he got them. "You wouldn't happen to know anything about that, would you?" Leon had drugged her with Ketamin. Maybe she knew where he got his stuff.

"Just from what I've seen on TV and in the movies."

She could probe, but she didn't want to dredge up those bad memories. Wendy was trying to recover from the same trauma she was. She decided to change the subject. "Hey, guess what? I'm your new neighbor."

She wrinkled her nose. "Huh?"

"I'm staying at the Parker estate. It's right around the corner from your place."

"Oh. That's nice." She finished the last bit of whipped cream.

Her indifference stung, but Miranda was glad she didn't ask any probing questions like 'are you staying there with Mr. Parker?' "So maybe we'll run into each other again."

"Maybe. Thanks for the banana split." She pushed the half-eaten dish away. Guess she was done.

"Do you need a ride home?"

She shook her head. "My mom's picking me up as soon as she's finished at the hairdresser's." She glanced out the window. "There she is now." She got up. "Better go."

Miranda paid the bill, and they went outside. From the sidewalk, she watched Iris Van Aarle's dark blue BMW pull up to the corner. The woman didn't get out.

She turned to Wendy. "Guess I'll see you around sometime."

"Guess so." She turned to go, then stopped and turned back. "You know, I never did get a chance to thank you." Not in person, anyway.

Miranda stared at her. "Thank me?"

"You saved my life."

"Yeah, I did, didn't I?"

Wendy had written her a note, which Miranda kept in her wallet, like a parent does photos of her kids. Apparently, Wendy thought that wasn't enough. She ran up to her and threw her arms around her tight. "Thanks." Her voice broke. It was more affection than she'd ever seen the kid express toward anyone. Then she pulled away and ran toward the car.

"Don't mention it." Her heart overflowing with emotion, Miranda stared at the car as Wendy opened the passenger door and climbed inside.

Iris adjusted her rearview mirror. Miranda wondered if she could see her and what she thought of her taking her daughter to get ice cream. But if the woman didn't like it, she didn't show it. She just leaned over and gave her daughter a peck on the cheek.

As the car pulled away, Miranda felt a pang of emptiness. But then, she was used to it. That hollow feeling was something she'd lived with for thirteen years.

CHAPTER THIRTEEN

By the time Miranda got back to the office, she'd decided to put Wendy Van Aarle out of her mind. Seeing the girl again had only broken her heart. And made her think of Leon. And how futile her search for her Amy was.

So much for the therapy session.

But Miranda had kept her word and gone to a shrink. Parker had better keep up his end of the deal.

When the silver elevator doors pinged open on the fifteenth floor, she marched right past the smug receptionist, through the double doors, took a left and headed straight for Parker's corner office.

His tall maple door was open, and she rapped on the trim when she reached it. "Pay up, Parker," she said, stepping into the large, elegant space.

The afternoon sun streamed in through the floor-to-ceiling windows and glistened on the glass credenza along the wall. The light reflected on the computers and the ethereal blue-and-silver of the walls and chairs. The color of paradise. Miranda always felt like she was stepping onto a cloud when she entered this place.

Impeccably dressed in a charcoal suit and red silk tie that set off his sexy salt-and-pepper hair, Parker sat at his glass desk, calmly going over some papers in a manila folder. He didn't look up, though he knew she was there.

"Pay up? Now that sounds interesting."

Miranda's gaze shot to the corner. Mr. P was sprawled in one of the blue chairs, his feet up on the glass coffee table, grinning like a Cheshire cat. He was wearing a navy classic pinstripe suit that looked like it had just been shipped from Italy. Didn't the Parker men ever break down and put on a pair of jeans?

"Hello, Mr. P," Miranda nodded. "It's good to see you again."

Southern gentleman that he was, Mr. P rose and crossed the room to shake her hand. "A delight to see you, Ms. Steele, as always."

This was the second time she'd seen him in two days. She wondered whether he always hung around the office before he'd checked into the nursing home. "Were you, uh, in the neighborhood?"

He smiled as if he understood the intent of her question perfectly. "I often drop by unannounced. I'm a member of the board, you know."

She didn't know that, but she nodded.

"But I try not to interfere in Russell's business. Just now I stopped in to tell my son about my wedding plans."

Parker didn't move. Miranda felt that familiar tension in the room.

"How are you enjoying your new home?" Mr. P asked.

"It's great. I really like that octopus shower."

He lifted a brow.

"The one with all the showerheads?"

He nodded with a chuckle. "Yes. Most of the ladies do."

She shifted her weight and glanced at Parker. He didn't react. Lucky for her, he didn't want to even hint to his father that they'd had a steamy rendezvous in the *other* bathroom last night any more than she did.

The air was getting stuffy. "Maybe I should come back later."

"Nonsense," Parker said without taking his eyes off his papers. "To what were you referring earlier, Miranda?" he asked blandly.

She put her hands on her hips. "You know perfectly well to what I was referring. I, uh, did what you asked me to. So now it's your turn."

Slowly his brow rose as he lifted his chin and eyed her with that piercing look of his. "Was it successful?"

She glanced over at Mr. P, feeling self-conscious. "It was okay."

"Will you be going back?" At least he was using vague terms. She appreciated that. And the fact that Mr. P seemed to be respecting her privacy and not asking questions.

But going back wasn't part of the original deal. He'd tagged that on this morning. "Not until you pay up. Have you started looking into you-know-what?"

"Pay up?" Mr. P asked again. Guess he was going to pick and choose which personal matters to be nosey about. He rubbed his hands together. "Is this a business deal? My mouth is watering already."

Miranda decided to play her hand. "It's about what happened to Desirée Langford at the Steeplechase last weekend, Mr. P."

"Oh?" His white brows rose in surprise. It wasn't the answer he'd expected.

"Delta Langford thinks Desirée's death wasn't a suicide. She thinks someone killed her sister."

"Really?" His voice echoed genuine shock. "Who would want to kill such a beautiful young woman?"

"That's what I want to find out. Delta wants me to look into it."

Inhaling slowly in that way that told Miranda she was trying his patience, Parker closed the file he'd been staring at and came around his desk. With that elegant air of his, he leaned against it and folded his arms. "There is still the matter of the client."

"Client?" Mr. P asked. "I thought Delta was the client."

Parker shook his head. "She hasn't hired the Agency, Father. And we know she won't."

There was a silent communication between them that Miranda couldn't decipher, but she knew it had to do with that secret Parker was harboring. That "unpleasant history" between him and Delta Langford. Of course, Mr. P would know about it.

After a moment, the elderly gentleman turned, slowly strolled to the window. He gazed out into space and scratched his chin thoughtfully. "Why can't I be the client?"

Parker stiffened. "I beg your pardon?"

Must be classy Southern for "WTF?"

Mr. P's voice suddenly lost its mirth and grew dark. "Eli Langford is my bitterest enemy. In business and in his personal life, he's a brute of a man. But if one of his daughters were killed, he'd want to know who did it. And so would I." He turned and gave Miranda a somber look. "I'll hire you to find out the truth."

Parker's jaw tensed as he stood. "Father, you can't be serious."

"Why can't I?"

"You have no idea what you're asking."

"Of course, I do, Russell. Didn't Ms. Steele here save your life recently?"

Parker's mouth opened, but it took a moment for words to come out. "Father, Miranda is—"

Mr. P raised a hand, shaking his head with a smile. "Don't worry, son. I can see Ms. Steele is far too headstrong to go off and get herself killed. I know how your business operates."

Parker's face tightened. His hands fisted at his sides. "There are many differences between your business and mine. A civilian can't comprehend all of them."

"I may be a 'civilian,' as you put it, but Ms. Steele isn't. She's your employee. She'll do an excellent job." He reached inside his jacket. "Now how much shall I make the check out for?"

Miranda beamed. She was really starting to like this old guy. "Guess we have a case after all, huh?" she said to Parker.

Ferocious anger burned in his handsome Magnum-gray eyes. She wanted to kick him.

Gently he took her arm, turned her away from his father, muttered gruffly into her ear. "We'll discuss it further this evening."

She ground her teeth like a prizefighter adjusting his mouthpiece. "Sure. Be glad to."

Miranda spent the rest of the afternoon agitatedly catching up on class notes, even did some more research on her computer about PCP. At five o'clock she tromped down to the gym, did five laps around the perimeter, then gave one of the punching bags a blistering. It felt good to get in some solid licks on something.

Dr. Theophilus was right. She did have a lot of pent-up aggression. She hadn't realized how much until she started to pummel the bag. Now this was therapy, she thought, smacking the leather hard.

But she didn't need to probe her psyche. Parker's reaction this afternoon was why she had so much adrenaline coursing through her veins. He didn't like his father's hiring her to solve the Langford murder. He wanted to "discuss" it, did he? She'd discuss it all right. If he wasn't going to let her work a case like this, she might just tell him where he could put his job.

And while she was at it, she just might tell him the only reason she'd gone along with Mr. P's idea about the mansion was to make him take it. If he really didn't want the freaking pile of rocks, she didn't either.

The idea that she might be out of a job and homeless tonight made her jab at the punching bag even harder.

She let go and gave it all she had.

CHAPTER FOURTEEN

By the time she showered, drove to Mockingbird Hills, and was walking up the stone steps to the majestic front porch of the Parker mansion, with its iron filigree railing and tall, white Grecian columns, Miranda was ready for a showdown.

The door of the three-car garage was closed. She wondered if Parker's silver Mazda was parked inside. Probably.

She pulled out her new key and unlocked the huge front door. As soon as it opened, a delicious aroma greeted her.

She followed it into the mansion's large, elaborate entrance hall, past the mahogany staircase, and through an arched doorway. There, a richly carved table of heavy wood sat on a Persian rug in the middle of a large room painted in dark, muted blue.

A matching china cabinet stood along one wall, with silver knick-knacks, finely etched plates, and embroidered boxes on display inside that made you curious about what was in them. On the opposite wall was a credenza next to a bronze statue of exotic lovebirds perched in a cherry tree.

Overhead a demure chandelier sparkled, while along the crown molding, stenciled Cupids smiled down at the room's occupants. Another memento of Mr. P's libido.

The table was set with a candelabra and flowers. There were two table settings of fine china and crystal.

After a moment, Parker appeared through a small door at the other end of the room, holding a bottle of wine. He'd showered and changed into a dark suit and tie with a matching dark blue striped button-down shirt. Rather formal for home, but then that was Parker.

As he studied her with that penetrating look of his, his gaze seemed wary. He was still pissed about his father and the Langford case.

"Honey, I'm home," she said flatly, meeting his intent look.

"So I see." He crossed the room and used the excuse to kiss her cheek.

She gestured toward the table. "I didn't know chef services came with the bodyguard."

She couldn't read his half-grin. "You have a cook."

"I do?"

"It was part of your agreement with my father."

Oh, right. "The part-time staff?"

He nodded. "The staff is here from midday until after dinnertime during the week. I merely made arrangements with the cook in anticipation of your arrival."

Thoughtful of him. Was this to soften her up for the bad news that they weren't taking the Langford case, after all? Steering away from the subject, she gestured toward the table, then at his suit. "My, aren't we formal?"

His lips curved dryly. "Forgive me. It's my heritage."

"Right."

"Shall we?" He gestured toward a chair.

She'd been planning on a bag of chips and salsa for dinner, but her mouth had been watering since she came through the front door. After all, she'd skipped lunch to go to Dr. Theophilus's 'Happy Time' session.

"Why not?" she shrugged.

He took her arm and seated her at the table, then opened the bottle of wine and poured some into her glass. "We're having salmon for dinner. I thought a nice Goisot Sauvignon would go well with it."

She wasn't much for wine. Budweiser served as her usual aperitif. It was Samuel Adams Black Lager when she really wanted to splurge, which wasn't too often, but she took a sip. It was good. Very dry. Very rich tasting. "Seems like a lot of amenities come along with the bodyguard service."

"We aim to please." He took a seat across from her, reached for a small silver bell, gave it a light ring. After a moment, a maid appeared dressed all in black, carrying two large plates filled with glistening salad. She set the plates before them.

Miranda blinked as she left the room. So now, she not only had a mansion, she had servants, too. No. Parker had a mansion. Parker had servants. She was just a temporary tenant.

"So tell me about your day." Parker picked up his fork and politely waited for her to start.

Miranda took a bite of the salad. Exquisite. The romaine was as fresh as if it had just come out of the backyard garden. And the dressing was downright exotic. Wine, vinegar, and spices snapped in her mouth. She couldn't imagine how it was made. For all she knew, Parker might have had the ingredients flown in from Istanbul that afternoon.

"My day at the *office*?" She stabbed a lettuce leaf with her fork, swirled it in the savory dressing.

"At the therapist." His tone was as dry as the Sauvignon.

She stopped chewing. Hanging around Parker was a little like being with a psychic. He could read her thoughts and knew her session had been a bust, just as sure as if he had been there. Or maybe he'd followed her again.

She swallowed her food and shot him a hollow grin. "It was peachy."

Now he stopped chewing. "Exactly what about it was 'peachy'?" he asked in that low, intimidating voice of his.

She picked at the Romaine and found a black olive, which she rolled around her plate with her fork. "It was a group session. Very relaxing. We tossed a ball around. The shrink called it our 'Happy Time.'" Something like that.

"I see." His timbre was a dark thunder roll.

They finished their salads in silence, then Parker rang the bell again and the servant came, took the empty dishes and replaced them with the main course.

Wild King Salmon drenched in a spicy cream sauce that smacked of garlic, thyme, and extra cayenne. The plate was edged with a colorful arrangement of avocado halves stuffed with a tangy mango salsa and onion roasted potatoes dotted with cilantro sprigs. It was almost too pretty to eat, but she was too hungry not to.

Deciding to concentrate on the food, she dug in. The argument that was bound to come could wait until after dinner. She didn't want to lose her appetite before she ate this meal. It was like something from a five-star restaurant.

When she was almost finished, she took another sip of wine and braced herself. "So, Parker," she said with a sigh. "Are you going to call off our deal because my therapy session didn't take?"

He wiped his mouth, laid the napkin on the table. "On the contrary. As promised, I've already started gathering information." He rose and retrieved a folder from a drawer in the credenza. "Have a look." He laid it next to her.

Shocked by his gesture, she put her napkin down as well. "What is it?"

"See for yourself." He returned to his seat.

Gingerly, she opened the folder, leafed through its contents. Her breath caught. Reports. Interviews. Photos. A toxicology report. The autopsy. This was a copy of the police file on Desirée Langford's accident.

She looked up at him in amazement. "You kept your word."

"I always keep my word."

"Where did you get all this stuff?"

His lip turned up in a wry half-grin. "My usual connections with the police department."

"Cool."

Parker watched her intently, sensing her excitement as she turned the pages. Her reaction satisfied him deeply. He had wanted nothing to do with Desirée Langford's case, but if it made Miranda feel alive again, he'd let her have it. Under his supervision, of course. And if it got her into that much-needed therapy, he would even risk coming into contact with Delta Langford.

It wasn't that he didn't care about Desirée's death. He cared more than Miranda could imagine. But it was a matter the police could handle. He believed the woman was suicidal, but her death was probably a bizarre accident that Ferraro Usher had had a hand in. In vengeance, Delta was lashing out at the artist in that hysterical way of hers. But Miranda wouldn't believe Usher was guilty of murder if the evidence didn't warrant it. Delta didn't know who she was dealing with.

Miranda narrowed her eyes at Parker. From the police department, huh? He had some strong ties with the cops. She couldn't help wondering who'd passed him this file. As the servant came in again to clear the plates away and serve coffee, she silently went over the list of possible informants.

Detective Tan's husband was a cop. There was Lieutenant Erskine, but he and Parker weren't always on speaking terms. Somebody Mr. P had rubbed elbows with? That could be anybody. The mayor. The governor. Parker was the most well-connected person she'd ever known.

But it didn't matter how he got the information. It was here.

Excitement danced in her stomach as she picked up one of the reports and studied it. "Bystanders at the Steeplechase said they saw Ferraro Usher and Desirée drinking together at a table near the barns. That wasn't the set of tables where we followed Simmons and Witherspoon."

"No. It was a similar arrangement on the opposite side of the field."

"And not so far from the barns, according to this chart." An officer at the scene had sketched out a diagram. "Delta was there, too. So were Dr. Kennicot and some other friends. Another witness heard the party arguing. She wasn't sure what it was about."

"There was definite tension among the group."

She picked up the autopsy. "COD: cardiac arrest caused by overdose of phencyclidine. One hundred milligrams of PCP was found in her bloodstream."

"Along with alcohol and cocaine."

She turned back a page. "A different witness thought he saw Desirée and Usher snorting coke." Good Lord, there were children there. "So Delta was right about the drugs."

"But the witness doesn't say which one of them was giving the illegal substance to the other."

True, but didn't that have to be Usher? She turned another page. "The toxicology report says an empty vial was found on the ground near that table. It had traces of PCP in it. The 'murder weapon'?"

"So to speak. That's where the lethal dose came from. Desirée had to imbibe it in liquid form to get that much. Though the coroner's report states that PCP was the cause of death, it was more likely CDI."

"CDI?"

"Combined Drug Intoxication. The interaction of substances in her system turned poisonous."

"But a hundred milligrams couldn't have been recreational. So it wasn't an accident. It was intentional."

"I would agree. The question is whether Desirée poisoned herself with the PCP."

"Someone could have slipped it into her drink."

"But wouldn't that person have been more careful than to leave the vial on the ground?"

"Maybe that person was intoxicated or distraught and dropped it accidentally." Though that seemed awfully careless for a killer. She turned another page and read some more. "There were no fingerprints at all on the vial. So the killer was careful enough." She thought a moment. "Desirée was wearing gloves that day."

He nodded, slowly sipped his drink, staring down at the golden liquid. "That detail supports the theory that Desirée killed herself."

She turned another page and sucked in her breath. "The suicide note."

"Yes."

An icy finger slithered down Miranda's spine as she read the words.

There's been so much pain in my life. So much torment. I'm so tired of it. I can't go on any longer. I want to die beside my beloved horses. This is good-bye. My final good-bye.

Her throat suddenly dry, she reached for her water glass. "It sounds pretty final."

Parker paused a moment to gauge her reaction, then spoke. "Less than a third of people who commit suicide leave a note."

She put the page down. "So this could be a fake?"

"Possibly."

Miranda sat back and folded her arms. How could the murderer fake a suicide note? Was it a letter Desirée had written in a different context? Did it have a different meaning? It sounded pretty definite. Did someone force her to write it? As usual, there were a lot more questions than answers.

Parker rose. "Come here and let's look at something."

Curious, Miranda closed the folder and tucked it under her arm. She picked up the wineglass she was still nursing and followed Parker down the hall and into a dark-paneled room that held a large, overstuffed black leather couch facing a huge flat panel television.

"Have a seat." Parker reached for the controls.

She eased down into the squishy-soft high-end leather, sighed at the thick padding. Then she set her drink down on a coaster on a side table alongside the folder and put her feet up on one of the inviting ottomans. This was the life.

The floor was polished parquet, in an intricate, herringbone pattern. A zebra skin rug lay near a fireplace in the far corner. It looked like some kind of entertainment room.

Parker sat down next to her and slyly slipped his arm around her shoulders, like a teenager on a date to the movies. She thought she knew what kind of entertainment he had in mind. She gave in and let her head rest against him. His chest was so strong, so muscular.

He pressed a button on the remote.

The TV flickered on, but it wasn't *The Late Show* or a romantic movie. Images from the Northwinds Steeplechase appeared on the screen. In particular, Farrah Simmons bumping and grinding with Lover-Number-Two.

Miranda sat up. "My recording."

"Yes," Parker murmured.

The big screen TV had much more detail than she'd seen on her little LCD laptop. The large image of Farrah Simmons and the moaning fluttering through the surround sound system didn't make Miranda's stomach feel very comfortable after that big meal.

Then the shotgun-like kicking came through the speakers. The commotion of the crowd. Miranda's footage of Calypso bucking and snorting outside the cell as the stable hands tried to control him.

The ground jerked as the camera covered her movement toward the stall.

Miranda pursed her lips. She'd better confess. "Uh, I've already seen this."

"Of course, you have. You played it on your home computer that afternoon."

She rolled her eyes. "Good grief, Parker. Who are you, Nostradamus?"

He grinned and eyed her with a hooded gaze. "It's my business."

Giving up, she sat back and watched the scene unfold. She took in the details, but all she saw was the same blue-flowered sundress, the smashed straw hat with the note under it, the white gloves, and that poor crushed, bloody face.

Ferraro Usher seemed bizarre, but she couldn't see any evidence that was incriminating. There was a little tic in his hand.

"What was Usher doing so close to the stall?" she asked, deep in thought.

"Not sure." Parker stopped the film and sat back. His eyes roamed over her.

She could guess what they'd be doing tonight. She wondered if it would be bubble bath this time or just twisted silk sheets?

"How does the film look after what you've read in the report?"

She reached for the folder and thumbed through it again. "There's a lot of suspicious activity in here. Why was Desirée doing drugs with Usher when she'd divorced him? What were they fighting about?" She closed the folder and put it down on the ottoman. "Too many open questions," she said flatly.

"So your determination is that the case warrants more investigation."

"Yeah." She grinned at him. "Aren't you glad your father hired us?"

His smile disappeared. "I haven't signed off on that yet."

She stiffened. "What do you mean?" After all this tantalizing evidence, he wasn't going to take the case away from her now, was he? She just might belt him if he did.

His gun barrel gray eyes bore into her. "I'll let you take this case under three stipulations."

She drew in a breath. "Which are?"

"One, you have to continue therapy."

She cringed. "And the other?"

"You're not to work on this case unless I'm with you."

83

She resisted the urge to spit. She'd made good progress on her own during the last case. In fact, she'd solved it by acting on her own. "And the third?"

"If at any time during the investigation I feel the case is too much for you, I reserve the right to pull you off. Is that clear?"

"Crystal." She stood up. "This is bullshit."

"I'm not asking, Miranda. As your employer, I'm demanding it."

She crossed the room to a panel bookcase. Her arms tight around her waist, she paced in front of it. "So I'm under your thumb all the way."

"No," he said calmly. "You'll be the lead on the case."

She stopped pacing. "The lead? You mean I call the shots?"

"Exactly."

The idea made her head spin. *The lead?* She didn't know what to make of his mixed signals, except that he was being his overprotective self.

He reached into his coat pocket. "I'll expect you to find your own therapist. One a little more reputable than Dr. Theodore Theophilus."

There he went again. Wade Parker, ace detective, clairvoyant, and busybody.

"But in the meantime, I took the liberty of making you an appointment with this one tomorrow afternoon."

He took out a card and handed it to her.

Irritated, she reached for it. "Dr. Arnold Chaffee." His office was on Piedmont. "What's so special about this one?"

"Something you'll like. He was Desirée Langford's therapist."

She blew out an exasperated breath. He knew how to tempt her.

He stepped toward her, took her chin in his hand and studied her. "So are we agreed?"

She didn't know why she wanted this case so much. Maybe because of the way Delta Langford had pleaded with her. Or because the weird way Usher had acted got her goat. Maybe just because she wanted answers. But she couldn't let it alone. And Parker was assigning her as the lead. It was too much to turn down, even with all his "stipulations." Deep down, she knew he'd insisted on them only because he cared about her.

Slowly she nodded. "Agreed."

"So where do you want to start?"

She looked down at the folder and thought about Usher at Desirée's funeral. "I'd like to talk to Dr. Kennicot."

"Very well. We'll go there tomorrow morning."

"No classes?"

"You can make them up."

She danced from foot to foot. "Hot dog."

Parker watched the eagerness in those deep blue eyes, his heart glowing with love. It was clear fieldwork made Miranda happy. He wanted her to be happy, but he would keep her in check for her own good. Fieldwork could also be dangerous. Leon Groth had hurt her so much. He refused to let anyone else hurt her again.

Still, it would be healthy for her to take charge of this case. He would enjoy watching her grow, helping her hone that keen intuition, that abundant talent of hers. Her zeal for investigative work made him think of his younger days. He found the thought intensely arousing.

He bent his head.

"Sealing the deal with a kiss?" Miranda sighed, as his lips reached hers.

"How else would we do it?" His low, sexy Southern murmur sent a thrill to her groin.

More than a kiss would follow. What kind of magic spell did he have over her to arouse her so much, so suddenly? It was Parker's raw, sensual magnetism. It exuded from him like the subtle smell of his expensive cologne. She couldn't resist it.

His hands slid over her back, down toward her bottom, then reversed course and went for her shoulders. He began to massage her between the shoulder blades. Just where she was sorest from her session with the punching bag earlier. His delicious movements made the spell complete.

"You're tense. You need to relax."

"You sound like Dr. Theophilus."

He chuckled. "We should go to bed."

"Too far," she murmured. He was a powerful man, a virile lover. He made her want him far too much.

"Oh?"

Suddenly emboldened, she grabbed him by the silk tie and pulled him across the room to the zebra skin rug. She began to loosen the tie as he slipped out of his jacket and tossed it aside.

His shirt and her blouse came off next. Then the only sound in the room was the zippers of their slacks going down and their ragged breathing.

It seemed like only another minute before he had her sprawled across the rug.

She groaned, more intoxicated than ever.

Why did she let him get to her like this? Did she really have a choice? His touch was as potent as strong whiskey. Intoxicating, enticing, irresistible.

His hand slid delectably up her thigh. When he reached his target, his fingers teased at her for a long moment.

She gasped.

He bent his head to her lips, chuckling, enjoying her moans. He knew he had her hooked.

Deftly, he rolled over on top of her, slipped inside and gently began to rouse her even more. She felt herself falling. Down, down, then up again. A sensual roller coaster ride of passion. As she rose toward the crest again, she suddenly remembered she'd intended to have it out with Parker about the house. If he didn't agree, she was going to leave. Mmmm.

Her mind clouded as his tongue plunged into her mouth, flaming her into a wild stupor, while their bodies worked together.

She guessed she'd let the topic of the house slide for tonight.

CHAPTER FIFTEEN

The next morning, Miranda was up bright and early. Brimming with excitement, she dressed in khaki slacks, a pert white cotton blouse, and a pair of black boots she thought might make her blend in with the horsey set.

Downstairs on the big redwood deck overlooking the richly landscaped backyard, Parker had the usual coffee and breakfast fare waiting for her. Along with the number for Dr. Gabriel Kennicot's veterinary office.

She gave him a grateful kiss on the cheek, pulled out her cell phone and dialed the number.

"I'm sorry," a staff member told her. "Dr. Kennicot is in the field this morning."

"Really? Where do you think he'll be? I mean, I really need to talk to him about my dog, Scruffy." Parker smiled at her knowingly. He was familiar with her penchant for making up stories about dogs she didn't own.

"I really don't know his exact schedule, ma'am, but I think he's at Aquitaine Farms all morning. Would you like to make an appointment for next week?"

"Uh, I'm not sure. I'll have to call back later. Thanks." She disconnected. "The vet's at Aquitaine Farms," she told Parker. "The Langfords' horse farm."

"And?"

"And?" She blinked at him.

Casually, he picked up his coffee cup. "And what should we do now?" he asked innocently.

He really was letting her call the shots, wasn't he? She wondered whether he just wanted her to get the need for this case out of her system, if he was testing her, or if he really had faith in her. If he didn't, she decided, by the time she was done, she'd make him believe in her. "Any reason we can't go out there now?"

"None at all." He took a final sip of coffee and rose.

A thrill spiked in her belly. "Then let's get going."

They went out a side door that led to the large, three-car garage, where Parker helped her into his silver Mazda.

"I knew you'd hidden your car in here last night," she said as he slid deftly into the driver's seat.

"There's room for two cars in here," he said as blandly as if he were commenting about the weather. "It is *your* house, after all."

She inhaled. That again. Did he think the sight of her beat-up blue Chevy would run down the neighborhood? "I never had a garage before. Don't see the need for one."

"It's up to you. However, if you change your mind," he reached into a tray and handed her a small electronic device. "Here's an extra automatic opener."

She took it, stared down at it. "Home sweet home."

He started the car. "Would you care to try it out?"

She gave him a sharp look, then pressed one of the buttons. The door opened behind them. He put the car in reverse and glided down the drive. As they moved past her old blue jalopy, she pressed another button, and the door went down.

She slipped the contraption into her purse, but she didn't intend to use it. She refused to get too comfortable with the accommodations. She'd made up her mind they were only temporary.

They shot down 400 to I-85, past the city office buildings and hotels and restaurants. They'd just missed rush hour, so the traffic was light for Atlanta, which made Miranda's nerves happy. South of Five Points, they took the ramp onto I-20 and headed east. Here the buildings became sparser, flatter, and the omnipresent trees took their place. It was a pretty monotonous view of concrete and green as they motored through Lithonia, Conyers, and Covington. Here the buildings disappeared, and the highway became lined with rows of tall Georgia pines.

They'd been driving over an hour, when Parker took an exit north.

Miranda lifted her head from the cushion, where she'd been half-dozing. "Are we there yet, Dad?"

"Almost."

They traveled several more miles, until Parker turned onto a country road. Here the landscape became even more rural, if that were possible, even denser with trees. After another mile, Miranda caught sight of a big, white wooden sign shaded by the rustling leaves of a large oak.

The words "Aquitaine Farms" were embossed on it in a fancy script. She half-expected to hear the theme from *Gone with the Wind*.

"Guess this is the place."

Parker peered out the window, his body tense. "It's been a long time since I've been here, but the landscape hasn't changed much."

That remark made her wonder again about his past with Delta Langford.

He made a right turn and the Mazda rumbled down a long dirt pathway. Slowly, the huge structure came into view.

The place was gorgeous. A majestic, sprawling, white plantation house done in antebellum Greek revival, with dozens of columns rising to tall stories, and rows of high Palladian windows. Framed by foliage, green pastures and acres of trees, it had a fresh, healthy feel. Where was that *Gone with the Wind* theme?

In the distance, behind the house, Miranda could see barns and paddocks. Several horses were outside. "Kennicot will be in the barns, no doubt."

"Let's head for the house," Miranda said. "I want to talk to Delta first." She felt she owed it to her to tell her she'd taken the case, though she wouldn't mention the client.

"Very well." Parker turned and headed that way.

"No protest?"

"I don't question the lead on a case."

Until he disagreed with her. And as long as he got to make stipulations. But it wasn't so terrible that he insisted sticking with her. There was a lot to learn from Parker. Professionally. As far as the personal part went, she guessed she was learning to be just as big a sneak there, too. What was she going to do about their pretend-this-is-all-normal living arrangements? Sooner or later, she'd have to do something about that. She'd figure out exactly what later.

As Parker steered the car up the circular drive, the sprawling Southern mansion loomed before them, its white columns like giant soldiers on guard. The smell of magnolias wafted through the car windows.

He parked just behind a row of Azalea bushes, so the Mazda wouldn't be seen from the large, Palladian windows.

Miranda regarded the yawning veranda. It was twice as big as the Parker mansion's porch, and that was no small potatoes.

She batted her eyelashes at Parker and put on a fake accent. "Why, Ashley. We're home."

His lip curled. "I thought you'd think of me as more of a Rhett."

"Yeah, sometimes you just don't give a damn."

He ignored her comment. "Why don't you go ring the bell?"

"All alone?"

He nodded.

She titled her head and grinned prettily. "Are you sure?"

He inhaled slowly. "If Delta is home, my presence won't make her talkative."

Must be that unpleasant history again. "You sure I can handle it? By myself I mean?" After all, he had said she wasn't to work this case without him. She couldn't resist rubbing it in.

He reached over and patted her hand. "I have the utmost confidence in you."

With a satisfied smirk, Miranda got out of the car and strolled casually up the stairs. At the door, she took a deep breath and rang the bell.

No answer.

She waited a minute and rang the bell again.

Nothing.

She gazed up at the huge domicile and had the feeling she was being watched from one of the upper windows. Once more she rang the bell. "Culligan man," she called out impatiently.

"Yes?" A young black woman dressed in a stiff, dark uniform answered the door. "May I help you?" Her accent sounded British.

"Uh, I'm here to see Delta Langford."

"I'm sorry, Ms. Langford's not home at the moment."

Miranda thought fast. "Is Mr. Langford at home?"

She lifted a sharp, dark brow. "Mr. Eli Langford? No. He's in town. Do you have an appointment with the Langfords, ma'am?"

The stiff formality was killing her. "Uh, no. I was just in the neighborhood and wanted to stop by and pay my respects. I understand Ms. Langford lost her sister recently."

The woman nodded solemnly. "Yes, she did. Shall I tell Ms. Langford you came by, Ms.—?"

"Oh, don't bother. I'll call. Thanks." She took a step backward, heading for the car, then turned back. "On second thought, tell Ms. Langford Miranda Steele came by. Tell her, uh, that matter we discussed is being looked into."

The woman nodded and closed the door. Miranda made her way back to Parker.

"No luck." She scooted inside the car. "Nobody's home but the staff. Let's try the stables."

The barn was a tall, rustic looking structure of treated wood with a high ceiling and big red doors, crisscrossed with yellow planks. It stood wide open, like welcoming arms.

In the nearby paddocks, riders were exercising some of the horses. Farther out, more animals grazed in a pasture.

Miranda got out of the car and headed for the open door, her boots kicking up the dry red earth on the path. This time, Parker came with her. She didn't mind the company.

Inside, it was bright and clean, the sun streaming in through the high windows. The air was thick with the smell of fresh hay. She could hear it being pitched somewhere, but didn't see any workers. Now and then she heard a low whinny.

Then she turned a corner and caught sight of a large man squatting down. In his hands was the hoof of a chestnut horse tethered to a post.

"Excuse me," Miranda said to him.

With a surprised frown, he turned his head, then gently put the horse's foot down and rose. "Can I help you?"

He seemed to be in his early fifties. Tall and broad-shouldered, he was rugged looking, with deep, weathered lines in his face and wavy graying hair, cut short. He had on khaki slacks and a green plaid shirt. Even in casual clothes, he had a professional air about him.

She approached him. "Are you Dr. Gabriel Kennicot?"

"Yes. Who are you?" So this was the notorious vet, Desirée's old flame. According to Ferraro Usher. He had green, wide-set eyes that gave him a quizzical look. Or maybe that was the scientist in him.

"My name is Miranda Steele. I'm looking into the death of Desirée Langford."

His thick gray brows drew together, making the furrows in his face deeper. And more defensive looking. "Are you with the police?"

Miranda shook her head. "No, we're private."

Kennicot gestured toward Parker. "Who is this?"

"Wade Parker of the Parker Agency." Smoothly, Parker reached into his jacket for a business card and gave it to Kennicot.

The doctor stared down at it a moment. "Detectives? Why are you looking into Desirée's death? It was a suicide."

"Some people don't think so." She folded her arms.

He blinked at them, looking genuinely shocked. Then he moved over to a stall and leaned against the wooden door to steady himself. "My Lord."

Miranda glanced at Parker. He raised an eyebrow and nodded toward Kennicot. He was going to let her handle the questioning. Well, that's what she'd been training for.

She took a deep breath and stepped over to the vet. "Dr. Kennicot, according to the Medical Examiner's report, Ms. Langford died of an overdose of phencyclidine. PCP. Angel dust, on the street."

"Yes," he said quietly. "I know that."

"One hundred milligrams of PCP were found in her bloodstream." She tried in vain to sound gentle.

He closed his eyes and nodded. The words were painful for him to listen to. "Yes."

Before she could ask another question, with a dazed look, the large man sat down on a bale of hay and put his head in his hands.

"My beautiful Desirée. I loved her so. How can she be gone?" He looked up at Miranda with pleading eyes. "Ms. Steele, do you really think someone killed her?"

"We don't know yet." Her heart went out to the grieving man, but she had to press. She took another breath. "As a vet, you'd have access to large doses of PCP, wouldn't you?"

His mouth opened in shock. He looked at Parker for a moment, then back at her. "Do you mean Sernylan? That drug was discontinued years ago due to its side effects."

She nodded in admission. "It's rare, but some veterinarians still use it." She'd noted that during her research the other afternoon.

Dr. Kennicot stood up, straightened himself and glared at her. "Sernylan can cause delirium, disorientation, hallucination. Not the type of effect my clients would want in a prize breeder or a racer. Not the type of effect I want to induce in the animals I treat."

Miranda looked down at her nails. "I hear Desirée Langford was often disoriented and hallucinating."

"What are you saying, Ms. Steele? That *I* had something to do with Desirée's death?"

She stood quietly, watched his eyes flame.

"I don't use PCP." His words were clipped. "You're welcome to check my office if you don't believe me." He pulled out a cell phone, his fingers shaking with emotion. "I'll have my assistant let you into my cabinets. You can search the entire place, if you like. I have nothing to hide."

Miranda held up a hand. "That won't be necessary." The doctor might have been protesting too much, but he seemed genuinely offended at her insinuation. Still, if he had PCP, it would have been smart to remove it from his office. Right now, though, she was inclined to believe him.

Slowly he put his cell phone back in his pocket and sank back down on the bale of hay. "I didn't have anything to do with her death, Ms. Steele, if that's what you're trying to imply. God as my witness, I loved her."

Miranda spotted another bale in front of the next stall. As Parker watched, she strolled over to it and sat down. Trying to simulate an intimate conversation with this man, she decided to play dumb.

"Loved her?" she said gently. "What exactly was your relationship to Desirée Langford, Doctor?"

His eyes narrowed. "We were close. We worked together here at Aquitaine."

She waited a beat. "Close?"

He let out a long breath. "Everyone knows she left that leech she was married to for me."

"Ferraro Usher."

"Yes."

"Usher was a leech?"

"Desirée supported him for years while he pursued his career as an artist. He couldn't have survived without her. Or become as successful as he now is."

Interesting. "So you encouraged Desirée to leave him?"

His jaw twitched angrily. "He was bad for her. I saw what that bastard was doing to her. I told her to leave him many times. I told her to stop using. She finally walked out on him last Christmas. The divorce was final three months ago."

Christmas? Santy Claus wasn't too good to the brooding artist last year. That parting scene couldn't have been a pleasant one. The two times Miranda had seen Usher, he'd acted like he was still in love with Desirée. Desperately in love. At her funeral, he said he was still seeing her and begging her to come back to him. Stalking her, perhaps.

What did Kennicot know about that? She leaned toward him. "Did Usher try to see Desirée after their breakup?"

He stiffened. "Not with my consent."

"But he did see her."

He nodded.

"How often?"

He shook his head, as if in denial about it. "I don't know. She kept it from me."

But he still knew about it. "Was Usher threatening Desirée, Dr. Kennicot?"

He looked at her blankly.

Dr. Kennicot didn't strike her as the type of man to let someone like Usher threaten his love interest. Maybe she was going down the wrong path here. Objectivity. Could Desirée have been playing the two men who were in love with her against each other? Boinking both of them at the same time? Like Farrah Simmons and her two lovers-on-the-side?

She wet her lips and swallowed. "Do you think Desirée was sleeping with Usher?"

His look grew even blanker.

She took a deep breath and decided to play her trump card. "Usher said Desirée was about to leave you and go back to him."

He stared at her a moment, then let out an anguished laugh. "Impossible. Desirée loved me since she was a teenager."

Usher had said that.

With a faraway look in his wide-set eyes, Kennicot continued. "She was sixteen when I came to Georgia and started my practice. Eli Langford was one of my first clients. She loved the horses and was always in the barn when I came to do examinations. I wasn't here a month before she caught me alone in a stall."

A young stable hand came and untethered the horse the doctor had been examining. He glanced over at the three of them. "Are you finished with Horizon, Dr. Kennicot?" he asked in a high-pitched voice.

The doctor nodded to him. "Yes. He's ready for his breeze."

The hand led the horse out of the barn.

When they were gone, Miranda turned back to Kennicot. "Caught you?" she asked.

He hung his head, as if embarrassed. "She threw her arms around me and started kissing me. She said she was madly in love with me."

"And you kissed her back."

He looked up, his eyes flashing. "No. I stopped her. I was thirty-three and married, for goodness' sake. I had two sons who were almost her age." He ran a hand through his hair. "I dismissed it as some sort of teenage obsession. I assumed she saw me as a father figure. She didn't get along with her own father. I often heard them arguing at the house."

Like Mr. P had said, Eli Langford didn't treat his daughters very well.

"I told her she was too young, and I was too old. I tried everything I could to discourage her."

"But it didn't work."

He shrugged. "She grew up, went to college, and came back home to breed horses. By then my wife had died. Heart attack."

"I'm sorry." The man had had it rough.

He took a breath and went on. "We began working together here at the Farm. After awhile, Desirée told me she still loved me. But I was too much in mourning for my wife to consider a relationship then. And I still thought she was too young. She was twenty-three. I was forty."

Rejected twice by the one you thought was the love of your life. That could bring on a depression. "And so?"

"She started hanging out with a wild crowd. Took up with a local artist group. That was where she met Usher. They used to have parties out here when her father was in the city. It was all for spite. She threw herself at Usher to get back at me."

Good Lord. "How did you know that?"

"She told me. Many times. She married Usher about seven years ago. The night before the wedding she called me and told me she could never be happy, but it was too late for us, so she had no choice."

Desirée had married Usher but longed for Kennicot all those years? Miranda supposed it was possible. She thought of her colleague Dave Becker, who was still pining away after his childhood sweetheart. You can get badly burned by an old flame.

"My sons had grown up and left home. As the years passed, I watched Desirée grow into a top horse breeder. More and more, her work brought us together. I admired her. Everyone did. Eventually, I fell as much in love with her as she had been with me in the beginning. Last winter, I finally got the courage to tell her so. It took her two full months to tell Usher it was over and leave him. We were planning to be married this fall."

"But she was still seeing Usher."

He nodded. "I couldn't stop her."

Miranda paused to take in what he'd told her. Then she drew a deep breath. "Witnesses saw them together at the Steeplechase before her accident."

"That's right. I tried to run Usher off, Desirée wouldn't let me. I got angry with her. If only I could have that moment back."

Must have been the argument some of the interviewees reported.

Miranda got up from the bale of hay and brushed off her slacks. She stared down at the poor, broken man before her, her heart aching for him. He was in genuine pain, in bitter mourning for someone he'd loved deeply. She felt terrible for having to pelt him with a lot of painful questions. But she needed just a little more information.

She sucked in another breath and fired. "One witness said Usher and Desirée were snorting coke at the Steeplechase."

Dr. Kennicot put his head in his hands again, looking weary and more bewildered than ever. He nodded. "She had a drug problem. She was an addict. She was in therapy for it and for her recurring bouts of depression. I wanted her to go to a clinic. She refused."

"So she saw Usher for drugs."

Once more, he nodded. "As far as I know, he was her supplier. He's the one who gave her that lethal dose of PCP." Then he looked up and fixed Miranda with a deep, penetrating look. "But Desirée's the one who took it."

CHAPTER SIXTEEN

Miranda slid into the passenger seat of Parker's silver Mazda and sat back. As he rolled down the dirt lane, she stared numbly at the tall trees. So many shades of green in their lush summer loveliness.

She blew out a long breath. "That was rough."

Parker drove on silently until they reached the paved road. Before he turned onto it, he stopped and gave her a long look. "I must remember to give Detective Judd a hefty raise."

"Detective Judd?"

"His training in interviewing techniques has produced excellent results."

She gave him a sad smile. "Thanks."

He nodded approvingly. "Natural talent helps, too."

"You think I have natural talent?"

"I do." He turned onto the road and took off.

Miranda rubbed her eyes. Parker's approval felt good. But she was exhausted, and she felt raw after raking the grieving doctor over the coals. "I'm not so sure about that. I hated having to put Kennicot through those questions."

"A natural reaction. Unfortunately, it's our business. Sometimes it's necessary to get the information we need. I don't like it either. But you did a fine job."

She nodded, smiled.

Parker took another side road and headed back to the Interstate.

"What a sad story. They loved each other for decades, and less than six months after they finally get together, Desirée is dead."

"Pitiful."

Miranda watched the expression on Parker's face. He was doing a good job of hiding it, but she could see that he identified strongly with Kennicot. He had lost his wife, too. And a young woman named Laura, long ago when he was young. He'd want to find Desirée's killer now.

"So what do you think?" she asked him.

He glanced over at her. "What do *you* think?"

He really was taking this lead thing seriously. She thought a moment. "I think Kennicot's telling the truth."

"So do I."

"And that brings us back to Usher. So what's the next step?"

He chuckled softly, a tinge of sadness in his laugh. "That's for you to figure out."

Well, she'd asked for it. She grunted aloud. "No help from the guru, huh?"

"I'm just the assistant."

She swatted him on the arm. "And the bodyguard. Don't forget that."

His eyes almost smiling again, Parker glanced at the digital clock on the dash. "You can ponder your next move over lunch. We'll have just enough time for a bite to eat before your session with Dr. Chaffee."

"Oh, yeah." She'd forgotten about that. Just now, she felt like she could use a therapy session. Or a nap.

Parker's idea of a bite to eat was a place called the French American Brasserie, a.k.a. FAB, on the northeast branch of Peachtree Road near Lenox Square.

The dining room's décor was elegantly simple, with black chairs, white tablecloths, and tall windows that must have been at least twenty feet high. They were outfitted with thick red velvet curtains, pulled back for a view overlooking the sunny, sophisticated Buckhead locale.

Parker asked for a table near the window.

While he schmoozed with their server and selected from the menu, Miranda watched the small army of waiters in white shirts and black ties scurrying about serving the lunch clientele.

A few minutes later, she ended up with *Pâté de Campagne* for an appetizer, followed by *Coq au Vin* for an entree, which turned out to be roasted chicken in a sumptuous gourmet wine sauce with pearl onions, English peas and egg noodles.

She knew Parker was trying to spoil her with all this pampering so she'd never want to leave him or his house, but she was determined not to let the royal treatment get to her. If Parker had his way, she'd feel toward him the way Desirée Langford felt about Dr. Kennicot when she was sixteen.

She cared about Parker. More than what was good for her. At times, he did make her feel like a giddy teen.

It was a nice fantasy, but they were both too adult not to know whatever this was between them couldn't last. Both of them had too many scars. She certainly had way too much baggage.

And yet her feelings for Parker grew more intense the longer she knew him. Who could resist his smooth, debonair ways? His top-notch skill at his craft? His strength, his kindness? He'd been good to her. To top it off, she'd never known what great sex could be like before she met him. Probably would never know it with anyone else. And yet, when she thought of anything that resembled a commitment to Parker, all she felt was…sheer terror.

She dragged a juicy piece of chicken along her plate to sop up the scrumptious sauce, put it in her mouth, and forced her thoughts back to business and her conversation with Kennicot.

He was the real victim in this crime, if it was a crime. Still clear in her mind was the doctor's pained look as he told her about Desirée and Usher. Suddenly she thought of something and nearly dropped her fork.

Parker's brows rose. "I'm sorry the chicken's not as spicy as you like."

She blinked at him and shook her head. "I just remembered something."

"What?"

"The day of Desirée's funeral, Delta Langford left a message on my phone. She said that Usher was challenging Desirée's Will. She insisted that all he cared about was the money." She lowered her voice. "If that's true, it would establish a solid motive."

Parker chewed thoughtfully for a moment. "That's very interesting. What do you plan to do with that bit of information?"

A little irritated with this hands-off routine, she drummed her fingers on the table. She couldn't ask Usher, of course, he'd deny it. He'd lied about Desirée coming back to him, after all. Or maybe that was just wishful thinking on his part. Or maybe Desirée had been leading him on. Still, he wouldn't admit challenging the Will if he were the killer.

She picked up her water glass and sipped thoughtfully. "It would be nice if I could talk to Desirée's lawyer."

"The one who drew up her Will?"

She nodded. "Or maybe the executor." She put down her glass and lifted her hands in exasperation. "I don't even know who to ask. Not someone I can trust, anyway."

Parker regarded her a moment, as if debating whether to make a move. Then he pulled out his cell. "Antonio might be able to help." He pressed a button to pull up his number and handed her the phone.

She looked down at it and grinned. Parker always came through. She took the phone and pressed "Talk."

After a moment that smooth Latin accent fluttered in her ears. "What can I do for you, Señor Parker?"

Antonio Estavez was Parker's surrogate son. When Antonio was a kid, Parker had picked him up off the streets, gotten him out of the Latino gangs he ran with, brought him into his home, and raised him. Now Antonio was one of the top criminal defense attorneys in the city with the law firm of Chatham, Grayson, and McFee. Parker was very proud of him.

"Hi, Antonio," she said into Parker's cell. "It's me, Miranda."

"Ah, Ms. Steele. How lovely to hear your voice." Antonio's flirtatious nature was an involuntary reflex.

"I was wondering if you could help me with something."

"I can try."

"I'm sure you heard about Desirée Langford's, uh, accident at the Northwinds Steeplechase last week."

"Of course. I read about it in the newspaper. What a tragedy. The police ruled it a suicide, did they not?"

"Yes. Well, it might not have been a suicide. I'm looking into it."

"Oh?" He sounded genuinely impressed. "What can I do for you?"

"Someone told me Ms. Langford's ex-husband might be contesting her Will. His name is Ferraro Usher. How can I find out if that's true?"

"So you're looking for motive, Ms. Steele?"

"Something like that."

"You came to the right place. I believe our senior partner, Charles Grayson, handles the Langford estate. Let me see if he's back from lunch."

He put her on hold and soft Musak came over the phone. She picked at her chicken while Parker looked on, satisfied with himself. She was too excited to eat any more. After a moment, Antonio came back on the line.

"You are in luck, Ms. Steele. Mr. Grayson tells me that Eli Langford was named the executor. Desirée Langford has a large trust fund. She also had some earnings from her work as a horse breeder. She owned no property. Upon her death, all her assets reverted to the Langford estate."

"So Eli Langford is her beneficiary, too."

"Correct. Mr. Grayson also said that no one has contested the Will at all."

"He knows that for sure?"

"Yes. The court would have informed him if someone did."

"Thanks, Antonio. That helps a lot."

"My pleasure. Give my regards to your boss."

"I will." She disconnected and handed the phone back to Parker. "Everything goes to Eli Langford. Usher didn't contest the Will at all. Delta lied to me." She was beginning to wonder whether there was anyone connected to the Langfords she could trust.

"Perhaps that was her impression," Parker said. "Perhaps Usher was intending to contest, then dropped the idea. Delta Langford can be given to exaggeration."

Hmm. Parker knew Delta Langford a lot better than she did. "Maybe it's you I should be interviewing."

He picked up his wineglass and took a sip. "Fire away."

She locked eyes with him, staring deep into that knowing face. She'd love to unlock his secrets, find out exactly what that "unpleasant history" was all about. But she was afraid she'd find only pain.

"Maybe later," she said at last. "I've got an appointment with a therapist to keep."

CHAPTER SEVENTEEN

Strange.

It was the only word Miranda could think of as she sat on the couch in Dr. Arnold Chaffee's eleventh floor office in a high-rise on Piedmont Street that afternoon, the hot, early June sun, burning brightly in through his tall window.

Dr. Chaffee was a big, burly guy, whose rugged build and thick, black, shoulder-length hair made him look more like a titleholder from the World Wide Wrestling Federation than a shrink. Dressed in a solid black suit and a solid black tie, he sat muttering to himself in a low, gravelly voice, with the air of an undertaker.

At last, he consulted the folder on his lap. "So you're here because of a problem with your ex-husband, Ms., uh, Steele?"

Miranda stiffened at the question, uncomfortable with the doctor's dark, penetrating gaze. Avoiding it, she glanced at the heavy mahogany shelves, laden with thick textbooks. There was a matching desk in the corner, covered with doodads. A small globe, a fancy pen set, a silver bell that she guessed the doctor might use to signal when his sessions were over.

She took a breath. "Something like that."

He rubbed his chin. "Are you an unwilling patient, Ms. Steele?"

Miranda remembered the main reason why she didn't like shrinks. They always got too personal. She shrugged. "I'm here, aren't I?"

He smiled and nodded mechanically. "That's a start." He picked up a page from the folder. "I take it from your file that you don't put much stock in psychotherapy."

He had her there. When she'd arrived, the receptionist had made her fill out papers for twenty minutes, including a long questionnaire.

She had gotten annoyed with the repetitious questions and became a little creative. Instead of checking True or False for "I think about my problems all the time," she'd scribbled in the margin, "Only when my paycheck bounces."

"I often worry about what people think of me." She'd written, "Only when I'm on a nude beach."

A sense of humor was a sign of mental health, right?

But since she wanted information from this shrink about Desirée Langford, she decided it might not be a good idea to piss him off in the first ten minutes. "Sorry about that." She grinned shyly at the doctor. "It's just that I think there are other people who need therapy more than I do."

That seemed to interest him. He leaned forward. "Such as?"

She shrugged. This was probably the best shot she would get to open the floor for her topic. "Desirée Langford, for example," she said, trying to sound off-hand. "What were some of her hang-ups?"

He sat back stiffly. "The unfortunate young woman who committed suicide last weekend? What made you think of her?"

"She's been on my mind lately."

He tapped his pen against the papers in his lap. "Do you often think of suicide, Ms. Steele?"

That question had been on the form. She'd written "Only when I hear the theme song to M*A*S*H." She pursed her lips. "Not really. I was just wondering what might have driven Desirée Langford to kill herself."

"But we're not here to talk about her."

"But we could. Why not? You were her therapist, weren't you?"

He cleared his throat. "There is such a thing as patient confidentiality, Ms. Steele."

She raised herself on one elbow and looked him in the eye. "The woman's dead."

He seemed to ponder that a moment, then slowly nodded. "Indeed."

Miranda knew patient confidentiality extended beyond the grave, but if she could make it about herself, maybe she could get this guy to talk. Some shrinks knew how to rationalize ethics. "I was at the Northwinds Steeplechase when it happened." She put an anguished tone in her voice, that was only partly false. "It might help me get over that, and my encounter with my ex if I understood why she took her own life."

Dr. Chaffee picked up another paper from her file, scanned it and frowned. "You're with the Parker Agency, aren't you, Ms. Steele?"

"Yes."

"Are you investigating Ms. Langford's death?"

Caught. This doctor didn't get his diploma by cheating on tests. "Sort of," she admitted.

He sighed. "I'll tell you what I can, only what is already public knowledge. Everyone knows Desirée Langford was a troubled young woman. She looked successful on the outside, but inside, there was a lot of turmoil."

He'd cracked. She should have been honest to start with. Excited, she sat forward. "Desirée had problems with her father, I understand."

With a sorrowful look, he nodded. "Yes. Both she and her sister did."

Like Mr. P had said, and Dr. Kennicot had implied. Nothing confidential about that. "And her relationship with Ferraro Usher? What was that like?"

He shook his head. "Tumultuous."

"They fought a lot?"

"Constantly."

"They used drugs."

He sighed aloud. "Yes. The use of stimulants and other recreational substances didn't help. They both tended toward narcissism. It was definitely what I would call a toxic relationship."

Narcissism. Shrink talk meaning they were both stuck on themselves. Usher had given Miranda that impression. "Was Usher ever violent with Desirée?"

He seemed surprised at the question. "They had loud fights and broke things, but I don't think he ever touched her. In fact, it was more the other way around."

She leaned forward. "Other way around?"

"During one of Ferraro's showings, Desirée publicly apologized for tearing up one of his paintings with a knife. Another time, she scratched his face badly enough he had to go to the emergency room for stitches."

Miranda remembered the half-inch long scar she'd seen along Usher's right cheek. Had Desirée put it there? Did Usher kill her to get back at her for humiliating him? She used to want to kill Leon for the things he did to her.

Dr. Chaffee cleared his throat. "Let's get back to your issues, Ms. Steele. I feel I've said too much about my deceased client."

Okay. She'd gotten some information—all nicely public information that wouldn't get the doctor in trouble. She probably wouldn't get much else, and she'd better give this session a shot, or Parker would have her hide.

"Sure." She leaned back, took a breath. "Go ahead."

"What was your childhood like?"

"My childhood?" She suppressed a groan. How many times did she have to tell a shrink about her childhood? But she'd do it once more or Parker might take her off the case. "Not good," she said. "My father left when I was little. I think I was about five."

She told him what she could remember of her father, a jovial man with red cheeks and nose, who always bounced his on her knee and made her giggle. A man who promised her a dollhouse for Christmas, but who, when Christmastime rolled around, had been gone. Later, she'd realized his red coloring was probably from drinking too much.

She described her mother, a cold, heartless woman who worked as a cleanup lady at a hospital in the Chicago suburb where Miranda had grown up.

By the time she got to her abusive relationship with Leon, she'd decided Dr. Chaffee must be a Freud man. Ask a question and let the patient talk without much comment. She'd always found that approach irritating.

Then she heard a low buzzing sound.

She opened her eyes and turned her head. Dr. Chaffee's eyes were shut, his chin nestled against his chest. He was sound asleep.

Without a sound, she got up, reached for her bag and headed for the door. She had a class to make up at the office. Then she turned back.

She tiptoed over to Dr. Chaffee's big desk, picked up the silver bell and gave it a hard shake. The shrill tinkling broke into the doctor's snores and had him raising his head in dazed confusion. Before he came back to life, she was out the door.

Shrinks, she thought, heading down the hall, ignoring the receptionist's plea to make another appointment. People who go to them ought to have their heads examined.

CHAPTER EIGHTEEN

When Miranda stepped into the Cupid-stenciled dining room that night, she thought someone might be opening a delicatessen in here. "What is all this?"

Parker strolled to the end of the table and examined the spread. "Gourmet cold cuts, European cheeses, freshly baked sourdough and multi-grain rolls."

"Did you order it?"

"I asked the staff to have some lighter fare set out for us this evening." He reached for a sterling silver pot and began pouring some of that wonderful coffee Mr. P got from St. Helena into a heavy mug.

"'Lighter' fare?"

He handed her the mug and held up his hands. She took it from him and sipped. Well, it was lighter than the rich lunch he'd treated her to. But Miranda was eager to get down to work.

Quickly, they slapped a couple sandwiches together, moved the rest to the credenza, and spread out all the information on the Desirée Langford case—the contents of Parker's police file and the notes she'd jotted down at the office after her therapy session.

Reports. Pictures. Interviews.

Munching her ham and cheese on rye, Miranda stood staring at it all, a hand on her hip.

"Here's what we know. Usher and Desirée had a hostile relationship. Maybe a love-hate relationship. They did drugs together. Desirée could be physically violent at times. Kennicot was the real love of her life. She'd been in love with the vet since she was a teen. She married Usher to get back at him. After seven years, she left Usher for Kennicot."

"But Usher was still in love with Desirée," Parker supplied.

"Right. Narcissistic artist that he was, he had to be pissed as a hornet about the way she'd treated him, the way she'd walked out on him. At Christmastime."

She thought about the lonely, brooding artist sitting alone near a decorated tree somewhere, drinking, getting high. And hatching a plan to get back. She pulled at her hair, perched on the edge of her chair again.

Parker swallowed the last sip from his coffee cup and sat back to study the woman pouring over the stacks of papers.

Some might call Miranda Steele merely pretty. To the objective observer, her looks might seem just above average. But to Parker, she was one of the most beautiful women he'd ever known. He loved watching her eyes flash as ideas burst inside her vibrant mind. He loved the passion for her work that was now growing into full bloom. They shared that passion for justice. In their core, they were alike. He felt a stronger connection to Miranda Steele than to anyone he'd ever known.

He loved her. If only he could tell her that without frightening her off. If only he could persuade her to think of a future with him.

He would. Slowly but surely, he would change her mind. And then? He smiled to himself. He couldn't wait to marry her. To watch her come down the aisle to him, adorned in some elaborate designer gown, in a cathedral filled with everyone he knew. But if that were to happen, his timing had to be impeccable. He'd pushed too hard the last time, moved too quickly. He couldn't risk doing that again.

"So what do you think?" he asked gently, eager to hear her analysis.

Miranda looked up, smirked at that penetrating gaze of his. He enjoyed watching the wheels in her head turn, didn't he? "I think Usher did it." She slapped her hand on the table. "I think he had a simmering rage underneath the surface that made him slip the PCP into Desirée's drink at the steeplechase."

"And your reasons?"

"He had motive, a wild temper."

"But…"

"But I can't prove it.

"No, you can't."

"Did Dr. Chaffee tell you about Usher's temper?" He set his plate aside and rose to move toward her.

"Yes. He said they had a 'toxic relationship.' Usher and Desirée fought loud and often. But it was Desirée who attacked Usher. She tore up one of his paintings once. And she scratched his face up bad."

"And so you're thinking…"

She nodded. "Revenge."

He gazed down at the papers and stroked his chin. "That's one way to look at it."

That took the wind out of her sails. "Do you see another?"

"There is still the possibility it could have actually been suicide, as the police concluded." He picked up one of the reports, studied it a moment and put it back down. "Or there might be another scenario we haven't found evidence for yet."

She pursed her lips. Patient Parker. For once, she was glad she had him to hold her in check. If this had been a month ago, she might have looked Usher up, hauled off and slugged him. Not anymore. It was good to have solid proof before you did something like that.

He regarded her for a long moment, then stepped behind her, began to rub her shoulders.

Oh, that felt good.

"And what did Dr. Chaffee do for you?"

She hung her head in exasperation. "Not much, Parker. I told you. I'm not good with shrinks." She ran a hand through her hair. It was tangled, as usual. "They don't help much."

Gently he pulled her hair back from her face. "You haven't found the right one yet." Softly, he brushed his lips against her cheek.

His touch made her melt, but it couldn't change her mind.

Parker nuzzled her sweet-tasting neck with his mouth, wanting to ravish her with pleasure. Make her feel things she'd never experienced. Make her feel loved. "Let's try a different bedroom tonight," he murmured against her delicious skin.

She inhaled, surrendering involuntarily to his magic. "What's wrong with the one we've, uh, been using?"

"I'd like a change. Something exotic, I think." His teeth just grazed her jawbone.

"Exotic?" She swallowed as a feathery tingle fluttered down her backbone.

He took the paper she was holding out of her hand and set it on the table. "Why don't we put all this away and have a nice weekend together?"

"Weekend?" It was Friday night. She hadn't thought about what their weekends would be like. Besides, she couldn't let this case go right now. She stared down at the papers on the table. "Shucks, I was going to ask how you felt about working tomorrow."

He stopped kissing her. "On Saturday?"

She turned around, gave him a sweet smile. "My boss pays well. Double time."

He raised a brow. "It seems I've created a workaholic."

She lifted her forefinger. "Another topic for therapy."

"Very well. What do you have in mind?"

"The scene of the crime. Do you think they'd let us onto the Steeplechase grounds?"

He thought a moment. "It's actually a private farm. I'll see what I can arrange." He took her hand and drew her close again, nuzzled her nose, then ran his tongue over her lips. "But tonight, let's think about other things."

Shivers dancing behind her knees, she gave in. "Okay." She let him take her hand and lead her to the staircase. "But only tonight."

CHAPTER NINETEEN

I pace the floor of the room, my temples throbbing with dread.

They're getting closer. What if they discover my secrets?

The fear has kept me up all night. The sun is rising over the horizon. Soon its rays will drench my window with light. Blinding light.

I run my hand over the damask of the chair where Desirée once sat. It's a pretty lavender blue. She loved the color blue. Her hairbrush lies on the dressing table. I pick it up, cradle it in my hands like a baby. We are one now. I am you, Desirée.

But what about Wade Parker? The very name stirs desire for murder in me.

And his associate, Miranda Steele. She's too bold. Too smart. Just a few weeks ago, she saved that little girl from being killed. If only that brute of an ex-husband she had would have killed her.

She'll figure it all out soon. I have to act before she does. I've thought of a plan, but can I execute it? No one will understand why I did it. If only people understood me. If only they would love me.

I lay the brush back down on the dressing table and stare at myself in the mirror. I know what I must do. It won't be easy. The last time wasn't easy, either. Yet, I did it. And I will do it again. I will do what I must. I will.

Sometimes, it's necessary for people to die.

And if I'm careful, if my plan works, Wade Parker and Miranda Steele will be dead before they can stop me.

CHAPTER TWENTY

Amazing, the things you could do with an old Southern mansion—or in one.

The next morning, Miranda awoke much later than she'd wanted to, and found herself propped up on a mound of colorful pillows where she'd fallen asleep, too exhausted to move.

Parker's idea of "exotic" had been a large, high-ceilinged room that looked like it had been a bedchamber in the Taj Mahal. A sensual feast in red and black and teakwood, it was filled with the scent of candles and lotus blossoms. The domed ceiling was hand-painted with suggestive figures along the gold cornice. Decorative tiger skin patterns of red and gold stretched across the walls, were echoed in the red-and-black spread and the piles of gold-tasseled pillows on the huge round bed.

Mr. P and his decorator had quite a naughty imagination. And his son took every advantage of it.

Oh, what Parker could do with those pillows.

The talented man had flooded her body with delicious sensations for hours. At one point during the night, she'd decided he must have studied the Kama Sutra, and would have asked, but had been unable to speak.

She didn't fully recover her vocal capacity until they were heading up I-75 toward Bartow County on their way to the Steeplechase grounds.

Sipping from the portable coffee cup he'd given her, she watched him from the corner of her eye and decided to remain silent a while.

Now awake, in broad daylight, she had a different question on her mind. How in the heck had she allowed herself to succumb to Parker's charms last night—again? Since she'd moved into his ancestral home, she'd spent every darn night with him. She hadn't had this much sex since… She'd never had this much sex. It was getting to be a bad habit.

Well, not all bad, she thought, remembering the luscious shivers he could give her with just his tongue. Her mouth grew moist as she remembered.

Mmm. How did he do that? She shook herself. It wasn't her fault Wade Parker was the sexiest, most desirable man she'd ever met.

Being with Parker was a fun habit. A nice habit. But not a wise habit. Or a smart one.

What she and Parker had together certainly wasn't anything like the occasional meaningless one-night stand she used to indulge in with an acquaintance from a job site or a drinking buddy.

What she and Parker had wasn't just sex. It was a warm closeness. A tender bond. A real intimacy. And feelings. Intense, mind-blowing feelings. The kind of feelings that came with…commitment.

Long-term commitment.

She guessed she was more old-fashioned than she realized. But she knew that closeness, that bond, that intimacy, those feelings—all those warm fuzzies could only lead to the one thing she could never let happen.

Sooner or later, as difficult as it would be, she was going to have to bite the bullet and break it off with Parker.

Just how or when, she had no idea.

The warm sun and fresh smell of grassy fields felt like a summer picnic spot when they reached the expansive farm where the Northwinds Steeplechase had been held. Gone were the crowds, the tents, the trainers with their horses. Except for a few riders practicing jumps along the track and a couple of people watching them, all that remained was the rolling landscape that seemed to stretch out forever. It was like being in another world. A nearly deserted one.

Was there really something here that would pin Desirée Langford's murder on Usher? If so, Miranda was determined to find it.

Parker pulled up onto the grassy slope that had served as a parking lot for the Steeplechase and stared out through the windshield. "Here we are," he said without fanfare.

He'd been unusually quiet during the trip and Miranda wondered whether her private thoughts about last night had been giving off unwelcome vibes. She dismissed the idea. They had work to do.

"Guess we don't need a special escort to get onto the grounds after all."

"The owner told me we're free to go where we want." Parker had called before they left.

She grabbed the papers she'd brought along and reached for her door handle. "Let's go."

"I'll get that." Parker turned the car off and walked around to help her out of the car. Being a gentleman was an automatic reflex for him. Like too many things about Parker, she was beginning to get used to it. And to like it.

He retrieved his silver investigator's kit from the backseat, and they headed down to the barn.

Miranda was glad she'd left her dress and high heels at home this time. Today it was tennis shoes, jeans, and a T-shirt. She'd stuffed her unruly hair under a ball cap.

Parker was in charcoal dress slacks and a light gray shirt that attractively set off his coloring, but no tie or coat. She guessed that was dressing down for him.

The warm, early summer air became a breeze as they approached the stables and the earthy smell of horses greeted them. Miranda had learned that bright, sunny days were the norm in Atlanta. This one was no exception.

As they neared the shelters, she stopped to look around.

"Where shall we begin?" Parker asked her, as if he had no opinion on the matter.

He was letting her take the lead again. Another thing she was beginning to like. It made her feel smart, competent. Taking charge of a case felt natural. Like something she was born to do.

She opened her folder and studied an interview with one of the Aquitaine Farms' trainers.

"The morning of the Steeplechase," she read aloud, "Desirée Langford and the party from Aquitaine Farms arrived at the grounds about ten o'clock for set up. Ms. Langford seemed in good spirits, laughing and joking with her crew. Dr. Kennicot arrived about half an hour later." She lowered the folder. "This witness saw Desirée and the vet holding hands, talking together, currying the horses."

Parker nodded as he scanned the now empty stables.

Miranda turned the page and summarized. "Calypso was scheduled for the first race. The crew got him and their other entries settled into their stalls. Then about an hour before the race, Desirée and Kennicot went to have something to eat at one of the stations."

She pulled out the sketch of the area. Following it, she walked to the opposite end of the barn, then paced off about fifty yards. Parker followed her, watching closely.

"This is about where the make-shift restaurant was set up," she said, gesturing vaguely when she reached the area. She studied the ground. There was nothing here now but grass. "Guess the cleanup crew did a good job."

"There might still be something to be found." Parker began to move over the ground, looking down as if examining each blade of grass individually.

Miranda consulted her folder again. She took a step, turned around, and planted herself on a spot facing the barns. "If this is where Desirée and Kennicot sat, then the empty PCP vial was found right about there." She pointed down.

Parker moved to the spot, bent down and peered at the grass. Then he ran his hand over it. "Nothing."

As if it had never been there. Maybe she wasn't in the exact place. It was only an approximation. She pulled another report out of the folder. "This interview of the waiter is the most detailed." She read from it. "Kennicot was drinking Bacardi, Desirée a daiquiri. After a while, Delta showed up. The waiter overheard the two women arguing. Desirée told Delta she was late. And that it was the last time she'd wear a stupid look-alike outfit to the Steeplechase."

"I recall the two sisters dressing alike every year."

Miranda thought a moment. "Delta told me it was their tradition. That confirms it. Guess Desirée didn't like the ritual. But her remark doesn't sound like she intended this to be her last steeplechase."

"Perhaps she hadn't made the final decision yet."

Miranda frowned. "To kill herself? What about the suicide note? She had to have written it already. If she was the one who wrote it."

"True." He sighed, deep in thought. "Suicide can be a cry for help or an expression of despair. Desirée might have been toying with the idea."

"On the bubble?"

He nodded. "Unsure until something set her off."

"Something that pushed her over the edge."

"It might have gone like that."

Miranda shook her head. Parker was a paragon of *Objectivity*, playing devil's advocate, but she didn't buy it. There had to be a clue that pointed clearly to Usher. She was determined to find it.

She went back to the pages in her hand. "The sisters had a few more sharp words, then Delta moved away and sat at another table by herself. After about fifteen minutes, Usher showed up and joined Kennicot and Desirée. Kennicot told him to leave. Usher said no. The two men shouted at each other, then Desirée asked Kennicot to give them a moment. He got up in a huff. Calling Usher a leech, he went back to the stables."

"The same term he used for him the other day," Parker observed.

Good point. "Because Desirée supported his art career." She turned a page. "After Kennicot left, the waiter says Usher and Desirée 'got cozy.' They drew their chairs close together, even started kissing." Miranda blew a breath out her nose. "She sounds like a two-timer to me."

Parker smirked half to himself. "The Langford sisters aren't known for their scruples."

She stared at him. Instead of something about Desirée, had she dug up a clue about Parker's "unpleasant history" with Delta? She wanted to know. "Did you have a personal relationship with Delta Langford?"

Shock was rare on Parker's face, but she saw it now, heard it in his smirk. "Hardly."

"And why do you hate the woman so much?"

The wind teasing the sleeves of his dress shirt, his frame took on the craggy, Gibraltar look. He wasn't going to give her an answer. "Are you finished with your investigation?"

"Hardly," she echoed. Okay, she wouldn't press him now. She'd store that one away for later.

She looked down at her papers again. "Desirée and Usher ordered more drinks. Desirée switched to gin and tonic. Usher had the same. Several rounds later, they asked the waiter for a straw. After he delivered it, the waiter saw Usher pull out a mirror."

"Insufflation," Parker said grimly.

Miranda nodded. "They were snorting cocaine, though the waiter pretends he didn't know what they were doing. Did he think Desirée needed the mirror because she had something in her eye? Another witness concurs that Usher and Desirée were doing lines, but others denied it. There wasn't enough corroboration to slap Usher with a drug charge."

She paused to take in the sprawling green fields, inhale the fresh, healthy air. Everything seemed so serene and peaceful up here. Heck of a place to snort coke. She smirked. "Hey, do you think we'll run into any dealers on this farm? Maybe a gang member or two?"

"Highly unlikely."

She turned another page. "After they'd 'messed' with the mirror a while, Delta came over again. The waiter said she argued with Desirée some more. A second waiter says Delta was trying to apologize."

"Eyewitnesses can be inaccurate."

"Sure, but if Desirée turned away from the table to talk to Delta," Miranda twisted her body to simulate, "it was the perfect time for Usher to slip the PCP into her drink."

Parker studied her pose. "Possible."

"Very possible."

"No witness saw the vial."

"True, but the police found it. And it had traces of angel dust." She turned back and read again. "Delta seemed very upset. She turned away from Desirée, ran toward the barn, and disappeared into the crowd." Miranda stared off in that direction. "So the last time Delta spoke to her sister, they'd had a fight." She felt sorry for the woman.

Parker didn't comment.

She continued. "Desirée and Usher stayed at their table and ordered more drinks, but Desirée was in a foul mood. Their conversation became heated and emotional. By now, they were both pretty sloshed."

"And stoned."

"It was time to get ready for the first race, but Desirée was in tears. The waiter heard her say something like, 'All you ever think about is your career.' At that point, Desirée got to her feet, called Usher a 'rotten son of a bitch,' downed her drink, and took off for the stables to check on Calypso."

"That was the drink laced with PCP," Parker said solemnly.

"Had to be. So what was the trigger that made her decide to commit suicide by pouring PCP into it? Her fight with Usher?"

"It's a possibility."

"Bullshit." Miranda started to walk toward the barns, as if she were Desirée on that day. "Desirée got lost in the crowd, like Delta did. Nobody saw her go into Calypso's stall. Nobody noticed Usher again until just after the incident. I was the first one to see him."

Parker gestured where he stood. "He might have stayed at the table until the commotion started."

"Or," she called over her shoulder, "he might have followed her when she left the table."

Parker joined her at the edge of the barn. Miranda strode over to the stall that had belonged to Calypso that day. She peered inside. The backboards had been repaired, and it looked new and clean, as if nothing gruesome and bizarre had ever happened here.

She looked at the dirt path in front of the building and pointed toward the right. "I was over there at the other end of the barn when Calypso had his hissy fit. Two men dragged the horse out of this stall. He was bucking and neighing furiously. A crowd started to gather. I ran over this way." She moved toward the middle of the barn. "A woman screamed, a man said Desirée was in the stall."

"That's when you entered it."

"Yes. I saw the body and tried to help, but she was already gone." She shuddered at the memory.

"And Usher came up behind you."

She nodded.

"Plenty of time to get there from the restaurant table."

She looked over at the spot. "Doesn't prove he came from there."

"Or that he didn't."

She grimaced. "Yeah, you're right. Usher could have sat there, smugly watching her. After he gave her that PCP, it was only a matter of time before she dropped dead."

"Then he couldn't have planted the suicide note."

She shifted her weight, uncomfortable with Parker's implication. "He might have given it to her earlier. And told her not to open it."

"He might have."

The devil's advocate was starting to bend. "Okay, so then a security guard came and threw Usher and me out of the stall. I moved over here." She stepped that way. "The crowd had swelled by that time. Usher pushed his way through the onlookers and took off that way." She pointed. "Back toward the restaurant tables." She wondered where he'd been going.

"Anyway, about here was where Delta stopped me and asked for help." She stopped on the spot and exhaled in frustration. "None of this is anything we didn't know already."

Parker stroked his chin. "True." The sun was getting higher in the sky and growing hotter. She saw sweat bead up on his forehead.

"Who commits suicide in a big crowd? Doing something you love?" She started to walk along the barn, trying to imagine the throng that had been there that day. Parker stayed behind to re-examine Calypso's stall.

She looked at the adjoining stalls where the other horses had been kept. Hay covered the floor. In front of the stalls, the red clay path was hardened from foot traffic. No shoe prints.

She reached the corner where the grass started up again. There, a row of bushes had been planted along the barn's side. Some decorator sprucing the place up, or trying to keep kids away. She stared into the bright green leaves.

Her breath caught. Something in there wasn't green. It wasn't a leaf. She bent down, peered into the bush. It looked like a flap of leather. Tan, mahogany colored.

She stared deeper into the thicket without touching the bush. A long, thin shape, like a stick with a knobby end, was wedged in there. She tilted her head and made out the fancy gold letters embossed on the tip. "FJU." The police report said that Usher's middle name was James. Good thing, or his initials would be "FU." But no. They were "FJU."

"Parker!" she shouted, her heart racing. "I think I've got something."

He trotted over to her. "What is it?"

She pointed toward the bush. "Look."

He bent down, squinted into the hedge. Then he smiled. "A riding crop."

Exactly what someone might have used to make Calypso go crazy after a buzzed Desirée had gone into the stall. "Look at the end of it."

His gray eyes twinkled in the sunlight. "Excellent work." Quickly, he set down his silver investigator's kit and opened it. "Don't touch it."

She rolled her eyes. "I know. I've passed Fingerprinting 101, you know."

"Indeed, you have. With flying colors." He took out a digital camera from his case. "Would you like to do the honors?"

"Sure." She took the camera from him, adjusted it, and took shots from several angles.

She handed the camera back to Parker and he exchanged it for a pair of rubber gloves. He already had his on.

Miranda donned the gloves and slowly, carefully, pulled back the leaves of the bush, eased the whip out of its hiding place. It was about two and a half feet long, made of top-quality leather.

"Got it." She beamed as she slid the crop into the long plastic bag Parker held open for her.

The look of pride on his face made her swell. Had she nailed Usher? It sure looked like it to her.

"We'll take this back to the house and print it," he said.

She grinned victoriously. "What are we waiting for?"

CHAPTER TWENTY-ONE

Parker's silver-gray Mazda shot through Kennesaw and down I-75 with the speed of a James Bond Aston Martin. Halfway back to Buckhead, he reached for his cell and ordered a pizza to go from Mellow Mushroom. No time for fancy restaurants this afternoon. They picked up their order, raced through traffic, nearly ran a few red lights along the way.

It was almost four o'clock when Parker pulled into the mansion's fancy garage. Miranda grabbed the pizza, and they hurried inside through the door that led to the kitchen. She laid the box on the stove, as Parker came up behind her and set his silver investigator's case down on the large stonework island in the middle of the room.

He gestured toward it. "Be my guest."

"You really are taking this lead thing seriously, aren't you?"

"You're doing so well, why stop now?"

She couldn't have been more thrilled. "Hand me a pair of gloves."

He obliged and with an eager grin, she pulled them on and gingerly eased the riding crop out of its plastic bag, being careful not to touch the handle.

Peering into Parker's case, she selected a fine, light gray powder and gave the whip handle a dusting. She blew on the surface and a nice specimen appeared. Cool.

Parker held the crop steady while she took the tape and lifted a fairly clear thumbprint from the handle. A pretty good forefinger print was just an inch away. That was all that were legible, but she could tell by sight that the ridge formations were similar.

She retrieved a black backing card from the case, filled in the information section with date, time and a short description, and carefully laid the tape across it. She looked up at Parker. He was wearing that look of pride that was becoming so familiar. The thrill of that look went right down to her toes.

"Now what?" she asked. "We don't have a place to process the prints."

He picked up the backing card that held her handiwork. "Now we run it through the database."

"Database? Here?"

Grinning slyly, he strode over to the fridge and reached for couple of beers with his free hand, nodded toward the door to the hall. "Follow me."

Miranda grabbed the pizza and tagged along as he went across the downstairs hall, up the carved mahogany staircase, down the upstairs hall, and into a large, open room.

She felt like whistling when she stepped inside.

The space was done up like an office. A very fancy office. Mostly in black and white, with classy silver accents, it was windowless, but it had track lighting along the ceiling, along with a few floor and table lamps with bases of pewter-colored, scrolling leaves. Against the walls were black lacquered credenzas and shelves showcasing books and magazines and decorative knick-knacks. On one shelf there was a silver desk clock, the kind with roman numerals and all the inner gears showing. Nearer the door sat a coffee table and a big white suede couch—a cozy little spot to lounge.

But the real eye-catcher was the three black lacquered desks, each with a huge, flat-screen computer monitor sitting on it, screensavers dancing merrily away.

This didn't look like Mr. P's taste. It was all very sleek, very sexy, very typically Parker.

Parker set the beer bottles down on leather coasters on the black lacquered coffee table. "I took the liberty of having some of my personal equipment brought over the other day. I hope you don't mind."

"Mind?" Miranda smirked.

"Since this is your house." He gestured toward one of the white suede swivel chairs at the desk nearest him.

"Oh, right. What self-respecting bodyguard doesn't need a few state-of-the-art computers lying around?" She set the pizza box next to the beers on the coffee table and sank down into the cushy-soft seat. She hadn't thought about what he'd done with the stuff in his penthouse. Guess he was making himself at home. That was good.

His eyes twinkled. "I'm glad you see it that way."

She looked at the backing card in his hand. "So what do we do with those prints?"

"We process them." Parker stepped over to a scanning machine on the credenza and ran the card through it. Then he sat down at the middle desk, punched a keyboard, and the fingerprints appeared on all three screens. He pressed a few more buttons. A nanosecond later, data began to flash and flicker.

He turned back to her. "It will take a while to find a match, if there is one in the database."

"Okay by me. A drug user's prints have got to be in there. Hey, this pizza's getting cold and I'm starving." She opened the box and grabbed a piece. She'd wanted jerk chicken, but had settled for the house special with everything on it when Parker had grimaced. She took a bite and moaned with pleasure. Right now, it tasted like filet mignon. She hadn't eaten since they'd left the house this morning.

Parker reached for a beer bottle, opened it and handed it to her. He shot her a wry smile. "Have I mentioned that you're turning into an excellent investigator, Miranda? I believe you were born for this work."

His compliment made her feel a little giddy, but she pretended to ignore it. "You forgot the glass," she teased.

"Do you want one?"

"Nope." She took the bottle and downed a swallow.

Parker opened the second beer and did the same.

She smirked. "I never thought I'd see you swig beer from a bottle."

"It's a difficult skill, but I believe I've mastered it."

She cocked her head at him. "So you're not a hundred percent highbrow, after all."

He gave her a look of mock incredulity. "What gave you the impression that I was highbrow?"

She laughed and took another pull. The cold liquid tasted wonderful, especially after the hours of tromping around under the hot Georgia sun. It was thick and dark, with just enough bite. She looked at the bottle. "What is this stuff?"

Parker reached for a slice of pizza. "Stone Imperial Russian Stout," he answered as she read the label.

"Sounds expensive."

"Moderately. About nine dollars a bottle."

Not a *hundred* percent highbrow? Drinking pricey beer from the bottle only counted for maybe five percent. The other ninety-five percent of Wade Parker was all class and sophistication. All polish and elegant, irresistible style. Though he was never haughty or uppity. Amazingly, he'd never made her feel less than an equal, except for the few times he'd pulled rank. But that was in his professional capacity, so she forgave him for it. Sort of.

She wiped her mouth. "It's good. A lot better than the brands I drink."

"Are your tastes changing, Miranda?" he asked in a low, provocative voice.

He probably wasn't talking about just beer.

She shrugged, took another bite of pizza and studied the screen intently. "It's way cool to have a crime lab in your own home." Except that it really wasn't her home.

She looked up. Parker was staring at her. "What?"

His smile was evasive. "You have the most fascinating line between your eyes when you concentrate."

A strange sensation, as sharp as the sting of the rich, heavy beer, flowed through her. She got up and moved over to the couch, reaching for another slice of pizza. "Detective Judd only taught us how to do manual methods of print analysis."

"Manual methods are usually too slow. This is print recognition software that accesses a national service the Agency subscribes to."

"AFIS. Automated Fingerprint Identification Service." She hadn't used it at work, but she knew about it from TV.

"Exactly. If Usher has a record, it will find a match. If those are indeed his prints."

"Still playing the skeptic, huh? Usher's a user. He's got a record of some kind."

"It's what I'm counting on."

Miranda sat back against the sofa's soft suede, took another swig of the delicious beer and watched the screens flicker. It was utterly cool to be with Parker. But all this was his stuff. Just like this was really Parker's house. Maybe it was time to come clean about that.

She ran her finger around the lip of her bottle. "Uh, you know what you said about bringing all this over?" she gestured vaguely at the furniture.

"What did I say?" He moved from the computer and sat down close beside her. He fixed her with that steady gray gaze of his.

She drew in air. It was always harder to breathe when Parker got this close. "Well, you said it was my house. How do you feel about that?"

He leaned closer, peered at her more deeply, more sensually. "You have a bit of tomato sauce at the corner of your mouth."

Before she could do anything about it, he bent forward and licked it off with his tongue. Her breath caught. All at once she was overcome by the erotic gesture.

His lips covered hers and the fire ignited. She reached over and managed to put her beer down on the coffee table without spilling it. Then as if they had a mind of their own, her arms slipped around Parker's neck and the two of them went prone on the couch.

As he began to tug at her T-shirt, he lifted his head, and the brief release cleared her mind enough to remember what she'd been trying to say to him. "Uh, Parker."

"Yes," he murmured, working his mouth over her hair. "I love the smell of your hair. Fresh, outdoorsy."

"I need to make a confession."

"Do you?" She felt him smile at her ear as his mouth moved over its folds.

She was growing dizzy and mindless again. Better spit it out while she could still speak. "I didn't mean it when I told your father I wanted this house."

"You didn't?" His voice rang with feigned surprise. Stubbornly, his lips moved softly over her temple, across her hairline.

She frowned. "No, I didn't. It was sort of a ploy."

"A ploy?" His breath grew heavy as his hands slipped under her T-shirt.

"Yeah," she swallowed, fighting to get coherent words out. "A maneuver to get you back in here."

"I'm shocked." His lips tickled her cheek, then moved to her neck.

"You knew. I thought you did."

His mouth went to her shoulder, sending little thrills over her. "I never would have thought you'd stoop so low."

"Hey, buster," she said in a hoarse whisper. "I did it for you."

"For me?"

"I couldn't see you lose your family mansion, your inheritance, just because of some testosterone-driven pride between you and your father."

He chuckled as one of his hands finally reached her breast. Slowly he ran his fingertips over her. "I'm glad you did it."

She groaned with the intense pleasure of his touch. Parker was like a rich piece of chocolate she couldn't resist. She tried to say no. She knew it would ruin her diet, but he was just too darn tempting.

"Glad?" she gurgled.

He raised his head and gazed into her eyes. "It means you care. Genuinely."

"So the bodyguard thing—"

He laughed darkly. "—was my ploy."

But she'd never really fallen for it. "Pretty transparent for an ace gumshoe."

"It worked, didn't it?" He lifted her shirt all the way, lowered himself to her breasts and did things with his tongue that made her mind whirl entirely out of control. Gently, he drew down the zipper on her jeans, reached between her legs and touched her soft spot.

She groaned even more helplessly this time. Yep, the ploy worked. It got him what he wanted. It wasn't fair. He wasn't letting her think straight. But he'd said she cared, and she guessed he was right. She did care about him. If only she could let herself admit it. But she couldn't think any more. Couldn't talk. Parker was flooding her with sensations too delicious for words. Her eyes fluttered as release rippled through her. Hard, long, as if it would never end. But then it did end, and as the sensation diminished and she drew in a breath, she heard a strange sound. A beeping.

She turned her head and opened her eyes. The computer monitor was flashing.

With a kiss on her cheek, Parker withdrew himself and rose. "We have a hit."

"Simultaneous." Weakly she pulled up her drawers and got to her feet.

Parker sat down at the desk and peered at the screen. "Usher was arrested in DeKalb County six years ago for possession of marijuana."

She sat down in a chair next to him. "Is that all? He's used since then. He's done coke. He's got to have connections with dealers."

"He's probably become more careful over the years."

"So those are his fingerprints on the riding crop."

"They are."

"And they're the only ones on it."

"Correct."

She sat staring at the data on the screen. For her money, this riding crop proved Usher was the one who had gotten Calypso so riled. After he'd plied his ex-wife with drinks, given her a line of coke and a fatal dose of PCP, he couldn't resist finishing her off with a vicious attack.

"So Usher stood there while Desirée was in the stall and whipped Calypso into a frenzy with that crop. That he used her favorite horse to do it only underscores his feelings toward her relationship with Kennicot. And probably toward her career, as well."

"Objectivity, Miranda." Parker murmured in that low voice. "This evidence is still circumstantial. It doesn't prove the scenario you just described."

She reached for Desirée's case file, furiously thumbed through the papers. "The trainers didn't mention any whip marks on Calypso. No one thought to ask about it, either." With a grunt, she got up and started to pace. She ran her hands through her hair. It was a mess. "What do we do now? We've talked to Kennicot, studied the crap out of this police file, we've even been to the crime scene." She strode back to the computer screen, trying to will more information from it. "If only there had been prints on that PCP vial. Or marks on Calypso. If only we knew who Usher's supplier was." She started to pace again, then stopped. "Where did Usher get the money to buy that much PCP?"

"Desirée was still supporting him."

"So he used her own money to kill her? That sick bastard."

Parker had a faraway look in his eyes. "A confession from the artist would be our best bet at this point."

She snorted. "And how in snot are we going to get that?"

Parker rose and went to the desk at the right. He opened a drawer, pulled something out of it, and handed it to her.

Miranda looked down and saw two rectangular cards with an orangey-red design and fancy lettering. "The Brentwood Gallery presents Ferraro Usher's 'A Moment in Time,' in memory of the late Desirée Langford. Ten o'clock." She looked up at Parker. "Tickets?"

He smiled his most sophisticated grin. "Are you feeling up to an art show tonight?"

"An art show? Tonight?" Parker truly was something else. She moved her head up and down in an exaggerated gesture. "Hot dog."

CHAPTER TWENTY-TWO

They had to go dress shopping again. According to Parker, nothing in Miranda's closet was suitable for a snooty art show, so they went to Phipps Plaza. Miranda despised looking for clothes, but Parker seemed to like picking out things for her. His choices were so numerous, so ultra-glamorous, so not-her, that after an hour, she was ready to spit and cuss.

Amused by her response, Parker finally selected a short black chiffon cocktail gown with a scoop neck and plunging back.

"Now that's nice," she sighed, despite her irritation.

"Very tasteful, isn't it?"

"Yep, that's the one. So are we done?"

Parker gave her that self-satisfied look. "What about shoes?"

"Oh, brother." It sure was rough going to the mall with a sophisticated man.

Studying herself in the full-length mirror in the master bedroom after they got back home, Miranda thought she'd made the right choice—of the five new outfits in assorted colors that Parker had bought her. She liked the effect of this little black dress, even if she did have to wear the three-inch Zanotti pumps with it. That was, except for the scars that marred the area just over her cleavage.

She grunted as she applied another layer of makeup over the healing wounds. "All the vitamin E and cocoa butter in the world won't erase these."

Parker came up behind her and kissed her neck. "Detective Judd says scars are a mark of honor."

She hissed through her teeth, despite the shivers his mouth was sending over her skin. "Detective Judd doesn't have to wear a low-cut gown to Usher's showing tonight." Though she guessed Judd had his share of scars and wounds. And she knew Parker did, too. She'd seen them, touched them when they made love. One on the lower side of his abdomen, one along his right shoulder blade. She hadn't asked who'd put them there.

Chuckling, Parker studied her in the mirror a moment. "Perhaps these will help cover them." He reached out and draped something around her neck.

Miranda swallowed hard. Pearls? No one had ever given her pearls.

One pink strand, the other a greenish-blue that set off the color of her eyes. Gorgeous. Stunned, she lifted a hand to touch them. "What are these? And don't say 'pearls.' I can see that."

His lithe fingers fastened the clasp. "*Tahitian* pearls. They belonged to my mother."

"Your mother?" Miranda whispered. She didn't know the details, but Parker's mother had died some time ago. This necklace must be very special to him. Embarrassment prickled her skin. She certainly couldn't keep them. "So they're, uh, a loaner for tonight. Right?"

She watched a flash of pain ripple across his face, then he stiffened. "Of course. A loaner for tonight." He removed his hands and stepped away from her. "Although since I attend a lot of fundraisers, this may not be the last time you'll use them."

It was an awkward moment. She expected him to get angry, but he didn't. He rarely got angry with her, unless she provoked it. All she'd ever gotten from Parker was understanding and compassion. She knew he cared about her deeply.

It wasn't fair for him. She couldn't return his feelings. She couldn't feel that deeply for another person after what Leon had put her through. She wasn't capable of it. The heady emotions Parker aroused in her were only a temporary thrill. Like a teenager's crush on a rock star. Not real. Not lasting.

She didn't want commitment. She didn't want a man in her life. And yet, here she was, living with Parker in his mansion. Go figure.

She glanced at the clock. "We'd better get going."

He nodded and silently escorted her down to the car.

The Brentwood Gallery was ablaze with streetlamps and floodlights when Parker pulled up in his hot, midnight blue Lamborghini and handed his keys to a valet. The place itself seemed modest. A three-story, modern-looking building on a residential side street off Peachtree Road.

But evidently, the staff knew how to put on the ritz, Miranda mused, as a second valet opened her door, and she stepped out and took the arm Parker offered to her.

A thrill knotted in her stomach as they climbed the rough stone steps to the entrance and stepped inside. She had to admit she was excited to be at this fancy shindig. Not for the contemporary art, but because they just might nail this self-serving artist tonight.

Inside she found a maze of white walls, with well-lit paintings hung every five feet or so. Soft guitar music played in the background. The air smelled of fancy appetizers and the expensive perfume of the patrons. In the many corners, odd sculptures stood on display. Most shiny, amorphous shapes in bright colors, that made Miranda think art was more about connections than talent.

There was a moderately sized crowd of people strolling about, studying the paintings. Nobody she recognized, though Parker greeted a few of them briefly. College-aged kids dressed in black silk oriental-style uniforms with red trim, moved through the rooms carrying drinks and hors d'oeuvres on silver trays.

"I don't see Usher anywhere," she muttered to Parker under her breath when they were on the third row of paintings.

He stopped strolling and rubbed his chin. With his salt-and-pepper hair, his blue silk tie and black suit, which she'd learned tonight was Ralph Lauren, he looked exquisitely classy. "Let's split up," he said. "We'll meet back at that statue in half an hour."

"Good idea." She took a casual glance at her watch, then pointed toward a corner. "The bright blue blob that looks like a large jellybean?"

He smiled. "That's the one."

"Gotcha." She headed toward the right, while Parker moved back in the direction they came from.

Fingering the pearls at her neck, she perused the abstracts as she moved along, trying to get some insight into Usher's mind. His paintings were weird and wild, his canvases filled with violent swirls of bold reds, golds, blues. Everything in an agitated, fitful style. Horses and women seemed to be favorite themes, all in the same fierce colors.

She turned a corner and heard a man speaking Spanish. For a minute she thought it might be Antonio Estavez, Parker's surrogate son, but then she realized the voice wasn't as refined. She stood still, watching a man with sharp eyes, black locks, shiny with styling gel, piled atop his head, and dark facial hair that circled his mouth and gave his chin a sharp, menacing look. Like the devil.

He wore black slacks and a blazer. His shirt, also black, was opened at the neck and he wore several heavy-looking gold chains around his neck. He was speaking quietly to two other Hispanic men.

One thin and garish looking in a gold paisley shirt, the other, dressed in dark clothes, with a protruding lip and a thick, heavy body, who sported a black wool cap.

They didn't look like art connoisseurs. They looked like…gang members. What were they doing in an art gallery?

The guy with the goatee seemed to be the leader. Was he…Usher's drug dealer? They seemed intent on some business that had little to do with art. Maybe they'd come to make an exchange. Maybe they'd come to collect. The leader pulled his coat back a bit and she thought she saw the hilt of a gun. A shiver snaked down her spine.

Luckily, they didn't see her. After a moment, the leader nodded, and the group moved toward the door. If they were here on shady business, she'd missed it.

She wanted to follow them out, but then she'd never find Usher. Where was the brooding artist?

Frustrated, she turned and headed into the next aisle. She took a few steps and stopped.

At the end of the wall was a large painting, maybe ten feet tall. It was all fiery oranges and blazing reds, like flames so searing she could almost feel their heat. She moved closer to scrutinize the face. It was horrific. A woman encased in a fiery gown. Those eyes. That expression, halfway between lust and hate, seemed almost…vicious.

But that face, those eyes were unmistakable. Desirée Langford.

"I didn't take you as the type to be interested in art, Ms. Steele."

She spun around, suppressed a squeal as she caught sight of Usher standing behind her, perfectly dressed, smug and full of himself. Not at all in mourning now.

Her target for the evening was wearing a conservative-looking dark blue suit. His bleached-blonde, shoulder-length hair was neatly combed. Tonight, his chin sported no stubble.

He held a champagne flute in his long, thin fingers. Toying with it, he stared at her with those large, seaweed-colored eyes that had been so full of shock and pain the day Desirée died.

She commanded herself to relax and smiled. "I'm interested in all kinds of things, Mr. Usher. I heard you were having a showing and I thought I'd check out your work."

He nodded haughtily, as if she'd just given him a huge compliment.

From the corner of her eye, she spotted Parker in the next row, pretending to examine a sculpture that resembled a large, green-spotted molar. He'd been tailing Usher. She was dying to know if he'd seen the artist with the three men who looked like gang members.

In her hand, she had a brochure that she'd picked up on the way in. It gave her an idea. "In fact, I wonder if I could get your autograph."

He tilted his head and eyed her carefully, as if debating whether he could trust her, but his ego won out. "Of course." He took a pen from his shirt pocket, reached for the brochure and stepped to a small table set against a nearby wall. He scrawled something on it and handed it back to her.

Miranda eyed the brochure. *To Ms. Steele. May your days be filled with loveliness. Ferraro Usher.* Perfect. "Thanks."

He looked up at the painting she'd been gazing at. "Were you admiring my *Medea*, Ms. Steele?"

"Your *Medea*?"

Casually, Parker came up between them. "Medea of Greek mythology?" he asked. "I couldn't help overhearing."

Usher looked unnerved, he gave Miranda a suspicious glance, and looked back at Parker. "Good evening, Mr. Parker. That makes two people I never expected to see at my exhibition tonight."

Parker gave him an easy smile, as if he thought that was a compliment. "You were saying? About your painting?"

"She was my inspiration, the Medea of the Greek legends. Wife of Jason."

Miranda vaguely remembered the story from high school English or maybe it was an old movie. "Jason? The dude who went after the Golden Fleece?"

"That's right," Usher nodded. "But he never could have captured it without the help of Medea."

"She was a witch." Parker eyed the painting.

"Ah, I can see my new patrons are very astute." With his champagne flute, Usher gestured toward the work with hunger in his eyes. His voice took on a dreamlike tone. "She had mystical, magical powers and when the god Eros caused her to fall hopelessly in love with Jason, she used those powers to help him get what he wanted."

Like Desirée had helped Usher get what he wanted.

"But Jason betrayed Medea," Parker said dryly.

The story was coming back to her. "He married somebody else, didn't he?"

Usher stared at the painting, as if he were in a self-induced trance. "He abandoned his true love for a political marriage."

Like Desirée had abandoned Usher for Kennicot.

"He was heartless," Usher said. "Medea threw herself at Jason's feet, begging him to come back to her. But he refused."

Like Desirée had refused to go back to Usher when he begged her to. "The cold-hearted bastard."

"As the story goes, Medea went mad. In the end, her only choice was revenge."

"Revenge?" That searing red blaze certainly looked like payback.

Usher's chest was nearly heaving. "Medea sent Jason's fiancée a lovely gown as a wedding gift. But the garment had a spell on it. When the bride put the dress on, it burst into flames and consumed her, burning her to death."

Miranda looked up at the painting. A case of life imitating art? Gave new meaning to the phrase *old flame*. "In your picture, it looks like Medea is the one wearing the fiery dress."

Usher gave a short, self-satisfied smirk. "It's my little twist on the story."

Uh huh. "Is that how you saw your late wife, Usher?"

Usher bristled. "What do you mean?"

He had been furious with Desirée for leaving him. The passions running rampant in that painting looked like enough to kill her. She tilted her head and put a finger to her chin. "The face is very recognizable. That's a good likeness of her. After all, this exhibition is in her memory, isn't it?"

Usher turned slowly and glared at Miranda with a strange look. "Desirée's face had interesting features. I used her likeness in many of my works. She always encouraged me to interpret things in my own way. Artistic freedom, you know."

"Oh really?" And he had destroyed that interesting face at the Steeplechase so Kennicot couldn't have it. "Does that freedom include snorting coke and taking angel dust?"

Usher made a slow hissing sound like a teapot. He looked as if he were about to bite her. "I don't have to listen to this."

Parker stepped toward the man and spoke in a low, dangerous tone. "You might be interested to know that in our investigation into your ex-wife's death, we've found some incriminating evidence."

Usher put a hand to his chest. "Evidence that incriminates *me?*"

Parker merely gave him a grim nod.

Usher clenched his hands together, open and shut them, as if they were too clammy to bear. He glanced frantically around the room. "Please, my patrons." He pointed off in the distance. "Let's go where we can talk privately."

CHAPTER TWENTY-THREE

He led them to a staircase that took them three flights up, to a roomy loft that was sparsely furnished and cluttered with canvases and easels. The large, open area seemed to serve as both living quarters and studio. A worn desk in the corner was overspread with brushes, palettes, tubes of paint. A single couch sat at the far end behind a coffee table littered with half-eaten fast food, still in the wrappers.

As they crossed the room, her heels clicking against the boards, Miranda sniffed, just to see if she could catch a whiff of Mary Jane. But the only smells were oil-based paints, turpentine, and stale whiskey.

Beneath the general mess, the place was elegant. Hardwood floors. Fireplace. A small kitchen with slate and limestone accents. The rent must cost a pretty penny. Desirée's money, she'd bet.

But what stood out most were the images of Desirée Langford.

They were everywhere. Desirée on a horse. In a field of daisies. Nude in a big, four-poster bed. The variously sized portraits took up most of the space. Looked a lot like an obsession.

"Quite a few paintings of Ms. Langford," Parker observed as they reached the kitchenette at the far end of the dwelling.

Usher waved a hand, grandly gesturing toward the canvases. "My late wife inspired much of my work. To me, she was more than a woman. She was an enchantress. My Medea, as I tried to explain downstairs. Temptress, seductress."

Vindictive witch? Miranda wondered, considering the artwork. Desirée's expression in these images was determined, but not as intense as in the Medea painting downstairs. The woman in that picture had evil in her eyes. These were tamer, sweeter. Maybe Usher had painted them before she left him for Kennicot.

The artist reached for a bottle of Kentucky bourbon on the granite counter. "Would either of you care for a drink?"

Miranda shook her head.

"No, thank you," Parker said.

"Did you and Desirée live here?" she asked.

Usher retrieved a shallow glass from the cabinet, some ice from the fridge, poured himself some whiskey. He took a swallow. "We moved in about three years ago when the gallery opened. I've had many productive hours here."

She strolled to the nearest image. One of Desirée on a chestnut horse. Could that be Calypso? "Did she pose for you?"

"Oh, yes." His lips twitched but there was pride in his tone.

"Even after she, uh," she waved her hand, as if searching for the right word, "began *staying* with Kennicot?"

He pressed his fingers to his temple, Kennicot's name must have given him an instant migraine. "Desirée was interested in my work. No matter how rocky our relationship became, she was always willing to pose for me."

Miranda played with the pearls at her neck. "But her work was at Aquitaine Farms."

He ran a hand through his long hair, took a swallow of bourbon, and nodded. "Even when we were married, she lived there part of the week."

And developed her relationship with Kennicot there. Miranda turned to face him, rocked on her toes. "Did you live at Aquitaine Farms the rest of the time you were married? Before you moved in here?"

Usher's seaweed green eyes grew sullen. "We started out there, but it didn't work for us. We stayed only a few years. A few difficult years." He took another pull of his drink, then set it down with a deep sigh.

Miranda stepped toward the counter. "Because of Kennicot?"

He focused on her, forcing back a sneer. "Because of the Langfords. I never got along with them. Her sister despised me. Her father thought I was beneath her. He called me her 'weakness.' He thought of me as a hobby of the lovely heiress. She was amusing herself by supporting the poor, starving artist."

Usher came around the counter, began to pace across the floor, his free hand fisting and opening in that agitated way Miranda had seen before. He was lying about something.

"But Desirée understood me. She believed in me. When we moved here, people started to recognize my talent. I couldn't have become a success without her."

The same thing Delta thought. "So she was a meal ticket for you."

His lip curled. "How dare you say such a thing? I loved Desirée. She was my life."

Or his obsession.

Usher picked up his drink and strolled to a wall where there were five or six eight-by-ten sized portraits of his deceased wife. He ran a hand through his hair and stared at the pictures.

"Desirée was a marvel." He whispered the words as if he'd just seen an apparition from Heaven. "I'm sure you both know she was one of the country's foremost horse breeders. She didn't believe in studying genetics and genomes and markers and all that. She was so instinctual, so fluid. It was a challenge to capture her essence. She understood horses. Their quirks, their traits. She could look at a stallion and a mare and predict whether their foal would be a winner. And which foal. Most of the time, she was right."

Parker stood eyeing Usher, his arms folded. Once again, he was leaving the questioning up to her. But Miranda could tell he was ready to pounce if things went south.

"Too bad Desirée wasn't so good at predicting people."

Usher came out of his reverie and glared at Miranda. "What do you mean? She had many friends."

"Is that why she ended up dead at the Steeplechase?"

Usher gritted his teeth, moved back to the kitchen and poured more bourbon into his glass. "The police said it was suicide, Ms. Steele. Why isn't that good enough for you?"

Miranda ran her hand along the counter, gazed at the cabinets, the stainless fridge. "Suicide from an overdose of PCP. Where'd she get that from?"

He blinked at her, unable to answer for a moment. "I have no idea." He raised his glass to his lips.

"Witnesses saw you plying Desirée with drinks and snorting coke with her half an hour before she died."

He lowered his glass, his face flushed. "You aren't the police. I don't have to tell you anything." His tone dripped with disdain.

Miranda took a step toward him. "No, but we can share what we know with the police."

Usher released a haughty laugh. "What do you know?"

Not yet, Miranda thought. "We know you and Desirée were both users."

With a huff, Usher picked up his drink again and took it into the studio area. "Desirée was the one who always wanted to experiment." He stopped in the middle of the room, put a hand to his head. He knew she had him on this point. "She said the drugs helped her. She had a history of depression. She was in therapy. You should talk to her therapist, Dr. Chaffee."

"I have."

He spun to face her, his eyes glowing with anger. "Then you should understand why she took her own life."

She folded her arms. "But why with PCP? Where did she get it from?"

His upper lip curled with irritation. "From Kennicot. I told you that at her funeral."

Miranda stepped toward him. "We've talked to Kennicot, too, Usher. He doesn't use PCP. But he told us Desirée left you for him. That she was in love with him since she was a teen. That gives you a motive. Jealousy."

"What?" he gasped.

"You know. The old 'If I can't have her no one else can' song and dance?"

Agitated, Usher began to pace the room again. Back and forth. To the desk. To the sofa. Over to another row of easels that held larger canvases of Desirée's likeness.

Miranda decided to plant herself at the desk. As she neared it, she looked down at the messy surface strewn with art supplies and saw one of the drawers was ajar. Inside, the handle of a handgun gleamed. Her pulse went into overdrive.

Parker came up behind her, saw it too. His eyes widened for an instance, but he gave no other appearance of alarm. He was as calm as if he were watching clouds float through the sky.

Usher was getting more uptight by the minute. Fitfully, he shifted his weight. "I don't know why she did what she did, Ms. Steele. Desirée had her whole life before her. But as I said, she had issues."

"What kind of issues?"

"Good grief, you ought to know if you talked to Chaffee." He was shouting now. "Problems with her father. With her sister, Delta."

Miranda played dumb. "What kind of problems?"

"The kind sisters have. Really, Ms. Steele." His voice broke with emotion. "How can you be so unfeeling at a time like this? She's only been gone a week."

For just an instant, a stab of guilt rippled through her. Was Usher telling the truth? Was he just a distraught, spurned lover who'd been caught up in a bizarre love triangle? No, circumstantial as it was, they had evidence. If anyone should be feeling guilty, it was this guy.

She inhaled to steady her nerves. "And yet you're ready to hold an exhibition."

His mouth flew open. "It was planned before her death. I wanted—I was hoping—"

"That she'd come back to you?" Like focusing on himself and his work would be irresistible to her. The pompous ass. She ventured another step toward him. "Is that what you were arguing with her about at the Steeplechase?"

A shudder went down the length of him. "You're not the police. I shouldn't even be talking to you."

"Desirée refused, didn't she? Even with this art show, she turned you down. You were devastated. Hurt. Furious enough to kill her."

"How can you do this to me? How can you be so cruel?" He glared at her, then at Parker. "Get out of here."

Nobody moved.

With a sudden jerk, Usher lunged for the desk. Miranda's heart ricocheted into her throat. He was going for the gun.

But instead, with one violent sweep of both arms, he heaved all the art supplies off the desktop. Tubes, palettes, brushes, all clattered to the floor. Paint oozed onto the hardwood. The oily smell thickened. "I didn't kill Desirée," Usher cried out, as if he were on the verge of a breakdown. "I loved her. I worshipped her. Leave me alone. Get out of my studio."

He began to weep.

Crocodile tears. Miranda pounced, getting up in his face, blocked him from the drawer. "We visited the Steeplechase grounds this morning, Usher. Guess what we found?"

His gaze circled the room, then finally focused on her. "I have no idea."

"A riding crop with your fingerprints on it."

He blinked, opened his mouth, stepped back in confusion, shaking his head. "No."

"Yes. The one you used to rile up Calypso. It wasn't enough that you got Desirée full of booze and coke and then laced her drink with PCP. You had to make her suffer. You used that crop to make her favorite horse kick her to death. All because she left you for Kennicot."

"No. No." Usher tore at his wild hair, screaming like a madman. "Isn't my life enough of a wreck? Why are you trying to destroy me?" He glanced down at the open desk drawer with the gun in it. It was too far away. Suddenly, he reached out with his bony fingers, going for Miranda's neck.

"Hey, asshole." She stepped back and was about to give the sucker a flying kick in the groin when Parker shot past her. With a single hand, he grabbed the deranged artist by the throat, lifted him up on his toes.

"Ferraro Usher," he growled in a dark, threatening voice that sent a sharp chill down Miranda's spine. "If you lay a hand on my associate, I'll see that you'll regret it for a long time. And remember, I'm not the police. I don't have to go by the book."

It was past midnight when they pulled into the mansion's huge garage. Exhausted, Miranda laid her head back on the seat. She couldn't wait to get out of the tight chiffon dress and into the octopus shower.

Parker turned off the Lamborghini and sat for a moment, staring at the empty space. "There's room in here for another vehicle," he murmured.

She still parked her beat-up old Lumina in the driveway. And there it would stay. Ignoring his implication, she shook her head. "Some confession we got from our number one suspect tonight."

He exhaled slowly. "It was less than satisfying." Parker was the king of understatement.

"That guy's guilty as sin and we can't get him to squeal."

He half-smiled. "Succinctly put. It takes time."

She smirked. How could he always be so patient? "I was ready to call Erskine to come arrest that jackass."

"All our evidence is circumstantial. Usher had motive, opportunity, and means, but we can't conclusively prove he killed Desirée." His voice flat, he sounded as worn out as she was.

"I know." With a groan, she put her hand on her brow. Her head hurt. "So what's our next step?"

He reached over and massaged her temple. It felt good. Oh, how she loved his touch.

After a moment, he took a deep breath. "For now, this case will have to be on hold."

Her head shot up. "Why?"

"I have to be out of town for a few days."

"What?" She pushed his massaging hand aside.

His face flushed with irritation. "I have another matter to attend to. It's pressing."

"Where are you going?"

"Washington State."

He was running out on her? Now?

Parker lifted his hand to touch her cheek, then thought better of it. The angry lines forming in her forehead annoyed him, yet the surge of admiration, of joy, he'd felt watching her work tonight lingered in his heart. That avenger's spirit of hers had been in full play. Motivated by what she'd seen in that stall, she hadn't flinched, hadn't backed down for a moment.

Miranda Steele would spend her whole being defending the helpless, the injured, the dead. On the outside, they were as different as two people could be. But at the core, they were just alike. Lord, how he loved this woman.

But the pain she suffered in her past made her more vulnerable than she realized. Not a good trait in this profession. He vowed he'd do all he could to try to heal it. That was the purpose of this trip, though he loathed leaving her.

In an effort he considered an exercise in futility, he'd sent emails to his former employees across the country, asking if they knew of any young girl who fit the sparse description he had of Miranda's daughter, Amy. Bill Malone, one of his first trainees, had answered last week. Bill ran his own office in Tacoma, Washington these days, and he had a client with a daughter who was Amy's age. The girl was adopted, had a birthmark on her neck, like Miranda's baby had. The timing was bad, but Parker had to check it out.

He refused to tell Miranda why he was running off to Washington, no matter how much he wanted to. No matter how much she wanted to know. He had no guarantees, and it would only get her hopes up.

"You do remember my rules?" he asked quietly.

Beside him, she tensed. "Your…stipulations?"

"Yes."

Slowly Miranda turned her head, stared into his eyes, that deep gray chasm had gone cold as steel. "I have to see a shrink."

"Correct."

She'd been to two. "You can pull me off the case anytime you feel like it."

"Anytime I feel there's too much danger," he corrected.

That couldn't be it, with all the compliments he'd been tossing her way. Her eyes widened. "I can't work on the case by myself. Meaning, while you're out of town."

He gave her his cocktail party smile. "I'm pleased you remembered."

Her blood starting to pound in her head, she grunted and folded her arms. "What about momentum?"

"Momentum? I'd say we just hit a wall."

He couldn't expect her to just stop cold. "I wouldn't do anything stupid,

Parker. I have learned a thing or two at the Agency, and as you recall, I can handle myself pretty well in a fight."

He patted her hand. "Just the same."

"What about all this 'you're getting to be such a fine investigator' crap?"

He scowled. "It's not crap. And it's not germane to this matter."

How could he hit her with this after what she'd just been through? She gritted her teeth, her chest heaving, her eyes starting to smart. So she was going back to classes. What was the point of them, if Parker was going to stifle her like this?

"Guess not." With a huff, she got out of the car, slammed the door and stomped inside to the kitchen.

Parker followed with a gait as casual as if they were on a stroll in the park together. "By the way, you never told me about your visit to Dr. Chaffee."

She spun around, glaring at him. "You want to talk about the *shrink*?"

"I do."

She kicked off her hellish high heels, tromped to the fridge, searched for a regular, normal beer. There was none. She grabbed a soda instead. Without offering Parker any, she shut the door hard, tore off the top and took a slug. "I already told you everything he said about Desirée."

"What did he say about you?" He reached for her.

She slipped to the other side of the island. Oh, yeah. That other 'stipulation' of his. She gave him a big, fake smile, lifted her arms. "It was just great. I'm cured of everything. I think he even healed my hangnail."

Parker stood, his whole body motionless, his gaze boring into her with an icy chill.

She let out her own angry growl, set the drink on the island, grabbed at her hair. "Shrinks don't work for me, Parker. The veritable Dr. Chaffee fell asleep while I was reliving my past."

His eyes blazed. "Your marriage to Groth?"

"Didn't get that far. Just my childhood."

His face creased with disappointment. He sighed aloud and reached into his coat pocket. He pulled out another business card and slid it across the island to her. "Here. This is the best psychologist I know. I've been to her myself."

Reluctantly, she picked up the card. "*You've* been to a shrink?"

"Yes."

For a moment she wondered why, then she realized the answer. "You mean after—?" She couldn't even say it.

"After Sylvia passed away. And when I've been involved in a particularly stressful case."

Well, that took the wind out of her sails. She didn't know what to say. "Particularly stressful" was another understatement. She'd heard Becker and Holloway talking about some of the rough characters Parker had tangled with over his career.

He ambled to the fridge, got a bottle of his fancy beer, fumbled in the drawer for an opener and popped the lid. "I don't like everything about therapy, either. But it helps."

"What don't you like?"

He took a swallow from his bottle and stared off in the distance. "Dredging up the past can be painful. I prefer to let it lie, as you do."

That was sure another understatement. He was more secretive about his past than she was. She looked down at the card. Dr. Valerie Wingate.

"Mention the Agency and she'll work you in whenever you want."

"You're leaving the appointment up to me this time? What is this? Reverse psychology?"

He leaned against the counter and studied his bottle. "I thought it was worth a try."

She pursed her lips and squinted at the card again. The name sounded familiar. Her mouth opened. "I know her. This is the shrink who came to see me when I was in the hospital. After...you know." She reached for the pearls covering her scars. "The fight with Leon."

"Yes, I know."

"What? I thought she was on staff." She blinked at him. "You sent her to me, didn't you?"

With that smug half-grin of his, he finished his beer and tossed the bottle in the recycle bin. "While I'm gone, I'll have Judd watch the house."

That comment woke up her rage, started it dancing over her skin again, like angry ants. Why did he treat her like a child? "I'm a big girl, Parker," she snapped. "I don't need Judd to watch over me."

"Just the same, since we've upset a temperamental artist with a gun who may have killed already."

She snorted. "I'm not afraid of Ferraro Usher."

"I know."

"I can take care of myself."

"I know you can. But you won't even know Judd's here." He leaned over to kiss her cheek.

She pulled away, spun toward the door. Leaving her fancy high heels on the floor, she headed upstairs. They undressed, showered separately. She left his mother's Tahitian pearls on his side of the dresser, climbed into bed without even a "goodnight."

It was the first night since she moved into the Parker mansion that they didn't have sex.

CHAPTER TWENTY-FOUR

Ferraro Usher sat on the couch in his loft, the shimmering whiskey trembling against the glass in his hand. He stared at the Medea painting he'd placed on his largest easel across the room after he'd had it brought up here about an hour ago.

He studied the colors, the brushstrokes he had used. So vivid. So passionate. So alive. He could never create that much vibrancy again. This was his masterpiece.

Feeling suddenly chilled, he rubbed his arm. The loneliness was excruciating tonight. A dark, hollow cave. Empty, echoing with memories that would never be again. Desirée.... Oh, darling. Why?

He looked up at the face staring down at him, cruel mockery in her eyes. It was a genuine likeness. He'd painted what he'd seen. And ironically had produced something...exquisite.

Others recognized that. He'd had an offer for the work tonight. An excellent offer. Lord knew, he needed the money, but he'd turned the buyer down. He couldn't sell this painting. Especially after those two "visitors" he'd had.

It was too risky. That portrait held too many secrets. If some bright investigator unraveled them, he was done for. Why had he let them into his loft? Why did he even speak to that conniving, smart-mouthed bitch, Miranda Steele? Because he'd look guilty if he didn't.

Rage pounded in his chest. How dare they do this to him?

And now Wade Parker was involved, too? Parker was the best investigator in the southeast. Just weeks ago, Steele had solved a high-profile serial murder. He should have strangled her when he had the chance.

Nerves prickled his skin, making it as sensitive as if he'd contracted a rash from his paints. He'd lost so much already. Would he lose his career, too? His life?

He swallowed the rest of his drink, stood, lumbered over to his desk. He stared down at the gun in the drawer. Miranda Steele had seen that gun. Would she use that knowledge to try to pin Desirée's murder on him? Perhaps he should use the weapon on Steele. She wouldn't be able to identify it if she were dead.

He reached out and softly touched the handle. He picked it up, held it to his temple. So simple.

Just pull the trigger. Bang. And all his troubles would be gone forever.

He put it back and shut the drawer, dragged his fingers through his hair. He wasn't the type for guns.

Agitated now, he hurried back to the kitchen, pulled a package from his pocket and laid it on the counter. Carefully he drew out a razor blade and worked the stuff into the right shape. It was like sculpting, he had always told himself. The shape of the line reflected the emotions of the cutter. He got a straw from a drawer, snipped it in half with a pair of scissors, put it to his nose.

Drawing it over the shape he'd formed, he inhaled deeply. Yes. Yes. That was better. He felt the effects immediately. The champagne of drugs. He sniffed, rubbed at his nose, glad he'd made the purchase tonight, though it was risky to do it here.

No, he wasn't the type for guns.

But his connections were. The people who supplied him with his recreational substances. Perhaps he could make a deal with them concerning Steele.

But that would cost money.

With a grunt, he turned and glared at the Medea painting again. Flaming corals and saffrons and golds and crimsons. His signature colors. Fire. Blood-red and white-hot. The colors of a seething inferno. Those eyes. Glowing. Burning. Blazing.

And that face. That inescapable face.

It seemed to ridicule him, pity him, scorn him.

Fear ripped through him. They would come for him. They would take everything, wouldn't they? They'd taken so much already. Soon, they would take it all. His art, his being, his life.

What had he done to deserve such disgrace? He'd only fallen in love with a beautiful woman. A haughty, heartless woman who didn't love him back. Who'd betrayed him with another.

Secrets. No one could ever discover his secrets. That would be the ultimate humiliation. He would not stand for it. If they got too close to the truth, if they learned too much, he would have no choice. He would have to do...something.

Perhaps the best course was to act and let the chips fall where they may. If he tried hard enough, he could find the courage. Besides, now that Desirée was gone, did it really matter if another woman died?

No, not really. Nothing mattered now. Nothing at all.

He grabbed the bourbon bottle, sauntered back to the couch, poured more into the tumbler on the coffee table. Lying back, he felt the drug taking effect. It was a pleasant buzz.

So, what to do? He had no idea. He picked up the drink, ran his finger around the rim of the glass, stared at the shimmering amber liquid. Desirée would have called him an indecisive fool. A coward.

He glared up at the painting. That exquisite face, so marred and broken. It was so wrong for her to die that way. And yet at the same time, fitting.

His mind grew fuzzy. Those blazing eyes seemed to bore into him from across the room, scorch him with their fire. The glass in his hand dripped with condensation, like blood. He put it down on the coffee table.

You see me, don't you? You're watching me, waiting to possess my very soul. Can I never break free of your spell?

His pulse hammered in his head. His whole body poured sweat. He got to his feet, tore off his coat. It wasn't enough. He picked up the drink again, desperate to cool his parched throat. Suddenly, the glass felt like a hot coal. It was the painting. It was Medea, setting him on fire.

"Will you never leave me alone? Will you always haunt me?" Crying out in sheer agony, he hurled the glass against the canvas.

It hit the face with a thud. The glass tumbled to the floor and shattered. Bourbon streamed silently down the face in the image. He sank onto the couch, buried his head in his hands.

He would never be free of her.

CHAPTER TWENTY-FIVE

Late Sunday morning, Miranda awoke alone in the chandeliered, blue-and-plum master bedroom, the sun streaming in through the gray-gauze curtains. Vaguely she remembered Parker kissing her and telling her he was leaving for the airport.

"Yeah, right," she'd grunted and rolled over and gone back to sleep.

She yanked off the covers and sat up to blink at the paintings, the chair arrangement in the corner, the copper bamboo fountain. You could rent the whole room out as an apartment.

"Too dang big," she muttered as she got up, ran her fingers through her unruly hair, pulled on jeans and a T-shirt. With a huff, she slipped her feet into a pair of sneakers and went downstairs.

In the kitchen, there was coffee, freshly brewed on a timer that Parker had set, guessing the time she'd wake up. In the fridge she found a fresh plate of *huevos rancheros* next to a bottle of extra hot sauce, with a note taped on it.

Cook is off today. Dinner is in the freezer.

Shaking her head, she popped the plate into the microwave and poured herself a cup of java.

Parker was a real good wife, she thought, tapping her foot as the microwave hummed. He was getting to know her far too well. Much better than she'd ever wanted him to.

After a minute, the microwave buzzed, and she grabbed a mitt and took the steaming plate, the bottle of hot sauce, and her coffee cup out onto the big redwood deck overlooking the backyard garden. She set her breakfast down on the tiled table, settled into an Adirondack chair, picked up her fork and took a bite.

Heavenly. The *huevos* were bathed in a delicious sauce, gooey with jack cheese, and had a great kick of heat, even without the Tabasco.

Okay. She might be furious at the man, but she had to admit Parker knew good food. That didn't make him any less pigheaded. Can't work the case

137

without him. Didn't he see he was choking her? What the heck was she supposed to do with herself?

She sat back and took a sip of Parker's sinfully delicious coffee and thought of that haunting portrait of Desirée Langford. Medea, huh?

A spiteful woman engulfed in the fiery red flames of her own vengeance. A bizarre emblem of her love-hate liaison with Usher. That face was crueler than any photos Miranda had seen of Desirée in the case file. It seemed older, haughtier. What had made Usher paint her like that? Her involvement in her own career? Their stormy relationship? Because she left him for Kennicot? Probably all of it. But one thing was clear.

Usher was pissed as all get-out at his ex-wife.

And then there was the gun in the drawer. What was a budding artist doing with a handgun? She couldn't even imagine him holding it in his shaky fingers.

Still, a volatile, emotionally unstable drug user could be capable of anything. Usher had been seeing Desirée before the Steeplechase. She went to his loft to pose, probably regularly. If Desirée had made him angry during one of those sessions, and the gun was in a nearby drawer, Usher would have pulled it out and shot her then and there.

Then Desirée's death would have been a crime of passion. A violent response provoked by…who knows what. The kind of spontaneous fits Leon used to have.

But Usher hadn't used the gun. He'd used PCP. That was much more calculating. A fit of passion she could buy. But calculating? Usher didn't seem the type to be calculating. He seemed half crazy.

And the suicide note was calculating, too. Could Usher have forced Desirée to write it? No, he would have had to do that at the steeplechase and there wasn't enough time, according to the reports. Was it a note Desirée had written that had some sort of double meaning? How could Usher have known about it if they were separated?

That left forgery. What if Desirée hadn't penned that note? Might be worth it to look into the handwriting.

She stared at the gorgeous landscape and thought about what she might do without arousing stealthy old Judd's suspicions.

Birds twittered in the trees. Around a rock garden, white day lilies and red roses swayed softly in their perfectly edged beds. Trees flowering with purple buds bordered the yard, along with tall oaks, firs and pines, all giving the spot a secluded feeling.

Lush green was the color of Atlanta. The way slate blue was the color of Portland, Maine, where she'd worked on a fishing boat for a few months. Or tan was the color of Denton, Texas, where she'd been a laborer on an oil rig for a time. Where Leon had found her.

Long ago she'd made up her mind not to stay in one place more than a year.

She thought of Dr. Valerie Wingate's card that she'd left lying on the counter in the kitchen. Parker was coddling her, trying to help her get over her past. He wanted her emotionally healthy enough to have a permanent relationship with him, she guessed. But he was in for a rude awakening. She'd never get over her past no matter how many shrinks she went to. No matter how good they were.

They'd admitted their "ploys" to each other about this house, and it hadn't changed a thing. If he wanted to be that stubborn about this piece of real estate, then there was nothing she could do. He'd left her only one choice.

After this case was over, she was out of here.

She reached for the hot sauce and shook it over the eggs, which had gone cold.

A latticework fence knit with climbing vines ran along the hedges bordering the neighbor's yard. From the corner of her eye, Miranda saw movement behind the leaves, near the ground.

Her breath caught in her throat. A faint noise rustled in her ears. She swallowed, got to her feet. That had to be Judd, right? Or had Usher surmised she was living at the Parker mansion and come to visit with his gun?

Then she heard a girl's voice.

"C'mon, Inky. Where are you?" Dressed in white shorts and a blue knit top, Wendy Van Aarle stepped out from the bushes, looking thoroughly exasperated. Shading her eyes with her hand, she scanned the yard, then caught sight of Miranda.

Miranda let out a breath of relief and strolled to the railing. "Good morning."

Wendy squinted up at the deck. "What are you doing here?"

"I told you. I'm your neighbor. Remember? After we saw that crazy therapist?" The Van Aarles lived a few houses away.

Wendy shrugged. "Oh yeah, right."

A zing of disappointment shot through her. Why should she feel let down that the girl hadn't remembered their trip to the ice cream shop? "And what are you doing here?"

She peered across the yard. "I lost my cat."

"I didn't know you had a cat." That must have been the movement she'd seen under the fence.

"I haven't had her long. She gets out sometimes."

"Inky, huh?"

Wendy nodded, heading toward the rock garden. "I was going to name her Mephisto, but my mother wouldn't let me. So I named her Inky."

"Guess she's black."

Wendy rolled her eyes. "Obviously."

Bad luck. Guess it fit both of them. "It's probably best to let her come to you."

Wendy scowled up at her from the middle of the yard. "What do you mean?"

"I'll show you. Hold on a minute." She went into the kitchen, found a saucer in the cabinet and a carton of milk in the fridge. She brought them back onto the deck and climbed down the long flight of wooden stairs that led to the grassy lawn.

She placed the saucer on the second step and poured some of the milk into it. "There. That ought to bring her around. C'mon up here so we can give her some space."

Wendy followed her back up the stairs and they sat together on a wooden bench along the railing.

"You want something to eat?"

"No thanks. I've had breakfast." She looked anxiously back at the yard. "I have to find Inky soon. My mother and I are leaving for Paris this afternoon. We have to take her to a vet to board."

"Paris?"

Wendy's eyes turned skyward again. "Mama says you can't really know the business until you get to Paris."

"I see." Miranda remembered Iris Van Aarle had an office for her cosmetics company there. Where she had carried on an affair behind her husband's back. A fling that was supposed to be over.

"My dad's coming with. He's playing in the Saint-Omer Open."

That was good. "I'm glad you'll be together."

"Yeah. Hey, any luck catching that guy?"

"What guy?"

"The guy who killed Desirée Langford. Or the guy who sold her PCP."

So she had remembered. "We're still working on it."

"Takes a long time, huh?"

"Yeah."

"Do you like being a detective?"

"Sometimes."

Wendy was quiet a moment. Her dark hair, with its new highlights, was pulled back in a band that matched her blue top. Even without the heavy mascara she used to wear, her dark eyes were intense. "I've been thinking."

"About?"

She gave Miranda's knee an impulsive shove. "Desirée Langford. She was wealthy, like my folks. So if whoever killed her was in her circle, they didn't do it for money or anything." Wendy fidgeted and gazed over the banister. "So it had to be for love. Don't you think?"

"That's an interesting deduction." Little Nancy Drew.

"I wish Inky would stop playing games with me."

"I had a cat when I was about your age," Miranda said. "My mother made me get rid of it."

"My mother didn't like the idea either. But I told my shrink I wanted one and she told my parents they should get me one. Guess shrinks are good for something once in a while."

"Maybe."

"I like mine. She's good."

She must be. Miranda saw a definite change for the better in the girl. "Who is she?"

"Dr. Valerie Wingate."

Miranda started. "Really?" The same one Parker recommended? She must be good. Wait a minute. "But she doesn't specialize in children, does she?"

"No. PTSD."

"I see." Post traumatic stress disorder. That made more sense. Maybe she'd give her a call.

A soft meowing came from down below. They craned their necks and saw Inky lapping from the saucer.

"It worked." Wendy jumped up and skittered down the stairs.

"Don't scare her off," Miranda warned.

But Inky must have been hungry. She stood perfectly still and let Wendy put both arms around her while her pink tongue scooped up the milk as fast as it could go.

"Bad girl, Inky. Don't ever run away like that again." She stroked her back.

Miranda fought back the sudden surge of tender emotions welling up inside her.

Oh, crap, she didn't want to feel this way. But all she could think of was what it would be like to watch Amy playing with a cat that way. What would it have been like to see her off on her first day of school? To bandage up her knee when she fell off her first bike? To feel a parent's pride when she got an A on her report card?

What would it have been like if Wendy had turned out to be Amy? For one thing, it would have meant a fight to the death with the Van Aarles. They may have neglected their daughter once, but they cared enough about her now to patch up their broken marriage.

It was a ridiculous thought. Besides, she'd given up the search for her daughter for now.

Suddenly a jolt went through her. Amy. Was that what Parker was doing in Washington? It would be just like him. That would explain his secrecy. Was he close to finding her? Oh, she couldn't even let herself think about it. She couldn't get her hopes up.

Inky finished the milk and began licking her whiskers.

Wendy picked her up. "I'd better get home. I need to pack."

"Right." Miranda's voice had gone hoarse.

"Thanks for catching her."

"Don't mention it."

Wendy turned and started back across the yard, the black tail curling around her legs.

"Have a good time in Paris," Miranda called, but the girl was already out of earshot.

After washing the dishes, flipping channels on Parker's big-screen TV in the living room, and watching a few hours of overenthusiastic women peddling turquoise jewelry and rose-shaped cake pans on the Home Shopping Network, Miranda couldn't take it anymore.

She got up and rummaged through drawers in the end tables, then the entertainment center, until she found a phone book. She opened it and began to hunt for a handwriting expert.

She was going to find out if Usher had forged Desirée Langford's suicide note, even if Parker would kill her for it. Well, he wouldn't *kill* her. He might take her off the case. But not if she found something good.

She'd learned at the Agency that the person she really needed was a forensic document examiner, but none of them would be open on a Sunday afternoon. So she settled for a graphologist named Madame Napier.

Pulling out her cell, she made a call and found the lady was open until six. Hot dog. Cautiously, she peeked through the front room curtains. No sign of Judd. She ran upstairs, got her purse, and headed out the front door.

As she pulled onto the street in her Lumina, she noticed a beige Audi several yards behind. "Well, Agent Judd," she chuckled to the rearview mirror, "you'll just have to go shopping with me."

She drove around for a while, feigning interest in a few clothing stores, then made a beeline for the colorful little shop off of East Paces Ferry. The building was a frame house with pink awnings and gaudy signs out front advertising a variety of goods. She hoped Judd would assume she was looking for a freaky necklace or a new energy drink. She found a parking spot along the street and went inside.

Definitely not mainstream, she thought, stepping into the cozy space. Red curtains on the windows, Zodiac symbols on the walls, and something that smelt like licorice in the air. Miranda browsed the glass shelves filled with supplements for hair growth and weight loss. She was examining a piece of blue crystal when she heard a Southern drawl behind her.

"I'm so sorry, ma'am. I didn't hear the bell."

A stocky, middle-aged woman with flaming red hair, penciled brows, and piercing dark eyes, swept in from the back, dressed in a flowing, multicolored chiffon cape over a peach pantsuit. She could have been someone's eccentric grandma.

"Are you Madame Napier?"

The woman smiled broadly with a lipstick-painted mouth. "I am."

"You have a lot of unusual things in here."

"There's always a good market for alternative approaches." Her accent was a rich Southern that spoke of old Atlanta money. Miranda wondered if Parker knew her. "Are you interested in something particular?"

Miranda put down the rock and shook her head. She'd stick to her own brand of vitamins. "I need a handwriting analysis."

The woman's penciled brows arched into her forehead. "I charge a hundred dollars for that."

Ouch. It took all Miranda had not to wince, but it was either pay up or wait for Parker to get back from Washington. She nodded.

"Very well, Ms—"

"Steele."

"Ms. Steele," she repeated. "Let's sit over here." Madame Napier guided her to a back corner and behind a beaded curtain where there was a small round table and two wire chairs that might have come from an old-fashioned ice cream shop. "Would you like some tea? I have chamomile, mint, catnip—"

"No, thanks." Wondering if the proprietress was going to whip out a crystal ball, Miranda drew in an uneasy breath and eased herself onto the seat.

"You look uncomfortable, Ms. Steele."

Miranda gave her a thin smile. "It's just that I was expecting something more—"

"Clinical?"

"Maybe." Graphology was considered pseudo-science, but she'd at least hoped for something that didn't make her feel like she was about to have her palm read.

Madame Napier gave her a look that told Miranda this wasn't the first time her methods had been questioned. "I've been doing this for eighteen years, my dear. I like working in this atmosphere. Would you like to change your mind about this?"

Miranda unlatched her purse, slid the five twenties she'd withdrawn from the ATM earlier across the table. This had better be good. "Let's do it."

Madame Napier pocketed the cash. "Very good. Now, please. Show me what you have." She opened her hand.

Miranda reached into her bag again, drew out the brochure from Usher's art show and laid it on the table.

Madame Napier's eyes grew round. "One of our local artists?"

Without answering, Miranda took out the copy of Desirée's letter from the case file and placed it beside the brochure.

The woman skimmed the paper and frowned. "Oh, my. Is this a suicide note?"

"Something like that."

She clasped her hands to her chest. "Oh, my, my. Is this that heiress who killed herself at the steeplechase last week? Desirée Langford?"

Everybody in Atlanta had heard the story. Miranda tapped her finger on the note. "Just tell me what you see."

Madame Napier picked up the brochure. "And this is the artist she was married to, isn't it? I heard that on the radio. Are you saying it *wasn't* suicide?" Tanya Terrance had done a fine job of spewing Desirée Langford's personal life all over the airwaves.

"Let's just say I'm doing a little investigation of my own into that story."

Madame Napier's eyes narrowed. "My family was once part of Atlanta's upper crust. Until my father lost his fortune in a real estate deal with Eli Langford." She inhaled slowly staring down at the colorful sheet in her hand. "But we've done all right for ourselves since then. And I certainly don't hold that against his daughter. Especially after what happened to her." She put the brochure down.

"I'm glad you feel that way." Miranda felt a sudden admiration for the woman whose inheritance had been lost and who'd had to live by her own wits.

"Very well, very well." Madame Napier lifted her hands, flittering them in the air like butterflies as she leaned forward to examine the scripts. Her fingernails were long and painted with an orange-and-pink-and-blue design that sort of went with her chiffon cape.

Gingerly, she eased the two documents until they lay side by side on the table. She shifted her weight, squinted at them, coughed, frowned. Then she reached behind her and into a pink wicker box and produced a magnifying glass. She picked up the brochure again, this time studying it like Sherlock Holmes.

She picked up the note, held it close, put it down again. She lifted the brochure again. "Hmmm. Interesting."

Miranda resisted the urge to tap her foot. "What do you see?"

She ran a gaudy fingernail under the lines Usher had written. "The flourish of the capital *T* in this brochure shows an artistic bent."

That would be obvious.

"But the downstroke of the *d*'s show a great deal of agitation. Much anxiety."

"In both documents?"

Frowning, she nodded. "Yes. And the looping of the *l*'s shows a particular, well, arrogance. Also in both copies."

Now they were getting somewhere. Leaning in, Miranda recalled Dr. Chaffee's comment. "Narcissism?"

"You could call it that."

"So would you say the handwriting is similar?"

"In some ways. But in this one," she tapped on the suicide note, "the vowels are rounded. While in this one," she pointed to the brochure, "they are sharp and pointed. This person was distraught."

Of course. Usher was upset last night when Miranda showed up at the exhibition.

"Madame Napier. What I need to know is whether these documents were written by the same person. Can you tell?"

The woman frowned. "It's very difficult to make such a determination. Some people can disguise their handwriting easily, though their moods can affect how they write. And then there are the people who do forgeries for a living."

"Of course. But don't you make *your* living seeing through that?"

Madame Napier's mouth became a grim line. "I generally confine my analysis to personality traits."

"Uh huh." A bust. She'd wasted a hundred bucks. Miranda got to her feet, reached for the papers. "Well, thanks anyway."

The woman raised a hand. "Ms. Steele, one moment."

"Yeah?" She waited as Madame Napier twisted her lips back and forth, as if trying to decide between chocolate or vanilla ice cream.

"I would say…"

"What?"

She picked up the documents, rose, and continued to study them as she led Miranda to the door. "This is just an opinion. But from the many handwriting samples I've seen over the years…"

"Yes?" Miranda said, taking back the papers as the woman handed them to her.

"My experience, my intuition tells me—"

Miranda hesitated at the door, turned back to Madame Napier. "That…?"

"I would say that these two documents were not written by the same person."

CHAPTER TWENTY-SIX

The suicide note and the signature on the brochure *weren't* written by the same person? What the heck did that mean? Miranda paced across the hardwood floor of Parker's den, her hands on her hips.

Was she supposed to believe that Usher was innocent? Impossible. They had his fingerprints on that riding crop.

With a grunt, she plopped down onto the cushy leather sofa and turned the two pieces of paper on the coffee table this way and that. She squinted at the downstroke of the *d*'s, peered at the loop of the *l*'s.

Nothing.

Was Madame Napier right? Or had she blown a hundred bucks on a carnival act without the cotton candy. How could she know? A second sample of Desirée's handwriting, that was how.

She pulled out her cell and dialed Delta's number. It rang and rang, finally the answering machine picked up.

"The Langfords are unavailable at the moment," said the clipped voice of a man with a British accent.

All she could do was leave a message. "This is Miranda Steele. Please tell Ms. Langford I'm making progress on our...arrangement."

Disgusted, she hung up and went to the kitchen to pop Parker's frozen dinner in the microwave.

It was after nine when she finished another round with the octopus shower and climbed into bed. She had just laid her head on the satin pillow when her cell rang. She picked it up off the nightstand where she was charging it—a habit she'd learned to acquire after her last case.

"Yeah?"

"What a delightfully warm greeting." Parker's smooth Southern tone caressed her ear.

"Oh, hi." She sat back, a little stunned, a little speechless.

"I'm fine. How are you?"

She rolled her eyes. So she wasn't much for protocol. Especially when she was pissed at the protocolee. "I'm doing okay." She pulled the black satin sheets up to her chin.

"That's good to hear. Did you find the food I left you?"

"Yeah. It was scrumptious. Thanks."

"You're welcome. Did you manage to find something to do with yourself?"

She narrowed an eye at the phone. Had that sneaky Judd squealed on her? She forced a yawn. "Mostly just lounged around the house."

He paused and she braced herself for a tongue-lashing. And not the kind he'd been giving her in this big bed lately. Instead, his tone grew somber. "I'm afraid you'll have to rely on the staff for a few more days."

She sat up. "What do you mean?"

"This case in Washington is taking longer than I expected."

"Oh?" She was surprised by the disappointment that rippled through her.

"I don't think I'll be home this week." He inhaled. "Possibly not until Monday." He sounded sad about that.

A whole week without Parker looking over her shoulder? Surely, she could solve the Langford case by then. She should be overjoyed. But instead, she felt a kind of hollow emptiness.

"Will you be all right until then?"

She narrowed an eye at the phone. "I think I can remember the way to McDonald's."

"I'm sure you can." For a long moment he was quiet. Had he sensed she'd guessed the real purpose of his trip had something to do with Amy? Talking to Parker could be a telepathic-like experience, the likes of which she'd never had with another human being. Perhaps because they both were a little shifty by nature.

"I know you must be disappointed, but we'll pick up the Langford case when I get back."

"Sure." She opened her mouth, about to spill the details about Madame Napier. Then closed it again. She couldn't risk kindling his ire. And there wasn't any need to. She'd have a break in this case before he got back. She'd show him what she could do on her own.

"Well, I better let you get some sleep." There was another long pause, until he murmured in her ear so low she barely heard him. "I miss you, Miranda."

Of its own accord, her heart somersaulted in her chest. *I miss you, too*, she wanted to say. But nothing came out of her mouth.

"Goodnight, then. I'll be home in a few days." Her heart ached with guilt at the pain in his voice.

"Can't wait," she managed to answer just as he hung up. She hoped he knew she meant it.

CHAPTER TWENTY-SEVEN

"What do you think this is, a geriatric unit? Get moving." The shrill Asian voice shot through Miranda's brain with the power of a machine gun.

Decked out in running shoes, sweats, and headbands of assorted colors, the class of IITs thundered around the perimeter of the Parker Agency gym.

"I said hustle."

Alongside Miranda, Holloway puffed and grunted. "This lady's a sadist."

On her other side, Becker's fists beat the air, like he was keeping time to *We Will Rock You*, as he tried to keep up. He spat out words between huffs. "I'd like to...tell her...where she can...shove it."

"Yeah, me too." But Miranda felt the sting of guilt. It was because of her that the maniacal Detective Tan had shown up in Judd's place this morning and decided to get everyone's attention with a hard run. Judd, of course, had been up all night watching over the caged bird in the gilded Parker mansion.

"What the hell is wrong with you lard asses? Move it!"

Tan must be the reincarnation of a gym teacher Miranda had back in high school, who made every girl want to claim she had her period every other class to avoid the torture. But that was before she married Leon and had learned how much of a disadvantage lack of physical strength could be.

Beside her, Holloway growled and Becker groaned.

She hated being the cause of their misery. She hated the insult of being babysat by Judd. Most of all, she hated being called a lard ass.

She broke into a hard run, sprinted away from her buddies, reached the guy out in front. When, at last, Tan blew the whistle to stop, she was twenty feet ahead of the pack.

Tan eyed her narrowly as she stood with the others, bent over, her hands on her knees, gasping for breath. "Pretty good, Steele. Let's see how you do with the bags."

She straightened as if she weren't worn out at all. "Sure, Detective Tan." With a sassy gait, she grabbed a pair of gloves off the hooks and moved over to the heavy bag hanging in the corner. She gave the bag a couple of hard kicks and landed a right jab against the red leather with a smack.

"Not so vicious, Steele," Tan warned. "You'll wear yourself out."

Wasn't that the point? Tan reminded her of a boss she'd had when she was a nail spotter in Syracuse. The type who thought insulting the employees would make them work harder.

But she nodded and slowed her pace, working on her side moves, alternating kicks and punches. The rest of the class was already at the other bags, and Tan moved on to give them her loving attention.

As she pounded and kicked, Miranda thought about Desirée Langford's suicide note.

Not written by the same person who signed that brochure, Madame Napier had said. Had she been barking up the wrong tree the whole time? Maybe the heiress's death had been a suicide, after all, as the police concluded. Maybe Delta had been overemotional, distraught after her sister's horrible demise, angry at Usher for what he'd done to her during their marriage. So she blamed him for Desirée's death.

But what about that riding crop?

She was missing something, but what? Her thoughts ran to Parker and his smooth style when he was working a case. Ignoring the pull at her heart, so like what she'd felt last night when he called, she focused on strategy.

Debonair, man-about-town that he was, Parker often attended fundraisers and fancy events. That habit could play into his hands when he knew a suspect was there. He'd told her people often reveal information in a social setting that they wouldn't face to face. With your peers around, the pressure to keep straight all the lies you've told can break a person.

If only she could corner Usher at some fancy event like that. She'd announce to the whole crowd that she'd found his riding crop outside the stable where Desirée Langford had died. That Usher had written her suicide note. That he kept a gun in his loft. She'd turn up the heat until that bastard sang.

But she couldn't get into a fancy-schmancy party without Parker. She didn't even know where to look for one. She didn't know the social calendar in Atlanta from the baseball schedule.

Tan's whistle pierced through her thoughts. "That's it, class. Hit the showers."

Miranda ended her assault on the bag and strolled over to Becker. He was clobbering the life out of a speed bag, his face twisted in an angry knot. She was surprised his hands were so quick. And glad she wasn't on the receiving end of those smacks.

Everyone stopped punching, but Becker kept going, like he wanted to kill that poor defenseless speed bag. And they said she had pent up aggression.

"Knock it off, Becker," Tan barked.

Becker came out of his trance, stopped punching, glanced around, embarrassed. "Sorry. I got carried away." His head down, he walked off by himself.

The class headed toward the stalls and Miranda caught up to Holloway. "Hey, what's up with Becker?"

Holloway shook his head. "He's still pining away for that girl I told you about."

"The one he knew in high school?"

"Yep. Still tied up in knots over a lousy dame. Pardon the expression."

Miranda smirked at his apology. "Love can be a bitch, can't it?" She was glad she'd been immunized against falling in love that hard.

"She left him flat. Broke his heart in two like a pretzel stick and he still wants her back."

"He needs to get over her and move on."

"That's what I keep telling him, but he won't listen. I tell him he should get out and meet people. Don't you know anybody? I mean *anybody* he could go out with?"

Holloway had asked her that before. The answer was the same. Maybe she should recommend a therapist, since she was getting so familiar with the shrinks in the area. Instead, she shook her head. "Sorry."

"I wish somebody did. Becker's fallen behind in his work. If he doesn't shape up, the Agency might let him go."

She stopped in her tracks. "Are you serious?"

"He says he can't study. He can't think straight. He's having trouble sleeping, too."

"That's terrible." She knew how bad dreams could mess with your mind. She didn't want to see Becker flunk out. "Being a part of the Parker Agency means so much to him."

"That's why I'm so worried."

She scratched her head. Becker and Holloway were her buddies. The first on this job to befriend her. But that didn't mean she could conjure up a girlfriend out of thin air. "I don't know what I can do, Holloway."

"Just about anything might help."

She nodded. "Give me some time. Maybe I can think of something."

She gave him a punch on the arm and headed for the women's shower.

Under the hammering spray, Miranda wondered what in the world she could do for Becker. Who was she to dabble in romance? Her own love life, if that's what you could call it, was such a tangled snarl, even shrinks couldn't unravel it. Besides, she didn't hang with girlie girls. She worked mostly with men.

But she'd hate to see Becker lose this job. He loved working for the Parker Agency. How could he let himself get so hung up over someone who'd dumped him back in Brooklyn? Maybe she'd just take him out for a beer and tell him to snap out of it, or else. Besides, she had a case to solve, and she only had until next weekend to do it.

She stepped out of the shower, grabbed a towel, and vigorously rubbed the coarse fabric over her skin. Finishing, she tossed the towel in a hamper, pulled on her underwear, then stepped into the pair of black dress slacks with tapered legs that she'd worn today.

Two of the other IITs—the only other females in the class—were standing at the sinks, primping. The tall, thin blonde with the short, curly hair was Smith. The tall, thin redhead with the long, sleek hair was Wesson. Their names had been a standing joke among the IITs since day one, but these two relished the attention. Especially when they took the spotlight away from Miranda.

Why hadn't Becker asked one of them out? They'd probably think he was too short.

"Hurry up, Steele." Smith shot her a sneer as she pulled a teal blazer over a pair of gray metro pants, then fluffed her hair in the mirror. "We'll be late getting back."

"I'm not waiting around for Steele." Wesson smoothed her short skirt and fastened her toffee-colored blouse, leaving the top two buttons open for the pleasure of the male IITs. "If we get back to class before she does, maybe we can beat her at something." She headed for the door.

Smith followed her with mincing steps on her four-inch heels. "I just hope we get to leave early. I've got a party to plan."

Jealous bitches. "Suit yourselves," Miranda called, as they left without her. She tugged on a black, short-sleeved sweater with silver studs that had only earned an eye roll from Gen when she walked in. One arm through the sleeve, she froze.

Party? Why couldn't she throw her *own* fancy party? After all, she owned a fancy mansion—just the place for it. Hadn't she just moved into the neighborhood? She could throw a housewarming. Why not? Invite some of the neighbors. A few other choice people. She'd tell them she'd come into an inheritance and had just bought the Parker mansion. *Come celebrate with me.*

And the party's guest of honor?

None other than the celebrated artist, Ferraro Usher. Though he wouldn't know it.

She'd invite Delta. And Kennicot. Peer group pressure. Psychological pressure. Seeing them in a social setting would make the sensitive artist break out in a cold sweat. She'd get him to break.

Excited, she slipped into her shoes and headed out and down the hall to her cube.

She wouldn't leave anything to chance. She'd plant some of those surveillance devices Judd had lectured about to record Usher's confession. She wouldn't tell Delta exactly what she was up to, just hint around. She was sure the woman would go along with the idea.

But could she get him to confess? She'd put all she had into questioning him at his art gallery and he hadn't broken.

She needed a statement. Something clearly incriminating. No innuendos. No double entendres. Something the police could use to put the guy away.

The truth.

Wait a minute. Wouldn't *Delta* be the ultimate pressure? If Miranda couldn't squeeze a solid confession out of Usher, Delta Langford sure could. With those catlike eyes that were so like Desirée's accusing him of murder, he'd crack like a walnut. All Miranda would have to do was record it. And set the scene.

Grinning, she reached her desk, sat down, and glanced at the calendar. Parker wouldn't be back for another week. Saturday would be the best day. That gave her five days to get everything ready. *Ready?*

Her stomach did a sick, queasy churn.

Miranda Steele throwing a high-brow party? Her idea of entertaining was a six pack and a couple of large pizzas. She had a cook at home, but she didn't have the foggiest idea what to tell her to fix. She could fake it, but what if somebody saw through it? The devil is in the details, they say. Crap.

She needed help, but who? Who did she know that wasn't connected to Parker and knew about fancy shindigs?

She put her head in her hand and closed her eyes. Think, dammit, think.

The memory of delicious-smelling Italian food materialized in her head. Desirée Langford's funeral. Her old buddy from the road crew who was a caterer on the side.

She clapped her hands and reached for the phone. No, she'd be at work. Miranda would have to give her a ring tonight. Good enough. Humming a little tune, she got to work on the stack of files on her desk.

She couldn't wait to get home tonight and call Fanuzzi.

CHAPTER TWENTY-EIGHT

"Well, if it ain't my best girlfriend. It must be my lucky night." Fanuzzi's sarcasm dripped through the receiver.

Rummaging through Parker's stainless-steel fridge for leftovers, Miranda winced. She'd forgotten to tell the cook what she wanted, and the woman had left without preparing anything. She couldn't believe Parker hadn't called and planned a whole week of meals for her. Must really be an interesting case he was working on.

"Hey, I called, didn't I?" In the cupboard, she found a bag of chips and a jar of salsa. Old standby. The salsa was extra fiery. Parker must have had the cook buy it for her. She put them on the counter, tore the bag open.

"I seem to remember you mentioning going out together last weekend? That you'd call?"

Miranda popped the salsa jar open, dipped in a chip, and shoved it in her mouth. It was extra fiery all right. She loved it. "Dang, Fanuzzi," she crunched into the receiver, "you act like I'm a hot guy who stood you up for a date."

The woman was silent a moment, then sighed deeply. "You weren't on the road crew very long, Murray, but we used to talk. You were the only other female. I thought we were friends."

Miranda stopped crunching. They had been, in a way. "What about Fat Mama?" she offered, hoping to get a laugh. Fat Mama had been one of the worse bosses she had ever worked for. She'd terrorized the entire crew until Miranda had given her a taste of her own medicine.

Fanuzzi exhaled. "Everybody has doubts about whether Fat Mama was really female."

"She wasn't male either. Space alien would be my guess."

Now Fanuzzi did laugh. She was softening.

Miranda strolled back to the fridge for a drink. "So how about I make it up to you for not calling?"

"The only way you could do that is to arrange a night with Wade Parker."

She stiffened with a sudden snap of jealousy. What was wrong with her? The woman had three kids. "I can't manage that." She picked up one of Parker's beers. "How about a bottle of Stone Imperial Russian Stout?"

"Say what? You're trying to bribe me with fancy beer?"

She knew the brand. Fanuzzi was definitely the one for this job. "I need your help."

Miranda could almost feel her grimace through the phone. "Let me get this straight. You want to make up for snubbing me with beer I don't like and asking for my help?"

She studied the bottle. "It's Parker's brand."

There was a pause. "How do you know what brand of beer Wade Parker drinks?"

Miranda shifted her weight.

A loud whine rang out in the background. "Mama, Charlie's hitting me again."

Fanuzzi muffled the receiver. "Knock it off, you two. I'm on the phone." Then she was back. "Okay, Murray. I give. What do you want?"

She put the beer away and did a little victory dance on the polished floor. "How about helping me throw a party? I need a caterer."

"How big of a party? I don't do small jobs."

"Oh, big enough to fill Parker's mansion."

She heard Fanuzzi cough. "Did you say Parker's mansion?"

"Yeah. The one in Mockingbird Hills."

As she reached for another chip, Miranda heard Fanuzzi gulp. Evidently, she knew the ritzy area. "Wait a minute. Why are you throwing a party in Wade Parker's mansion in Mockingbird Hills?"

Miranda sighed. Her former coworker wasn't going to make this easy, was she? "I'm sort of, uh, staying here."

"With Parker?" Her Brooklyn accent took on a breathy quality. "You're *sleeping* with Wade Parker?"

This was getting way too personal. Maybe she should have found a caterer in the phone book. Miranda shoved the chip back in the bag. "Are you interested in the business or not?"

There was a pause while Fanuzzi weighed her options. "Sure. When's the party?"

"This Saturday night." She'd need the whole day to get things set up.

"That's pretty short notice. How many people?"

"Maybe a dozen or so. Can you come over tonight so we can start planning?"

"Tonight? To the mansion?"

"Where else?" Miranda smiled slyly.

It didn't take long for Fanuzzi to make up her mind. "Let me see if I can get a babysitter."

Feeling triumphant, an hour later Miranda opened Parker's ornate front door and grinned at the short, dark-haired woman in a red shirt and tan slacks standing on her porch with a notebook, a briefcase and a basket in tow.

Miranda faked a British accent and stretched her arm in a grand gesture. "I'm so pleased you came."

"Good to see ya, Murray." With the same swagger she used to have on the job site when she bossed around big men on heavy machinery, she stepped into the foyer. "Mother of gawd."

Miranda strolled across the intricate marble tiles, came to a halt in front of a Grecian urn atop the rosewood credenza with gold inlay. "Didn't know you were Catholic."

Her mouth open, Fanuzzi turned in a full circle, staring at the twinkling chandelier, the huge paintings on the high walls, the grand mahogany staircase with its carved banister. "I feel like genuflecting. This is as fancy as Notre Dame."

Miranda spread her hands. "Home sweet home."

Fanuzzi's dark eyes sparkled with envy. "You lucky dog, you."

Miranda nodded toward a door. "C'mon. We've got work to do."

"Are you kidding? You gotta give me the grand tour first."

With a grunt, Miranda grabbed Fanuzzi by the arm and ran her through the airy living room with its big-screen TV, the Cupid-decked dining room, the dark-paneled entertainment room with the zebra skin rug, which she eyed suspiciously as if she could just imagine what Miranda and Parker had done there, and a few other rooms Miranda had never been inside before.

Fanuzzi oohed and aahed the whole way.

Her mouth was still open when they finally reached the kitchen. This was the last stop. No way Miranda was showing her the bedrooms upstairs. Especially not the Taj Mahal room.

Gawking at the gleaming stainless steel appliances and black granite counters, Fanuzzi set her basket and book down on the stonework island in the middle of the huge room. "Holy moly, Murray, is this where you cook?"

Miranda opened the bag of chips she'd abandoned earlier and offered Fanuzzi one. "Heck, I don't cook." Since she left Leon, except for the microwave and the fridge, she'd never used any kitchen appliance.

Fanuzzi ignored the bag, her eyes growing even wider. "You've got servants, don't you? Holy tamole."

"Parker has servants," Miranda corrected.

Fanuzzi scooted onto one of the island's iron-edged stools and reached into the bag, greedily. But her greed wasn't for the chips. "Tell me about you and Parker."

Miranda gauged her options. Fanuzzi wanted to be friends. She was trustworthy. She was even like Miranda in some ways. Maybe it wouldn't be so bad to confide a little to her. Might even be therapeutic.

She got the salsa, a roll of paper towels, placed them on the island and leaned a foot on the rung of a chair. "Parker and I have...I guess you'd call it a relationship."

Sucking in her breath, Fanuzzi looked at her like her skin was turning green. "What *kind* of a relationship?"

Miranda felt her skin turn not green, but several shades of purple. "A *working* relationship."

Fanuzzi scowled at the dodge.

Miranda went to the fridge and pulled out a couple of bottles. "Sure you don't want one of these Stone Imperial Russian Stouts?"

The woman licked her lips. "Actually, I've never tasted one."

She popped them open and handed her one. "Try it."

"Thanks." She took a sip. "Wow. That's some brewski. Tastes as rich as Parker."

Miranda glanced up at the clock. "We don't have a lot of time. Can we get to the party?"

"Sure, sure." Fanuzzi scowled and opened her book. "What kind of party is it?"

"A housewarming."

Her brow rose. "Housewarming?" she asked, in a suggestive tone.

"Sure. I just moved in."

"Uh huh. You just moved in with Wade Parker, the richest, the most eligible, the most desirable bachelor in Atlanta. Okay. Do you want the party in the late afternoon or evening?"

Miranda tapped her fingers against her lips. Later would be better. "Evening. Maybe seven or eight."

Fanuzzi made a note in her book. "And you said about a dozen people?"

"There about."

Another note. "I'm thinking fancy appetizers and drinks."

"Sounds good."

"Budget? Guess the sky's the limit."

Miranda gave an awkward little laugh. "Uh, not exactly."

Fanuzzi stopped writing and looked up, her eyes demanding an explanation.

"Parker's not paying for it. I am."

She put down her pen. "So what have you got to work with?"

Miranda ran her hand up and down her beer bottle. "Not a lot. Can you do that? And still make it look, you know…ritzy?"

Fanuzzi's inhale was like a low growl. "Yeah, I've worked a few miracles in my time. How come Parker's letting you pay for it? Is he really a cheap bastard under all that charm?"

Miranda reached into the bag for a chip. Instead of eating it, she broke it into little pieces on the paper towel. This was getting complicated. She'd better come clean. Fanuzzi would figure it out sooner or later, anyway. She wiped her hands and let it out. "Parker won't be there. He's out of town."

Fanuzzi looked like a kid whose puppy just ran away. "So you're having a housewarming in his house without the host?"

"Right."

Her air turned stiff, exquisitely professional. "Do you have a guest list?"

"Sort of." Miranda walked over to the counter and picked up the pad where she'd scribbled down a few names.

"Let me see it." Fanuzzi held out her hand like a grade school teacher.

Miranda handed her the pad.

She looked it over and scowled. "These are the principals from the Langford funeral. They don't live in this neighborhood."

Miranda folded her arms. Why did Fanuzzi have to be so nosey? All she wanted was some party planning. But if she didn't let her old coworker in on the real plan, her curiosity just might ruin the evening.

Miranda took a swallow of beer to bolster her courage. "Look, Fanuzzi." She sidled up to her at the island. "Whatever else Wade Parker is, he's also my boss. I'm working a case for him." It wasn't much of a stretch.

Fanuzzi's thick dark brows shot up to the high ceiling. "Is *that* what this party's about?"

She nodded. No need to tell her Parker didn't know about it. "I'm investigating Desirée Langford's death and I sort of need to see some of these people, well, in action."

Her mouth dropped open even wider than when she'd stepped inside the mansion. She ogled Miranda awhile, then slowly shook her head. "You sure are something else, Murray."

Miranda forced a grin. "That's me. Full of surprises."

"How are you going to do that and play hostess at the same time?" Feeling more at home, she reached for her beer.

"I'm going to bug the rooms and tape conversations."

Fanuzzi almost spat out her mouthful of Stone Imperial Russian Stout. "Holy guacamole. This is real detective stuff."

Miranda nodded. "Mum's the word." Best not to tell her one of the guests might be bringing drugs. Or even packing a handgun. Maybe she should have Judd frisk everyone at the door.

Oh, crap. She'd forgotten about Judd. It didn't matter. By the time he told Parker, the party would be over.

And the case would be solved.

Suddenly, Fanuzzi grabbed her hand like her long-lost best friend. "Oh, you can trust me. I swear on my grandmother's grave, God rest her soul, I won't breathe a word. I'll take care of everything. It'll be perfect. Absolutely perfect. And don't worry about the cost. I'll do it gratis."

"You don't have to—"

She held up a hand. "It's not every day I get to be in on a real murder investigation." She snickered gleefully and looked over the list. "Who else are you inviting?"

"Uh, I'll have to work on that." Miranda watched Fanuzzi's eyes dart over the skimpy list, as eager as a bloodhound on a trail. Relief washed over her. The woman was a real friend, after all. She should have let her in on the plan right away. This was exactly the kind of help she needed.

She could focus on the guest list and the surveillance while Fanuzzi handled the party details. She'd borrow some equipment from the Agency, but it would be a pain to install and impossible to check by herself. She thought a moment.

She'd get Holloway and Becker to help. She'd have to tell them something about the case and swear them to secrecy. Could she trust them? She'd have to chance it. She couldn't risk the equipment not working. At least Becker would be excited about something for a change.

Wait a minute.

She studied her new friend's short frame, her dark eyes and hair. Not bad looking. Bright, hard-working. "You seeing anybody these days, Fanuzzi?"

"Me?" she said in her Brooklyn accent. "Who has time? Why? Parker got a brother?"

"Just wondered." Fanuzzi even hailed from the same part of the country as Becker. This party would be the perfect opportunity to introduce them. Yep, Joan Fanuzzi might be just the person to get Becker to forget his old flame.

She peered at the container on the counter. "What's in the basket?"

"I almost forgot. Samples." Fanuzzi opened the woven lid and took out a small jar and a roll of crackers. She opened the jar and spread a bit of the contents on a cracker with a plastic knife. "Try this and see what you think."

Miranda took a bite. A salty tang snapped in her mouth. "That's okay. What is it?"

"Beluga caviar. But that's probably not going to be in your budget. I mean, *my* budget. I'll have to come up with some ideas."

"Cool. I really appreciate this."

She looked at her watch. "This is enough for me to get started. I'd better get home. It's a school night."

"Right."

Miranda helped her gather her things and walked her down the hall and through the majestic foyer.

"You know, this entrance hall would be a good spot to centralize the festivities."

Miranda looked around. Nice, open space for her victims to face each other. "Sounds good to me." She opened the front door. "Thanks for everything, Fanuzzi. You've been a big help."

"Don't mention it. What are friends for? I can't believe I'm going to be involved in a real live sting operation."

"You can't tell anybody, you know."

"Of course not. I'm not stupid, Murray. Besides, who would I tell?"

"Okay. Oh, and be sure to wear something nice."

"I always dress nice when I cater."

"Make it extra nice."

She narrowed an eye at her. "What aren't you telling me?"

"You'll find out soon enough."

Giving up, Fanuzzi shook her head and went through the door with a spring in her step. "A real live murder investigation under the guise of a housewarming party. Well, Murray, I always said you had balls."

Was it balls she had, or was she just crazy? She didn't know why she wanted to close this case so badly, unless it was the vision of Desirée Langford's face that had begun to haunt her nightmares, along with the faceless man that always chased her.

Parker didn't call that night. Or the next night. Or any night that week. Except the time he'd called during the day, when he knew she'd be at work, and left a message on the answering machine confirming he wouldn't be home until Monday.

She should have been glad she didn't have to listen to him boss her around, but instead she felt an uneasy void in the pit of her stomach. Didn't he want to speak to her? Had Judd figured out what she was up to and tattled to him? Was this his way of punishing her? So what? He couldn't stop her. Parker certainly wouldn't hop on a plane and fly across the country just to chew her out. Why should she let it make her so angry? It didn't matter.

Parker would beam with pride when he saw she had put Ferraro Usher behind bars. Even if she did it without him.

She decided not to worry about Judd or Parker. She was too busy with party plans.

CHAPTER TWENTY-NINE

Scented candles in accent colors flickered on golden stands, artfully placed about the imposing entrance hall. Fresh-cut wildflowers graced crystal vases, their aroma blending with the smell of good food being set out on a long table near the majestic staircase. Against a wall leading to the hallway, stood a makeshift wet bar. From hidden speakers, Barry Manilow crooned softly.

Tonight, Miranda would nail Ferraro Usher.

She descended the carved mahogany staircase in a deep red, open-shouldered gown with a fitted skirt and jeweled cuffs. For once, she was glad that Parker had insisted on buying her more than one dress the day they went clothes shopping. She hadn't had a spare minute to get a new outfit.

She'd been wrong about being able to let Fanuzzi handle the details of the party. The woman had insisted on her input on everything.

To get tonight's little shindig together, Miranda had spent every evening this week with the caterer-slash-road-crew-worker, either at the mansion or, when she couldn't get a babysitter, at Fanuzzi's little bungalow in Avondale Estates with her three kids. They'd gone over the decorations, the invitations, what to serve, protocol. Until Miranda had gone blue in the face.

They ate junk food with the kids, laughed, told stories about the road crew. It was the most time Miranda had ever spent with another female. Fanuzzi was becoming—a friend.

The time spent had been well worth it, she thought, gazing over the banister at the beautiful hall and beaming with pride. Fanuzzi was something else. Exactly the right choice to manage this soiree. She watched her black-clad staff scurry about, then caught sight of her talented caterer putting the finishing touches on the canapés.

She'd worn her hair in a French twist, caught by a shimmering silver comb. Her dress was midnight blue sequins and taffeta. Strapless, with a fitted top and a slit up the side.

Sexy, Miranda thought, as she stepped across the floor. Becker was going to go ape when he saw her. "Everything looks great."

Fanuzzi turned and gave her a satisfied smile. "I told you I'm a fantastic caterer."

She touched her arm. "You sure are. I'll give you a great reference after tonight. And you look great, too."

"Thanks. You're not so bad yourself."

Miranda had worn her own hair down, chiefly to hide the wireless bud in her ear. She'd dressed quickly, having spent the whole afternoon with Holloway and Becker, placing and testing cameras and listening devices everywhere on the first floor, before sending them off to get dressed.

They'd acted like two starving dogs who'd just spotted a steak when she told them about this case. She'd revealed only the barest of details and sworn them to secrecy several times. That would have to do.

The trap was set.

"So what's the big surprise?"

"Surprise?"

"The reason you asked me to dress up."

"Oh, that." Maybe she should give her some warning. "Well, there's this g—"

The doorbell rang.

Uh oh. Miranda inhaled a mouthful of nerves. "Our first guest." She hoped she could pull off this ruse.

Fanuzzi gave her hand a motherly squeeze. "You'll do fine."

She straightened her shoulders. "Of course, I will." She turned and strode to the front door. When she opened it, the breath went out of her like a balloon. It was Mr. P.

Dressed in a black tuxedo, not a hair out of place, he stepped into the foyer with his new fiancée on his arm. "Ms. Steele," he cried, as if she were a movie star. "How wonderful to see you."

As usual, the charismatic gentleman oozed the same good looks and sensual magnetism he'd passed on to his son. With a flourish, he took her hand and gave her a kiss on the cheek. Laying on the charm, like his son, too.

Beside him, Tatiana smiled a warm, thick-lipped grin. "Good evening, Ms. Steele," she said in her heavy Ukrainian accent.

"Good evening." Miranda shook her hand. "I'm glad you could come, Tatiana."

"How kind of you to invite us both to this festive celebration." Mr. P's eyes twinkled with expectation.

Miranda leaned over and whispered. "You can drop the social act, Mr. P. You two are the first ones here."

He nodded and winked at her.

"Come on in." She led them into the entrance hall.

Mr. P strode over the marble floor, taking in Fanuzzi's handiwork. His pure white mane of hair gave him the look of an elderly lion surveying territory that had once belonged to his pride. "This place looks even better than when I lived here." The note of nostalgia in his voice made Miranda wonder whether he might be changing his mind about the house.

He turned to Tatiana with a hungry look. "My darling, do you remember the room I told you about?"

Her eyes widened and she nodded.

Mr. P pointed toward the staircase. "It's up the stairs and down the hall on the left. Fourth room." He was talking about the Taj Mahal bedroom. "Why don't you go take a look at it?"

She turned to Miranda, excitement in her eyes. "Do you mind?"

Miranda nodded in the same direction. "Knock yourself out."

With a giggle, she shot up the stairs.

Miranda shook her head at Mr. P. No doubt he'd join her up there in a bit, but right now, he'd sent his fiancée away so that they could have a moment alone.

This past Tuesday night, Miranda had been sharing a bowl of popcorn on the couch with Fanuzzi and her kids, Charlie, Tommy, and Callie, while the woman nagged about finishing the guest list, when Mr. P had popped into her head. She'd let out a yelp that woke the family's golden retriever.

It hadn't been her fault that she wasn't able to come up with a list of people to invite to her housewarming. It was Parker who knew the high and mighty of Buckhead, not her. Except for the Van Aarles, who were in Paris, the Todds, who were in Rome, and the Oglethorpes, whom she hadn't met, she didn't even know who her neighbors were.

But Mr. P had turned out to be a regular social registry. After bawling her out for not keeping him informed about the Langford case, he gave her a list as long as her arm, including several art connoisseurs who admired Usher's work.

Rocking back on his heels, he chuckled to himself. "Very impressive, Ms. Steele. If only Russell could see your handiwork tonight."

She swallowed. "But you promised not to tell him."

He gave her a wink and put a finger to his lips. "I won't say a word."

Of course, he wouldn't. He was enjoying their little secret too much. She was glad now that he'd charmed the real purpose of tonight's soirée out of her.

His face warmed with sincerity. "How are you feeling?"

"A little nervous," she admitted.

He took her hand and patted it, in a fatherly manner. "You'll do just fine. You were trained by my son." He glanced around the room again. "And the entrance hall is absolutely perfect."

"That's my caterer's doing."

To some, it might be considered *trés gauche* to introduce the hired help, but Miranda didn't care. "Fanuzzi," she called out. "Come meet Mr. P."

Fanuzzi stopped what she was doing and scurried across the floor, her hand out. "Glad to meet you, Mr. Parker, Senior. I've read so much about you—I mean, about your real estate dealings—in the paper."

He chuckled with delight, took her hand, and breathed a light kiss over it. "I'm always glad to meet a fan. Especially such a lovely and talented one."

Fanuzzi sucked in her breath. For a minute Miranda thought she might faint.

"Don't let him turn your head, Fanuzzi. He flirts with all the women."

"Ms. Steele. I'm astonished." He put a hand to his chest. "I'm simply well-bred."

And his genes included the Parker family's abundance of charm and testosterone.

He narrowed his eyes. "Is she—"

"Yes," Miranda whispered. "She's in on it."

"Very well." He glanced around once more. "Is all the equipment ready?"

"Checked and double-checked."

"I hope you get the information you need."

"I will." If Delta Langford played her part right, by the end of the evening, Miranda would have Ferraro Usher's confession to her sister's murder on state-of-the-art DVR.

The doorbell rang again.

Miranda took a deep breath. "Show time." She fairly glided to the front door.

By nine o'clock, the foyer of the Parker mansion was shimmering with the sheen of satin lapels, silvery jewels, leopard prints and bare shoulders. And echoing with the flirtatious laughter of strangers whose names Miranda couldn't remember. And smelling of eau de money.

But the principals still hadn't shown up.

Dr. Kennicot, the horse vet, Desirée's first love. Usher, the famous artist, Desirée's first husband—and her killer. Delta Langford, Desirée's only sister, who was the key to tonight's scheme. What if they'd all decided to stand Miranda up?

After sending out the invitations, Miranda had called each of them personally. Good thing she had. Getting them to agree to come tonight had taken more persuasion than a late-night infomercial.

Delta had flatly refused until Miranda told her the real reason for the event and that she couldn't bring Usher down without her. When she added that Parker would be out of town, Delta had agreed.

Getting Kennicot to say he'd be there was a little easier. She'd only had to hint that she might be able to put the squeeze on Usher.

The artist himself was the hardest sell. She'd had to grovel. With a sick feeling lining her stomach, she'd told Usher she was ashamed of how she'd treated him at his art gallery. That she'd only been trying to impress Parker, and that he'd reamed her out for her sorry behavior. Usher had relished her fawning, as well as the opportunity to tell her no.

So she'd pulled out all the stops. She'd made pouting sounds and told him if she couldn't have the famous artist at her party, it would be a complete flop. The ego ploy got him. With the condescension of a medieval monarch, he agreed to show.

When she put down the phone, she'd needed a barf bag.

Heck, maybe all three of them were liars, Miranda thought, eyeing the silk-and-satin-clad strangers wolfing down Fanuzzi's appetizers and guzzling the faux champagne. If she'd gone to all this trouble for nothing, she'd really be pissed.

Once more, the doorbell rang.

Fanuzzi, who'd scolded her earlier for answering her own door, crossed the room and opened it.

Miranda let out a breath of relief as the tall, rugged-looking veterinarian entered the room with a slow gait.

He ran a hand over his wavy gray hair and gazed about the foyer, his lined face looking more worn than the day Miranda had questioned him at Aquitaine Farms. He nodded to a few people he recognized, then made his way to Miranda.

She offered a hand, and he took it with a motion that was almost warm.

"Good evening, Ms. Steele." He still wore that puzzled look that gave him an intellectual air.

"Hello, Dr. Kennicot. Thank you for coming."

He bent his head politely. "I only hope this evening turns out as you promised it might."

"I'll do my best."

His wide-set eyes scanned the room. "Is he here?"

"Not yet."

The same doubts she'd been having seemed to flitter across his weary face.

"Until he shows, why don't you relax and make yourself at home."

"That would probably be best."

"Have something to eat." She took his arm and walked him to the table holding large platters of appetizers.

Fanuzzi had outdone herself with prettier food than one of Parker's classy restaurants. There were bits of parsley and fake crab on slices of cucumber Fanuzzi had scored, dates wrapped in bacon, seasoned cream cheese sitting in little crisps she called fricos, and colorful little cakes that looked like they were gift wrapped.

"I'm sorry, Ms. Steele. I'm not very hungry." He nodded politely and sauntered across the marble floor to speak to one of the strangers. The way they shook hands and fell into easy conversation made Miranda believe the man was a colleague. Mr. P had probably invited another vet or two for Kennicot to schmooze with. Good thinking, Mr. P.

The bell rang again. This time, one of Fanuzzi's staff got it.

Miranda slipped a cucumber cup into her mouth and turned toward the door. She could hardly swallow. Her heart began to pound at the sight of the reddish curls and catlike eyes as Delta Langford entered the hall.

The woman stood a moment, scanning the room. In a short, black fitted gown with horizontal draping, puffed sleeves, and long satin gloves, she looked as much the vixen as the little girl. The same contrast Miranda had noticed in Usher's paintings of her sister.

She seemed tense, flustered. Was she ready to play her role? Then she caught sight of Miranda and closed her eyes in relief. She started for her, was halfway across the hall, when the front door opened again, and Usher's lanky figure appeared.

Delta stopped, turned toward him, as did half the guests. The man had presence.

He had on a lilac-colored suit with a matching vest, black shirt, spats on his shoes. His streaky, bleached-blond hair, which seemed freshly washed, spread out over his shoulders, like some medieval warrior, like he was trying to blend a look from the twenties with the fourteenth century.

As soon as he stepped inside the room, he spotted the woman and glared at her as if she were a spitting cobra. "Delta."

She glared back. "Ferraro."

He looked past her, spotted Miranda. His lip curled in hateful disgust. He'd better not turn around and leave.

Quickly, Miranda bypassed Delta and made a beeline for her secret guest of honor.

"Mr. Usher," she gushed, putting a teen-swooning-over-Justin-Bieber note in her voice. "I'm so thrilled you decided to come. This party would be a disaster without you."

He raised his nose in a move stiffer than Fanuzzi's cake fondant and opened his mouth.

She cut him off. "There are so many art lovers here tonight." She tugged on his arm like he was an old chum, led him away from the door. "They would have been so disappointed if they didn't get to meet such a celebrity."

As if on cue, two young women scampered up. One was a brunette and wore a black strapless number with a gathered skirt, along with an oyster bed of pearls around her neck. The other had highlighted hair that went from brown to blond to red. She was clad in diamonds and red satin. Both had legs like giraffes.

"Mr. Usher," the one with the multi-colored hair squealed, handing the artist a brochure from his showing. "May I have your autograph?"

Miranda grinned. Good thing she'd stopped by the gallery this week and picked up some copies of that brochure to scatter around the room.

The brunette was bolder. She reached for his arm and started to gush. "I so adore your work."

A few more ladies came scurrying up, and soon, Usher was surrounded by a small gathering of adoring female fans.

Once more, ego got the best of him. "I don't normally do this, but I'll make an exception tonight." He signed the first brochure, then another and another.

Where did Mr. P find these people? Miranda owed him big time. She slipped away, was about to head for the kitchen, when Delta reached out for her.

She squeezed her arm tightly with her gloved hand. "Ms. Steele, I'm not sure this was such a good idea. I can't stand to be in the same room with that man."

Miranda patted her hand. "Relax, Ms. Langford. You just got here."

She shook her red curls. "I shouldn't have come. I shouldn't have let you talk me into this."

"Yes, you should. You'll be fine."

Delta glanced around and saw Kennicot, still talking to his colleague. She stiffened. "You didn't tell me he would be here."

"Just a little added pressure."

"There are so many people here. I'm still in mourning. Really, I should go home."

A zing of panic shot through her. Delta couldn't leave. She forced herself to speak gently. "I need you to play your role. You do remember our plan, don't you?"

She looked at her blankly.

Miranda lowered her voice. "You have to get him to confess. If you accuse him of killing Desirée to his face, he'll crack." At least, she was betting the house that he would. "I've got hidden surveillance equipment set up in all the rooms on this floor. Everything you say will be recorded. Once we get his confession, we can turn him over to the police."

She rubbed her arms. "I'm not sure I can do it, Ms. Steele. I'm not sure I can face him." She narrowed her catlike eyes at Usher and his new fans and Miranda saw a vicious fire in them. She really despised the man, didn't she?

"Yes, you can. Trust me. Remember, this is for Desirée."

She closed her eyes dramatically. "Very well. I'll do my best. Can we do it soon?" She sounded like a child begging to stay up for five more minutes.

"Not too soon, or it won't look natural. He can't suspect it's a setup."

Delta just stared at her.

"Maybe in an hour or so. Give Usher the chance to loosen up. Take him off guard."

She didn't like the answer, but she nodded. "Just be as quick as you can." She moved away and sat down on a chair near the staircase.

Exhaling her nerves, Miranda stationed herself near a carnation-decked pedestal to keep an eye on her fidgety guests.

Usher was at the bar now, trying to get a drink while pretending to fend off the devotion of his fans. When he'd finally gotten his hands on a martini, he turned and saw Kennicot, who was sampling one of the finger sandwiches. Kennicot caught his stare.

Daggers flew between them.

With a few long strides, Usher left his groupies and headed for the vet.

No. Miranda started for the artist. They met in the middle of the room.

"What is the meaning of this, Ms. Steele?"

She tilted her head. "Something wrong with your martini?"

166

He brushed his long hair away from his drink with an arrogant flip. "You know what I'm talking about. What are Kennicot and Delta Langford doing here?"

"Aren't they your friends? I thought you'd be more comfortable with people you knew. Though everyone seems to want to be your friend."

The honey coating didn't work this time. "Comfortable? This is an outrage. I have a good mind to—"

She slipped her arm around his. "Please, Ferraro. Don't make a scene. You wouldn't want your fans to see you in a bad mood."

He caught her meaning. If he acted like a jerk, it wouldn't endear his followers. And with Delta here, some of them might start gossiping about his connections to the Langford family. Some of them might even put two and two together about Desirée's tragic death.

"All right, Ms. Steele, you win." He spoke through gritted teeth, like a growling grizzly. "I'll behave myself for now. But at the first opportunity, I'm leaving." With a huff, he pulled his arm out of Miranda's grip, slugged down his drink, and went back to the bar for another.

Well. That put a wrinkle in her plans. She'd wanted the narcissistic artist relaxed and in an open mood when it came time for Delta's scene. And now she had to make sure he got that way before he decided to leave.

She gazed across the room. Maybe Mr. P could help out.

Through the Saturday night traffic, Parker drove up I-75 from Hartsfield airport, feeling bone weary and bitterly disappointed.

The first night he met Miranda Steele came to mind. The vision of the angry woman pacing in a Fulton County holding cell, her black hair wet with rain, her clothes torn and streaked with mud from her struggle with a cop. He'd had to coax the information from her about Amy. He'd been moved by her story, by her tenacity. She had such spirit, such strength, despite the years of frustration she'd endured.

He remembered the night she confessed what Leon Groth had done to her, melting into his arms with tears he'd thought would never end. And then she'd faced the bastard that had caused her so much pain, and nearly killed him. To protect others.

If only he could find Amy for her. But perhaps it wasn't meant to be.

He'd had such high hopes when he met the daughter of Bill Malone's client. She had curly dark hair, like Miranda. Bright, clear blue eyes, an infectious smile. It had taken longer than expected to convince the parents to help. When Parker revealed to them selected details of Miranda's past, they agreed to let him take a DNA sample. For the match, he'd stolen another sample from Miranda's toothbrush before leaving town. Not wanting to wait weeks for the results, Parker had called the lab and persuaded them to give him an appointment next Monday. Yesterday they called with an opening. The meeting was short.

Negative. The young girl was not Amy.

He took the exit onto Northside Drive. Almost home. The mansion he'd always thought of as his father's house. Could it be a home for Miranda and him now? He thought of their tense phone call a week ago, her terse responses. She thought he was overbearing with his rules, but he had to protect her. As far as their relationship went, he'd decided he'd been pushing too hard and forced himself to stop calling, stop making arrangements for her. She needed her independence. Her space, as they say.

He'd even told Judd not to report in unless it was an emergency. That had taken all the strength he had.

She knew what his trip had been for. She'd figured it out. She was sharp. Intuitive. They'd both sensed the other knew, but neither of them had said anything.

The possibility of failure was too great. Parker couldn't bear the idea of disappointing Miranda again. Of coming home empty handed. He wished with all his heart he could give her Amy back. But he couldn't. All he could give her was himself.

Did she want him?

He could sense her feelings for him growing stronger the longer they were together. She trusted him more. They worked well together. But she was still skittish, restless, reluctant to settle down, to give in wholly.

Perhaps her longing for her lost daughter was the key to it. He hadn't thought of the possibility of more children before he met Miranda, but if that would make her happy, he'd consider it.

Would that be enough? He didn't know. He only knew that tonight, when he stepped inside the house, if he saw that glow in her eyes that told him she had missed him, he would take things to the next level. He would give her something he hadn't imagined offering to anyone since Sylvia passed.

He only prayed she would accept it.

He turned onto Sweet Hollow Lane, glad to be home after the long week. He longed to be alone with Miranda. To feel her warmth and vitality in his arms once again.

Then he noticed a row of luxury cars along the curb. He turned the corner. The entire house was ablaze with lights. Music came from inside.

What on earth?

Miranda Steele was the least social person he'd ever known. It wasn't like her to throw a party while he was away. Especially not with this set.

Where was Judd? He found a spot for his Mazda down the street. He searched for his employee, instead spotted his father's Bentley and several vehicles he recognized. Then he saw a silver Porsche with a vanity tag reading simply "Usher."

Now it made sense.

He got out of the car, stood rubbing his chin as irritation rumbled in his chest. She'd broken his rules. Again. Would she never learn? Why had she lured a man who might be a killer into their home? Obviously, she thought she'd set some kind of trap. At least there were other people around. Judd had better be inside watching over her or he'd be looking for a new job.

He decided to go in the back way.

CHAPTER THIRTY

The guests were on their fourth round of appetizers and were hitting the open bar hard. Everyone was loosening up and getting louder. The music had gone from Barry Manilow to Bon Jovi and some of the revelers had started to dance.

Miranda wandered over to the table where Fanuzzi was busying herself making sure everyone had food and drink, and popped what her new friend called a Swiss Pear cracker into her mouth. Could use some spice, but it still tasted rich as a five-star eatery. Fanuzzi was something else with the faux haute cuisine.

Miranda scanned the crowd. Almost time for Delta to make her move.

Mr. P and Tatiana were flirting with each other and keeping Usher occupied at the bar, just like she'd asked them to. Though the artist still looked pretty surly.

The other two principals were sulking in their respective corners, trying to ignore each other. Three sullen party guests in a roomful of strangers. They were spoiling the mood.

The rooms on the mansion's lower floor were open for viewing, but Fanuzzi had placed a red velvet rope across the stairway entrance to keep visitors from going upstairs. As people wandered through the elegant parlors and sitting rooms, Miranda could hear snatches of conversation through her earbud.

"Oh, look at this gorgeous vase," said a female voice.

Another woman gave a low, cynical laugh. "Wade Parker was always an ostentatious bastard."

"You're just jealous."

"I'm direct. And who is this bitch giving the party? Why is she buying a house from the Parkers?" Miranda had mentioned that little detail in her invitations to make the party more plausible.

Must be a couple of Parker's jilted girlfriends. Focus, she told herself sternly, anger fluttering down her spine.

The anger quickly turned to nerves. She should give Delta the signal and get on with it. But something told her to wait a little longer. She was going on pure instinct now.

And where were Holloway and Becker? They were supposed to help monitor the surveillance equipment and should have been back an hour ago. She was going to introduce Becker to Fanuzzi so her buddy would get over his old flame. That, at least, ought to go right. They had a lot in common.

The only other person missing was Parker. He'd be pissed as Hades if he could see this.

She looked across the room at Usher. Mr. P almost had him cracking a smile. Delta wandered in from the hall. It was time, Miranda decided.

Nursing a cocktail, trying to look sophisticated, she was about to give Delta a nod, when movement overhead caught her eye. She glanced toward the stairs—and nearly dropped her glass.

Speak of the devil...

Freshly showered and dressed in an elegant black suit, his thick, salt-and-pepper hair perfectly styled, Parker descended the staircase.

Where in the world had he come from? How had he gotten upstairs? He wasn't supposed to be back until Monday. What would everyone think he was doing up there in *her* house?

He lifted one end of the red velvet rope, stepped onto the main floor and deftly replaced it. Smooth as a silkworm, he began working his way across the room, greeting various guests as he went. All class and sophistication and good looks, he was the handsomest man in the room.

And yet, there was weariness behind his smile, disappointment in his eyes. He hadn't found Amy. She fought back a sudden wave of heartbreak.

After a moment, he reached her side. "Good evening, Miranda." His deliciously low, Southern voice reverberated with an all-too familiar rumble.

What are you doing here? she wanted to say. But all that came out was a weak, "Hi."

"In case you're wondering, there's a back staircase you evidently haven't discovered." His hand went around her shoulders, slipped down to her waist, then to her butt. He gave her a hard pinch.

"Hey, buster." She glared at him, but her heart leapt at his touch, in spite of his brash move.

He lowered his voice. "You must have forgotten my instructions."

She bristled. "What are you talking about? Can't I have a party in my own house?"

A sexy brow rose. "A party with Dr. Kennicot and Delta Langford?" He glanced toward the wet bar. "And Ferraro Usher as the guest of honor?"

"He's not the guest of honor."

"Not ostensibly."

She narrowed her eyes at him, livid that he could see through her so easily.

"Why is my father here? And what is Detective Judd doing in the corner?"

"Mr. P's my guest, and Judd's keeping an eye on things, like you told him to," she snapped, furious at the man. Why had he shown up now? And why was her heart doing cartwheels in her chest at the sight of him? She hadn't missed him that much, had she?

He studied her with a dark, piercing gaze, then spoke in a whisper. "Have you found the Agency's surveillance equipment satisfactory?"

She tilted her chin. "I don't know what you mean."

He brushed her cheek with his lips. "That's a lovely bud in your ear."

Erotic shivers slithered across her shoulders, down her back, and ended at her tailbone. He knew her too well.

She took a small step away from him. "You're ruining my concentration."

Parker inhaled slowly, forced back his temper. He refused to embarrass her with a tongue-lashing in front of her guests. Besides, the sight of her playing hostess in that gorgeous red dress that set off the blue of her eyes, and the black of her hair, had melted his heart the instant he'd entered the room.

Her ingenuity impressed him. It was a good trap. He glanced over at the disgusting artist drinking his whiskey. And since the trap was already set, might as well use it.

Giving in to feeling, he put a hand under her hair and drew her close. "Lord, I've missed you. And your rebel spirit."

He kissed her. Right in front of everybody, though it wasn't a long kiss.

Guess he wasn't too upset, Miranda thought, relishing his seductive embrace. "What happened? You weren't supposed to be home until Monday."

He released her, his face suddenly grim. "The case was closed. I caught an earlier flight."

"Uh huh." She fought back a new wave of pain, not wanting him to see it.

But he sensed it. All his irritation with her evaporated when he saw that sad look in her eyes. With his whole heart, he wanted to give her Amy, the world, and anything in it she wanted.

Gently he took her hand and kissed it. "I'm proud of you."

"What for?"

"Even though you went against orders, this party is a clever scheme. I couldn't have thought of a better one myself."

Really? Or was he trying to make up to her for his lack of success in Washington? The compliment still felt good. The party was a good idea, even if it was hers.

"So what's the plan?"

She opened her mouth, then spotted Delta glaring at her like a passenger on the Titanic who'd missed the last lifeboat. Her gaze went back and forth between Miranda and Parker. Uh oh.

"Excuse me. I have to go to work now."

She glanced over at Usher, still huddled at the bar, a thumb hooked in the pocket of his lilac vest. He was actually laughing, apparently at a joke Mr. P had just told him. Good time to catch him off guard. She caught Delta Langford's eye. *Now.* She mouthed the word across the room.

The woman nodded. After another searing glower at Parker, Delta crossed the room to the bar.

Miranda watched as Delta spoke stiffly to the artist a moment. Then they took their drinks and disappeared down the hall.

What was she doing? She was supposed to confront him right here in front of everybody. She must have lost her nerve. She'd better play her role right, or this could blow up in everyone's face.

As casually as she could, Miranda sauntered toward the hallway and watched them step into the library.

"I see what you have in mind," Parker said slowly, approval in his voice. "Did you use the zoom cameras?" he asked so softly only she could hear him.

She nodded. "High-def color." Since there were *only* a dozen rooms on the mansion's ground floor, she'd been able to hide several of the thirty-two cameras in each one. She'd put three in the library. "One in the plant in the corner, one in a book on the shelf, one in the smoke alarm."

"Thorough."

Miranda didn't have time to relish Parker's praise. Usher's voice was coming through her earbud.

"What do you want, Delta?"

After a long pause, Delta said something about being surprised to see him here. Her voice was scratchy.

Usher answered, but his reply was muffled.

"Sorry," Miranda said to Parker. "I've got to, uh, go see what's cooking in the kitchen." She spun on her heels and hurried down the hall.

The granite counters in the huge kitchen were piled high with trays of fresh appetizers. Recycle bins filled with empty bottles of booze and beer were stacked on the floor.

Miranda stomped over to the pantry where she'd hidden the DVR. She yanked open the door and glared at the monitor. Delta and Usher were facing each other like two cowboys in a showdown.

She turned a knob. *Say something, dammit.* There was a voice. Still muffled. *Move to the plant, Delta.* She adjusted the knob again and watched the signal.

"Ferraro. What are you doing here?"

"Same as you. I was invited."

That was better. Nice and clear. A thrill rushed over her skin.

"But you didn't have to come. Why did you?"

Pause. Noise again, but it was only Delta setting down a vase too near the mic.

"I wanted to see what Ms. Steele was up to."

She could almost feel the gasp in Delta's throat. "Why do you think she's up to something?"

There was a sharp rap. Miranda jumped, then realized someone was at the door that led to the deck.

"What the heck?" With a grunt, she yanked the bud out of her ear, closed the pantry, went to the window and peeked out. It was her two work buddies. Fine time for them to show up.

She jerked open the door and put her hands on her hips. "You're late."

Holloway stepped into the kitchen wearing a sheepish look. "I'm sorry, Steele. It took me an hour to convince Becker to come back."

Becker shuffled inside behind Holloway, his hands in his pockets, his head down. But at least he'd combed his thick black hair and worn a suit. Might have even trimmed his eyebrows. He didn't look half bad. "I just don't feel like a party tonight."

"You haven't felt like a party in weeks," Holloway scolded. "I keep telling you, you need to get out. Steele was nice enough to invite both of us to this shindig and look how you act."

Miranda held up a hand. Now that they were here, she had to get rid of them and get back to Delta. "You'll both love this. Parker's here."

"Parker?" they said in unison, both pairs of eyes glowing. Becker seemed cheerier already. But that hadn't been the idea.

She took the short man's arm. "Come on into the foyer, Becker. There's someone I want you to meet." She'd do a quick introduction, then get back to the surveillance.

"Parker, right?"

"You know Parker. You see him all the time at the office. He teaches a martial arts class once in a while."

"Not the same thing as getting to talk one-on-one with him."

This might not be as easy as she thought. "Just wait till you see who—"

Before she could take another step, Fanuzzi swung through the door, an empty tray in one hand, a drained wine bottle in the other.

"Well, here she is."

The caterer froze. Staring at Becker, she craned her neck, blinked hard, frowned as if she were trying to remember something.

"Dave, I'd like you to meet—"

Becker stiffened, cocked his head. "No," he murmured. "It can't be."

"What?" Miranda looked back at Fanuzzi. Her mouth was open. She stood as stiff as a board. What was wrong?

Becker wiped his lips with the back of his hand. "Joan?"

Fanuzzi didn't move. "Is that you, Dave?"

"You two…know each other?" That was good, right?

Becker took a step forward. "I can't believe this. I've been looking all over for you."

Fanuzzi stepped back. "What do you mean?"

"I, uh, I mean I've been looking at some of those 'find-your-lost-classmates' websites, trying to find you."

Fanuzzi's face went white, then red. "Oh, you have, have you?"

"Yeah. I wanted to find you."

Darts were flying from Fanuzzi's eyes. "After all these years?"

Huh? *Joan Fanuzzi was Becker's old flame?* Holy crap.

Becker blinked, stunned at her harsh tone. "Yeah. Are you still upset about what happened between us? What was I supposed to do after you broke up with me?"

"I broke up with you? Other way around, buddy." She made her way toward the sink, sputtering like a leaky faucet. "What the crap are you doing here anyway, Dave?"

He nodded toward Miranda. "I work with Steele. She invited me."

"What?" Slowly, Fanuzzi turned her head and glared at Miranda. "*You* invited him?"

Miranda shifted her weight. "Yeah. I thought I'd introduce you to each other. Guess I don't need to."

"We went to Brooklyn High together," Becker said. "Maybe we could get together sometime, Joan. Heck, like maybe now."

"Like when hell freezes over. I'm working, here." She glanced over at Miranda, her blazing eyes said, *I'll get you for this.* With a loud clatter, she set her stuff on a counter, picked up another tray, and left the room.

Miranda raced after her, caught her by the arm. "Fanuzzi, wait. What's going on?"

She spun around. "You tell me, Murray. I don't appreciate people sticking their noses in my personal business. I thought you were my friend." She brushed her off and stomped back to the appetizer table.

Miranda turned and saw Becker and Holloway standing at the other end of the hall. Becker looked bewildered.

She went over to him. "I'm sorry, Becker. I was just trying to get you out of your funk."

"I—I guess I should go home."

"At least stay and have a drink. It's on the house." Her lame joke fell flat.

Just then, a crash came from down the hall. Miranda's heart jumped to the ceiling. Was that gunshot? No.

There was a shriek. Everyone turned in the direction of the sound.

Miranda ran to peer down the hall just as the library door burst open and Delta emerged. With a wild look in her eyes, she raced down the passage, holding a hand to her cheek.

"What happened?" Miranda demanded as the woman reached her.

"He struck me. That monster struck me. Ms. Steele, I can't stay here another second." She rushed through the foyer and out the door.

Parker was at her side as they raced back to the library. She peered through the open door and saw Usher standing there alone.

"What happened?"

"What was the idea of inviting Delta Langford here tonight? I've never been so humiliated. I have a good mind to bring charges against the Parker Agency."

With a fierce growl he stomped past them and left.

175

CHAPTER THIRTY-ONE

Beside her, still in his suit, Parker stretched. "It's past midnight, Miranda. How many times are you going to relive this party?"

They were in the room with the zebra-skin rug, reviewing the digital recording on the big screen TV. The guests were gone. No one had stayed long after Delta and Usher had their blowup.

Fanuzzi had cleaned up and left without another word.

Miranda had had enough faux partying for a lifetime, but doggedly, she ran the recording back, trying to find a clue. She hit the Pause button and caught Usher's face, his bloodshot eyes wild with emotion.

Parker pointed at the screen. "That look is rather interesting."

She sat forward on the leather sofa, willing the image to reveal something. Parker ran a hand over her back, massaged the taut muscles between her shoulder blades. "Oh my, that feels good." She'd missed that glorious touch of his. It was almost enough to distract her.

"You did a good job tonight."

"Except that I failed to get Usher's confession. The whole point of the thing."

"The effort was still commendable."

She snorted in disgust at herself and sat back.

He studied her a moment, drinking in the features he had longed for a whole week. "I need to find a way to reward you."

She gave him a knowing glance. "I'm sure you'll come up with something."

He held her with a deep, intimate gaze, not unlike the one he used when they made love. Her heart fluttered.

"I was thinking of something unusual," he said in a sultry voice.

She looked away, reached for the soda she'd set on the coffee table. "Is this part of the Agency's bonus plan?"

"You could think of it that way." He stretched his arm across the back of the couch in that easy way of his. "If you could have anything in the world, Miranda, what would it be?"

176

She put down her drink, picked up the remote, and settled against his shoulder. "You know what I want. To find Amy." She was sorry she said it as soon as the words were out, but it was what she felt.

He lifted her hand and tenderly kissed her fingers. She felt his compassion course through her. And his frustration at being unable to give her the thing she wanted most. "Something else," he murmured after a moment.

She shrugged. "To solve this case."

He shook his head. "That's in your hands. Something material."

Did he really want to give her a present? She thought a minute. The first image that came to mind was riding along State Route 51 with a gnarly work buddy who called himself Yosemite Sam, her hair blowing in the wind. That was it.

"A motorcycle," she said with a grin.

Parker laughed out loud, relishing the sudden sparkle in her deep blue eyes. She was so unlike anyone he'd known. Other women wanted diamonds or pearls. Sylvia had always asked for exotic trips. But Miranda Steele wanted a motorcycle. How he adored her. "Is that really what you want?"

"I had a pal in Phoenix who taught me how to ride a few years ago. We'd go out together on weekends. He let me drive most of the time. I loved it." She'd wanted one ever since, but could never afford it.

His gaze was thoughtful. Miranda couldn't imagine Parker on a motorcycle.

"I might have guessed you'd ask for something like that. What color?"

"Red."

He eyed the cleavage of her dress. "You do look good in red. I'll see what I can do." He took the remote out of her hand and laid it next to her soda. Kissing her cheek, he murmured gently against her skin. "You should go to bed. You'll have a better perspective on the case in the morning."

Hmm. Bed. She longed to have Parker in her bed again. She turned and saw again the deep weariness in his eyes. He'd had a long flight. A long, disappointing week. Her heart melted for him. And herself.

"You go up," she told him softly. "I'll be there in a minute." She picked up the remote.

"Very well." He rose, kissed her tenderly on the forehead and left.

Glad he was home, she pushed the play button and the scene in the mansion's library began to move again.

The camera caught Delta, stiff, rigid, full of anger for the man before her. "I came here for Desirée."

"For Desirée?"

"Remember, Ferraro, it was *I* who introduced you to my sister."

"Need you remind me?" Usher flipped his bleached-blond hair over his shoulder and paced beside a bookcase. He shoved his hands into the pockets of his lilac suit and stopped to study one of the landscapes on the wall, as if critiquing it.

Miranda hadn't known Delta had introduced them. But she could imagine how guilty the woman must feel about it.

"Why shouldn't I? Since she's been gone, I'm reminded every day of the things you did to her."

Usher took his fists out of his pockets and began to open and close them. "What things?"

"What things? You made her life wretched, miserable."

Usher's lip quivered as it curled into a snarl. "It was her family who made her life wretched and miserable. You and her father."

"I'll admit Eli Langford is a poor excuse for a father, but Desirée and I loved each other. We were all we had."

Usher turned and stared at Delta as if he couldn't believe his own ears. "Hah," was all he could say.

"It was you who gave my sister drugs until she became hooked on them. You who drank with her night after night until she was ill."

He took a step toward her. "How would you know? You never paid attention to her."

"It was you, Ferraro, who gave her that fatal dose of PCP."

His eyes flamed, then comprehension flashed in them. "Who got you to come here tonight, Delta?" he demanded with a sneer.

"Miranda Steele invited me. She's with the Parker Agency."

"I know she's with the Parker Agency."

"Then you must know why she invited you."

He put a hand to his head, as if he were getting a massive migraine. "What are you talking about?"

"You put that fatal dose of PCP in Desirée's drink that day at the Steeplechase." There was a vicious glow in Delta's eyes that Miranda hadn't seen before.

"Shut up," he snarled.

"I know it. The press knows it. The police are about to know it. You won't get away with what you did to my sister much longer."

"Stop it, Delta." He made a sound like a wounded animal.

"Everyone knows you killed my sister, Ferraro. Miranda Steele is going to prove it."

He put both hands on his head, as if it were about to explode. "For heaven's sake, Delta. Leave me alone."

"You're going to jail, Ferraro."

His eyes rolled back in his head like he was going insane. "Shut up!" he screamed again. "How can you do this to me?"

"You'll rot in there. And then you'll rot in hell."

"Shut up! Shut up!" He shoved her hard.

She caught herself on the desk, knocking over a decorative pencil holder. "I can't tell you how much I hate you." She reared up and got in his face. "Murderer!"

"You bitch, you." He moved to her, slapped her hard.

"How dare you strike me?" She slunk away from him. Her fingers found a round green vase on the shelf. She picked it up and hurled it at him.

He ducked. It crashed against the wall. She ran from the room, crying.

Miranda stopped the recording and took a deep breath. Her pulse was pounding, her mind cloudy with the need for sleep.

But she couldn't let it go. Something wasn't right. Why did Delta seem like the aggressor and Usher like a whipped puppy?

One more time. She rewound to the place where Delta came into the library.

"What do you want, Delta?" Usher said as he stepped into the room.

This time, Miranda switched to the other camera and focused on Delta.

As if she didn't hear him, Delta moved to the bookcase. She ran her gloved hand over a set of books, a tender look in her eyes. She removed one from the shelf, opened it, and smiling, put a hand over her mouth. It was a sentimental smile, full of tender emotion. She closed the book and put it back, then turned toward Usher.

Miranda hit the Pause button. What was that about?

She rose and went down the hall to the library. It didn't take long to find the spot where Delta had been standing. There on the shelf, just at eye level were Parker's yearbooks from Westminster High School. One of them stuck out farther than the others. Delta hadn't lined them up evenly.

Miranda pulled it out and turned to the "Ps." Her heart skipped a beat. There was Parker at age eighteen. Young, full of life and vigor. So handsome, every girl in the school must have walked the halls with her tongue out. The same knockout that had grown into a mature man.

Across the page were the "Ls." In the upper left corner was a picture of Delta. She was no slouch, either. Gorgeous face. Thick, gold-red curls, big, bright green cat-like eyes. There was a look of longing in them.

She'd signed the book across the bottom of her photo. Slowly, Miranda ran her hand over the words written decades ago.

To Wade, Thou art to me a delicious torment.

Delicious torment? A shudder went through her. Good Lord. Delta Langford had been in love with Parker. Really in love. "Unpleasant history," her behonkus.

She tucked the yearbook under her arm and headed for the master bedroom.

CHAPTER THIRTY-TWO

"Okay, Parker. What the heck is this 'delicious torment' crap?" Miranda shoved the upstairs door open.

The room was dark. She plodded to the side of the bed. Parker was already under the covers, his eyes closed, his bare chest rising and falling under the satin sheets.

His masculine scent teased at her nose and her heart melted. He was exhausted. Okay, she'd talk about the yearbook tomorrow. She turned around to head for the closet, felt a tug on her skirt. She turned back. Parker's fist clung to the hem he'd snatched.

"Don't go," he said gently.

Her heart was in her mouth. "You were asleep."

"Not really." He pulled her to him, and as she leaned against his hard body, took her mouth in a fierce, sensuous kiss.

Welcome home, she thought giddily.

He reached around her, aiming for her breast and found the book under her arm. "What's this?"

She pulled back to regain her balance and got to her feet. Jealousy flooded her when she thought of that school photo of Delta Langford. It was a silly reaction. Childish. But she couldn't help it.

Okay. He'd asked. She turned on the light on the nightstand and flipped through the book till she found the right page. "What does this mean?"

Raising himself on one elbow, Parker squinted down at the book, a wisp of hair falling sexily over his forehead. She watched the lines in his face as memories registered. "*Delicious Torment*. It's a quote from an essay by Emerson."

She grimaced. "I wasn't checking for plagiarism."

He looked up at her. "What do you want to know, Miranda?"

"I want to know just what this 'unpleasant history' is between you and Delta Langford."

He exhaled heavily. This wasn't what he'd expected after being away a week. Memories of the past tore at his heart. Delta. His father. Laura.

Impatient, Miranda snatched the book out of his hand and laid it on the nightstand. "You don't have to tell me if you don't want to. It's none of my business, anyway." She walked away, started to pull off her party dress.

With a grunt, Parker sat up and ran his hands through his hair. He watched her hang up the dress, move to the dresser and wrestle herself into the gray T-shirt and the bikini-cut cotton panties she liked to wear to bed. She didn't flinch changing in front of him, now that they had been living together for over a week, but that didn't mean she wasn't irritated. Though she was blithely ignorant of the power her body held over him.

He wanted to ignore her question and simply take her in his arms and make love to her. But that wouldn't be fair. He glanced at the chairs that sat in the corner of the room.

It wasn't so long ago that she'd bared her soul to him in that very corner. How could she truly belong to him, if he were unwilling to share his own secrets with her?

He patted the mattress beside him. "Sit down."

Miranda turned around. Parker sat on the side of the bed, wearing only his underwear and his classic look of patience. Her body cried out with desire for him, but if he was ready to talk, she wanted to hear it. Holding her breath, she crossed the room and sat down gingerly next to him.

She waited.

He studied the carpet. "I was sixteen when my mother died. I had pneumonia that winter. She contracted it from me. She had a weak constitution."

"That's terrible. I'm so sorry," she said in a whisper, wondering if he blamed himself for her death.

He stared off into the distance, consumed by the painful memory. "My father and I had never gotten along, but her passing made things worse between us. I often wondered if he blamed me for her loss."

Mr. P? That was even worse than blaming yourself. So that was the heart of the rift between them. She'd never have guessed. "How awful," she murmured, not knowing what else to say.

"My older sister was already a freshman in college. My father said he didn't know how to raise a teenage son."

She blinked. "You have a sister?" He had never mentioned her.

He nodded. "Evelyn. She ended up helping my father run his real estate business, since I never wanted to. We don't see each other much. My reluctance to follow in my father's footsteps was usually at the center of our arguments."

Not the happy family she'd pictured. "Go on."

He let out a measured breath. "Two years later, my senior year at Westminster, I met a girl named Laura Turner. She was seventeen. I was eighteen. She went to a different school."

His eyes grew wistful. "There was a district Science Fair we both attended. She had a project comparing the vitamin content of various brands of grape juice." He smiled tenderly. "She wanted to be a nutritionist. I invited her to a school dance. We started dating."

Miranda's stomach twitched.

"Laura was young, sweet, pretty. Dark hair cut to her shoulders, intoxicating brown eyes. She was the oldest in her family. Both her parents worked, and she took care of her two younger brothers. Her father was a painter. He worked irregularly, had a problem with alcohol. He was an angry, violent man."

"Did he...?" her voice trailed off.

Parker turned to her. "Beat her?" His face grew grim. "I suspected it, but Laura would never admit it."

Miranda clenched her teeth. "Did he do...anything else?"

"I don't think so. I believe she would have told me that." Memories of Laura's bright eyes and infectious smile invaded his mind. She was always happy, despite her family problems. So long ago.

Miranda squeezed Parker's hand, knowing that what he'd said so far wasn't the worst of it. "Go on."

"I gave her my class ring. We called it going steady, but it was much more serious. I started driving Laura home from school every day. But it wasn't easy for us."

"Why?"

"My father, for one thing."

"Mr. P?"

He nodded. "He didn't like it a bit that I was dating a girl from the 'other side of the tracks,' as he called it. We fought bitterly over it. I always thought that if my mother had been alive, she could have made him understand. But she wasn't there. When I told my father I was in love with Laura and wanted to marry her, he said I couldn't see her again."

"No." It was hard to imagine Mr. P being so mean. He really must have mellowed over the years. It sounded like a different person from the one Miranda knew.

"So I started sneaking out to see her. My father didn't keep close tabs on me, so it wasn't very hard. He was absorbed in his business and starting to date himself about that time. Laura and I saw each other as much as we could. Our plan was to marry right after I finished high school. I wanted to get her out of her house." He paused at the memory of the tiny yellow clapboard home on Millege Road.

Miranda's heart ached. Parker's need to protect had surfaced early. She waited, glanced over at the yearbook on the nightstand. "What's all this got to do with Delta Langford?"

"Delta and I both attended Westminster. The Langfords had a home in Buckhead before Eli moved out to Aquitaine Farms. We were both seniors that year and had several classes together."

It was hard to picture the younger versions of Parker and Delta sitting at desks in a classroom. "And?"

He sat back against the pillows and raised his palms. "Delta 'claimed' me, for lack of a better word."

Miranda twisted to look him in the eye. "'Claimed' you?"

"Even then, she had emotional problems. She was obsessive." He looked away again with a scowl. "Somehow, she got it into her head that we were meant to be together. Our fathers were in the same business. It was almost as if we were related, she said. She decided that I belonged to her."

"And you knew this because…"

"She told her closest girlfriends, who told their boyfriends, who told me." He sighed in near disgust. "And then there was the time she caught me alone in an empty classroom and kissed me and tore at my clothes until I forced her to stop."

Oh yeah? "She fell in love with you hard."

He nodded slowly.

"But you weren't in love with her."

"No. She never appealed to me."

A sudden wave of relief hit her at that news. "So…?"

"She became…obsessed."

"Obsessed?"

"She told me she couldn't live without me. That she loved me desperately. She followed me. Left love notes in my locker. Called me at home."

"She stalked you."

"You might call it that."

Miranda tried to imagine the young Delta pining over Parker. Somehow, it seemed to fit with the little she knew of the woman. She'd always appeared emotionally distraught, but Miranda had assumed that was because of what had happened to her sister. "What did you do?"

"I didn't want to hurt Delta, but I had to tell her the truth. I arranged to see her. I told her I was in love with someone else who went to another school. She insisted on knowing who it was. I never should have told her."

She almost didn't dare to ask. "Why not?"

He took a breath as if it were painful to inhale. "There was a tall oak tree outside Laura's school building. It had a small hollow spot, where we would leave notes to each other. When I could get away, I'd leave her a note telling her when and where to meet me. Laura was driving by then and I chose various spots where no one would think to look for us. Where we could get away and be together, talk about the future. One time, Delta followed me and found out about the notes and our secret meetings."

"Did she tell your father?"

"No, I wish she had."

Again Miranda waited, almost not wanting to hear the rest of it.

"It was the last week of school. I was studying hard for exams, and I told Laura I couldn't see her until they were over. Delta knew that. She wrote a note to Laura pretending it was from me and hid it in the tree. She told Laura to meet me at Wisteria Park at ten o'clock that night. Even back then, it wasn't a safe place to go at night." He put his head in his hands.

"Did she go? Didn't she realize the note wasn't from you?"

"She might have. She should have known I would never ask her to meet me in a deserted spot like that. But she went anyway. She was trusting. She didn't know about Delta's obsession. I never told her. That was another mistake."

The silence hung in the air like a death knell. Miranda held her breath.

Parker lifted his head and continued. "It was the next day that my father came to me and told me Laura was missing. He'd heard it on the news. I hunted for her. The police hunted for her. But there was no trace of her anywhere." He ran his hand over his eyes. "A week later, they found her body in Peachtree Creek. She had been raped and stabbed to death."

Because she'd gone alone to a park at night. Like Miranda had gone to a bad part of town years ago. Her hand trembled, went to her mouth. "Someone raped and killed her? Who?"

"No one knew. I went to the police and demanded answers. They said they were working on it and if I really wanted to help, I'd join the force. There was an intense recruiting program going on at the time. As soon as I graduated, I did."

Miranda blinked, remembering he'd told her about this incident in cloaked terms before. This was his first case. The one that started his career. "And you found the killer."

He nodded. "A few years later, after I'd been promoted to detective and assigned to Homicide, I resurrected the case. The perpetrator turned out to be a sex offender who had been roaming the area looking for vulnerable prey. He killed a few other young girls as well around the time."

Miranda shuddered, her heart aching for the tragedy he'd been through. "And Delta?"

"After Laura's funeral, she confessed to me what she had done and said she was sorry. She never meant any harm to come to Laura. She just wanted to break us up." He smirked bitterly.

"Oh, my."

"Then she suggested that now Laura was gone, there was hope for us. I told her I never wanted to see her again."

Miranda stared at him, rubbing her arms. What a horrible thing for a young man of eighteen to go through. "No wonder you don't care for Delta Langford."

"That," he said with a twisted smile that wasn't a smile, "is an understatement. For a long time, I blamed her for what happened to Laura. I blamed my father. I blamed myself. But the years passed, and the pain lessened."

Unless someone reminded him of it. "I wish I'd never asked you to take on Desirée Langford's case."

"A professional puts his or her own feelings aside."

He'd done that for her, just so she could get her feet wet being the lead on a case. Why was he so good to her? She glanced at the yearbook sitting on the nightstand where she'd shoved it. "Sorry I reacted so…ridiculously."

He grinned, but there was still sadness in his eyes. "If the past weren't so painful, I'd have rather enjoyed that part."

Guess she'd admitted with her actions that she cared for him.

Tenderly, he reached for her hair, took a strand in his fingers and studied it. "Old memories. Old loves. I'd rather live in the present. You're the one I care about now, Miranda."

His fingers glided through her hair, moved to the back of her head to pull her close. He pressed his mouth to hers, laying her back on the bed. His lips tore into her, greedily, lovingly, savagely, as if his could push the past away by force. He lifted her T-shirt, cradled her breasts, lingered a moment, then slid down and clutched at her panties until they were gone.

He didn't wait. He plunged into her, frenzied, furious, as if he was trying to drive both of their demons away with the strength of his body.

Her hands slid over the hair in the middle of his chest, felt the smooth, muscular skin just over it. Reaching around him, she traced the impression of the scar on his shoulder and met him with her hips, just as full of need as he was, of fierce desire to think only of this instant. To feel only this moment. Only the two of them. Only now.

They came, fast and hard and together.

Parker buried his face in her hair as the throbbing subsided, his heavy breath beating against her ear, her neck. They lay there together, arms and legs entwined, and suddenly she wished she could hold onto the moment forever.

Parker's breath slowed. Kissing her, he murmured against her neck. "Be mine, Miranda."

Her throat tightened. His? What did he mean by that? She escaped from his arms, scooted up on the bed, heading for her pillow.

She ran her hand along his cheek in a conciliatory gesture. "It's late, Parker. I'm drained and I know you are, too. Let's talk tomorrow." She straightened the pillow and laid her head down. There was something hard underneath it. She frowned "What's under here?"

"I can't imagine." Parker raised himself on one elbow, studied her with a strange look in his eye.

Sitting up, she reached beneath the pillow and pulled out a small box. It looked suspiciously like a jewelry box. Ring size. Her mouth went dry. "Parker?"

He pulled himself nearer to her and smiled, traces of sadness reappearing around his eyes. "Perhaps the Tooth Fairy left it."

Her lips tightened. "I haven't been in any fights and lost a tooth lately."

"Open it."

Did she dare? Did she have a choice? Holding her breath, slowly, carefully, she lifted the lid. Her heart did a flip. Not a heady pulse of romantic thrill. This flip was fear. Pure dread.

Sure enough, inside the box was a ring. A gorgeous ring with an old-fashioned design. A center diamond, surrounded by alternating bands of smaller gems and blue stones. Probably sapphires.

She forced out a weak laugh. "I guess the Tooth Fairy has the hots for me."

"It belonged to my mother," he said quietly, watching her in that intent way of his.

Oh, no. She swallowed. This ring belonged to the mother Parker had lost at sixteen? Did he mean—? Was this—? No, not now. They were both dead tired. "Why do you want me to have this?" The innocent note in her voice quivered with deceit.

His hard gaze roamed to the tall windows a moment, then shot back at her with the force of a pistol. He edged closer to her on the bed. "Why do you think I want you to have it?"

She paddled with her elbows, her heels slipping against the satiny sheets as she inched away from him. She laughed again. "For doing a good job on the Desirée Langford case?"

Parker drew back. Inhaled. Exhaled. Stared down at the rumpled comforter that made a little wall between them. "If you'd rather have something more ostentatious…"

Her teeth clenched as she struggled with the waves of emotion that were now mostly anger. More ostentatious, her rear end. "Heck, Parker. What's this ring supposed to mean?"

"What do you want it to mean?" His voice reverberated with that low, penetrating tone.

"Dammit, stop being a detective for a second and answer the question," she snapped.

His gaze scanned the wall over her head. He wore the same look she'd seen when he was trying to decipher a clue to a murder. After a moment, with that casual air, he pulled himself up toward his pillow. "The conventional interpretation implies a promise of permanent cohabitation. Vows and such. But, being the renegades you and the uh, Tooth Fairy, are, you can put your own interpretation on it." His tender sarcasm hung in the room like a swamp fog.

She closed her eyes, fighting the urge to smack him. Why was he doing this? Was he really asking her to marry him? She couldn't marry him. She wasn't the marrying type. It would never work. But how could she tell him she couldn't take this ring after the things he'd revealed to her tonight? He'd bared his soul to her. How could she hurt him after that?

"What if—" She batted the air with one hand. "What if we don't come up with the same interpretation?"

His mouth turned in a grim half-grin. "All life is negotiation."

Negotiation, huh? Miranda closed the box with a sharp snap and put it on the nightstand. She lay down and pulled the comforter to her chin. "I think I need to sleep on it."

He watched her a long moment before he spoke. When he did, his voice was even sadder than before. "I thought you might say that. Take all the time you need." He reached for the light, turned it off, and rolled over on his side.

Away from her. He wasn't happy.

With a huff, Miranda turned over, faced the windows and stared into the darkness. All the time she needed? And how long did Parker think that would be? How long did it take to work up the courage to say no—again.

In the dark, she glanced over at the nightstand where the ring box sat. She couldn't see it, but she didn't need to. She squeezed her eyes shut. Good Lord, she couldn't marry again. Even if she wanted to. Even if she thought they might have a fighting chance. Because they didn't have a fighting chance. They didn't have any chance at all. She was a basket case when it came to marriage. Marriage for her and Parker would be a disaster. A catastrophe. A regular tsunami. Why couldn't he see that? Stubborn male testosterone. That was why.

But there was another question nagging at her heart. A question that had been hiding in the recesses of her mind ever since they'd first made love. A question she barely dared to think.

Did she want to marry Parker…anyway? Her breath caught. Did she want to throw caution to the wind, take the plunge, just do it, and any other cliché she could think of? Did she want to marry him, despite the failure that was sure to come? Despite the pain, the bitterness, the heartache for both of them? Did she? That was the sixty-four-thousand-dollar question.

Take all the time you need. Right.

As she closed her eyes and listened to his steady breathing, Miranda wondered just how patient Wade Russell Parker was going to be.

CHAPTER THIRTY-THREE

Monday morning, Judd was back at his instructor post at the Agency, with his characteristic panache—total deadpan. The current topic of study was firearms. Only the tall, lumbering, craggy senior investigator with the booming monotone voice could make shooting a gun sound boring.

Of course, they weren't really shooting. They were going over evidence for a crime scene shooting, and all the safety rules for using a weapon. Every rule. Word by word.

In a few weeks, those who had passed all the tests would be allowed on the practice range. The Agency would determine which employees would be allowed to carry on a case-by-case basis after graduation. So it was just an exercise.

Miranda sat in her chair, resisting the urge to drum her fingers on the desk. She didn't even have anyone to make snide remarks to. Holloway and Becker had planted themselves as far away from her as they could, on the opposite side of the classroom. Neither had even said so much as hello.

She ought to tell Parker about the Fanuzzi fiasco. That would show him how good she was with relationships.

Parker.

She thought of the ring still sitting on her nightstand.

"Take all the time you need," he'd said. But she knew he wanted an answer. And the longer she waited, the longer she stayed in the same bed with him and went on as if things were just peachy, the more she implied the answer was yes. She couldn't go on misleading him.

As soon as she'd gotten in this morning, she'd called Dr. Valerie Wingate's office. There was a slot available that afternoon at three. She'd taken it.

She was going to get this muddle in her heart worked out one way or the other.

She thought of the secrets Parker had told her and the vision of the young man grieving for his murdered fiancée reverberated in her heart. The man who trained himself to go after her killer with the tenacity only a brokenhearted lover could have. She felt...in awe of him.

More than that, she felt something deep within her being resonate with him. She didn't want to feel so close to Parker. She wished to high heaven she'd never asked him about Delta Langford and her "delicious torment" line. She wished she'd never gotten involved with the case.

But Desirée Langford's battered face still haunted her. She had to solve this murder.

Yesterday she'd watched the recording in the library again and come up with nothing. Delta had hit Usher hard with her accusations. Much harder than Miranda thought she was capable of. But he hadn't cracked.

Why? If he were so sensitive, how could he stand the things she'd said to him? Could he really be innocent after all? And where did that leave her?

She'd have to think about that one. Then it came to her.

The drugs. If she could pin the PCP on Usher, that would prove he killed Desirée.

But how was she going to do that?

Judd finished his lecture and dismissed the class for lunch. Miranda looked over at Becker. He glanced away.

Okay, be that way. She'd planned to treat him at the Horseradish Grille on Powers Ferry Road to make amends. But since he was being an ass, she'd just go by herself. If the food was good, she'd rub it in his face when she got back.

Miranda found a parking spot and strolled up the walkway to the restaurant's rustic exterior. Its white tin roof and cheery windows seemed to welcome her, as did the hedges, trees and flowers that lined the stony path to the entrance. There was an outdoor patio where diners chatted and ate in wrought iron chairs under green umbrellaed tables.

The friendly design was repeated on the inside with white walls, wooden floors, and white-tablecloth booths that overlooked the garden. At this hour, the place was crowded with businesspeople on lunch break.

As Miranda followed a hostess down a red carpet runner along the row of booths, she spotted a familiar face. A lean, professional-looking woman with dark brown hair pulled back in a simple elegant chignon. She was sitting by herself. Dressed in a plain gray suit, she was absorbed in paperwork she'd spread out on the table.

Wilhelmina Todd. The criminal defense attorney who worked at Antonio Estavez's law firm. When Parker introduced them at a party a few weeks back, Miranda had felt an instant connection to the woman.

"Would you like some company?" she asked, stopping at the lawyer's table.

Wilhelmina looked up, her eyes brightened. "Miranda Steele. It's good to see you. Yes, of course. Have lunch with me." She moved her papers to give her room.

"I'll sit here," Miranda said to the hostess, who nodded and handed her a menu. She turned back to Wilhelmina as she opened it. "I thought you were in Europe."

With a sad sigh, she finished packing her papers into her Gucci briefcase. "Felicia and I got back last week. I'm too much of a workaholic to stay away from the firm for long. And she missed her friends."

Miranda nodded.

Wilhelmina had had it rough lately. Shortly after her younger daughter was killed, she discovered her husband was having an affair. Her response was to divorce him and leave for Italy with her older daughter, Felicia.

A waitress came and took their orders. Miranda skimmed the menu. The only thing that looked both appealing and cheap enough was the catfish fingers with spicy mustard coleslaw. She ordered it. Wilhelmina ordered a green field salad.

"You look good," Miranda said after the waitress left their table.

"Thank you." She smiled, but Miranda could see the lingering grief behind her eyes.

She hesitated a moment, before she spoke. "I know the last month must have been hell for you."

The last time she'd seen the woman, she'd been hysterical over the death of her daughter.

She reached across the table and gave Miranda's arm a warm squeeze. "I never got to thank you for…everything. For finding Tiffany's killer."

Miranda shrugged. "All in a day's work."

"I suppose, but it means a great deal to me and Felicia."

Miranda nodded, wishing she could bring back the woman's daughter.

The waitress delivered their orders. They both began to pick at their food. The conversation wasn't conducive to a hearty appetite.

Wilhelmina lifted her chin and tried to sound breezy. "So what has that sexy slave driver of a boss of yours got you doing these days?"

If she only knew. But she saw no reason to hide the truth—about her work. "Desirée Langford's death."

Wilhelmina frowned. "I read about that in the paper. At the Northwinds Steeplechase, wasn't it?

Miranda took a bite of catfish and nodded. The food was good.

"Didn't the papers say her death was a suicide?"

"Some people don't think so." Miranda wiped her mouth with a napkin.

"Hmm. It was a PCP overdose, wasn't it?"

She nodded. "That was the official COD."

"But you think there was more to it?"

"Don't know yet."

Wilhelmina raised a hand. "I didn't mean to pry. I, of all people, should know the rules of confidentiality."

Confidentiality. A good excuse to use when you couldn't prove squat. She changed the subject. "How are things going at the law firm?"

"Busy, but it's my own fault. I asked for a heavy caseload when I got back. I just need work to keep my mind off of...things."

"Right." Again, Miranda's heart went out to her. She eyed her a moment. "I don't mean to sound judgmental, but I've always wondered how someone does a job like yours."

Wilhelmina gave her a sly grin. "You must have worked with a few defense attorneys in your career."

"Some." A couple of times, she'd been appointed a public defender when she was jailed for a bar fight. And then there was Antonio who got her out on a murder rap. Wilhelmina didn't know about that. Miranda intended to keep it that way.

"I know we can be annoying. The standard answer is that everyone deserves a fair trial. But the truth is it's all about billable hours and highbrow clients who can pay them. Not unlike the PI business." She took a sip of iced tea.

"Touché." The longer Miranda knew Wilhelmina Todd, the more she liked her. She sat back. "Did you ever have a client you couldn't defend?"

"Do you mean because I knew the client was guilty as sin and my conscience wouldn't let me twist the facts?"

Miranda nodded.

She put down her fork and thought a moment. "Not many, but I can think of two recent cases."

"And did you have to defend them anyway?"

"Oh, no. Chatham, Grayson, and McFee has its scruples. The firm let me recuse myself. Of course, the clients didn't like it, but they found another firm to take their cases."

"What were they guilty of?"

"One was a child predator." Her eyes narrowed as she stared out the window a bit.

She was thinking of Leon Groth, Miranda knew.

"And the other was a young, ambitious drug lord."

"Drug lord?" Now that was interesting. "Here in Atlanta?"

She nodded. "A local gang leader. You probably know that for about a decade now, the higher-ups in the Colombian drug cartels have broken up their organizations into smaller units."

She didn't know that, but pretended to. "Street gangs."

"Sometimes. The leaders of those gangs often have as much clout as the old drug lords, in their own areas. This one does. He's young, good-looking and ambitious. His group is large and growing."

"Charismatic leader, huh?"

"Very." Wilhelmina leaned forward, her face suddenly bright with interest. "But this guy's selective. He likes to prey on the rich. He likes his toys, too—cars, motorcycles, booze, parties, women."

Not in that order, Miranda bet. "And he deals drugs?"

"Best business in town." Wilhelmina attacked her salad like a witness on the stand.

Nerves and excitement shimmied up Miranda's spine. She asked the obvious question. "Do you mean he might have clients like upcoming artists and wealthy horse breeders?"

Wilhelmina stopped chewing, tilted her chin. "You mean Desirée Langford, don't you?"

Miranda grinned. "And Ferraro Usher, her ex-husband."

Her eyes glowed. "Far be it from me to ask you about your suspects, but come to think of it, that's exactly the type of client this guy would prefer."

Miranda played with her napkin. "The hundred milligrams of PCP that killed Desirée Langford had to come from somewhere. If I can find out who sold it, I might be able to find out who bought it. Desirée herself or her killer."

Wilhelmina pointed her fork at her approvingly. "I can see why Wade Parker hired you, Miranda. You're good."

Not good enough, yet.

"If this guy didn't cut the deal himself, he'd know who did."

"He has that much power?"

Wilhelmina nodded. "Unfortunately."

Dave Becker had done her a big favor. By snubbing her for lunch, he'd let the clue she'd been searching for all these weeks fall right into her lap. Her heart thumping, trying not to grin too hard, Miranda leaned close to her lunch partner and whispered. "So what's this guy's name?"

Wilhelmina gave her a satisfied look that said she had just read Miranda's mind. "Carlos Santiago."

When Miranda got back to the office, she had just enough time before Martial Arts class to do some research on her computer. She looked up Carlos Santiago and found several articles on him describing his arrests in various drug busts and gang-related shootings. A slippery guy. Though Wilhelmina Todd had refused to be his lawyer, he'd found an attorney who was able to help him beat every rap.

Her lunch partner was right. This was one bad dude.

She went through another set of links and finally found a picture of the drug lord after his release.

Black curls heavy with styling gel. A pronounced widow's peak. Eyes sharp as razors. Black mustache and beard, trimmed to a point. His arms and hands folded in a gang gesture, he was dressed all in black with heavy gold chains around his neck, one a thick cross. Must be real devout.

She sat back in her chair, gasping like the wind had been knocked out of her. *It was him.* The guy she'd seen in Usher's art gallery the night of his showing.

Excitement pulsed through her veins. She was close. She knew it. Her mind whirled with the details she's just read. Then her heart sank to the seat of her chair.

What in the world could she do with the information?

A reminder popped on her computer. Time for class. She closed the browser and got to her feet. She didn't have an answer yet, but she'd figure out something.

CHAPTER THIRTY-FOUR

Miranda fidgeted in the semi-comfortable chair in Dr. Valerie Wingate's office. The therapist sat across from her at the obligatory forty-five-degree angle waiting with the patience of Job, for her to open up.

Dr. Wingate was a petite woman with fine blond hair she wore pulled back from her face and intense, perceptive, brown eyes. Eyes that now studied Miranda from behind a pair of square-shaped glasses. She wore a charcoal gray pants suit, a plain white shirt, very little jewelry.

Obviously, the serious type.

Miranda took a breath, searching for words. She didn't know how to act with a shrink she halfway respected.

At last, Dr. Wingate broke the silence. "If you don't have something specific you want to discuss, we can treat this session as a consultation, Ms. Steele. Just time to feel each other out and see if we want to continue with further visits." Her voice was warm, soothing. No pressure.

Miranda remembered the sound of that voice when the doctor had come to see her at Saint Benedictine's after Leon slashed up her chest. That voice had given her hope then. Hope of what, she wasn't sure.

She stared down at her hands, which were laced together in her lap. "I do want to talk about something specific."

"Go on, then. Whenever you're ready."

Miranda scanned the office. It was bright and cheery, with a tall window, a very neat, simple oak desk, bookshelves with medical texts and pictures of what must have been the doctor's family, a nice set of framed diplomas on the wall.

She took a deep breath. If she didn't get on with it, her time would be up. She couldn't wait another week. "I have sort of a...relationship. With this...guy." She exhaled. Dang, why was this so hard?

"What kind of relationship?" The doctor's voice was so quiet, it was almost as if her words came from Miranda's own head. Pretty good shrink trick.

"That's what I'm here to figure out."

"I see." She sat forward.

Miranda smirked. Why speak in cloaked terms? "I guess you know who I'm talking about."

She smiled compassionately. "Wade Parker."

Pretty straightforward for a therapist. She rubbed her forehead.

"Nothing you say will go outside this room, Ms. Steele." she said in a sweet, reassuring tone. "Patient confidentiality is something I hold very highly."

Miranda folded her hands, unfolded them again. "I wasn't worried about that."

"Good." She sat back. "What are your feelings about this relationship you mentioned?"

"My feelings?" Her mouth opened, then shut.

The doctor waited.

She rubbed her nose. "The sex is pretty good."

"That's encouraging."

"I guess." Or it would be, if it were a serious relationship. They couldn't keep on being just fuck buddies.

"Have you considered why the sex is so great?"

She laughed. "It's Wade Parker."

The doctor smiled. "Yes."

The most desirable man in town. But that didn't really explain it. Miranda didn't care about his money or his status. Was it his skill, his essential, core sexiness? That didn't account for it all, either. It must be his tenderness, the care she could feel in his every touch, whether gentle or rough. And how much he wanted her. And the feelings he aroused in her. For him.

Dr. Wingate spread her hands. "Do you love him?"

Miranda blinked in surprise. This shrink shot straight from the hip, didn't she? She ran her tongue over her teeth.

Were those feelings…love? Was it love that made the sex so fantastic? If that were so, then she'd loved him weeks ago. That couldn't be right. She shook her head. "I can't say."

"Does he love you?"

Of course, he did. He showed her in a thousand ways, though he'd never said it. Not since the time she went into orbit at those three little words and walked out on him. He was too smart to make the same mistake again.

She shrugged. "He seems to."

"And?"

"And?" Miranda echoed. She blew out a breath.

Love. That was the problem. She understood fear, despair, disappointment and pain. She didn't know what to do with love. "He gave me his mother's ring."

"Oh." Dr. Wingate sat up. "What do you think he meant by that gesture?"

Miranda smirked. "What else? Commitment. Permanence. Forever after."

"And?"

"And I froze. I have no idea what to do. What to tell him."

Dr. Wingate's face grew serious and thoughtful as she nodded. Leaning forward, she spoke in that gentle voice again. "It's hard to trust after what you've been through."

From her visit to the hospital, the newspapers, and the short discussion they'd had at the beginning of this session, Dr. Wingate had the gist of her past.

Miranda didn't know what had possessed her to mention the time Leon went after her with a coat hanger when she'd forgotten to iron his favorite shirt, on the preliminary forms she had filled out in the reception room. Or the time Leon called her a filthy whore and threw her out of the house. That was after she'd been raped by a stranger.

She stared blankly at the wall where Dr. Wingate's diplomas hung. "I've got so much anger stored up inside me, there's no room for love."

The doctor was silent for a long moment, taking in her words. "And yet, you feel something for Wade."

Miranda winced. Wade. She lived in his house, worked in his company, ate the meals he had prepared for her, slept in his bed. And yet she couldn't even bring herself to call him by his first name.

"That's just it. I think I feel something, but I can't connect with it. It's like something's dead inside me."

"We talked about that when I came to see you in the hospital."

Miranda nodded. That cold deadness she felt after her fight with Leon. Dr. Wingate had said it would pass.

"Has it gotten any better?"

Miranda thought a minute. "I've been working a case. I feel normal when I'm doing that. Excited. Alive."

"Sounds like a good career choice for you."

Miranda stared at her. It was, wasn't it?

"But you can't let yourself feel 'normal' about Wade Parker?"

She squirmed in her chair. "Parker's a good man. Even a great man. But he's not perfect."

"What do you mean?"

"For one thing, he's demanding. And overprotective."

The doctor nodded.

"And he pampers me too much. I don't want to be dependent on a man."

The doctor sat quietly.

No, that wasn't it. Those were things they could work out. Parker would listen if she told him how she felt. He'd understand. He was so dang understanding.

Miranda stood up. She couldn't sit in that chair another minute. "And he's bossy," she said, dragging a hand through her hair. She thought of those stupid stipulations of his. "He doesn't treat me like an equal. Like he'd treat my peers." She felt like a whiny little kid.

Again, the doctor nodded.

Miranda stomped to the tall window. Hugging herself, she stared out of it. Down below a willow tree bowed its branches low to the ground. A rose bush climbed a nearby white fence.

That wasn't true. Parker had lavished her with so much special treatment, Becker and Holloway were purple with envy. She knew Parker's "stipulations" were just his way of protecting her after what she'd been through. After what he'd been through with his first love, Laura.

From across the room, the quiet voice spoke again. "Are you afraid he'll hurt you? Physically?"

She sucked in a shallow breath. Was that what she was really afraid of? "I can't imagine Parker doing that," she heard herself say.

Another pause. "So there's some level of trust." She sounded pretty sure of that.

That was right, Dr. Wingate knew Parker intimately. She'd been his therapist, too. The doctor knew she couldn't make a case for thinking he'd get violent in a relationship.

There was another pause, then the doctor spoke, sounding like the voice in her head again. "So what *are* you afraid of, Miranda?"

She stared out the window. She stood so close, her breath formed a film on the pane. She traced the outline of the willow tree on the glass as her mind slowly cleared, and the aching reality emerged from the fog. "Sooner or later, Parker will get sick of my problems."

That was it. The truth. She closed her eyes as the waves of pain tremored through her. "I have so much rage inside me. So much hurt. I'll lash out at him. I'll find a way to punish him for what others have done to me. I won't be able to stop myself. Sooner or later," she forced down a gasp, slapped herself on the chest. "Sooner or later, I'll become the abuser. And Parker won't take that. He'll get fed up."

Dr. Wingate watched her for several long moments. "And leave?"

"Or tell me to." What if Parker threw her out of his house the way Leon had done years ago? "I don't think I could handle that." Her voice cracked.

She turned away from the window, went back to the chair, held her head in her hands. It was pounding. She wanted to cry. She wanted to scream. She wanted to let it all out. All of it. But her eyes were dry. She raised her head and peered at Dr. Wingate. "So it's best not to get started, isn't it?" But it was already beyond that point.

The doctor studied her carefully a moment. "Your past haunts you, doesn't it?"

Miranda looked down at the floor and nodded. The woman could read her soul.

"You've made progress, but I don't think you can have a healthy relationship until you heal more."

"That's my problem, Doctor." She blinked in surprise as the tears finally formed in her eyes. "It's been thirteen years. I've been to therapists, tried all sorts of things, but I can't get over—"

"What?"

"This rage. This anger inside. It eats away at me. Drives me away—"

"From people?"

The tears rolled down her cheeks. She covered her face with her hands and sniffed.

Dr. Wingate rose and came to her side, handed her a tissue. Gently she touched her back. "Your problem is that you let what happened long ago drive you away from the present. You have to learn to distinguish past from present. You have to stand your ground. Face your fears. Defeat them instead of letting them defeat you."

She looked into that wise, pretty face. "How?"

"One step at a time." Dr. Wingate looked at the clock. "We're past our hour. Would you like to make another appointment for next week?"

Miranda wiped her eyes with the tissue. "Yeah," she said absently. "Next week is good."

But for now, she had something more immediate in mind.

Tapping her foot on the worn, sterilized carpet, Miranda rode the creaky elevator to the third floor of Brandywine-Summit Memorial Hospital. She had gone straight back to the mansion after her session with Dr. Wingate this afternoon, stopping only long enough to call the office and give the receptionist an excuse about car trouble for not coming back to work.

Finding nothing in her closet, she'd gone on a quick, impulsive shopping spree. Now she scratched at the itchy elastic waistband of the draped teal blue dress she'd selected at Belk's for this mission. She'd tucked her dark hair under a broad-rimmed straw hat with a matching ribbon that she'd found, and had donned a pair of silver earrings and leopard heels that were on the bargain table.

A pair of dark sunglasses completed the outfit. At first glance, Parker himself might not have recognized her.

At the reception desk, she passed herself off as the patient's sister, Emily, from out of town. He'd had a sister Emily who'd died at birth. She was banking on the overworked staff being unaware of that fact. They were, and she got the room number.

Two sixty-one.

When the elevator doors opened to the Trauma Center, she sidled past the nurses' station, hoping no one would spot her. Fortunately, the workers were too busy tending to the injured patients.

She followed a sign pointing to room two sixty-one around a corner and saw a policeman stationed at the door about halfway down the hall.

She stopped and ducked behind a wall. She waited, then peeped out from her spot. The guard didn't see her. After a moment, he settled down into a metal chair next to the door and crossed his arms. She waited longer.

Five minutes later, his chin was on his chest, and Miranda could hear steady puffs of air coming from between his lips.

Keeping watch over a near corpse for days on end must get pretty boring.

Noiselessly, she emerged from her hiding place, shimmied down the hall, quietly turned the doorknob to two sixty-one and stepped inside.

The room was silent except for the measured beep-beep of the heart monitor and the steady pump of the breathing machine. The dry, stuffy air had that inconsistent hospital smell of medicine and bodily odors.

Slowly, she moved to the side of the bed. *Face your fears*, Dr. Wingate had said. No other reason to be here.

With a shudder, she forced herself to look down at the patient.

Leon lay motionless, except for the strained, regular movement of his chest up and down. His face was pale, cold. His hands lay still over his chest. For a long while, she simply stood there, listening to the rhythm of the machines, as though in a trance.

He was here because of her. She'd put him in this bed, in this condition, and she wasn't sorry. She stared down at his large, knobby hands.

She felt sick.

He had been in a coma for over a month now. And yet, standing here, she was afraid of him. Terrified. As if he might open his eyes at any moment and reach up with one of those thick hands and grab her throat.

She remembered the night he'd done just that after they'd been married a few months. It was the first time he'd attacked her. She'd thought he was going to kill her then. And several times after that.

She'd married him to get away from her mother. The dark, lean stranger in a black leather jacket and jeans who'd hung around the high school was the James Dean type. Dangerous. Exciting. Her mother had hated him. Miranda hadn't cared. He was her way out of the dreary, monotonous life she had at home. A life with no promise of anything. No future, but scrubbing floors and toilets, like her mother did.

It wasn't long after she'd married Leon that she'd begun to think the floors and toilets might have been the better alternative.

She thought of the time he didn't like the tuna fish casserole she'd made for dinner. He'd picked the bowl up with one of those big, gnarled hands and hurled it against the dining room wall. Noodles and mushroom soup and broken glass everywhere. Then he'd made her clean it up.

He'd apologized afterward. He always apologized. But he'd always do it again. Each time a little worse.

And then she was raped when he sent her out to a bad part of town late at night. And she got pregnant. And all he felt for her after that was hate. A murderous hate that had followed her for thirteen years. Haunted her. Driven her from place to place, as though he were stalking her. It hadn't been until a month ago that she'd learned he had been stalking her.

Face your fears.

"You can't hurt me anymore, Leon," she whispered to the comatose body. "You can't control my life." But her words were hollow.

Control her life? Leon Groth had ruined her life, dominated it, even when he wasn't there. No matter how hard she'd tried to escape him.

She fingered Parker's ring in her pocket. Before she'd gone shopping for her disguise, she'd picked it up off the nightstand where it had sat since the night Parker gave it to her. She squeezed her eyes shut as regret washed over her.

She had found a man who truly loved her. A man who treated her with tenderness and kindness and respect. Wade Parker was the best thing that had ever happened to her. But Leon would ruin that, too.

She loathed him for it.

She loathed him for all of it. He'd taken her daughter. He'd taken her soul. He'd taken everything.

Why wouldn't he die?

She glared at the ventilator, the thick blue tubes coming out of it. There was a round white connector that joined the main tube to the machine. She could loosen it. Just a turn or two and the machine would malfunction. She could stand right here and watch the life seep out of him, just as he'd made any hope for happiness seep out of her. Would it be worth it to go to prison for the rest of her days? For an instant, she thought it might be.

Hesitating, she stared at the machine. Her heart beat in her ears. From the corner of her eye, she watched those hands of his. Suddenly, one of them moved.

Yikes. Her hand went over her mouth, her heart jack hammering. Was she going crazy?

Across the room, the door opened. Slowly, a nurse entered. "Excuse me." She stared at Miranda with a disapproving frown.

"How is he?" she asked, trying to sound concerned.

The nurse moved to the bed, efficiently checking the tubes and the IV. "Not well." Her voice was a sharp whisper.

"How long…has he got?" It would help to know that.

"The doctors don't know. The coma could be indefinite."

"Indefinite," Miranda echoed in a hollow murmur.

The nurse finished with the IV and shot Miranda another scowl. "I didn't know this patient was allowed visitors. How did you get in here?"

"I'm his sister." Maybe she could stir up some compassion.

Her look remained cold. "Leave your personal information at the front desk."

"Sure. I was just going, anyway." Miranda brushed past her and out the door.

It hadn't worked. Dr. Wingate meant well, but facing her fears hadn't done a thing. How could it? She'd never get beyond the horrors of her past.

But her visit to the therapist had made her see the truth at last. The history of abuse ran through her veins just as strong and sure as Parker's vaunted lineage ran through his. Sooner or later, she'd betray him. Sooner or later, she'd turn on him like a rabid dog. No man, not even a saint like Parker would put up with that. She'd been right all along.

They never had a future.

As she pushed open the revolving doors of the hospital and headed for her car, all she could think of was that she wanted to get drunk. Maybe she could talk Fanuzzi into going slumming.

CHAPTER THIRTY-FIVE

Fanuzzi was prickly as a rabid porcupine in heat when Miranda called. But after a half hour of empathy over the agonies of the single life and the road crew job, Miranda had her eating out of the palm of her hand. Or least softened up enough to have a drink on the Buckhead strip.

It was around nine o'clock when they sat down at a table in a noisy, upscale yuppie bar on Peachtree Road. Miranda was delighted when Fanuzzi ordered a dollar Bud. None of that fancy Russian Stout crap.

"Nothing drowns your sorrows better than cheap beer," she said.

Fanuzzi nodded. "Got that right."

After a couple more bottles, they decided to make the rounds.

Heading south down Peachtree, they hit Bliss, Uranus, Tongue and Groove, the World Bar. The gaudy neon lights glimmered happily along the vibrantly painted buildings, and with each stop, life seemed a little brighter.

By the time they slid into a booth at Locos, they were both pretty sloshed. Miranda tapped her hands on the thick wooden table, in time to the loud seventies music a DJ was playing. He wore a big, blond Afro, a tie-dyed T-shirt, and a smile like a Jack-o-lantern. On a stand, he'd suspended one of those old-fashioned reflecting disco balls, and with his hands raised in the air, he cast weird shadows on the walls as he danced along to his own tunes.

"Now there's a guy who knows how to have fun," Fanuzzi smirked.

"Yeah, right. I think it's time to order some food and sober up a bit," Miranda said. If that guy was starting to look appealing, they needed to slow down. Besides, neither of them could afford a DUI.

Fanuzzi agreed and ordered a burger and fries. Miranda decided on the Looney Bird, which was smoked turkey and Swiss cheese. Kind of bland, but the chicken wings sounded anemic. They ordered a couple more beers as well. Had to have something to wash it down.

"Men," Fanuzzi said, taking a swig from her bottle after the waitress set them down and left. "You can't kill 'em. And you can't kill 'em."

Miranda pointed a finger at her. "Dang straight." She took a slug of her own bottle. It was nice and cold, but starting to get a little boring. She wanted to switch to something harder, but she'd better just quit.

After another song or two from the DJ, the waitress brought two big plates of food. They both sat staring at them awhile.

Miranda glanced up at Fanuzzi's drawn face. She looked worn out. It was rough working two jobs and taking care of three kids. "I'm sorry about that mess at my party."

"Party?" Fanuzzi frowned a minute, as if she didn't remember. Then she waved a hand. "Sorry I acted so pissy. You were just trying to do something nice."

Miranda picked up her sandwich and took a bite. Pretty good. She wiped her mouth and swallowed another swig of beer. "So why did you? Act so pissy, I mean." Might as well find out, since they were starting to get chummy again, and their tongues were getting loose.

Fanuzzi's brows shot up, then she shrugged. "I don't know. It was just…"

"What?"

She grabbed the ketchup bottle and squeezed a small puddle onto her plate. "When I walked into your kitchen and saw Dave Becker standing there, I just freaked. Talk about a blast from past."

"Guess I should have warned you."

"It wouldn't have helped."

Now she was curious. After all, Becker was her buddy. "So how come you freaked? Didn't you like him? Back in high school, I mean?"

Fanuzzi chewed on her burger and stared dreamily at the cascading lights of the disco ball, as if she were reliving a scene from her youth. "Like him? Heck, we were crazy in love. We wanted to get married."

A bit of sandwich stuck in Miranda's throat. She forced it down and blinked at her friend. "Married?"

"We went steady. He gave me his class ring. I wore it around my neck on a chain. We always talked about getting hitched after we graduated."

"Jeez, Fanuzzi. What happened?"

She took sip of beer, then picked up a fry and dragged it through the ketchup on her plate. "My folks were against it. So were his. We were only sixteen."

"So you didn't run away together or anything?"

She made circles with the fry in the ketchup. "We were planning to, but before we could, my dad got a different job. We moved to Yonkers, and I transferred to another school. Dave was so mad, he made me give his ring back."

"And that was that?"

She lifted the fry and bit off the end of it. "I wrote him, tried to apologize. We kept in touch for a while, but you can't keep up a relationship that way when you're young."

Miranda picked up her sandwich again. "Guess not."

"By the time I graduated, I had met Daryl."

"Daryl?"

"My ex. He made me forget Dave. So I wrote him a 'Dear Dave' letter and told him it was over."

"Ouch." But the new love didn't last. "What broke you two up? You and Daryl." She studied her bottle. Must be the suds that were making her so nosey tonight.

Fanuzzi leaned on the table and put her chin in her hand. "He was a cop. A good one. Too good. Married to his job. The longer we were married, the less I saw of him."

"Rough, huh?"

She nodded. "I put up with it for a long time. Told myself he was just doing his duty and I shouldn't complain. I don't know how we managed to conceive three kids, he was gone so much."

She got that dreamy look again. This time it was bitter. "He didn't mean to neglect us. He really didn't even know he was doing it. He'd stay away, working on a case, sleep at the station. Being a single mom isn't all that much different."

"Sounds awful."

"One day, I'd had enough. It was our anniversary. Daryl had promised to take me out. He didn't show. Didn't come home for three days straight. I took the kids and went to my mother's."

Miranda put down her beer. "Then what?"

"He comes home so exhausted, he doesn't even realize we're gone. Next day, he gets up and goes back to work again. A few days later, he calls my mother and asks if I'm there. Mother of gawd." She shook her head bitterly. "It had been a whole week by then. A whole freaking week it took him to figure out I had left him. That was when I knew for sure it could never work."

Miranda frowned with sympathy. "That's too bad, Fanuzzi. My ex was a cop, too."

"So you know what it's like."

Miranda smirked. "It would have been better for me if my ex had stayed away like Daryl did."

Fanuzzi's eyes shot open. "I'm sorry, Murray. I forgot what a psycho you were married to."

Miranda took another swallow from her bottle. "It's okay. Wish I could forget." She let out a laugh. "We're a couple of real headaches aren't we?"

"Guess we are."

Miranda looked around at the other customers. She'd been itching for a fight, but there was nobody obnoxious enough to give her an excuse to punch. Too bad.

Fanuzzi waved her hand. "I don't want to talk about me anymore. Hey, how's your investigation going? The one the party was about?"

"Kind of stalled. But I got sort of a tip the other day."

"What? Can you tell me?"

"Sure. It was about the guy who might have sold Usher the PCP. He might have been a drug lord."

Fanuzzi's chin dropped. "Did you say *drug lord?*"

Miranda drained her beer, set it on the table with a nod. "Yep."

"Holy crap, Murray. Daryl used to work undercover. He knew some gang creeps and told me stories that would make my skin crawl. What are you going to do?"

She had no idea. Yet. "I'm working on it." Something was bound to click in her head sooner or later. With a yawn, she pushed back her plate. "Where to now?"

Fanuzzi looked at her watch. "I'd better get home, Murray. Charlie has soccer practice in the morning."

Laughing, Miranda handed the waitress some cash. "Never thought of you as a soccer mom."

"Hey, he likes it. And it gets rid of some of his aggression, so he won't beat up his little brother so much."

The joys of parenthood. There were some advantages to being childless, Miranda told herself, as they headed out the door. But it might have been the beer talking.

They'd had to park a good distance away from the main road, due to the volume of Friday night revelers on the Buckhead strip. They strolled together along Peachtree, passing storefronts and groups out for a good time. The lights were almost as bright as daylight.

At a traffic light, they turned right onto a side street and walked another block. There were cars parked along both curbs, but no one was around. The streetlamps grew fewer, the sidewalk darker as they went. They had just reached the parking lot of a strip mall when an engine roared on the road next to them.

Miranda heard male voices. A bit of Spanish.

"A C note says my hog can beat your streetfighter, amigo."

"You're on."

She turned her head. Two men on motorcycles cut into the entrance in front of them, forcing them to stop. Engines revving, they took a couple of turns and came to a halt right in the middle of the parking lot.

One of them got off his cycle, leaned against it like the bad guy in a video game. He pointed his chin, along with its black goatee, straight at them. "*Buena tarde, señoras.*"

Miranda's pulse spiked. She felt every hair on her body come to attention as she took in sharp eyes, the slick black curls, the widow's peak. Black boots and jeans, metal chain belt hanging low on his waist, a sleeveless black tank top, revealing the barbed and twisted tattoos that climbed along his muscular biceps. Around his neck hung a single gold chain with a heavy cross at the end. Just like in the picture she'd found on the Internet.

Carlos Santiago.

He must be dressing down tonight. She remembered Wilhelmina Todd said he was expanding his operation. Were his followers becoming a motorcycle gang? Or had he just been out bar hopping? Buckhead would be his style.

Beside her, Fanuzzi shivered. "What the heck is going on, Murray?" she whispered.

"Not sure yet. But it looks like a street race."

"You sure that's all it is?"

Santiago chuckled. "What are you ladies doing out so late?"

"Minding our own business," Fanuzzi said. "We were just leaving. C'mon, Murray."

"Wait a minute." Miranda didn't budge. She stared at the cycles. Santiago's was a low riding black and silver. V-Twin engine, shiny chrome exhaust.

Francisco's was a big, aggressive-looking hog with a wide rear tire and stainless steel, drag-style handlebars. It was blood red. The glossy spokes and fenders glimmered under the streetlights. Miranda lusted to feel the power of one of those engines. Besides, if this wasn't opportunity, she didn't know it.

She nodded toward the bike Santiago had just dismounted. "That's a cool-lookin' chopper."

He folded his arms and grinned. "You have good taste, *señora*."

"The name's Miranda."

"Miranda," he repeated, rolling the r in that sexy Latin way.

"I didn't catch your name."

He lifted a sharp brow. "Carlos."

Bingo. She knew it was him. "Glad to know you, Carlos."

He seemed very amused. "Do you like motorcycles, Miranda?"

"Do I," she said.

"Francisco and I were just debating which one of these beauties was superior. We were about to settle it with a little Mat Rempit."

Yosemite Sam, the buddy who'd taught her to ride, had told her about Mat Rempit. It was a Malaysian term for illegal street racing. Her hunch had been right. She pointed toward the red one. "My money's on the hog."

"Do you think so?"

She waited a beat. "I'd be surer if I was driving it."

Next to her, Fanuzzi suppressed a squeal.

Santiago chuckled. The sinister man took a step toward them. "Are you challenging me to a race, Miranda?"

A frosty shiver went through her that was both excitement and dread. She fought to keep her breathing steady. She hadn't been on a bike in years, but it would come back. She put her hands on her hips. "What's the matter, Carlos, can't take the heat?"

Fanuzzi hissed in Miranda's ear. "What the world are you doing, Murray?"

"My job," Miranda muttered back.

"Are you out of your freaking mind?"

She had a point. The guy who'd taught her to ride had also warned her to stay away from motorcycle gangs. The way they treated women made Leon

Groth look like a Sunday school teacher. But this wasn't Hell's Angels, it was Carlos Santiago's gang. Maybe that was worse.

But a woman was dead, and her killer was getting away with it. Miranda was supposed to be a professional investigator. If this guy was the one who sold the lethal dose of PCP that killed Desirée Langford, it was her job to find out. But first, she had to take care of Fanuzzi.

She turned back to Santiago. "Uh, my friend here's had a little too much to drink. She needs to go home."

Santiago's black eyes gleamed in the streetlamps. "Are you chickening out, Miranda?"

"Not me. Her." She turned back to Fanuzzi and put her mouth to her ear. "Get out of here now. I'll keep them distracted."

"Are you insane? I can't leave you here."

"I can take care of myself."

"No."

"I promise I'll be okay. You've got your kids to worry about, Fanuzzi. Now get, or I might not be able to help you later."

The bit about the kids got her. Slowly Fanuzzi nodded. There wasn't an opportunity to argue. Her eyes almost glowing red with shock, she took a few steps backwards, then turned and walked quickly down the sidewalk.

Miranda turned back to Santiago and his big escort, and wished she had one of those concealed weapons Judd had been lecturing about in class.

She spread her hands, trying to look nonchalant. "I'm game, if you are, Carlos. And if Francisco here will lend me his Harley."

The sidekick didn't budge.

"Francisco?" Santiago said to him with an oily grin, his voice as steady as a mother's lullaby.

Francisco knew the score. He shook his head in submission, let out a bull laugh and got off his bike. "Okay, if you say so, boss. This I've got to see. It'll be worth giving up my hog a little while for such entertainment." He bowed and gestured toward the seat. "Here you go, little lady."

"Thanks." She strode over to the hog, grabbed the handlebars, and swung a leg over the seat. It was big and hard. She hoped she could get her bearings fast.

"Just remember, if you wreck it," Francisco said, "you pay for it."

She had a feeling he didn't mean with money.

Santiago fixed her with his black gaze. "We head south on Peachtree, take a left on Pharr Road. Then right on North Fulton. We end at the parking lot behind the Marta station. It's a half-mile. *Exactamente.*"

"*Exactamente,*" she repeated with a grin and turned the throttle to rev the motor.

He tossed his head back and laughed. "I like a woman with balls. Are you ready, Miranda."

"Ready, willing, and able."

He grinned lustily. Might not have been the best choice of words.

Francisco gave the signal, and they took off.

They cruised up the side street between the parked cars, each of them taking a lane. Miranda prayed no other vehicles would come down it.

Santiago went slowly at first, to let her get used to the bike. Awfully fair for a gang leader, but he must have wanted a real challenge.

Then they turned onto Peachtree, and he took off. She held her breath and hit the accelerator hard.

It was all she could do to keep up. They whizzed around a Toyota, past the iron railing of the Cheesecake Factory, around a bus stopped along the curb.

Now Santiago was several feet ahead. She gritted her teeth, shifted into high gear and gave it the gas. Her palms were wet on the leather handles. She glanced down at the speedometer. Seventy-five. Lord Almighty.

The wind shot her hair straight back. The legs of her jeans whipped around her legs. Neon bar signs blurred as they whizzed past. Glimpses of pedestrians on the sidewalk flitted in the corner of her eye. One gave them the bird and shouted obscenities. Others cheered. But there was no time to reply.

When they wheeled onto Pharr Road, they must have been doing ninety. Miranda's heart ached in her chest. She struggled to keep up. If she could win, she'd gain Santiago's respect. It was one step toward getting the information she wanted from him.

Then just behind them, a siren rang out. No. Last thing she needed now was a cop.

The squad car whipped around the turn. She glanced in the mirror and saw him gaining.

Throttle. She gave it more gas. They spun onto North Fulton. Her front tire reached Santiago's back one. Finally, she was gaining on him. She heard him curse as she passed him. But her glory was short lived.

Ahead, another squad car pulled onto the road from a side street. Lights and sirens blazing, it swung around and blocked the road. An officer jumped out, his gun drawn.

Brake! she thought madly, pulling on the lever, trying to stop without skidding and getting plummeted off head first.

"*Hijueputa,*" Santiago growled beside her.

Gasping for breath, she squealed to a halt not two feet in front of the officer.

Santiago ground his streetfighter to a standstill and turned off the engine. The cops and the riders glared at each other. Everything went quiet, except for the sound of heaving chests.

Miranda blinked at the officer pointing his pistol at her. Short curly hair of a nondescript color, wide-set eyes, and a perpetual questioning expression on his face. She'd know him anywhere.

Officer Chambers.

CHAPTER THIRTY-SIX

Miranda stared up at the lime green concrete walls of her holding cell. This made her third trip to Fulton County jail since she'd come to Atlanta—all three courtesy of the same cop. The place was beginning to feel like a home away from home.

She rubbed her eyes and glowered at the mattress she sat on, wishing she could lie down and take a nap. Coming off of an adrenaline rush like the one she'd been on tonight was exhausting. Especially after all the beer she'd sloshed down.

But her mission wasn't accomplished yet.

She looked up and saw her best bud, Officer Chambers, strolling toward her cell.

He stopped and shook his head. "Well, well. If it isn't little Ms. Miranda Steele, come to visit us again." Back on North Fulton, he'd been so silent and smug when he'd handcuffed his two lawbreakers and shoved them into the back of his cruiser, she'd thought he hadn't recognized her. No such luck.

"What's a matter, honey? You get homesick for the boys here at the station?"

She curled a lip at him. "I just thought your left jab needed some practice."

His wide-set eyes grew surly. The first time Chambers arrested her, Miranda had just about kicked his balls in. She'd gotten him demoted to patrolling Peachtree on the midnight shift. Guess he still had a grudge.

He clucked his tongue. "What's a nice girl like you doin' hanging with the likes of Carlos Santiago?" He nodded to one of the adjacent cells. Santiago must be within earshot.

"None of your business, Chambers." She wished he'd just shut up and go away. "Where's Erskine, tonight?"

"Out on a call. For the life of me, I can't see why someone with a job like yours wants to—"

"Shut up, Chambers." Dammit, he was blowing her cover.

209

His eyes blazed. "Don't you tell me to shut up, missy. You might remember you're the one who's incarcerated."

She made a face and nodded her head in the same direction he'd indicated before.

"What you making faces at me for? What an ornery bitch you are. Lord have mercy, I don't know why Mr. Park—"

She shot to her feet. Before Chambers could blink, she reached through the bars and grabbed him by his uniform collar. "I'm working undercover here," she hissed under her breath, "and you're blowing it."

His eyes widened in shock. Then he frowned, like he didn't believe her. "Lookie here—"

She pulled him closer to her. "If you want to discuss it, take me to an interrogation room."

He jerked loose of her grasp. "With pleasure."

It took longer than it should have to convince the hardheaded rookie she was on the level. She had to go over her story several times, explaining that she'd just happened on Santiago tonight.

She sat back in the stingy excuse for a chair in the interrogation room. "You know, Chambers, if I hadn't been racing him, you would have had his partner on your hands instead."

He gave her a you-think-I-couldn't-handle-that? look. "Oh? And who would that be?"

"A big dude named Francisco."

She watched his Adams apple go up and down. "Francisco Sanchez?"

"Didn't say his last name."

"He's Santiago's enforcer."

She raised a palm. "Well, there you go."

Chambers's face turned grim. Maybe he was angry he didn't get the collar for Francisco, too. Or maybe he was reconsidering his cocky attitude. "That still doesn't tell me why you were racing with the drug lord."

She exhaled. She'd have to spill it all. "Okay, Chambers. But this is strictly hush-hush."

One brow quivered. "I am a cop, you know."

Right. "It's about the Desirée Langford case."

"Desirée Langford, the heiress? Thought that was a suicide."

"I don't think so. I think her ex-husband laced her drink at the Northwinds Steeplechase with PCP. Drugs he got from Carlos Santiago."

Chambers stared at her in that baby face way of his for several minutes, shifted his weight. "Guess hanging around Wade Parker has done you good."

She wasn't sure that was a compliment or an insult. She let it slide. "I've learned a thing or two at the Agency." She got to her feet. "You gonna help me or not?" If he could help prove the wealthy horse breeder's death was a murder, it would get him off the shit list with his superiors.

His face said that idea had just dawned on him. He'd learned a thing or two since they'd first met, too. "What do you have in mind?"

"Here's the plan."

When Chambers walked her back to the cell, she had to hide the spring in her step. She'd turned an adversary into an ally, just the way Parker had done with Erskine years ago. Chambers had even given her his cell number, in case she ever needed it. And she had a link to the underworld in Santiago. Two good contacts in the same night. Not bad for an IIT.

But after the cop shoved her into Santiago's cell and the bars closed behind her, she almost lost her nerve.

They'd taken all his chains, including the one with the cross. With his muscular, tattooed arms crossed over his black tank top, the drug lord wore an expression that could bring on another ice age. "How nice of you to join me, Miranda."

The rolling *r* was losing its charm. "How nice of you to invite me." She sauntered in and plopped down on the cot.

He scratched at his beard. "I don't recall doing that."

"Sorry, Santiago," Chambers said with a grunt. "It's a busy night and we're short of cell space." He turned the key to lock the door.

"I thought it was against the rules for males and females to be together."

Chambers chuckled. "It is. I just wanted to teach this one a lesson." He gave her a wink. "You two play nice, now." He turned and strolled away, whistling.

"Freakin' cop." Miranda gave him the finger behind his back. Had to make this look good.

Santiago studied her.

Her gut twisted inside her like a hangman's rope. Hoping he wouldn't see her shivering, she leaned back and put her feet up on the dingy mattress with a careless air. "I must say, I thought a man of your means would have nicer digs."

"My downtown residence is quite elegant. Perhaps you would like to see it some time." He smiled and his white teeth glistened as his gaze traveled the length of her body.

A miniature glacier slid down her spine. Not the best pose. She'd been aiming for fearless. She sat up.

"Sure." An idea came to her, and she shot him a grin. "Maybe when I do, you can help *me* out."

"Help you out? With what?"

"Oh, I don't know." She eyed him carefully. "How come a man like you hasn't been sprung yet?"

"A man like me?"

"You know, they said some crazy things about you in there." She gestured down the hall.

"Oh? Like what?"

"That you're the head of a large and lucrative organization."

He nodded. "True. I'm a businessman."

"So why are you still here?"

He smiled that oily grin. "My lawyer is on his way." He took a step closer to the cot. "Now what would you like my help with?"

Miranda stood up and crossed to the wall. "Oh, I don't know. Maybe…a little weed from time to time. A little blow. From what they said about you, you're just the type who'd know where I can get some." She sniffed and rubbed her nose the way a coke addict might.

He chuckled and came closer to her. "You're not as good an actress as you think, Miranda."

She steadied her breath. "What do you mean?"

"For one thing, the police don't put women in cells with men. And they don't put anyone in a cell with me." He put one hand on the wall next to her face. She tried not to shudder. "Do you really know who I am?"

Time to lay her cards on the table. "Yeah, I know who you are. Or at least, I've heard of you."

His black eyes scanned her body, this time with caution. "And what do you really want? Who do you work for?"

Uh oh. He must have overheard bigmouth Chambers when he came to her cell. She swallowed. "I'm not sure what you mean."

His eyes narrowed to hard slits. "Are you an investigator?"

Cover. Blown. "Something like that."

He was so close, his breath whispered over her face as he spoke. She could smell the pomade on his jet-black curls. "And just what are you investigating?"

She didn't answer.

He leaned closer. She watched the jagged lines of a gang tattoo around his neck move as he swallowed. "They have found prisoners dead in these cells from time to time."

Nice. Miranda's mind raced. Maybe he thought she was FBI, some RICO investigator trying to bring him down. Desirée Langford's death would be small potatoes compared to that.

She had to take the chance.

She raised her chin. "I'm investigating a murder. A wealthy horse breeder was found dead at the Northwinds Steeplechase last month."

His face relaxed. He drew back. Miranda exhaled a slow breath.

"I read about that in the newspapers. Terrible tragedy. And why do you think I would know anything about it?"

She studied him a moment, decided to take another leap of faith. "I saw you at Ferraro Usher's art show. He has motive to want her dead. She died of a PCP overdose."

He nodded slowly, thoughtfully, ran a hand over his slicked-back hair as he stepped aside. Then he laughed. "You have a lot of balls for a woman. I like you, Miranda."

Nice to be liked. She could still feel her heart beating in her ears.

He stepped away, walked to the sink. He ran some water and splashed it over his face. "Yes, Miranda. You are quite correct. I have a relationship with Ferraro Usher. We do business."

She knew it. "Did you do business just before the Northwinds Steeplechase? Maybe some coke? Maybe some angel dust?"

"Oh, I don't remember such details."

Bull. "Liquid form of PCP? Hundred milligrams? Ring a bell?"

He grinned. "So you surmise that Ferraro Usher made such a purchase. Exactly the dosage that killed his ex-wife, as I recall from the newspapers."

She stood and waited.

He put a hand on his chest. "You think that *I* sold him that dosage?"

"That's what I'm asking."

Chuckling, he moved toward her again. Once more he put a hand on the wall next to her. He spoke softly, as if to child. "If you were to think that, Miranda," he grinned, "then you would be correct."

Hot dang. A break. A real break.

Santiago lifted his hand, twirled a strand of her hair around a finger. "Now that I have shared that secret with you, Miranda, what can you do for me in return?"

Uh oh. She hadn't planned on paying him back.

She opened her mouth, but before she could answer, the door at the end of the hall clanged and footsteps sounded.

Santiago moved away from her with a look that told her he wasn't finished with this business.

An officer appeared at the iron barred door. It wasn't Chambers. "Miranda Steele?"

"That's me," she said.

He opened the door. "Come with me."

First time in her life she was happy to obey a cop's orders. She gave Santiago a shrug and left with the flatfoot.

CHAPTER THIRTY-SEVEN

"What's going on?" Miranda asked the officer as he led her down the hall to Processing.

"You've been sprung."

Sprung? But when she saw who was at the desk waiting for her, she didn't need any further explanation.

Parker stood next to another officer, dressed in one of his fine suits, his arms folded, his face like iron.

"Hi," she said when she reached him. "Sorry about this."

"I don't want apologies," he snapped.

Well, what a pissy mood he was in. She finished the paperwork, got her things and scurried down the hall with him. She had to trot to keep up with his pace.

"Thanks, Parker. I know you're thinking, 'How'd she get herself in jail again?' but this time it was different."

He opened the door for her without a word. He didn't speak until they reached his Mazda.

He opened the passenger door. "I had someone retrieve your car and bring it home."

She got inside and he shut the door with a slam.

What was wrong? She watched him slide into the driver's seat, every muscle taut.

She tried to lighten the mood. "Hey, how'd you know I was here, anyway?"

He drew in an angry breath, started the car and pulled out of the parking space. "Joan Fanuzzi called me just before one a.m." At the parking lot exit, he braked before turning onto the road and glared at her. "Do you know how worried I've been about you all evening when you didn't come home?"

She bit her lip. How could one look from him make her feel so guilty? "I'm sorry, Parker. I should have called. But let me tell you what I was doing. I think I've got a break. A real piece of evidence to prove Usher killed Desirée Langford."

"Oh, do you?" He pressed the accelerator and jerked the wheel for the turn onto Ponce de Leon, making the tires squeal.

She was crestfallen. He wasn't taking her seriously at all. "Look, I said I was sorry. I didn't mean to worry you, but there's no need to act like a butt."

His jaw tightened. "You think you have a break? Let me show you something."

They rode in silence along I-85. There was little traffic. It was, after all, three in the morning, according to the time on Parker's dash. When he turned onto Peachtree and headed south, she knew something was very wrong. The mansion was the other way.

Her heart started to pound. "Where are we going?"

"Somewhere you've visited recently."

As they pulled up to the curb on the side street along the Brentwood Gallery, Miranda felt sick to her stomach. Police cars with their flashing lights were everywhere. Yellow crime scene tape barricaded the area.

She got out of the car and followed Parker up the stone walkway.

"Tell me what's going on," she demanded.

"You'll see for yourself in a moment. Erskine called me half an hour ago. He's waiting for us upstairs."

He led her up the steps to Usher's loft. It was crowded with police officers.

Erskine stood with his head down near the far wall, along a row of canvases, talking to an assistant. Miranda followed Parker as he made his way to the police detective.

"What's going on?" she asked again. But this time, she didn't need him to answer.

As she stepped past the coffee table and looked down, her hand went to her mouth.

Usher lay on his back in a pool of blood, his long hair spread out, his tall, thin body stretched over the polished floor. His eyes were wide open. What looked like his last gasp of surprise was chiseled on his face.

Usher? Dead? "Good Lord," Miranda gasped. "What happened?"

"It was short range. Handgun," Erskine answered curtly.

She looked more closely and saw the entrance wound in his chest. Didn't Usher owe Santiago money? Helplessly, she looked up at Erskine.

He glared at her, then at Parker. "You two have no business here. Unless you have something to add, I suggest you leave."

Miranda looked at Parker.

He folded his arms over his chest. Why had he brought her here? She turned to Erskine. "We questioned Usher here about a week ago. When we were here, we saw a gun in his desk." She turned and pointed. "In that top left drawer."

Erskine motioned to a female officer. Wearing gloves, she gently pulled open the drawer and lifted out the handgun. "Doesn't look like it's been fired, sir."

"Bag it anyway."

While the technician busied herself, Miranda surveyed the room and spotted the Medea painting. The vengeful woman in a flaming red dress. Her mouth open, she stepped toward it.

Someone had moved it up to the loft and done...something to it.

Streaks ran down the figure's face, smearing the paint, distorting the features, though the eyes blazed just as hatefully. Shards of glass were scattered on the floor beneath it. Like someone had thrown a drink at it.

Erskine's bark bellowed over her shoulder. "Ballistics is going over the evidence, Parker. If we find anything more, we'll let you know."

"Thank you, Hosea. For tonight, Ms. Steele and I will get out of your way."

CHAPTER THIRTY-EIGHT

She must have fallen asleep on the drive home. She didn't remember Parker carrying her inside or pulling her clothes off, but when she awoke on the big mattress in the master bedroom, Miranda realized he must have. It was morning.

Rolling over, she reached for him, then sat up. He hadn't slept here. Man, he must be pissed.

As last night's events came back to her, a hollow emptiness settled in the pit of her stomach. Ferraro Usher was dead. Definitely murdered. Who could have killed him? And why?

She got up and pulled on jeans and a fresh T-shirt. Okay. So she should have called Parker last night. She hadn't meant to worry him. But surely, he couldn't still be upset over that. They had more to worry about now. Usher was dead.

In the kitchen, she found bagels and coffee on the counter, but Parker was nowhere in sight. A skimpy meal for him, she thought, grabbing a plate and smearing a dab of cream cheese on the bread. He'd always loved pampering her with exotic breakfasts. Something was up.

She took the plate and a coffee cup and went out onto the deck. There, she found him.

His back to her, Parker stood under the redwood trellis, the climbing vines circling over his head like a regal canopy. He wore what he considered dressing down—a pale blue dress shirt and black slacks. His hair was damp from a shower. As she set her food down on the tiled table, she caught the faint scent of his cologne.

He didn't move, though his slight flinch told her he sensed her presence.

Causally, she settled into an Adirondack chair and took a bite of her bagel. "Top of the morning," she said when she had swallowed.

He didn't answer.

She put the bagel down and took a deep breath. "Parker, I'm really sorry I didn't call last night. I've had a lot on my mind and—"

He didn't budge. By now she had noticed the rigid tension in his shoulders, his neck. The mounting strain that was almost audible. The fire of a volcano ready to blast.

She ignored it and picked up her cup. "Okay, if you don't want to discuss that, let's talk about Usher. Do you have any thoughts about who might have killed him? Because I think—"

His dark voice rumbled from the corner. "I told you at the police station I didn't want apologies."

She set her cup down with a clatter, folded her arms over her stomach, her teeth involuntarily gritting. "What do you want?"

He turned slowly. His face was dark and worn, like he hadn't been to sleep. But his gray eyes were as cold as the barrel of Usher's handgun. "Compliance."

She glared at him, attempting to match the coldness of his gaze, but there was too much fire in her. "Compliance?"

Parker watched her eyes flame with that wild, rebellious spirit he now knew he could never tame. Struggling, he fought back the fuming adrenaline coursing through him. In his entire life, he'd never been so angry with a woman he loved. How could she have been so reckless? How could she have put herself in so much danger—after what she'd been through with Groth?

"Did you think I was joking when I gave you the stipulations for taking this case?"

Miranda grunted out loud. Parker and his stipulations. "I thought you were being overprotective."

"It's my prerogative as your employer to protect my investment in you." Spitting out the words, he took a step toward the table.

"Hah," she snapped. "You weren't protecting me as an employer. It was personal."

His eyes narrowed. "It was professional."

"Bullshit."

He shot a hand out, dismissing her comment. "That hardly excuses last night."

She closed her eyes, fighting the mounting frustration. "I said I was sorry."

He gave his head an exasperated shake. "This isn't about a phone call. Do you expect me to be pleased that you went street racing in the middle of the night with a notorious gang leader?"

So that was it. She flicked a nail against her cup.

"Did you have any idea what kind of ruthless killer you were dealing with?"

She met his piercing gaze. "Yeah. I had an idea. Wilhelmina Todd told me about him."

"Wilhelmina?" Now it was his turn to stare.

Heck, it wasn't like she had chased Santiago down. She spread her hands. "I wasn't looking for the guy. He happened along. It was an opportunity. What was I supposed to do? Walk away?"

His jaw tightened. "That's exactly what you should have done."

He couldn't be serious. "Oh yeah? Is that what you would have done?"

He ignored her question. "Carlos Santiago? A notorious drug lord who tortures and kills anyone who opposes him? Who'd just as soon rape a woman as look at her? Are you out of your mind?"

"Okay, it was a little dicey."

"A little dicey?"

"Isn't investigative work dangerous at times? Doesn't a good investigator take a calculated risk once in a while?"

"Calculated, not reckless."

"It wasn't reckless. I wasn't jeopardizing the investigation, Parker. I was only putting myself at risk." And there was the rub.

His lips became a hard line. "You're intractable, Miranda."

"What?"

"Difficult to control. Impossible to manage."

She laughed. "Me? Intractable?" Well, if that wasn't the sauté pan calling the deep fryer black.

His eyes blazed. "For heaven's sake, Miranda, you're an IIT. A trainee."

She clenched her hands, forcing back a wave of anger. "You forgot to say 'mere' trainee," she sneered and got to her feet. "But you know what? It was in your classes I learned that a good PI takes calculated risks. It's Judd who always says a good PI uses her instincts. Last night, my instincts said, 'go for it.'"

His entire body igniting with rage, Parker turned away from her. He leaned against the railing, glared at the rose beds lining the yard. What if those instincts had been wrong? What if he'd gotten a call telling him she was dead?

Slowly, he willed control back into his voice. "The fact remains that you broke the rules."

Miranda's eyes stung with disbelief. How could he be so blindly stubborn? "Is that how you got to be such a hot shot PI? By following rules? By playing it safe and never taking risks?"

His grip on the rail tightened.

She put a hand on her hip, took a step toward him. "Isn't that why you quit police work? Because you were frustrated with the red tape and having to follow the rules while the guilty got away?"

He turned to glare at her, opened his mouth, then shut it.

Got him.

She folded her arms around herself tightly, struggling not to shake with the anger peppering her nerves. "You should be proud of what I did last night. I got a real lead. Carlos Santiago told me he sold Usher the PCP that killed Desirée Langford. He might have put a hit on Usher."

Parker grunted, raising his hands in the air. "My point exactly."

Her lip curled. "Do you think I can't take care of myself? Hey, I was tussling with men bigger than me long before I met you, bud."

He glared at her. "But did you take on a bloodthirsty drug lord?"

She blinked, unable to respond. One for one.

"Do you expect me to be happy that you flirted with a man like that? That you talked an officer into letting you share his jail cell?"

He just didn't get it, did he? "Yes, I do. I got a lead. You ought to be happy." Tears stung her eyes. She'd risked her ass. How could he demean it? She glared at him. "Am I a real detective, Parker? Or am I just someone you're playing detective with?"

He took a step toward her, his face blazing "I don't play games when it comes to my profession."

"Like hell, you don't."

He closed his eyes, drew in a tight breath as he turned to stare out at the garden again. Several silent moments went by. "You're wrong, Miranda," he said softly. "I'm not playing. Insubordination is insubordination." His tone was intensely quiet. The eye of a hurricane. It took her breath.

"What are you saying?"

Parker ran a hand through his hair, regretting this moment with all his being. He despised having to clip her wings, but she gave him no choice. He'd thought she would flourish under his careful watch. Grow to maturity. But she was too headstrong. Too uncontrollable. He'd lost two women he'd loved to death. He wasn't about to lose another.

He turned to her, calmer. She was safe now, after all. He'd do all he could to make sure she stayed that way. "I'm taking you off the case."

His words were like a punch in the chest. "What?"

"You'll finish your training with the rest of the IITs. No more special assignments."

Make that a one-two punch. "No more working with you, you mean."

"Correct. When training is complete, you'll have a choice of doing background checks or working with the clerical staff."

Her throat went dry. Was this the same man she'd been making love to all these weeks? The same man who'd heaped praise on her? "You expect me to be a secretary?"

"Not a secretary. You would transcribe testimony, examine collected evidence, review field notes for worker's comp and insurance fraud claims."

"Paperwork. Yippee." Her knees suddenly felt like jelly. She wanted to throw up.

"No outside cases," he continued. "No field work."

"No murder investigations, you mean."

He took on a lofty, authoritative air. "Perhaps, after a number of years. After you've developed some discipline."

"*Years?*"

The pained look on her face tore at his heart, almost making him change his mind. But the decision was made. It was for her own good. If he didn't stop her, she would get herself killed.

"Years?" she repeated.

"That's what I said."

She pulled herself up. "And what if I refuse?"

The gray coldness was back in his eyes. "There's always the option of resigning."

She dug her fingers into her hair, reeling from the shock of his words. How could he take this case away from her? She thought he loved her. She thought he understood her. She thought she'd found the impossible—a man who respected her. What had all those compliments been for? Had it just been a sham to get her into his bed? Had he been stroking his own ego because he'd trained her? Or was he just as big a control freak as—

She stepped to the table and picked up her plate. She put it back down. Let the servant get it. Or Parker. She turned to him again. "You know what? I'm sick of this bullshit."

"I assure you, Miranda, this is no bullshit."

"Yes, it is. All of it. We've both been playing games, haven't we? Pretending we're really working together. Pretending I'm a real investigator. I guess we've been pretending we have a relationship, too." She turned and headed for the kitchen.

He rushed to her, caught her by the arm. His sudden grasp almost hurt. "What do we have, Miranda? I've waited for an answer from you, and you've given me nothing."

She glared into his face. How dare he bring that up? All she felt was rage and insult. She wanted to hurt him back—just like she knew she would. "That's because we have nothing," she spat. "We never did."

He let her go, stepped away from her.

"You know, I think I'll take that last option you mentioned. Consider this my resignation from the Parker Agency." She reached for the door handle, then stopped. "And you know what else? I'm moving out. This house belongs to you. It always has. I sure as hell don't want it. I'll call your father and cancel my lease."

"Miranda," he said sharply.

She spun around. "What?"

She'd never seen such a dark look on his face. "If you walk out again, this time I won't take you back."

Anger hammered in her chest. She could hardly breathe. *Take her back?* Don't worry, buddy. I won't be back. She narrowed her eyes at him, wishing her gaze could bore holes through his stubborn heart. "Go to hell, Parker."

Fighting back tears of frenzied rage, Miranda charged up the steps of the carved mahogany staircase as fast as she could go.

When she reached the master bedroom, she stomped to the closet, pulled out the boxes she'd stored there.

Her heart felt like it had been pummeled with a meat pounder. Heaving with pain, she stopped and looked around. It was too much. She wasn't going to make twenty trips down to her car while Parker watched.

She grabbed a duffle bag and threw as much underwear, clothes and toiletries she could stuff into it. Then she reached for the laptop she hadn't used since she'd moved in.

She'd come back for the rest of her stuff later. When Parker wasn't home.

Tossing the bag over her shoulder, she scrambled down the stairs and out the front door, slamming it as hard as she could.

She sprinted to the driveway, threw her things into the passenger side of her old blue Lumina. She knew there was a good reason she'd never parked her car in the garage.

It made her final exit easier.

CHAPTER THIRTY-NINE

Bewildered, she drove around aimlessly for over an hour. Her head throbbing, her heart in agony, she alternated between stinging pain and dead-cold numbness.

How could Parker do this to her? Okay, she got that he had been worried. And furious at her. She could accept that. But how could he suddenly be so aloof and indifferent? How could he take her off the Desirée Langford case? She'd been making progress. She'd wheedled important information out of Santiago. But Parker hadn't even asked for an explanation about last night. He'd just dismissed it as if it meant nothing.

And he wanted her to wait years before he'd let her on another murder case? *Years?* How could he be so cruel?

She glanced at the bright red flowers filling the median, blinked at the steel-and-glass high-rises lining either side of the street. She was on Peachtree again, headed south. She'd been driving in circles. Impulsively, she took a side lane and found herself on a road alongside a city park.

She pulled over to the curb, turned off the ignition. She sat there awhile, feeling dizzy with shock, sick with the sense of loss. Finally, she put her head down on the steering wheel, and let herself cry. More than cry. She bawled.

Her shoulders heaved as she sobbed like a baby. It wasn't just this case. It wasn't just her future at the Agency.

It was Parker. She realized that now.

She'd been sucked in by his charm. Drawn in by that suave allure. Mesmerized by his magnetism. Duped. Bamboozled. She'd let herself care about Parker. She'd let herself fall in love with him. Hard. That had been her first mistake.

She didn't even know who he was any more.

She'd always told herself being with Parker was too good to be true. That it would all come crashing down on her head. And now it had. She just didn't think it would be so soon. Well, better sooner than later.

Raising her head, she wiped the tears from her cheeks with both hands. A jogger passed her car on the path beside the road, plodding away. Fountains blithely spouted water into the air. The jogger turned at a strange-looking statue. Circular and rust-colored, it reminded her of a sculpture she'd seen at the Brentwood Gallery.

Anger roused in her gut. Ferraro Usher was dead. They ought to be figuring out who killed him. Instead, Parker takes her off the case. She couldn't believe her work meant so little to him. That hurt as much as losing him.

She put a hand to her aching head. She'd gotten spoiled by his compliments. Used to the thrill when he said she had promise. Addicted to the glow when he told her she was becoming an "excellent investigator."

Had he meant any of it?

Once more she saw Desirée Langford's battered face in her mind. The woman had been murdered, and nobody cared enough to find out who did it. Except her.

Two months ago, she wouldn't have given a rip. Oh, she'd have been sympathetic, but she wouldn't have felt this driving need to solve the case. Why did she care so much now? She couldn't answer that. She only knew she did. That she wanted to solve this case with all her being.

And now she never would.

Parker once said she was born for this work. Whether he'd meant it or not, it was true. She knew that now. Knew it in her bones. The need to set things right, to discover the truth no matter the cost, was in her blood. She *was* born for this work.

She sat up, blinked, stunned by the revelation. And her mind began to clear.

She could solve this case. She had all the data. All she had to do was put the pieces together. She didn't need Wade Parker. She could do it herself. She could be an investigator, and a darn good one, without him. She didn't need anyone's permission or approval. Hadn't she already solved the Taggart case?

There was the little matter of a license. She hadn't needed one while employed by the Agency. But technically, she still worked for them until they processed her exit papers. That would take a few days, at least. Maybe more if Parker stalled, waiting for her to change her mind about his offer.

Hah. She'd solve Desirée Langford's murder before they finished.

And after that? She drummed her fingers on the steering wheel. In Georgia, it was the Agency itself that was licensed. To open her own office, she'd need to pass tests, wait for results.

Heck, she didn't need to stay in Georgia. She'd go to some state where they didn't require PIs to be licensed. Wyoming, maybe. Then she could take her own cases and handle them exactly as she saw fit. No more therapists. No more rules about not working on her own. No more "stipulations."

No more Parker. Her throat constricted as the urge to cry again came over her. She shook it off.

Leon always told her she was nothing. Her mother thought she was stupid. No wonder it took her so long to see her life's calling. But here it was, right in front of her. And she didn't need Wade Parker to see it.

He may have started her on this path, but she didn't need him to continue it. It was her own identity, not his. It felt right. It felt good.

She reached in her bag for a tissue and blew her nose.

Right now, she needed a place to stay. And to work. She could go back to her old apartment, but her landlord would insist on a six-month lease.

She still had the lease agreement with Mr. P. She could go back to the mansion and kick Parker out. She smiled at the thought, but only for a moment. She couldn't face him again. And with his arrogance, Parker would assume she was crawling back to him. Or that she couldn't live anywhere but a mansion now, like the kind of women he was used to. He'd never get that satisfaction.

Maybe she'd look for a fleabag hotel, though she ought to save her money if she was going to open her own business.

She turned the ignition and started out of the parking spot.

She'd lived in her car before, and she'd do it again if she had to. She'd just need a spot near a wi-fi. She didn't need luxury. She didn't need Parker. She didn't need anybody.

Men. What good were they? Just like Fanuzzi said last night.

She turned onto Peachtree and grinned. That's where she could go.

When she pulled up to the single-story bungalow in Avondale Estates and saw Fanuzzi's station wagon filled with toys, she felt a tad guilty. The single mother had enough on her hands.

But it wasn't just a place to stay she needed. She wanted someone to talk to. And a place to work. Just until she solved the case.

Then she'd be off.

She grabbed her laptop and duffle bag and trekked up the walk to the front door. She rang the bell.

No answer. Then she heard footsteps inside.

Gosh, Fanuzzi worked second shift. She'd probably been asleep. Miranda was about to turn away when the door opened and Fanuzzi appeared in a bathrobe.

"Murray." She sounded shocked.

"Sorry to bother you. I didn't mean to wake you up."

"You didn't."

Miranda eyed the bathrobe. "Are you sick?"

Fanuzzi ran a hand through her disheveled hair. "No, I'm not sick. I'm glad to see you're okay. I called Parker last night."

"I know. He told me. In fact, we had a big fight."

"A fight? Good grief, Murray."

"I, uh, kind of need a place to stay."

"That bad of a fight?"

"Yeah. Can I come in?"

She glanced inside the house, nervously. "Uh, sure." She opened the door.

Miranda stepped into the small kitchen and set down her duffle bag. There were breakfast dishes in the sink and two coffee cups on the dinette table. Did Fanuzzi have "company"?

"If I'm an imposition, I can go somewhere else."

Fanuzzi picked up the cups and took them to the sink. "It's okay, Murray."

"I'm sorry. I don't intend to be here long—"

"Joan?" A familiar male voice rang out from down the hall.

Miranda swiveled toward the opposite end of the kitchen just in time to see a man emerge wearing nothing but a towel around his waist.

He stopped cold and blinked at her. "Steele?"

"Becker?" She turned to her friend. "Gosh, Fanuzzi. I didn't mean to interrupt, uh…anything."

Fanuzzi's ruddy face flushed. She scratched at her hair. "Would you excuse us for a minute, Dave?"

Becker's face was redder than Fanuzzi's spaghetti sauce. "Sure." Sheepishly, he nodded and tromped back down the hall.

"Gosh, I'm sorry."

"Stop apologizing." Fanuzzi took Miranda by the arm and drug her into the living room. As she sank onto the cozy couch, her friend peeked out the window. "The kids are playing outside in the yard, thank goodness. They love that waterslide Dave bought them."

Miranda could hear their squeals. "Dave Becker bought your kids a waterslide?" Seemed she'd missed an episode or two of this soap opera.

Fanuzzi crossed the room and sat down next to her. "When I got home last night, there was a message from him on my answering machine. He said he was sorry he'd made a mess of things and wanted to talk. He said he couldn't sleep and to call back any time. I couldn't sleep either. So I called him and he came over." She shrugged toward the backyard and rolled her eyes. "After stopping at an all-night Walmart. How could I say no to that? We sort of decided to pick up where we left off all those years ago and see what happens."

"Really?" Miranda felt a warm glow.

"It wouldn't have happened without you. Thanks, Murray."

She was actually embarrassed, but she couldn't hold back a smile. "I didn't know I was such a Yenta." She glanced back at the hallway. If things were heating up between them…. "If I'm in the way, just say so."

Fanuzzi shook her head. "He's not staying here. I want the kids to get used to him first. If it goes that far."

"Do you think it will?"

"Maybe. And I…" She was blushing like a teenager. "I kind of hope it will." Then she gave Miranda's hand a squeeze. "What happened between you and Parker?"

Miranda squirmed. She didn't want to tell Fanuzzi the things Parker had said to her. It would be too humiliating. "We had a professional disagreement."

Fanuzzi's face wrinkled with suspicion. "Professional?"

"We didn't see eye to eye about this case."

"The one you're working on? Seems like a strange reason to breakup with someone as hot as Wade Parker."

Miranda sighed. "Like I said, we have a weird relationship." Or had one. She slapped a hand on Fanuzzi's knee. "But I've decided I'm going out on my own."

Fanuzzi's eyes grew round. "As a PI?"

Miranda nodded.

"Here in Atlanta?"

"Probably not here."

She was crestfallen. "You're leaving?"

Miranda shook her head. "Not until I figure out who killed Desirée Langford. That's why I need a temporary place to stay. And to work."

"Sure," Fanuzzi said with enthusiasm. "*Mi casa es su casa.*"

"I'll pay for room and board."

"No, you won't."

Miranda got to her feet. She'd leave some money in an envelope. "Did you hear Ferraro Usher was shot dead last night?"

Fanuzzi gasped. "That artist who came to your party?"

Miranda nodded. "Yep. In his loft."

"Holy moly, Murray. Do you think Santiago had something to do with it?"

"I don't know yet."

"Well," she said getting up and starting down the hall. "You'd better get to work, then, Ms. PI."

Fanuzzi gave her Tommy's room, and she settled in among the dragons and wizard figurines, the GI-Joes, footballs, and video games.

She sat down in the small chair at the desk, opened her laptop and fed it the flash drive she'd used to backup the reports and pictures she'd scanned in from Desirée Langford's file on Parker's computers. She really didn't need them. She had most of the details memorized.

What next? She'd type up a report. Her own report. Parker had been taking care of that detail up to now, having a clerk type up dictated notes. Now it was up to her to track the case.

As she stared up at the plastic human skeleton on the bookshelf, her thoughts began to gel. Her fingers moved over the keyboard. She started from the beginning, summarizing her findings. The police interviews, the coroner's report. Her conversation with Kennicot. The PCP found in Desirée's bloodstream. The riding crop with Usher's fingerprints. His violent reaction when she questioned him in his loft. His sudden death.

By the time she finished, hours had passed. Exhaustion was starting to wear her down, but she pressed on. She stood up and stretched, hooked her laptop up to Tommy's printer and made a hardcopy.

Fifteen double-spaced pages. When the last page came out, she snatched it and lay down on top of the colorful solar system spread on the small bed. She went over it page by page.

What was she missing? There had to be something here. Right under her nose. She could feel it. But she couldn't figure out what it was.

A yawn came out of her mouth. She rubbed her burning eyes, then turned back to the beginning and read again. Before she reached page five, she was asleep.

CHAPTER FORTY

Parker sat on the redwood deck, watching the late afternoon shadows grow in the garden, a whiskey sour that he hadn't touched in his hand. He hadn't done much but sit out here since this morning.

How could he have let Miranda Steele walk out on him a second time?

Impetuous, impulsive woman. Rash, uncontrollable. All the things he loved about her. All the things he deplored in her. She frustrated him beyond his endurance. How could he have fallen so deeply in love with her?

How many times had she told him it could never work out for them? He had refused to listen, but she'd been right. He closed his eyes, trying to will away the pain of that reality.

Where she would go, what she would do, he couldn't tell. He couldn't let himself care. He could only try to heal somehow and go back to life as he knew it before she came along.

The thought made his stomach clench.

He leaned back in the chair and remembered how she'd cried over Madison Taggart the first night he saw her in a jail cell. How doggedly she'd pursued the little girl's case. How she'd wept in his arms when she told him about Leon.

If only she had let him help her. But she didn't like being helped. She was so darn independent. She wanted to do everything herself.

Whether it was because they were too different or too much alike, he'd never know. The only thing he knew for certain was that it was over. Even if she wanted to make amends, which she didn't, he couldn't open himself up to this kind of pain again. It was done. He was done.

A phone rang inside the house. He opened his eyes. *Was it her?* No, she'd be too proud, too stubborn to call him. Perhaps she wanted the things she'd left. He didn't want to talk to her now. He'd let the answering machine get it.

The ringing stopped. A moment later, it started again. Had she come to her senses? Seen his point about her reckless behavior?

He rose and plodded into the kitchen. He picked up the receiver on the last ring.

229

"Hello?"

"Wade? I'm so glad you're home."

He let out a surprised breath. It was Delta Langford. "Hello, Delta. How…are you?"

"As well as I can be, I suppose."

"Of course." He forced sympathy into his voice as he searched for a way to end the call quickly.

"I want to apologize for the scene I caused at your party last week."

It wasn't his party. It was Miranda's. He thought of the yearbook she'd found. The things he'd told her that night. His mother's ring. Every muscle in his body ached. "Think nothing of it," he murmured into the receiver.

"Oh, but I do think of it. It's bothered me terribly since that night. I want to do something to make it up to you."

Make it up to him? Delta Langford was a woman who thought only of herself. She'd never tried to make up for anything in her life. "What do you mean, Delta?"

There was a pause. "I was wondering if I could get you to come out to the farm tonight and have a talk with me."

"We haven't spoken in years."

She gave an awkward laugh. "That's just it, Wade. It's been so long and there are so many things I need to say to you."

"You can say them now."

She hesitated. "Oh, no. I need to do it in person. And I need to do it tonight. I have my courage up. I don't know if I can later, if you put me off."

Suspicion prickled the back of Parker's neck. The last person he could trust was Delta Langford. She could never make up for what she'd done years ago. But what she had to say might give him a clue about her sister's murder. He might as well take up the case where Miranda had left it.

He glanced up at the clock on the kitchen wall. "I can be there about eight."

She exhaled audibly. "Oh, thank you, Wade. This means so much to me. I'll be waiting."

He hung up the phone and headed upstairs to shower and dress. But first, he checked his cell on the hall table. Fully charged. That was good. He would need it to record everything Delta told him.

When Miranda awoke in Tommy's bed, it was late afternoon. The pages of her report were scattered on the floor. She picked them up and squinted as she turned on the light.

She could hear voices outside the door. She laid her report on the desk and opened the door.

Fanuzzi and her kids were in the kitchen. Callie and Tommy were at the table playing a board game, while Charlie made faces at them. Fanuzzi was at the sink, pouring noodles into a strainer.

"You're just in time for homemade spaghetti," she called out.

"Sounds delicious." She just realized she hadn't eaten since morning.

"Go wash your hands and join us."

"Yes, Mommy." Miranda grinned and headed for the bathroom.

She washed her face and hands, stared at herself in the mirror. She looked haggard, tired. She'd been through hell today. A broken heart, a broken career, a broken life. No, she'd fix them. All of them. But she still had little on Desirée Langford's case.

She sat between Tommy and Callie, listening to them pepper Mommy with questions about the new man in her life, and watching Mommy squirm. No, Fanuzzi told them, Mr. Dave wasn't staying overnight. She wasn't sure about the relationship yet. She would take it one day at a time. But beneath the parental sternness, Fanuzzi was beaming.

And so was "Mr. Dave." With a forkful of pasta in his hand, he caught Miranda's eye and mouthed, "Thank you."

Her heart swelled. "No problem," she mouthed back. She was genuinely happy for both of her friends.

She ate two plates of spaghetti, then excused herself and went back to Tommy's room.

She picked up the report again and paced the floor as she skimmed it.

Despite her efforts, she was still short on hard facts. All she knew for sure was that Carlos Santiago had sold Usher that fatal dose of PCP. Usher had to have bought the drug to kill his ex-wife, right? And Santiago had him killed because he owed him money. Was that it?

No, there was something missing. Think, dammit. She sat down at the desk, closed her eyes and let her mind drift. What were the facts?

Desirée Langford and Ferraro Usher. Two narcissistic people, absorbed in their careers. She marries him on the rebound from Kennicot. They have a tumultuous relationship. She gets physical at times. She's prone to depression. So is he. They take drugs together. They go to therapy. His career blossoms. Hers does, too.

She leaves him for her old flame. He begs her to come back. She says no, but still sees him as a model, plays the two men against each other. She swallows a fatal dose of PCP at the Steeplechase. Her favorite horse kicks her face in.

Miranda exhaled. It had to have been Usher who'd riled that horse with his riding crop, didn't it? But why had he seemed so genuinely shocked when he first saw Desirée's body in the stall?

Over and over, Usher had said he hadn't killed her. He'd insisted he'd loved her. Then he winds up dead. Had he killed himself out of remorse? That scene didn't look like suicide.

So who killed Usher?

She thought of the paintings of Desirée in Usher's gallery. The angelic ones in his loft. The Medea painting that had been on display downstairs. That somebody had moved to Usher's loft.

She leaned an elbow on the desk and stared at the report.

Medea. The vindictive witch, full of jealousy and hate, with those mysterious, cat-like eyes. Desirée's, she'd assumed.

Her head shot up. The recording of Usher and Delta in the library at her party. Delta had goaded the artist, taunted him, almost as if she'd relished tormenting him. When she called Usher a murderer, the glow in her eyes was vicious…just like the eyes in that painting.

Miranda dropped the report in her lap. That Medea painting wasn't a portrait of Desirée.

It was Delta.

Her mouth opened as the breath left her body. That was it. The missing piece. Now it all made sense. Why hadn't she seen it before?

She sprung up from chair, grabbed her duffle bag, started tossing things on the bed. It was in here. She'd held onto it after the party, thinking it would be fun to secretly record Parker making love to her and tease him with it afterward.

She winced at that thought, but kept looking. It had been in a drawer with her clothes, and she'd scooped it up with them. There it was. At the bottom of the bag. She pulled it out. A small, silver digital recorder, about the size of a cigarette lighter. Extremely discreet. With a high-powered microphone that worked up to thirty feet away.

Quickly, she stripped off her T-shirt and jeans, put on a nice blouse and a pair of slacks with deep pockets. She slipped the recorder into the right one. Then she grabbed her purse and headed for the hall. She told Fanuzzi she was going out and didn't know when she'd be home.

"Where are you going?" Fanuzzi called after her as she hustled into her Lumina.

"Aquitaine Farms. I'm going to pay Delta Langford a visit. And I might just catch myself a killer."

232

CHAPTER FORTY-ONE

"Oh, Wade. I'm so glad you're here. I was so afraid you wouldn't come."

Parker tensed as Delta Langford took a tight hold of his arm and led him through the foyer of the Aquitaine Farms estate. She was all in satiny reds and pearls tonight. An attempt to look seductive, he assumed. Her ploys had never worked on him. They weren't working now.

But he'd always pitied her, despite his distaste for her. And he was ashamed of the sick knot in the pit of his stomach as they strolled down the hall and into a small private room.

There was a table set for two. Flowers. Candles. Very intimate.

"What's all this?" he asked cautiously.

"I remember how you always liked Chateaubriand. Are you still fond of it?"

He stiffened. "I'm not really hungry, Delta."

"Oh, please don't refuse me, Wade. I'm trying so hard to make up for..." Her voice trailed off as she laid a delicate hand against her cheek. Her fingers trembled. "I don't suppose I ever can."

He softened. After all, he'd always pitied the woman. From the time she was a young girl, with more beauty and money than she knew what to do with, to even now as a handsome woman just gracefully beginning to show the signs of age.

"Very well, Delta," he said with a sigh. "I'll have dinner with you." If all it took to get her to talk was eating a steak, he would comply.

He seated her at the end of the small table, then took the chair across from her.

Her servants appeared, noiselessly serving the elaborate meal without fanfare. He ate what he could of it, as he watched her green eyes glisten in the candlelight and listened to her chatter on about high school and what the Langford family had been back then. She dwelt on the years they had spent together at Westminster.

"Do you remember that funny little boy you used to always hang around with? He was such an intellectual."

"Jackson Taggart. He's a grown man now," Parker said, attempting to nudge her back to the present.

She laughed in that half-flirtatious way that had always annoyed him. "It's strange what we turn into as adults. Who would have thought that gawky boy would grow up to become Chief of Staff of St. Benedictine's?"

Parker picked at the remains of his meal with his fork. "I don't find it odd at all. We carry the seeds of what we'll become within us from childhood. Jackson was a fine person then, just as he is now." Unlike others.

She waved a hand. "Oh, I don't mean it that way, Wade. It's just that it takes social skills to rise to a position like that. I never thought Jackson had any."

If she was trying to win his affection, she should know insulting his best friend wouldn't help.

She raised a wineglass to her lips. "On the other hand, you always had wonderful social skills. And you've used them well. It wasn't hard then to see that you'd grow up to be enormously successful."

He decided a little flattery might loosen her tongue. "I could say the same for you."

"Me?" she scoffed. "I've had two failed marriages. I'm over forty and I live with my father, for heaven's sake. I wouldn't call that successful."

"No, I suppose not." He'd wanted to tell her she was successful in ways that couldn't be measured by outward values. But it would be too much of a flat out lie.

He watched the servant clear away his plate of half-eaten Chateaubriand.

"Didn't you like the steak, Wade? Perhaps it was a little tough. You were always so discriminating when it came to food." Her tone had the mixture of pleading and disapproval that had always sickened him.

He wiped his mouth with the napkin. "It was fine, Delta."

"Perhaps you'll enjoy dessert better. It's blueberry cheesecake. Freshly baked."

He forced a smile. He'd always hated cheesecake. Delta didn't know him as well as she liked to pretend. Nonetheless, he allowed the servant to place a slice before him.

He lifted his fork and picked at it. "So what was it you wanted to tell me, Delta?"

"Tell you?" Her eyes glowed with faux innocence that annoyed him.

"You said you wanted to talk. You said you had your courage up."

Her face grew sullen. She nodded. "Yes." She waited a moment for the servants to leave the room, then leaned toward him. "Wade, it's been a long time." She looked down at her hands. "I was wondering. After all that's happened—Laura, Sylvia, my two husbands, my sister, and now Ferraro. They're all gone from our lives."

She raised her chin, her eyes watery with emotion in the candlelight. "Is there any chance for us? Any hope of regaining what we once had?"

He swallowed hard but didn't answer right away. He hadn't expected this. Was she still in love with him after all these years? For his part, he felt the same as always for her. Nothing but pity mixed with a tinge of revulsion.

"Delta, I—"

"Don't say it." She raised a hand, then put it to her mouth. Her lips trembled as she shook her head. "I didn't really think it was possible. I just had to ask."

With an elegant move, she rose and moved to the decanter table. Silently, she poured two sherries. She turned back, handed him one.

She sat down and stared out the window with the saddest look he'd ever seen. "Delta, I'm sorry."

She shook her head slightly. "It doesn't matter."

With a heavy sigh, he lifted the sherry to his lips. He had to get out of here. He'd been wrong. Delta wouldn't be any help to the investigation of Desirée's death. She was too disturbed, too wrapped up in her own troubles. He swallowed half the sherry, hoping that would be enough to placate the woman.

He set the glass down and looked up at Delta, intending to say good-bye.

"I had wanted…I had hoped…" Her lips moved, but suddenly, he couldn't make out her words.

He tried to stand. The room swayed. He caught himself on the table before he fell.

Too late, he sensed the warm liquid on his tongue and knew the taste of it wasn't right. What could be so fast acting? Have such a kick? "What did you put in that drink, Delta?"

She smiled bitterly and waved a hand. "Oh, a pain prescription the doctors gave my father after his knee surgery last year. Oxycodone, I think."

Ground oxycodone would work fast. And could be fatal if there were enough of it. Irritation prickled at the back of his neck, but it was a dreamlike sensation.

Blinking hard, he raised his head and saw Delta through a hazy cloud. She was pointing something at him. A handgun. Through sheer force of will, he brought his mind to attention. He stared at the barrel, made a deductive leap. "The gun that killed Ferraro Usher."

"Why, whatever do you mean, Wade?" Her voice echoed as though she were standing in a tunnel, but he could hear the viciousness reverberate in her tone.

Slowly he forced his hand into his pocket and turned on the recorder on his cell phone. "Are you going to shoot me as well, Delta?"

"You hurt me so much, Wade. You broke my heart."

"You broke mine, too. You took my first love from me."

"She took mine." She put both hands on the pistol. "We can't do this here. Besides, there's something I want to show you. Raise your hands, turn around slowly and head through the door."

He did as she said, relieved that she seemed to be in no hurry. With time, he could catch her off guard. If he could stay conscious. "Where are we going?" he asked.

"Out to the stables."

Miranda raced down I-20 toward Conyers, cursing her old beater and wishing for the speed of Parker's Lamborghini. After an eternity, she turned off the exit and followed the country road to the white wooden sign reading "Aquitaine Farms." Giving the Lumina the gas, she sped up the long dirt path under the rows of trees, hoping that her clunker didn't blow a gasket.

As she reached the house, she realized she was shaking with rage. She had it all planned. She would tell Delta she had a lead on her sister's case. She'd tell her what she knew. Delta would see that the evidence pointed to her. If she didn't, Miranda would point out that fact.

Oh, but she knew she was innocent. All she needed was for Delta to explain the details that incriminated her. With any luck at all, she'd either get a frank admission or a cover-up with enough contradictions to hang her. And she'd be recording every word. How was that for objectivity? Too bad Parker would have to read about it in the newspapers.

She pulled her car under the same row of azalea bushes where Parker had hidden his Mazda the day they drove out to the place. She got out and looked up at the building. Had Delta been watching them that day? Had she seen the nose of the Mazda? Surmised Parker was with her?

Miranda didn't know, but something made her hesitate.

And then she saw it around the corner.

Parker's Mazda. *What was he doing here?*

With the smell of honeysuckle and hay in her nose, following instinct, she strolled around to the side of the house and stood on the rise overlooking the barn where she had questioned Kennicot.

The sun had almost set and in the dusk, she couldn't see much. She shaded her eyes and squinted. Finally, two figures came into focus, lumbering along a dirt path, heading toward the barn. They stepped into the light of one of the overhead lamps and at last, she could make them out.

Shock ripped through her. No. She had to be imagining things.

Parker? Going out to the barn with Delta? Why?

Then she saw that Delta seemed to be forcing him along. He had his hands in the air. Was that a gun she was pointing at him?

No. Please, no.

She stood, holding her breath as they shuffled to the barn and went inside. Her heart hammering in her chest, she reached for her cell and punched in the number Chambers had given her. It rang. Thank goodness, she had service out here.

He answered right away. "Yeah?"

"Chambers," she whispered, muffling her voice with her hand.

"What? I can't hear you."

She turned around and dared to speak a little louder. "Chambers, it's me. Miranda Steele."

"My old buddy. Heard you got sprung last night. How are you liking your freedom?"

"Shut up and listen."

"Lookie here, you—"

"Chambers, this is an emergency. I'm out at Aquitaine Farms."

"Aquitaine Farms? The Langford estate near Conyers?"

"Yeah. I've got a problem. Someone with a gun. If I don't get help fast, there could be another murder."

That got Chambers's attention. Stopping a murder would be a feather in his cap. Not to mention his pledge to serve and protect. "Conyers is out of my jurisdiction, honey."

"What can you do?"

"I'll get hold of the local yokels and tell them to bring backup. How many you need?"

"As many as you can spare. Send EMTs, too." She had a feeling this wasn't going to be pretty.

"I'll work on it."

"Move your ass. Otherwise, the next victim could be Wade Parker."

"Wade Parker?" he gasped. "Why didn't you say so? I'll get right on it." He hung up.

Miranda put the phone back in her pocket and raced up the slope toward the barn. By the time she reached the structure and slipped through the big, open door, her whole body was shivering.

Her eyes took a moment to get used to the darkened space. There was light in the distance, but she didn't see anyone. She stood a moment, listening hard, catching her breath.

Then she heard voices coming from one of the stalls.

"I'm so sorry things had to turn out this way." Delta's voice.

Quickly, Miranda took in the area. Behind a pole, there was a wooden staircase leading to a platform that ran over the stalls. Some sort of hayloft or storage area.

"If only they had played out differently." Delta again.

She moved quietly to the wooden stairs and began to climb.

"Why couldn't you make things turn out differently, Wade? Why?" The woman sounded like she was about to cry.

Parker wasn't saying anything.

At last Miranda reached the top. There were bales of hay and boxes piled high on the platform. A narrow wooden handrail ran along the border of it. She grabbed onto the railing and inched along the ledge. Slowly, she slinked as silently as she could, praying that the floorboards wouldn't creak.

"Delta," she heard Parker say. "How long do you think you can get away with this?"

Hay rustled below as Delta shuffled her feet. "I don't care about getting away with it. Not anymore. If I can't have you, my life is over."

Miranda stopped in her tracks, dizzy at the words. Her life was over? Was Delta Langford still in love with Parker? Like she had been in high school?

More hay rustled. "Tell me what happened." Parker's voice lacked the strong, confident force it usually had. *What had Delta done to him?*

Biting her lip, she crept another few feet until at last she could see the tops of their heads. Peering over the handrail, she saw Delta's flaming red curls, Parker's sophisticated, salt-and-pepper mane.

They were both dressed up, Parker in his usual debonair suit, Delta in a red satin knee-length dress. A string of pearls, heels. She sure wasn't dressed for pitching hay.

They stood facing each other inside a large, open stall, near the spot where Kennicot had bared his soul to her. A chestnut horse stood in the opposite corner blinking at the intruders.

Calypso? Just like Desirée. No.

Delta turned. There was a gun in her hand.

Miranda clamped a hand over her mouth to keep from crying out.

"What happened to Ferraro, Delta? What will it matter if you tell me?" Parker was trying to get the truth out of her.

Carefully, Miranda slipped her hand into her pocket and pulled out her recorder. Her heart thumping wildly, she crouched down and slid it onto the floor near the edge. She pushed the Record button, then grabbed onto the railing to watch the scene below.

Delta wiped her forehead with her free hand. She took a step forward, a step back, rustling the hay again. Then her shoulders slumped, and she let it out. "I fell in love with Ferraro Usher the moment I met him."

Delta? In love with Usher? Oh, man. Miranda's heart was tripping like a machine gun. It all made sense now.

"Then I made the horrid mistake of introducing him to my sister." Delta said the word *sister* with such hatred, Miranda felt like she'd been shocked with a live electrical cord.

"Of course, he immediately fell in love with Desirée. Everyone fell in love with Desirée. He became obsessed with her. They married, but I knew Desirée didn't love him." Delta's voice took on a high-pitched, pleading tone. "How could she do that to me? She was everyone's favorite. My father preferred her over me. She was more popular in school than I was. She could have had anyone. Why did she have to take the man I loved?"

"Delta," Parker tried to soothe her.

"And you," she snapped. "You fell in love with that snippy little creature who wasn't even good enough for you."

"Calm down, Delta," Parker took a step toward her.

"Get back." She waved the gun.

The horse whinnied.

Delta shifted the gun and patted his neck. "There, there, Calypso. Not yet."

Now, Parker. She's distracted. Now's your chance to get the gun. He didn't go for it. What was wrong with his reflexes?

Delta glared at Parker. "I watched them together all those years they were married. They'd fight. They'd take drugs together. Ferraro was miserable. Why couldn't he see *I* was the one who could make him happy?"

She meandered away from the horse, coming closer to Parker. Hay rustled as he stumbled back, his hands up. "Ferraro was a fool," he said, his voice a tad stronger.

Delta didn't seem to hear him. "And then she left him for Kennicot last Christmas. Of course, I was overjoyed. I went to see him in his loft. I told him I loved him. That he deserved better than the way Desirée treated him. He should have married me, not her." She sniffed, as if about to cry. "He made love to me. Over the next few months, we had an affair. I was so happy, so insanely in love with him. And then, I realized he was only pretending to love me. All along he'd been pretending I was Desirée. He even painted it. He said I was like Medea and so was Desirée. His canvas captured both of us in one portrait. He was such an arrogant ass."

She had that right. Usher's relationships were getting sicker by the minute.

"Delta, how awful for you." Parker risked another step toward her.

Delta was too engrossed in the past to respond. "He wanted her back," she moaned. "He'd do anything to get her back. She refused. But she used him to get the drugs she needed. She told me that was all he was good for."

She put a hand to her temple, steadying herself. "And then one night I saw that vial on his counter. I asked him what it was. He said it was a strong dose of PCP. I asked what it was for. He wouldn't tell me, but I knew he was going to kill himself with it. And so I took it when he wasn't looking. I couldn't let Ferraro destroy himself for my worthless sister. That was when the idea came to me. Why not use it to destroy *her* instead?"

Miranda glanced down at the floorboards. The recorder was still going.

"The Steeplechase was the following weekend," Delta continued. "It would be the perfect opportunity. And so I wrote a suicide note for my sister, mimicking her handwriting. Our writing was always similar. I was good at imitating it."

Like she had imitated Parker's handwriting in high school when she put that note in the oak tree for Laura Turner.

"On the morning of the Steeplechase, I had second thoughts and decided I couldn't go through with it. But Desirée was so cruel to me when I saw her. She brushed me aside. She scoffed at our tradition of dressing alike for the Steeplechase. She ridiculed the outfit I'd had made for her. She said she hated the thought of being identified with me. I thought of the suicide note I'd tucked under the bow of her hat."

Delta closed her eyes, shook her head. A second opportunity. Wake up, Parker. He rocked on his feet, as if about to fall into the hay. What had that bitch done to him?

Delta spun toward the horse. He snorted, pawed the ground. With Parker in that condition, the animal could tear him apart with his hooves if the crazy woman riled him.

"I was so hurt, so angry, that morning. When Desirée's back was turned, I slipped the vial I'd taken from Ferraro's loft into her drink. She drank it all. She didn't even notice it."

Miranda stole another look at the recorder to make sure its light was still green. It was. At last, she had the confession she'd wanted so badly.

"At first it seemed as if the drug had no effect. Desirée told Ferraro she was going to check on Calypso and headed for the stables. She seemed fine. Ferraro got up and left, but he left his riding crop behind. I picked it up and followed Desirée to Calypso's stall."

"You were wearing gloves," Parker said. Miranda felt a wild rush of relief to hear his voice again.

"Yes, we both were. They were part of our outfits."

That was why only Usher's prints showed up on that riding crop.

"I watched Desirée go into the stall. The trainers were away on a break. No one noticed me. By then, she was staggering. The drug was taking effect, but I couldn't be sure it was enough. And I wanted to punish her for her cruelty to me. I watched her stumble to the back of the stall. She didn't even know where she was anymore. I raised the crop and beat Calypso's head, the way I wanted to beat her."

She took the horse by the halter, patted him again. "You always were excitable, weren't you, boy?" She clucked her tongue.

Then her voice took on a dreamy, faraway tone. "Calypso reared up, went into a frenzy. I remember the sound of his hooves against the wall. The dull thud came right away. His hooves struck Desirée's body, her face. Once, twice. She went down. I took one look at her crushed face. That face she'd used to take Ferraro away from me. She never would again."

She moved her head, as if reliving the scene. "Calypso became uncontrollable. People would start to notice. Before anyone saw me, I ran from the stall and hid the riding crop in the bushes. I realized Ferraro's fingerprints were on it. That I could frame him for Desirée's murder. That's why I asked your assistant to take the case. I read about her history in the papers. I knew she would sympathize with my plight."

Miranda clenched her teeth. Be a pushover, she meant. Bitch.

"I told Ferraro if he would marry me, I would call off the investigation. But he refused."

No wonder he'd acted so violently when Miranda grilled him. He knew who the murderer was all along but was afraid to tell the truth. He was terrified of Delta.

"After that awful party, he told me he was going to the police and tell them the truth."

"And?" Parker said quietly. Did she hear strength returning to his voice?

"And so I killed him. With this very gun. I went to the loft to beg him to take me away. He wouldn't do it. He said I belonged in jail. His words made me wild with grief. I had this gun in my handbag. I always carry it for protection when I go into town. I pretended to look for my keys. My fingers slipped around the handle as if they had a mind of their own. I couldn't stop myself. I pulled the gun out and shot him." She started to sob like a little girl who had lost her favorite doll.

Parker didn't move. Where were those local yokels Chambers promised?

"It happened so fast. My heart broke the moment I saw him crumple to the floor. What had I done?" She gasped as she put a hand to her mouth. "I left the loft and drove home in a panic. But on the way, I thought of the party you gave last weekend. You were so stunning, so handsome. Just as you had been in high school. And then I realized the truth. It wasn't Ferraro I truly loved. It was you, Wade. I've always loved you."

"Delta."

"But you refused me, too. Just like Ferraro did."

The woman was crazy. A raving lunatic. Miranda peered over the handrail. Parker looked like he wanted to strangle her on the spot. But he kept calm.

"Delta," he said. "I never knew you had such courage." He took another step toward her.

She lifted the gun. "Get back."

"If I had known what you were really like—"

"Are you saying you're changing your mind about me? About us?"

"I've never seen you like this."

Man, that was a good act. Could Parker pull off the deception? Too easy.

"Do you really think I'm so stupid as to believe you, Wade? You've had your chance."

"Give me another."

"Oh, no. Now it's my turn to refuse you."

"You can't refuse me, Delta. Put that gun down."

Good try, Parker, but this bitch was too insane to charm.

"Stay back, I said. I've thought it all out. I'll say you came out here looking for evidence. I thought you were a prowler. You tried to take my gun before I could recognize you." Without taking her eyes off Parker, she moved to the wall and grabbed a riding crop. She waved it ominously. "And then the horse spooked. It was an accident. A dreadful, horrible accident."

"Three accidents in a row? The police will see through that, Delta."

Her stomach in a vice, Miranda stooped to shut off the recorder. The cops Chambers was sending would find it here. Slowly, she rose, grasped the handrail with both hands, and swung a leg over it.

"You know the connections my father has. Besides, it doesn't matter what happens to me. What matters is that those who hurt me are punished." Delta gave the whip a snap.

Calypso whinnied, began to prance on his forefeet.

Medea, Miranda thought. Usher had hit the nail on the head. She watched Delta maneuver herself within shooting distance. There was only one way to stop her.

She swung the other leg over and held tight to the rough boards. She shook a little as she steadied her heels on the ledge.

"Delta, think what you're doing."

"I know exactly what I'm doing."

Miranda's breath hitched. Don't lose your nerve now. C'mon. She'd worked on skyscrapers in New York. But she'd had a vest to protect her from falling then.

She looked down.

The loft was low, only about eight or nine feet high. There was lots of nice, soft hay on the floor to land on. Several bales were stacked up just beside Delta. She'd hit them dead on.

If she got the angle right.

"I'll miss you, Wade. It could have been so beautiful for us. I'll always love you. You'll always be my delicious torment. But this is goodbye." She raised the pistol.

"Like hell it is," Miranda yelled.

Delta glared up at her just as she let go of the railing. She sailed through the air like Superman without his cape. Downward. Fast.

Her aim was good. She landed right on top of the bitch. She grabbed at her arm, trying for the gun. They hit the floor. Miranda heard Calypso neighing with nerves. Delta twisted. Her arm curled under her.

"No." The shot exploded in Miranda's head as pain shot through her legs, her arms. Beneath her, the woman was still.

She lay stunned for a second, then heard the horse's frenzied cry. She looked up and saw the hooves coming straight for her head.

Roll. She rocked, swiveled herself away just before Calypso's deadly hooves came down. They landed with a sickening thud on of top Delta's body. Once, twice, three times, battering it like a limp rag doll. Then the stallion reared up again, came down on the hay, and bolted out the open door.

Her head spinning, Miranda grabbed her arm. It felt like it was on fire. The bullet must have gone straight through Delta's body and into her. With all the strength she had, shakily she got to her feet.

She looked down. Her forearm was soaked in blood. She strained her head to the side, despite the pain. There was a hole in the side of the stall.

She spun back around. Parker. Where was Parker?

She saw him fall to his knees in the corner. No. It couldn't be. What had that bitch given him?

Her whole body aching, her arm blazing, she rushed over to him. She reached him just as he tumbled over.

"Parker," she screamed. Sirens blared in the distance. At last, Chambers had come through. Thank God.

She ran her hands over his face. Was he breathing? Frantically, she knelt beside him, pulled his mouth open, pinched his nose with her fingers and blew into him.

Slowly, she told herself. It was hard to control her own quivering breath, but she had to. She couldn't lose him. She couldn't let him die.

On the third breath, he sucked in air, pulled away. He opened his eyes groggily. Did he even recognize her?

Then he smiled that gorgeous sexy smile of his. "My guardian angel," he said. And pulled her to him in a bold, hard kiss.

CHAPTER FORTY-TWO

Miranda pulled her old blue Lumina into the long drive of the Parker mansion and turned off the engine. She sat there awhile, watching two blue jays hop along the lawn, squawking and poking the ground together.

It had been four days since the shooting. Her forearm had a bandage and still ached from the bullet that had grazed the inside of it. They'd kept her in the ER for twenty-four-hour observation, but the shot hadn't done any nerve damage. There'd be a scar, of course. But it went well with the ones on her chest. Battle wounds.

The ambulance and local police had arrived just after Parker came to. Chambers had been with them and took charge. EMTs took Parker away, pumped his stomach, treated him for an oxycodone overdose. They'd put her in a different ambulance.

They'd also pronounced Delta Langford dead.

There was the usual lengthy police questioning. She had explained what happened and told them where she'd left her recorder. They'd found Parker's in his pocket still running. When they played them both, there wasn't much left to do except write up the paperwork.

And bury the dead.

Delta Langford had been a pitiful case. Neglected by her father, scorned by the men she fell for, she was desperate for anyone to love her. Miranda would have felt sorry for her…if she hadn't killed her sister. Or tried to murder Parker. Or been responsible for what happened to Laura Turner.

She hadn't called Parker in the hospital, but she learned they'd released him yesterday. Now that he was home, she'd said goodbye to Fanuzzi and come here to pick up the rest of her things. It was time to be off.

Nothing had changed between them. She knew better than to trust that big juicy kiss he'd planted on her on the floor of the barn at Aquitaine Farms. The man had been delirious.

But she hoped to tell him about her plans to become a private investigator. He'd done so much for her, after all. He'd given her a start in the business.

She gazed at the big, beautiful house. Good memories here. She'd carry them with her.

Might as well get it over. Taking a deep breath, she opened the car door.

When there was no answer at the big front door, she used her key and went inside.

"Parker?" Miranda called out, stepping into the big, echoing foyer.

There was no answer.

Well, she wasn't going to hunt him down. She'd just pack and go. She started up the carved mahogany staircase, heading for the master bedroom. If she didn't see him again, it would make things that much easier.

Still, the thought of being in the bedroom where they'd slept together made nerves dance in her stomach. But it had to be done. Hoping he wasn't asleep up there, she hurried down the hall.

"Parker?" she said again, stepping through the open door.

Still nothing.

He wasn't in one of the lounge chairs, or at the bar, in the walk-in closet, the bathroom or the bed.

To heck with it. She marched to the closet and started pulling out the boxes she'd stored there. First load. She lifted two and took them down to her car.

When she came back up, she grabbed her spare duffle bag and put it on the bed. She pulled open a dresser drawer. She'd left a lot of stuff here when she'd gone before. She'd been too angry to be methodical. And she'd accumulated more than she usually carried since she'd gone to work for Parker. Maybe she'd leave some of it.

She folded some underwear and T-shirts and laid them in the bag. She turned around, ready to tackle the next drawer…and saw Parker standing in the doorway.

"Hello, Miranda."

She stared at him. He was handsome as ever. Alive as ever. Strong, well groomed, not a hair out of place.

But something wasn't right. He was dressed in jeans and a light blue short-sleeved knit shirt that set off the steel of his eyes. It was open at the neck, showing off the beginning of his delicious chest. She'd never seen him dressed casually before. He'd always been either in a suit or naked. For some reason, his clothes made her uncomfortable.

"I didn't mean to startle you."

"You didn't," she lied and gestured toward the bag. "I just came by for the rest of my things."

"I see that."

"Hope this isn't a bad time. Maybe I should have called." Her heart was full, melting at the heat he radiated just standing there.

"No need. I believe your name is still on the lease."

She smiled sadly. She would swing by Mr. P's office after she'd packed and cancel her agreement.

He folded his arms and leaned on the doorpost. "Do you intend to leave town?"

Opening another drawer, she nodded. "I'm better now. It's time I started looking for Amy again." She looked up at him as she gathered her socks, raised her chin. "I'm going someplace where I can become a real detective." She turned back to the bag.

His voice came low and strong. "But you are a real detective."

Her heart leapt at his words, but she couldn't imagine what he meant after the things he'd said to her. "I'm going to a state where the licensing requirements aren't so stringent. Someplace like Idaho or Wyoming."

He stepped toward the end of the bed, stared down at her bag. "Are there many high-profile murder cases in Wyoming?"

Bristling, she put a hand on her hip. "If there are, I'll find them and solve them."

He nodded, scratched his handsome chin. "You might have to do some background checks to make ends meet."

She brushed past him as she went for her jeans in the next drawer. "Uh huh."

"And then there's the clerical work of running your own office."

She stood up and exhaled loudly. "I'll do what I have to. At least I'll be calling the shots."

"Something you're good at."

Now he was starting to annoy her. She went to the bed, stuffed the stack of jeans into the duffle bag. Instead of a smart-ass reply, she decided to be civil. After all, she'd be a business owner soon.

"Parker, I want to thank you for getting me started on this career." She had wanted to sound warm and sincere, but the words came out stiff. She picked up one of the shirts she'd laid out on the bed and folded it. "I've come to realize it's in my blood. Something I was born to do. I've never felt that way before."

"I'm glad to hear it."

"Are you?"

He was quiet.

She put the shirt in the duffle and turned around.

He stared at her a long moment, studying her. She couldn't read his face.

"Oh. I almost forgot." She dug into her pocket and pulled out his mother's ring. "I need to give you this back."

Pain colored his expression, stinging her with guilt. "Keep it," he said in almost a whisper.

She scoffed. "I can't do that." She held it out to him.

He refused to open his hand. She laid it on the dresser. "Here."

She reached for the next drawer. His hand stopped her. "Don't."

She looked up at him. "What?"

Parker's jaw clenched tight as he studied her. Those sharp blue eyes, that wild dark hair that matched her wild spirit. He had almost lost her twice, three times, depending on how you counted it. He wasn't about to let her walk out of his life now. But it wouldn't be easy to change her stubborn mind. "You don't need to pack the rest of your things," he said darkly. "I'll have them sent to you."

Miranda stared at him. Was this a way to get her address? But he could get it anyway. Maybe he just wanted her out of here. "You don't have to—"

"If you're resuming your search for Amy, I have something that might help."

She frowned at him, confused.

"Come downstairs. I'll show you." He pointed toward the bed. "Oh, and bring that bag along. You'll need it."

What kind of game was this? She stepped to the bed, zipped the bag and slung it over her shoulders. He was in an awful hurry to get rid of her, wasn't he? Her heart sank as she followed him through the hall and down the staircase. Maybe she shouldn't have lost her temper the other day, but dang, he could be such a hardass.

It didn't matter, anyway. He'd obviously come to the same conclusion she had. That it would never work between them, no matter how much they wanted it to. There was no use to argue about it. It was high time to say good-bye.

She followed him out to the kitchen. He opened the door to the garage for her as they reached the far end.

"So what are you sending me off with, Parker?" She couldn't imagine what he'd been talking about upstairs. Or what he could have that would help her find Amy.

Then he switched on the light. She stopped dead in her tracks and sucked in her breath.

Two shiny new Touring motorcycles sat next to Parker's Mazda. One blue. One red. Matching helmets hung from the handlebars. Stunned, she eyed the bat-wing fairing, the fancy windshield for wind and rain protection, the cast aluminum wheels, the gleaming exhaust pipes. They were absolutely gorgeous.

"I bought them the day after your party. They've been sitting here waiting for you to open the garage door."

She turned to him, dumbfounded. "Are you saying I can use one of these to search for Amy?"

"Mobility is always an asset, when the weather is good. Of course, you'd have to get a trailer for your Lumina."

She scratched her head. Seemed like a stretch. How would a cycle help her search for Amy? Might attract some kids.

He nodded toward the red bike. "There's room for some of your things in the saddlebag." He pointed to the compartment under the seat as he strolled over to the blue one, slung a leg over it, started it up.

The purr of the motor gave her goose bumps. He reached for the remote and opened the garage door. With a grumble from the engine, he shoved off and took a turn around the drive.

Dang, if Parker couldn't ride a cycle.

When he came back, he eased the bike inside the garage again and studied her as he turned off the motor. "I've been rethinking our last discussion."

Discussion? The one they had the day she stormed out? She folded her arms. "Oh?"

He inhaled slowly. "I've decided you had a point. My position at the time was more personal than professional."

Her mouth opened. What was he saying?

"This business of ours can be a dangerous one. Risk comes with the territory. If I don't give you your head in some situations, you'll never be complete. You'll never realize your full potential. You'll never become a 'real' detective, as you call it. With your strength, your intuition, your desire, that would be a terrible waste."

Her knees went weak beneath her. Did he mean it?

"Besides, since that bold, brash spirit of yours saved my life the other day—for the second time, I might add—I've come to the conclusion that it might not be wise to suppress it."

She laughed softly, her heart filling with warmth. "Guess we are two for one."

"We are," he conceded. Then she saw a flicker of that wry grin. "So here's the way I see it. If you really want to open your own office, you can take that bike and go off to Wyoming. Or, once you finish your training at the Agency, you can study for licensing exams. The Agency has many resources to help you."

Her mouth dropped open again. Stay at the Agency and get licensed, too? If he was going to be reasonable, maybe she could stick around until graduation. The Parker Agency's training was top notch.

"And after that?" she asked cautiously. Did he still intend to keep her chained to a desk doing background checks?

His eyes sparkled with that familiar admiration. "We'll see what comes along. You've proven the Taggart case wasn't a fluke. And that you're too good to sit in an office. In fact, Erskine said what you did at Aquitaine Farms was amazing."

She swallowed hard. "'Amazing?' Erskine said that about me?"

"He did." Parker's brows knitted in a handsome, deliciously amused expression. "He also said I was darn lucky to have someone like you on my staff to save my backside." His heartfelt chuckle warmed her.

She laughed out loud at the thought of the brusque Lieutenant saying that to Parker. "Well, it's a very nice backside."

"Thank you. And I'd prefer to keep it. Oh, and your new-found friend, Officer Chambers, has been promoted to assistant detective."

"Really? Cool."

"It was very smart of you to solicit his help."

She turned her head away, trying to hide the blush at his barrage of compliments. If she was supposed to be so bold, why was she shaking? "What about looking for Amy?"

He sighed as his expression grew sober. "You know I've been trying to find her since you told me about her, don't you?"

She nodded. "I gathered that." Though he'd been as secretive about it as a Russian spy with herpes.

"I'm sorry to say I haven't had a bit of success."

She bit back a disappointed huff. "So do you think it's hopeless?"

He paused, his face thoughtful. "I have one more idea."

"You do?"

He nodded as his gentle smile returned. "I'd like to discuss it with you tonight over dinner." He gestured toward the bikes. "So where will it be, Miranda? Wyoming or the North Georgia mountains for the weekend with me?"

She stared at him.

"Would you prefer Myrtle Beach?"

She didn't know what to say.

His Magnum-gray gaze shot straight through her with such emotion, her heart broke. "I love you, Miranda."

Her breath caught. He'd said it. He said he loved her, and she didn't blow up or want to run away. This was progress.

She looked into that wonderful face and saw wisdom, courage, compassion. She closed her eyes, trying not to cry, not knowing what to say to him. Yes, she wanted to go away with him.

A lump caught in her throat and suddenly she knew for sure. She loved him, too. Truly loved him.

But she couldn't say it. Not yet. How could she let him know before it was too late?

Then she knew that, too.

She opened her eyes. "We can't go yet. I left your ring upstairs."

His eyes twinkled with a knowing smile. "No, you didn't." He reached in his pocket and held it out to her.

The sneaky sleuth must have picked it up as they left the bedroom.

She took it from his hand, watched its brilliant blue sapphires and diamonds blaze with fire. It was a beautiful, sincere token of love. Of trust. "I'm not sure I can wear this yet."

He cocked his head. "What if I buy you a chain so that you can wear it around your neck?"

"Like going steady?"

He shrugged. "Something like that."

She bit her lip and wrinkled her nose. "That would be just too high school."

"Well, then?"

Face your fears, Dr. Wingate said. It was now or never. Sucking in her breath, she slipped the ring on her finger. It seemed to glow even brighter.

Parker grinned with delight. "Easier than leaping from a ledge in a barn or taking a bullet in the arm, wasn't it?"

"Just a little." She stared down in wonder at the dazzling jewels gracing her hand. Then she wagged a finger at him. "But this doesn't mean you own me."

He laughed out loud. "No one could ever own you, Miranda." He turned the key on the cycle, revved the motor, tempting her beyond endurance.

She picked up her duffle bag, opened the compartment under the seat of the red bike, and stuffed it inside. Then she hopped on, slapped on the helmet, and switched on the engine. It hummed like a tiger, thrilling her almost as much as the thought of a night with Parker in the North Georgia mountains.

She turned the throttle and cozied up beside him. "C'mon, Parker. I'll race you to Peachtree."

"No racing," he laughed. After Parker donned his own helmet and lowered the garage door with the remote, they headed down the drive. "We both need to stay in one piece for what I have in mind tonight."

Hmm. Until they got on the open road, she thought, slyly.

As they turned onto Sweet Hollow Lane, Miranda wondered, with a thrill, what exactly he had in mind. Her stomach quivered with anticipation. And as they glided under the big green oaks rustling in the summer breeze, she also couldn't help wondering what adventures a life with Parker might bring her.

The only way to find out was to give it a try.

Giving the throttle some juice, she sped up and inched past him for just a moment. Then, relishing the feel of the wind against her face, she settled in at his side.

THE END

ABOUT THE AUTHOR

Linsey Lanier writes chilling mystery-thrillers that keep you up at night.

Daughter of a WWII Navy Lieutenant, she has written fiction for over twenty years. She is best known for the popular Miranda's Rights Mystery series and the Miranda and Parker Mystery series. Someone Else's Daughter has received several thousand reviews and more than one million downloads.

Linsey is a member of International Thriller Writers, and her books have been nominated in several well-known contests.

In her spare time, Linsey enjoys watching crime shows with her husband of over two decades and trying to figure out "who-dun-it." But her favorite activity is writing and creating entertaining new stories for her readers.

She's always working on a new book, currently books in the Miranda and Parker Mystery series (a continuation of the Miranda's Rights Mystery series). Other series include the Maggie Delaney Police Thrillers and the Wesson and Sloan FBI Thriller series.

For alerts on her latest releases join Linsey's mailing list at linseylanier.com or check out her store at **store.linseylanier.com**.

Edited by

Donna Rich

Editing for You

Second Look Proofreading

Gilly Wright
www.gillywright.com